# NIGHT
## OF THE
# ACCIDENT
## Heather Chavez

**HEADLINE**

First published in the USA in 2022 by
William Morrow, Harper Collins Publishers

First published in paperback in Great Britain in 2022 by
HEADLINE PUBLISHING GROUP

1

Cataloguing in Publication Data is available from the British Library

ISBN 978 1 4722 6479 4

Printed and bound in Great Britain by Clays Ltd, Elcograf S.p.A.

Headline's policy is to use papers that are natural, renewable and recyclable
products and made from wood grown in well-managed forests and other
controlled sources. The logging and manufacturing processes are expected
to conform to the environmental regulations of the country of origin.

HEADLINE PUBLISHING GROUP
An Hachette UK Company
Carmelite House
50 Victoria Embankment
London
EC4Y 0DZ

www.headline.co.uk
www.hachette.co.uk

*For Jacob and Maya,*
*the inspiration for everything.*
*Except the evil parts. Those are all me.*

# NIGHT
## OF THE
# ACCIDENT

# 1

For several months after the accident, I awoke with the same two questions: What would go wrong that day? And would my sister, Izzy, be the cause of it? During those first months, I bit my nails to nubs and bought my antacid in multipacks.

But by that morning in late June, it had been five years. Now I awoke with a different set of questions. Had I signed Julian's permission slip for the field trip to the library? Did we have cereal? Milk?

So when Izzy's boyfriend, Mark, called much too early asking to meet, I didn't worry. Not like I should have.

The first clue that I should've worried more was the couple in the matching San Francisco Giants hats. I had just pulled into the Chevron on South Cloverdale Boulevard and climbed out of my truck when a car stopped behind me. Summers in Northern Sonoma County are hot and dry, and that day temperatures were predicted to hit triple digits by midafternoon. Even though the car's windows were rolled up and its engine was off, the couple stayed in the cab.

Through the sedan's untinted windshield, I could see both of their faces. The man's graying hair curled beneath the bill of his hat and wrapped like an invasive weed around protruding ears. Sallow skin stretched over the sharp bones of his face. He seemed to be studying the screen of his phone. Then he glanced up, his eyes widening and narrowing in nearly the same instant.

The woman sat next to him, her gaze even more intense than his. Her lips were pressed so tightly that they disappeared into her face as if she'd swallowed them.

As a woman in my late twenties, I was accustomed to a certain level of unwanted attention. But this felt different. I unglued my ponytail from the nape of my neck and coiled it into a knot, grabbing one of Izzy's tortoiseshell barrettes from the cup holder to secure it. It did little to stop my sweating. My eyes locked with the woman's, and I tilted my chin in defiance. Who was she to make me look away? When I was a teenager, I would've backed down immediately. Back then, I gravitated toward stillness. Toward being that quiet brunette in the background whose name no one could quite remember. The nerdy girl in advanced calculus. It was exhausting. It's not as easy as you would think, being forgettable.

The woman's eyes released mine as she brought her phone to her ear. I turned away and pushed the button on the pump to select the cheapest grade of fuel. Almost immediately I again felt her attention as heat on my back. The man's too. Even in my modest shorts and T-shirt, I felt abruptly too exposed.

As I positioned the nozzle in the tank of my F-150, I pricked my ears. Raising a four-year-old had made me an expert at listening—for glass breaking, doors squeaking, guilty pauses. Behind me, the silence seemed to be thick with hostility. The strangers—whom I was certain I had never seen before—both buzzed with it. Why?

While my tank filled, the warmth on my back spread to my neck, causing the hairs there to stand on end. When, finally, the car door slammed, I inhaled sharply. Fumes burned my nose. I heard the shuffle of feet on concrete and a soft whispering. They had gotten out of their car. I glanced over my shoulder, toward the couple in the matching hats who for some reason didn't like me.

After a moment, the man had returned to the car, but the woman stood staring, one hand in her pocket, the other wrapped around her phone. I studied her face. Briefly I considered whether I did indeed know this woman. Perhaps I had given her child a failing grade? Was she the new neighbor I had yet to meet, upset that my lemon tree blocked the sun she needed to grow her tomatoes? But the intensity of her gaze suggested something more than an F in middle school math or withered vegetables.

I squared my shoulders and called to her: "Do I know you?"

The woman scowled as if the question offended her. She retreated to stand near her car's rear bumper and began pumping her own gas. Every thirty seconds or so, her glance darted in my direction.

I wiped the sweat from my neck and swore under my breath. What was wrong with me? It had been years since I had been this jumpy. But maybe it wasn't just the strangers who unnerved me. Maybe the idea of meeting Mark left me more anxious than I had originally realized.

That morning on the phone, Mark had been calm enough. *We need to talk about Izzy.* But those words always set me on edge.

*Is everything okay?* I'd asked.

*I just need some advice.*

In the moment, I had allowed myself to believe it might be

about a ring—my parents and I knew Mark was on the verge of proposing. Or maybe he and Izzy had fought. He often joked that I was an Izzy whisperer, the only one who could make sense of her complicated moods. I doubted that was true anymore. Not after what had happened. Years later, I could still feel her breath, hot and sour on my face, on that last night she had really trusted me.

The nozzle clicked, snapping me out of my memories. I didn't want to linger with them anyway.

I replaced the nozzle in its holder and grabbed my purse. Even before Mark had called, it hadn't been the smoothest of mornings. I had misplaced my keys, and I'd had to add water to the milk so there would be enough for Julian's Cheerios. The banana I had intended to eat had gone brown, and I was late dropping Julian off at preschool. Later I would hit the grocery store, but for now I needed something quick and plastic-wrapped to get me through the morning.

Before heading into the convenience store, I glanced again toward the strangers in the Giants hats. They both stood next to the pump, though they seemed more interested in my truck's bumper than filling their tank.

I shook off my disquiet. I'd spent too much time thinking about the past that morning. That's all. Even Julian had felt it, eating his cereal in silence. Rare for any four-year-old, but especially for Julian.

The door to the store was propped open with an orange construction cone. Already, artificially cooled air blasted across the threshold. Inside, snacks were loaded on shelves and carousels, beer and energy drinks stacked along walls and in refrigerated cases, a counter dedicated to dark-roast carafes and a cappuccino machine. I grabbed a bottle of water and a cranberry-orange muffin and headed to the register.

"Hey, Frankie," the cashier greeted me.

"Morning, Lucy." Near the register, rubber bugs—green centipedes, black spiders, yellow bees—were piled in a basket in colorful heaps. Julian had recently developed a fascination with bugs, whether it be the roly-polies he hunted in our backyard or the spider that spun its webs in the corner of our living room. I grabbed a centipede and placed it on the counter next to the water and muffin.

Lucy smiled. "Julian'll love that."

I returned the smile, but my stomach churned. Too many times, I'd ignored my instincts. That hadn't gone well. So as Lucy scanned the items, I glanced out the window toward the couple. My shoulders tensed. The woman had taken a few steps closer to my truck, her head bowed.

What was she staring at?

When Lucy looked up, I gestured toward the couple. "Do you know those two?"

She nodded. "Sure. The man's Bill, I think. Or Phil? His wife's Amy. They're regulars. Why?"

I thought of the way they had looked at me—as if they were judging me. "They give me the creeps."

She leaned in to whisper, "Honestly? Amy gives most people the creeps." Lucy wrinkled her nose. "She's a bit of a racist, and nosy as hell. But they're both harmless enough."

I bristled on the word "harmless." And a *bit* of a racist? Was that like being a bit dead?

I slid my debit card through the reader and grabbed my items, mumbling a thanks as I hurried toward the front of the store. But in the doorway I stopped, frozen by an unreasonable urge to check in with Julian's preschool. Chilled air blasted my neck while gas-fumed heat flushed my cheeks, and I juggled the water and muffin as I fumbled for my phone. I found it at the same moment I sensed movement near my truck. When I looked up, Bill or Phil or whatever the hell his name was had cupped his hands against the windshield.

Phone temporarily forgotten, I shouted: "What are you doing?"

The man turned, crossed his arms, but it was the woman who charged me, finger wagging. "Where the hell's the kid?" Her words a challenge.

I thought of Julian, and my stomach knotted. Instinct pushed my attention to my phone. No missed calls. Just a missed alert. Relief came, warm and quick. Then I read the notification more carefully, and suddenly I understood.

Mill Valley, CA AMBER Alert: White Ford F-150. It included a partial license plate number: 7RO. The number and two letters matched my own plate.

That didn't make any sense.

I slipped the rubber centipede in my shorts pocket and transferred my bottled water and muffin to my left hand, using my right to unlock my phone. I selected the preset number for Julian's preschool. There must be some confusion on their end. A new teacher not paying attention. An overly cautious parent.

One ring. Two. Three. At five rings, I hung up.

Certain I had misdialed, I tried again. This time, I didn't hang up until I saw the police cruiser pull up alongside my truck.

# 2

The officer circled my Ford F-150, peering in the window as the couple had done, then headed in my direction. The tag on his shirt gave his name as Quinn. He was about my age, tall and thin-legged, but with a broad stomach and shoulders. He had the appearance of an inverted bowling pin about to tip.

My throat grew tight as he approached. An aggressive sun had already swallowed half the shade near the store's entrance, the sky overbright and the air thick with the burgeoning heat.

"This your vehicle?" he said. Friendly. Practiced.

I nodded, my hands full with muffin, water, and phone.

"Anyone traveling with you?"

I shook my head, my hands tightening on the muffin. Mashing it.

The officer glanced past me into the store. Then his attention landed on me again. My thumb pierced the plastic wrap.

"Can I see your driver's license?"

I looked down at my hands, at the muffin I had mangled. I tossed it in the garbage can—I'd lost my appetite anyway—and tucked my water under my arm, my phone back in my pocket.

From my purse, I pulled out my driver's license and handed it to him.

While he scanned it, I looked for the couple in the Giants hats. Had they left? A moment later: Of course not. They had merely relocated, moving their car to a spot near the vacuum station. Out of the way but close enough to observe the action.

"Francisca Barrera?"

"Frankie."

"How about your registration, Ms. Barrera?"

Officer Quinn followed me to my truck, a step behind and to the side. He watched as I unlocked it and placed my water on the truck's roof. When I opened the passenger's-side door, he hovered. He positioned himself so he could better scan the interior. I thought maybe it was a good sign that he allowed me to get my own registration. If he thought I was dangerous, he wouldn't let me near the glove box, would he? Still, I felt him tense as I opened it.

A sense of foreboding vibrated in my chest. I held out the registration with an unsteady hand. He took it, read it, handed it back.

"Is Julian okay?" I asked.

Quinn cocked his head. "Julian?"

"My . . . son." It was hard to get the word out. Hard to get oxygen in.

"This isn't about your son."

My throat dilated. I could breathe again. "If it's not about Julian, what's it about?"

"Just following up on something." He tried a smile, but his eyes were wary. "Okay if I look inside your vehicle?"

Even in the morning's warmth, I shivered at his request. Did he even need my permission?

I hesitated, afraid of appearing uncooperative but also wary of yielding my rights. I was innocent, but I knew that didn't always matter. "Sure," I said, trying to sound confident, but betrayed by the tremor in my voice.

He gestured to his left. "Why don't you wait with Officer Callahan for a minute?"

Confused, I looked in the direction Quinn pointed. There, a second cruiser was parked behind the first. How had I not noticed that? The officer standing beside the car was even younger than Quinn, his hair yellow—not blond, but canary—and his mustache so sparse that I wondered if it was intentional, or if he'd just forgotten to shave.

My focus returned to Quinn, his top half buried inside my truck. Even though he had assured me the alert had nothing to do with Julian, my unanswered call to the preschool unsettled me. I opened my mouth to ask if I could call again, but then I remembered: Julian was on a field trip to the library. That was why my call hadn't been answered.

Officer Quinn lifted Julian's booster seat. On days when there were field trips, I usually gave the preschool the booster, marked with a piece of masking tape bearing Julian's name. The tape from the last trip still stuck to the plastic, though it had started to flake, the n that ended his name half gone. Since the library was within walking distance, Julian's booster remained in my truck.

As Quinn examined the booster, I remembered the day Julian had graduated from his car seat. We had celebrated with cherry-flavored snow cones. For the first week, Julian hadn't allowed me to remove the old car seat, handing it down to Mr. Carrots, a love-worn bunny whose ear I'd stitched back on several times.

Then Julian had decided Mr. Carrots was safer riding in his lap. Mr. Carrots still had a cherry-syrup stain on his back. Some had also dribbled on the then-new booster, which Quinn now probed as if it held evidence of Very Bad Things.

Even knowing this wasn't about Julian, I couldn't tear my eyes away from that booster seat.

While I waited beside Officer Callahan, Quinn finished inspecting the interior and moved to the bed of the truck. He opened the tailgate. A heavy-duty zippered bag was secured to the sides with bungee cords. I mainly used it for stashing bags on trips home from the grocery store, but it currently held tools I'd borrowed from my dad. The bag could be rolled up and stowed when I needed the space, but most of the time I didn't bother with that. Quinn unzipped the bag. For one horrible moment I thought: *What if he finds something inside?* There was room enough for a child. The juxtaposition of my memories of Julian and that thought made me queasy. I reached out to steady myself but I had nothing to hold on to. Quinn couldn't think me capable of such a horror, could he?

But of course he could. He didn't know me.

The thought lodged in my brain, its barbs burrowed deep: If he did know me, he might trust me less. Better that I was a stranger to him.

I watched as Quinn searched the bag. I exhaled only when he abandoned his search.

Quinn returned, his face neutral.

"Where were you headed?" he asked.

Mark. I had momentarily forgotten about our meeting. "On the way to see a friend."

"Where does your friend live?"

"Petaluma."

"And where were you coming from?"

"Home." Then I shook my head. That wasn't exactly right. I needed to be exactly right. "I mean, we were at home, then I dropped Julian off at preschool. He's four." My voice wavered.

"Where were you last night?"

"What time?" Stupid question. It didn't matter what time. The answer was the same. "I was home."

"All night?"

I managed a nod. "I got home around six. Stayed there all night."

"Anyone else have access to your vehicle?"

"No." Did Quinn notice the hesitation?

"And at home, it's just the two of you?"

"Just me, Julian, and Mr. Carrots."

Quinn cocked his head. "Mr. who?"

"Sorry. A joke. That's my son's stuffed rabbit."

Quinn smiled, but it didn't reach his eyes. "Officer Callahan will take you to the station, if that's okay." He said this as if it were an invitation and not an order. "We'd like to ask you some more questions."

I glanced at my truck, but I knew it wasn't mine to take. While Quinn had ruled out the presence of an abducted child, there were probably other, smaller tasks that required swabs and special lights. Would they need a search warrant for that? Should I be worried? Should I get a lawyer?

"Of course," I said.

I realized Quinn still hadn't told me what had triggered the AMBER Alert.

From her spot near the vacuum station, the woman in the Giants hat continued to stare, arms crossed, a look of self-satisfaction playing across her face. As if I were a killer she'd helped bring to justice, and not a single mom trying to figure out if she'd be home in time to pick up her son from preschool.

When I stepped from beneath the awning's shade, the sun abraded my eyes. I shook off the unease stirred in me by the stranger. She was just a nosy woman who had spotted my license plate and then reported it to the police. That was all. She didn't think I was a killer. There was no way she could've known about that.

# 3

In the back of the cruiser on the way to the station, I remembered a similar trip when Izzy was six and I was twelve. She had decided to run away. Something to do with the tyranny of a forced bedtime. She had asked me to come with her since she wasn't yet old enough to cross the street alone. Really, she had just wanted the company, and I, as always, had wanted to keep her safe.

We had set out near dusk, her wearing a backpack that contained fruit roll-ups and a few of the rocks she collected, and me with a flashlight we didn't really need. As we walked, I waited for Izzy to change her mind, to get anxious, especially as it started to grow dark. But my sister was stubborn. Fearless. She only stopped when her legs started to cramp.

That had happened a block from the police station. An officer had offered us a ride home, and in the car, Izzy had fallen asleep with her head in my lap. Now my fingertips grazed the seat next to me, remembering the smile she had worn as she dozed. Even at that age, Izzy found joy in resistance.

A deep sigh rattled my chest. Of course, I remembered my sister's subsequent visits to the police station with less sentimentality.

Now Officer Callahan led me inside the boxy tan building to a small conference room. I expected Quinn or Callahan to do the questioning, but when I entered, a woman with brown skin and a lavender blouse stood on the other side of the table. She waited for me to sit before she did the same.

She introduced herself: "Detective Amelia Pratt." Then she passed a piece of paper across the table.

I took the paper, which turned out to be one of those "missing" flyers. The kind posted on telephone poles and in market windows. Always heartbreaking to see, but worse when the face staring back belonged to a child. Like this one.

Her name was Marina Wagner. Five-three, 135 pounds. Seventeen years old. The same age I had been when I was accepted to Sonoma State. The age Izzy had been the first time she had gotten grounded for staying out all night.

In the picture on the flyer, the missing girl's blond hair was pulled back, two tendrils framing a face caught mid-smile. Forced? Her face was round, her blue eyes wide-set. She wore a collared blouse, the kind teenage girls usually wore only to family functions. That was something, at least: she had someone in her life who nagged her to wear her special-occasion clothes. The flash had washed out the girl's face, softening her nose and muting any color in her cheeks. Half of her ear was cropped too. Who had been cut out of the picture?

Beneath the photo was a description of my truck.

"Do you know her?" Pratt asked.

My tongue felt chalky, and my lips stuck to my teeth. I hadn't had the chance to drink the water I had purchased at the gas station. Where had I left it? Then I remembered: I had left it on the roof of my truck.

"She doesn't look familiar," I said.

"You sure?"

I studied Marina Wagner's face until my head pounded, but I didn't recognize her any more than I had the couple at the gas station.

When I looked up, I found that Detective Pratt was studying me just as intently as I had studied the flyer. She leaned forward and folded her hands on the tabletop. "You're a teacher. You must come across a lot of girls like Marina."

"It says here she's seventeen. I teach middle school."

"Still. The big sister of one of your students? A babysitter?"

I shook my head, which made my temples pulse.

"Officer Quinn says you were at home last night."

"Yes."

"Tell me what you did yesterday."

Having skipped breakfast and suddenly very thirsty, I felt the ache in my head intensify. It took longer to respond than it should have. "I'm not teaching for the summer, so Julian and I spent most of it at home." We made chilaquiles for breakfast, then we hunted bugs in the backyard. I washed some laundry. None of those details would've helped Detective Pratt find the missing girl, so I didn't share them.

I continued, "We stopped by my parents' house for a couple of hours in the afternoon. They live near Cloverdale City Park, so we go there most days during the summer."

"Then what?"

"We went home."

"You didn't go back out?"

I shook my head. "We had a pizza delivered around seven. Both of us were asleep by nine." I shrugged. "My life's not that exciting."

It also didn't make for much of an alibi. I had done nothing wrong, but five years of guilt lodged in my throat.

"What happened?" I asked. "To the girl?"

"She was abducted, late last night."

The subtext was unmistakable: Marina Wagner had been taken while I had been sleeping, with no one to prove it.

On the table, I noticed a coffee ring, faint and broken. From a detective's mug, or a paper cup offered to a suspect to put them at ease? It made me think of the history of this place, and of all the thieves and liars and killers who'd sat in this chair before me. People like me. How many of them had confessed in this room? I fought the urge to confess myself, even though I'd done nothing wrong. Not this time.

"You sure she's not a runaway?" I asked. Hope warped my voice, suddenly an octave higher, even though I knew better than most people that bad things happened to runaways too.

Pratt quickly skewered my optimism. "An AMBER Alert wouldn't have been triggered for a runaway." Pratt paused. For effect or waiting for me to fill the silence? As she watched me, she twisted the ring on her left hand. Finally, she said, "There was a witness. The mom saw Marina being forced into a white Ford F-150."

My stomach clenched in that way it always did when tragedy struck other parents' children. "How horrible."

"Quite." Pratt continued twisting her ring, which made me wonder if she had children. Did she feel the same thing I did: relief that her own children were safe, and fear that it was only luck that kept them that way?

When Pratt caught me noticing her ring, she released it and placed her palms flat on the table. "So you've told me where you were last night. What about your truck?"

"Quinn already asked me that."

"Now I'm asking." She made no effort to soften her comment.

I rubbed the bridge of my nose, worrying a rough patch of skin where my reading glasses often rested. I had nothing to offer the detective, and to sit here repeating answers I'd already given seemed a waste of our time. Worse, it seemed a waste of Marina's. "The truck was with me."

"No one else had access to it?"

"No." In the moment, the answer was an honest one. Still, doubt started to form. I pushed it away. But as was the case with many uncomfortable truths, it was insistent.

"A neighbor doesn't have a spare set of keys? You know, to help you out when you go on vacation."

"I don't often take vacations." Even I recognized how ridiculous my answer was.

I was grateful that Pratt didn't call me on it. "Where do you normally park?" she asked.

"In the driveway."

"And your truck was in your driveway last night?"

"Yes."

In her expression, I sought evidence that I was convincing her, and that she was on my side. Of course she wasn't. She was on Marina's. I blinked hard against my blooming headache.

"Where's your bedroom?" Pratt asked.

"What?"

"I'm trying to get a feel for your house. How the rooms are laid out."

Too late, I realized I had given Pratt an opening. Still, I couldn't lie. It would've been too easy for her to disprove. "My bedroom's in the back of the house, near Julian's."

"So someone could've taken your truck, and you wouldn't have known. Being asleep and all."

*Being asleep and all.* I didn't like the way she said that.

The lie came easily, too easily, and almost without warning. "I slept on the couch last night," I said. "Fell asleep reading. The living room is right next to the driveway, so I would've heard if someone took my truck."

Why had I lied? I had no part in Marina's disappearance, and even from the back of the house I should've heard the truck start. But of course I knew why.

Pratt's eyes narrowed. "You sure about that?" Her voice nearly a drawl.

What was she asking? If I was certain I would've heard the truck, or if I had really fallen asleep on the couch?

"Anyone taking my truck would've had to break into my house to get my keys, and I would've noticed that." My words were more careful now. "I have a four-year-old. I'm a light sleeper."

And just like that I remembered: the keys I'd misplaced. I always left them on the hook by the kitchen sink, but that morning they had been on the counter near the toaster.

Pratt must've noticed the shift in my expression, because her eyes narrowed. "You might think you're protecting someone by keeping their secrets, but you're only making it worse," she said. "For them, and for you."

While what Pratt said was true, my spine went rigid, a reflex born from years of defending Izzy. Other than math, the thing I did best was keep my sister's secrets, no matter the consequences.

I tapped my finger on the "missing" flyer, Marina's face staring up at me as if in accusation. "You only have a partial plate, right? One number and two letters."

"True."

"The Ford F-150 is one of the most popular vehicles in the country. That's one of the reasons I bought mine. Easy to get parts."

"The next closest match with that partial is in the Central Valley."

"And trucks don't, you know, move? Isn't that what they're built to do?"

"That particular vehicle has a non-op on file with the DMV."

"And people don't lie?"

She stared at me for several seconds. "All the time."

My face flushed. I'd stepped into that one.

"You said it happened late last night? The mom could've gotten the plate wrong. Obviously, she didn't get a good look if she only got a partial."

The detective's eyes went flat. "She was preoccupied by her daughter being pulled into a car against her will."

Though her voice had an edge to it, I nodded. "Exactly. She was distracted."

"The Wagner family's had it rough." That edge sharpened. "I imagine Anne Wagner would be careful who she accused."

The way she said it implied the Wagners' bad luck extended beyond Marina's disappearance, but the set of Pratt's jaw made it clear that questions on that subject wouldn't be welcome.

"Look, I'm cooperating here," I said. "I have nothing to hide." Spoken like someone who did, indeed, have many things to hide.

Pratt's words came back to me: *You might think you're protecting someone by keeping their secrets, but you're only making it worse.*

"Then you won't mind if we search your house?" she asked.

"Not at all."

As soon as the words left my mouth, I regretted them. While I didn't expect there was anything for them to find, I also had never expected I'd spend a morning being interrogated by the police. At least not about the disappearance of Marina Wagner.

# 4

Julian and I lived in a yellow-and-white Craftsman in one of Cloverdale's older neighborhoods. Built in 1903, it had two bedrooms, a single bath, and a porch I restored myself. It was the only project I had completed since buying the house two years before, though that had only been because I had fallen through one of the rotted planks a month after we moved in.

Inside, the wood flooring was original, though the stains now covered by an area rug definitely weren't vintage. When I had first toured the place, the real estate agent had dismissed these stains, focusing instead on the tongue-and-groove installation, as if I were supposed to understand the significance of that. Something about extra stability, according to the agent.

But what had sold me on the place was the overgrown backyard, larger than the house itself, and the bathroom. True, the floor sagged a little in one corner—original floors, the agent had stressed again when she caught me noticing. But the exterior of the claw-foot tub had been painted blue, the hummingbird wallpaper was charming, and the large window looked out onto the lemon tree. Besides, if it had been in better repair, as a middle school teacher I couldn't have afforded it.

Now, while I waited just across the threshold, the police rummaged through the cabinets in need of painting, lifted the rug covering the stains, and went into our bedrooms, probably to check our closets for proof Marina Wagner had been here.

A current flowed between my shoulder blades. I would've been less nervous if I hadn't remembered my misplaced keys.

Detective Pratt stood at a distance, but her attention landed on me every so often. I felt each of these glances like pricks on my skin.

When my phone buzzed, I flinched and pulled it from my pocket slowly, not wanting to appear anxious. Pratt's gaze lingered. I worked to control my breathing. Under the circumstances, nonchalance was a hard look to pull off.

I checked the screen, biting the inside of my cheek to keep from scowling. I hadn't realized how late it was. Julian would be out of preschool soon. I had also forgotten my appointment with Mark. A text from him was what had made my phone buzz.

What happened?

I felt Pratt's eyes on me and bowed my head. I typed: Long story. Tomorrow?

Bubbles appeared, indicating he was typing. Then: Really need to talk. You home tonight?

Yes. What's up?

Better if we talk in person. At work now. Can I stop by around 7?

Sure.

Then: Don't tell Izzy.

My stomach dropped. Why?

Later.

Frowning, I tried to recall the other times Mark had texted me outside of a family group chat. He'd reached out a few times while we had been planning a surprise party for Izzy. Another time, he'd wanted a restaurant recommendation. And once, early in their relationship, he'd texted when Izzy was running late, before he learned that for my sister a half an hour late was early. Had there been other times too? If so, I couldn't remember. I scrolled through our previous conversations, when it was just us two. I read them carefully. Typos and abbreviations. Limited punctuation. The occasional thumbs-up emoji. None of them carried the same urgency, or had been as carefully composed, as these latest texts.

Izzy had to be drinking again. Or what if it wasn't alcohol this time? She had experimented with drugs before, mainly cocaine, though I had found a couple of pills on her nightstand once that I thought might've been Ecstasy. What had I missed while my sister set about ruining her life?

But, no, if it was that serious, Mark wouldn't have waited for a meeting. He would've called in sick to work and driven straight to my house. Could it be something more innocuous? More joyful? Maybe Mark really intended to propose. But when it came to Izzy, my mind always wandered to the darkest corners first. I couldn't help but wonder if it was about the missing girl.

I took a deep breath to calm myself. I would know what Mark wanted to talk about soon enough. At the moment I had other worries, like the evidence technician who was dangerously close to knocking over a vase Julian had made me for Mother's Day. Or was it a mug? Hard to say. But if she broke it, we would have words.

"Everything okay?"

Detective Pratt stood beside me, appraising me with that un-blinking gaze of hers. Distracted by my thoughts, I hadn't noticed her approach.

"It was my sister's boyfriend. Wondering where I was."

She nodded. "Earlier you mentioned you'd been on your way to see him."

My turn to nod. Pratt held out her hand. "Mind if I take a quick look?"

*Yes. Very much.* But I couldn't think of an excuse to deny her request. Heart thundering so fiercely I was sure Pratt could hear, I placed the phone on her upturned palm.

I watched as the detective scrolled, but she kept the phone an-gled so I couldn't see the screen. Would she find something that might make me appear guilty? Or, worse, that might implicate Izzy?

It had only been minutes since I'd texted Mark, but I couldn't recall exactly what we'd said. Except for three words: Don't tell Izzy.

Pratt returned my phone, and I calmed. Until she said, "Would you mind unlocking this for me?"

She had navigated to *System services. Significant locations.* I un-locked it with facial recognition and handed it back. I had nothing to hide, but still my temples pulsed.

A minute later, the phone rang. I immediately recognized the ringtone and my pulse quickened. With the workout my heart was getting, how had it not exploded?

Pratt's eyes thinned to slits, and she handed back the phone.

"Guessing you need to take this."

I accepted the phone and connected the call to Julian's pre-school. It was his teacher, Candace.

"I noticed we missed a couple of calls from you," she said. "Is everything all right?"

Pratt remained uncomfortably close. Across the room, an officer stuck her head in the fireplace. I wanted to answer, *I'm not even close to all right*. Instead, I said, "Just wanted to check on Julian."

With a gloved hand, the officer sifted through ash from a fire I'd made months ago. She wrinkled her nose, leaving me suddenly insecure about my housekeeping skills and what she must think of me. And then the thought, sudden and sharp: Did she think I had burned something there other than an oak log? Pratt's attention also shifted to the officer.

"We were on a field trip this morning, to the library," Candace said, obviously confused.

Now I also felt like a bad mother. Julian's father had never been in the picture, so I felt this failure even more acutely. I was all he had. "Yes, I remembered that after I called. Which is why I didn't leave a message."

That and the police cruiser that had pulled up behind my truck.

"Julian loves the library. He's one of the few kids who's learned to sound out words. He's actually quite good at it."

I smiled. "He loves books." Eric Carle's were his favorite. *The Very Quiet Cricket. The Grouchy Ladybug. The Very Clumsy Click Beetle*. And, of course, *The Very Hungry Caterpillar*. Julian had memorized all of them and at bedtime would pretend to read to me. When he was especially groggy, he would hold the book upside down or skip pages, but he always got every word right. Lately, he had started recognizing words in unfamiliar books too.

"He's been looking forward to it all week," I said. Pratt left to join the officer at the fireplace, and I released a long breath.

But my relief was short-lived. On the other end of the line, Candace cleared her throat. "Yes, well . . . when you pick up Julian this afternoon, I was hoping you might have a few minutes to chat."

That didn't make sense. We'd just had our check-in the week before. "Of course. Is everything okay?"

I waited for her to laugh, reassure me there was nothing to worry about. Tell me that I needed to update my contact information or that it was my turn for snack duty.

"Julian's fine," she said. "But we should have a quick chat. See you at one-fifteen?"

My mouth went dry, and my tongue felt as if it had been coated in ash. "See you then."

I disconnected but continued to stare at the screen, as if it might give me a clue what Julian's teacher meant to tell me. It couldn't have been urgent, I told myself. If it had been, she would've asked me to come right away. But as with Izzy, the dark thoughts were more insistent. Probably because of what had happened five years earlier, or how Julian had entered my life. I knew how tenuous happiness could be. How easily taken.

I called my sister but she didn't pick up. I left a message and then, anxious, texted: Call me.

"We're done here." I jumped at Pratt's voice and her sudden presence only a few feet from me. How did she keep doing that?

Pratt gave me her number, which I programmed into my

phone only because she was watching. "In case you remember anything," she said. "They've released your truck, too, if you'd like a lift back."

I thanked her but told her I would take an Uber. I was as eager to be rid of her as she was of me.

# 5

After picking up my truck, I headed to Julian's preschool. His happy place. Usually mine too. But that day, I worried.

Inside, the letter of the week was M. Near the alphabet rug, M's had been cut from red and yellow construction paper and taped to the wall, next to pictures of monkeys and mice. Bags of colored macaroni, balls of string, and pairs of safety scissors sat at the art station, and books featuring the letter were stacked on the center table.

*M for Marina.*

*M for murder.*

*M for stop being so morose, Frankie.*

Candace stood at the art station, wiping the tabletop with disinfectant wipes, scrubbing at spots marked by pen or glitter glue. "Good afternoon, Ms. Barrera."

"Frankie's fine."

She nodded, but I knew she wouldn't call me that. "I'll be just a sec." Then she resumed scrubbing. The way her brows and mouth knitted, those stains didn't stand a chance. I imagined her pointing to one of the construction paper *M*'s and lecturing the students: *The word of the day, kids, is meticulous.*

While I waited for Candace to finish, I watched Julian on the playground. Through the window I could see him at the top of the slide. He pulled up his shirt, reaching for something tucked near his hip. Mr. Carrots. Stuffed animals were allowed at the school, but they were supposed to stay in the cubbies during school hours. My son had contraband. I fought a smile as he pushed the bunny down the slide. A blink later, and Julian was at the bottom of it too. I watched, unseen, as he climbed the slide's steps and repeated the process. Then he tucked Mr. Carrots back into his waistband and ran over to play in the dirt.

My thoughts returned to how the police had ransacked our home. Had they left a mess in Julian's room? In a hurry, I hadn't checked before I'd left, and now I worried that there would be toys missing and drawers emptied onto his bed. I was abruptly relieved Julian had Mr. Carrots, at least.

"Thanks for coming, Ms. Barrera." Candace balled up the wipe she'd been using and dunked it in the trash, the wisp of a smile forming. *Take that, microbes.* Then she pointed to a table near her. "Come. Sit. The kids will be outside with Sophie for another few minutes."

I took the spot Candace indicated, a student's blue chair with a slotted back and tubular steel frame. In front of me, four-ounce stickered cups filled with beads were lined up in a row. I could tell which cup Julian had decorated: the one with the cricket stickers and hand-drawn spiders. In my tiny chair staring at the tiny cups, I felt like a giant.

Candace helped herself to a squirt of hand sanitizer, then held out the bottle to offer me a squirt too. I started to decline, but her expression suggested that wasn't an option. After we were both done sanitizing, Candace took the seat across from me and folded her hands in her lap.

"I'm glad you could make the time."

"For Julian, always. What's up?"

She cleared her throat, a habit of hers that usually preceded bad news. I braced myself. "Julian said something that was—concerning."

My gaze flew toward Julian, still happily playing in the dirt, handfuls of it slipping through his caked fingers. "What did he say?"

Candace paused. She reached across the table, as if to pat my hand in sympathy. But, you know, germs. She dropped her hand on the table, just short of the tiny cups at its center. "Before I tell you, I'd like to explain something first," she said. "By the time children get to be Julian's age, they're starting to recognize what's real and what's not. But that doesn't mean they can't still believe in Santa Claus, or have an imaginary friend."

Anxious, I didn't want a lesson in child psychology. I wanted her to get to the point. "Are you saying Julian has an imaginary friend?"

"Not at all, though as an only child, such a thing wouldn't be uncommon. What I'm saying is even if four-year-olds are developing a better understanding of reality, their imaginations are also developing, and they can sometimes become confused. Especially when they're tired. Their dreams, too, are becoming more vivid."

"Did Julian have a nightmare?" I could hear the impatience in my voice. "Is that what you wanted to talk to me about?"

"No, that's not it." She pulled her hand back and rested it in her lap. "Julian said you left him alone in the house."

I shook my head, hard. "What? I would never . . ."

"I know, Ms. Barrera. That's why I started by explaining a child's relationship with reality."

"When? When did Julian say I left him?"

"Last night. He says he heard you leave the house."

My skin tingled, the prickle of a thousand invisible ants. "I didn't go anywhere last night."

"Like I said, I'm sure you didn't. But what's important is that he believes you did."

I wasn't sure I wanted to know, but still I asked, "What exactly did he say?"

"He was quieter than usual this morning, which surprised me, since he had been so looking forward to the field trip."

Earlier, I had noticed the same thing—how he'd eaten his Cheerios in silence—but I had been too preoccupied by Mark's call to wonder why.

She continued, "When I asked him about it, at first he didn't want to tell me. He was afraid of what might happen."

I didn't understand. "I've always encouraged Julian to tell the truth. He would never get in trouble for that."

"He wasn't worried about something happening to him."

I glanced out the window, toward Julian, then back at Candace, trying to make sense of what she was telling me. "He was worried about me?"

She nodded. "He said he once saw his aunt get taken away in a police car, and he was worried that if he told, the same thing might happen to you."

I remembered. That was the time Izzy had been so wasted she'd broken into my neighbor's house thinking it was mine. When he told her to leave, she had thrown the pan of minestrone he'd been preparing at him. It would've been so much worse if Izzy's aim had been better. I was surprised Julian remembered that. It had happened nearly a year before.

"Julian told me that he heard the truck, and he and Mr. Carrots hid under the bed until he heard you come back."

"It wasn't me," I insisted, but I was fuming.

*Damn it, Izzy. What did you do?*

# FIVE YEARS BEFORE

MERCURYVILLE, 7:50 P.M.

Standing in the Grocery Outlet parking lot, Rachel Stroud should've been the kind of girl anyone would notice right away. Pretty. Almost translucently pale. Copper-colored hair that would've glinted in sunlight, but seemed rather drab in the burgeoning dusk. Still, it took Izzy a solid minute to notice that Rachel existed, distracted as she was by the man next to her.

Piper had warned Izzy about the incredibly attractive Ben Wesley: an art school dropout who, at twenty-four, was several years older than the rest of them. As Piper put it, Ben was the kind of guy who made a party fifty percent cooler by showing up, but who you also needed to watch carefully in case he tried to spike your drink.

Piper elbowed her in the ribs. The gesture clearly said: *Get it together, Izzy. Don't embarrass me in front of my friends.*

Ben introduced himself with the grin Piper had also warned her about. Did he practice that grin in the mirror? He'd gotten it exactly right.

Izzy managed to keep her jaw closed, the nonchalance firmly in place. "Hey. I'm Izzy."

"I know." The grin twitched up at the corner. *Yeah, he practiced.*

Rachel stepped forward. "Cool hair."

Distracted as she was, it took Izzy a second to realize the other girl was talking to her. The week before, Izzy had made the change from platinum to blue after deciding she wasn't meant to be a blonde. So far, blue was suiting her better.

"Thanks," she said.

Rachel turned to Ben. "So where're we going?" she asked.

Ben shook his head. "Where would the fun be if I told you?" His forehead wrinkled. "Where the hell are they?"

As if summoned by the force of Ben's will, two vehicles entered the lot. From Piper, Izzy knew this would be Rachel's brother, Tobin, and his roommate, Chuck Romero.

They were the geeks in the group, according to Piper. Izzy decided Tobin had smart eyes, his gaze sharp and unflinching. Not as obviously handsome as Ben, he was pale and his ears stuck out a little. Less leading man, more self-deprecating sidekick. But that had always been Izzy's type.

*This could get interesting*, she thought.

In comparison, Chuck didn't make much of an impression. He was thin, with eyes that watered and, though in his early twenties, a receding hairline. According to Piper, Chuck was pre-pharmacy.

Except for Piper, they were all strangers to Izzy. She didn't usually care what people thought about her, but at eighteen she was the youngest in the group. She didn't want to screw it up. Getting along with them was important to Piper, so it was important to Izzy.

Ben clapped his hands. "Caravan," he announced.

Only Rachel hesitated. The others immediately positioned their cars behind Ben's and waited for him to make the signal. After Ben climbed into his car and Rachel into his passenger seat, he reached out the window and pointed to the road. Izzy fell in behind, driving Piper in the sedan Izzy had borrowed from her mom. "Borrowed" being a relative term, since she hadn't asked. Tobin and Chuck followed in separate cars.

Though Ben had kept the location a secret from the others, on the drive Piper admitted to Izzy that he'd told her where they were headed. Piper had always been good at uncovering secrets.

They were going to a spot not far from the Geysers, a geothermal field located in the Mayacamas Mountains. Mercuryville, as it was called, was founded a couple of decades into the gold rush, when cinnabar had been discovered. The scarlet and highly toxic mineral contained mercury, a liquid metal once found in thermometers and, more importantly, used to extract gold from ore. The demand for cinnabar led to the forming of the aptly named Mercuryville. Unfortunately, the demand was short-lived, and the town's many bars and single church quickly shuttered. The population dwindled, too, mines abandoned and left to rust until they were consumed by wildfire less than a century later. Now all that remained were patches of concrete and metal framework well hidden among the weeds and rocks.

Izzy was pretty sure Ben had been attracted to the spot by its isolation. There would be no one to complain if the festivities got a little loud, which was likely, since she had seen in the back of his car at least two bottles of vodka and several dozen cans of hard seltzer. Even if someone thought to complain, it would've taken a good twenty minutes, probably longer, for police to respond. Izzy thought it was appropriate that a ghost town once known for its abundance of bars and the brawls that started there had become a drinking spot for young people avoiding law enforcement.

Izzy parked along the shoulder, with Chuck pulling in behind. A little farther up the road, Ben and Tobin stopped in a turnout next to a gate. When Izzy got closer, she could read the sign beside it: WESTERN GEOPOWER. There was also a warning against trespassing. Not that Ben seemed at all deterred.

The others, though, looked dubious. Tobin stood next to his open door, as if not yet willing to commit to staying. "Why the hell did we come to the middle of nowhere?" he asked. "Things can get dangerous out here at night."

Izzy had been wondering the same thing.

Rachel's face seemed to have grown paler than it had been back in town. "Why don't we go back to your place?" she suggested.

"Why would we do that?" Ben grabbed the alcohol from his backseat and handed it to Tobin and Chuck, then he slammed Tobin's door, nearly clipping him. Though it still wasn't fully dark, Ben switched on a lantern. He climbed over the gate without looking back, confident the others would follow. Tobin, Chuck, and Piper did, though Piper tossed a few creative obscenities in his direction.

Rachel stayed frozen in place, which led Ben to call over his shoulder, "Come on, Rach. This is Izzy's first time hanging out with us. You know how important first times can be."

Rachel looked at Izzy, who had just landed on the other side of the gate. Her eyes were wide, and she seemed unsure. Was she looking for an ally? But the moment passed, and Rachel climbed over the gate after the others.

# 6

While I helped Julian into his booster seat, I asked him about what he had told his teacher. Julian had nothing to tell me that Candace hadn't already shared: The night before, he'd heard the truck start and had hidden under his bed. He had fallen asleep, so even if he'd had a better concept of time, he couldn't tell me how long before the truck had returned.

Then, face tilted to stare into mine, he asked, "Where'd you go when you left me?"

His eyes were as wide as I imagined they had been the night before when he'd hidden. Though I was an expert at deflection with Julian, I'd never been able to lie to him. I mean, other than that one big lie, but there had been no getting around that.

"I didn't go anywhere last night," I said, mussing his hair. "I would never leave you alone."

By the way his face scrunched, I could tell he didn't believe me. "I heard the truck."

I smiled. He could be as stubborn as his mom.

"Aunt Izzy borrowed it."

Relief melted his features, and he beamed, my favorite sight in all the world.

I steadied myself for more questions, but they didn't come. Probably because of his time on the playground, he seemed to have recovered from his rough morning. Wish I could've said the same. My muscles ached from being knotted all day. Even now, when I tried to breathe through it, the lump between my shoulders hardened and pulsed. I didn't think playing in the dirt with Mr. Carrots would work for me.

As I drove, half listening to Julian's happy chatter, I considered what I knew. The night before, Julian thought he heard my truck being driven from our driveway. *Thought.* It was the memory of a groggy four-year-old.

The same night, a seventeen-year-old named Marina Wagner had been abducted from Mill Valley. Seventy-five miles from Cloverdale. That one was firmly in the facts column. It would've taken hours to drive there and back, even if the girl's abductor had exceeded the speed limit. And how likely was that if there was a kidnapped girl in the truck? Still, since I'd slept for seven hours, it was easily doable.

Marina's mom got a look at the truck and part of the license plate, which matched my own. There was always the chance she had lied—even Detective Pratt acknowledged that people lied all the time. Of course, I was pretty sure she had been directing that comment at me. Not that she was wrong.

Then this morning I'd found my car keys on the kitchen counter instead of on the hook where I usually put them. That detail was indisputable, too, though there could be other explanations. I could've been mistaken about returning them to the hook.

Or Julian could've taken them. He liked the "music" they made when jangled, and I kept them on a butterfly key ring. Sometimes that combination proved too irresistible for him.

Keeping my eyes on the road, I half turned to Julian. "Did you play with my car keys yesterday?"

"No. We played bug hunt, remember?"

I smiled. "I mean after we got back from visiting your abuelos."

"No."

So that theory was shot. Still, it didn't matter, because all of the facts taken together pointed in the same direction: My truck had been taken from my driveway and used in the abduction of a seventeen-year-old girl. And only one person had a key to my house: my sister.

I headed to Izzy's apartment. This being a weekday afternoon, Izzy was likely home. During the summer she volunteered at a grief camp for kids and picked up server shifts through her roommate, Piper, who had a regular catering gig. But this wasn't a volunteer week for Izzy, and she mostly worked weekend shifts, covering weddings at nearby wineries. She would be home, and, if I knew my sister, probably just pouring her first cup of coffee.

At Izzy's complex, I backed into one of the visitor spots. There were several dozen units, but from the driver's seat I had a clear view of my sister's front door, painted a shade of brown only slightly darker than the exterior walls. It had surprised me when my sister had chosen this place. I had always pictured her renting a room in a brightly colored bungalow or parking a retro RV next to a copse of trees somewhere. I could even picture her living in one of those trees, on a platform with only a sleeping bag and a pile of books. But Izzy didn't belong in a stack of brown boxes.

Izzy and Piper lived on the second floor, the first apartment at the top of the stairs. Julian and I climbed the stairs. He insisted on ringing the doorbell four times. His lucky number.

While we waited for Izzy to answer, I thought of ways to occupy Julian while Izzy and I talked. The apartment wasn't large, but with a closed door between us, we would be able to keep him from overhearing. As long as we didn't raise our voices.

I needn't have worried. Though we waited a solid five minutes, no one ever came to the door.

BACK HOME, MY ANXIETY corrupted a simple game of hide-and-seek. During the three minutes it took to find Julian, giggling in the closet, I wondered: What if this happened for real? What if Julian went missing just as Marina Wagner had? The thought that Izzy could be somehow involved soured my stomach.

When it was my turn to hide, I climbed into the bathtub and watched my phone. I was still staring at it when Julian peeked around the shower curtain I hadn't bothered to close and proclaimed that I wasn't a very good hider. Then he climbed into the tub, landing with an emphatic thud on my stomach, and laid his head on my chest. "Can we have pizza for dinner?" he asked.

I swore silently, remembering I hadn't made it to the grocery store. Fortunately, leftover pizza was the one thing we did have in the house. "Sure. Getting hungry?"

He nodded. The hard edge of the tub cut into my neck, the bristles of his hair tickling my chin.

"Then I guess we should eat."

He shot up with enthusiasm, coming down hard on my stomach.

"Easy," I said, catching my breath. "I'm not a trampoline."

His eyes widened, and I realized my mistake. "We should get a trampoline." Now he was the one breathless. "Can we, Mama? Please?"

"Maybe for your birthday," I said. Julian wouldn't turn five for eight months. That should allow plenty of time for him to forget the request.

As he often did, my son saw through me. "Why not sooner?"

"Not sooner." I nudged him. "Now let's get out of the tub and heat up some pizza."

A few bites in, my phone finally rang. I checked the display. *Izzy.* I took a couple of deep breaths, left Julian with his pizza, then answered.

"Hey, Izzy."

"Hey, Frankie."

"I've been trying to reach you."

"What's up?" Nonchalant, as if she hadn't received my many texts and voice mails.

"We need to talk," I said. It would be easier to read Izzy if we were talking face-to-face.

She must've recognized this, too, because she said, "I'm at Mark's, but we were about to grab something to eat."

I checked the time on my phone. A little after five. Mark and

I were supposed to meet at seven, and his house was about forty-five minutes away. Maybe longer with commute traffic.

"Mark's with you?" Though it felt like a betrayal, I texted Mark: You with Izzy?

"Yeah." But she hesitated, and I sensed the lie.

I gave Mark a few seconds to respond. When he didn't, I pushed. "I really need to talk to you. And it needs to be in person." I wanted to see her face when I asked her about Marina. Not all of Izzy's lies were as obvious as her last one.

She paused, probably searching for an excuse as to why that wasn't possible.

"I can't." I recognized the tone: she wouldn't be convinced.

*Challenge accepted.*

"You in the hospital?" I asked.

"No."

"Jail?"

"No."

"Kidnapped by aliens?"

She sighed. She knew where this was going. "No. Like I said, I'm at Mark's place."

"And you're grabbing a bite. Yes, I know. Where're you going to eat? I can join you."

Mark still hadn't responded, so I typed: We still on for 7?

"We haven't decided," Izzy said. "I'm busy, Frankie. Tomorrow."

"We've already established you aren't in the hospital, in jail, or being held hostage by aliens. You're not working until Sunday. So what are you busy doing?"

"I told you. I've got plans with Mark."

"So do I." It slipped out. *Don't tell Izzy*, Mark had texted. I felt a pang of guilt.

Izzy didn't answer for a few beats. Then: "What do you mean?"

"Mark called earlier today, saying he wanted to talk."

"About what?"

*About you. Obviously.* "I don't know. But if I meet him at his place, it'll save him a trip to Cloverdale. Then you and I can talk too. How efficient is that?"

"I'm busy," she said again, but her voice cracked.

"Doing what? Abducting young girls?"

This time the silence stretched for so long, I knew she wouldn't be the one to break it. But it gave me my answer. "You're involved, aren't you?"

"Involved in what?" Still playing dumb.

I didn't want to say more about the missing girl. Not on the phone. But there was something I did want to say. It wasn't about the creepy couple at the gas station, or the hours I'd spent at the police station, or how my home had been searched. Those things might not have convinced Izzy.

"Last night, Julian heard the truck start," I said, my voice low. "He heard it drive away. He thought I'd left him alone. So he hid under the bed. For hours." I emphasized each detail. "We're talking tonight, Izzy. In person. Seven?"

She exhaled sharply, a sudden gust that signaled her frustration. "Whatever," she said.

In that moment, I knew I had her. Or thought I did anyway.

By seven-thirty, it was clear neither Mark nor Izzy was going to show.

# 7

Though Izzy had a key to my house, I found her the next morning in the bed of my truck. It had happened enough times that I knew to park in the shade.

I climbed on the tailgate and waited for her to crawl to a sitting position. The day promised to be hotter than the one before, and already the truck's bed had started to warm. When full sun hit it in an hour, it would scald.

As I told Izzy about the AMBER Alert and my interrogation the day before, I watched her face for signs of guilt.

Finally, I asked, "What's going on?"

Izzy raked her fingers through her short hair, which was matted on one side. She had bitten her unpolished nails to the skin and she had lost enough weight that her favorite jeans now required a belt. But her eyes were clear. I took solace in that. "Mark and I lost track of time. But I'm here, aren't I?"

"You took my truck Thursday night." I had intended it as a question, but it didn't come out that way.

She shook her head but broke eye contact. I had been right to have this conversation in person. I easily spotted the lie.

"You went to Mill Valley and took that girl." Again, not a question.

We held eyes as a pause stretched between us. "I know I screwed up," she said.

Though it was what I suspected, her admission was a gut punch. "What did you do?"

"No, not that," she said quickly. "I had nothing to do with that girl. But I did borrow your truck."

"When you take something without asking, it's not called borrowing." I'd thought that had become clear after she *borrowed* Mom's car for that ill-fated trip to Mercuryville.

She shot me a look: *Come on, Frankie.* She had spent years perfecting that look. "I needed to run an errand."

"In the middle of the night?"

"It wasn't the middle of the night." Exasperated, but it felt forced. "This, right now, feels like the middle of the night to me. Unlike you, I'm not in bed by nine every night."

*Nine-thirty.* "If that's true, why did you need my truck?"

"What do you mean, if it's true?" Indignant. "A friend needed me to help him move a desk, and he didn't get off his shift until eleven. And, of course, by the time he called you were already asleep. I figured you wouldn't notice." She hesitated, her voice softening. "I'm sorry. If I'd known it would upset Julian . . ."

The apology, given countless times before, made us both uncomfortable, as it always did.

"It upset me too."

She shot me that *Come on* look again. "I haven't been drinking. I'm just tired." She hadn't needed to add that last part. I heard it in her voice.

"You've lost weight."

I had also noticed the swelling beneath her eyes, her pallor, the jerkiness that suggested she was trying to climb out of her own skin.

"I've lost a few pounds," she admitted. "Stress."

"Which friend needed help with the desk?"

"Kent Hardy."

I knew Kent well enough to know he would lie for her. "And where does Kent live now?"

"San Francisco."

Smart. San Francisco was half an hour from Mill Valley. Even if my truck was placed near the Wagner home, she could claim she was just passing through, or that Anne Wagner had mixed up the license plate because Izzy had been in the area at some other time. My sister had planned her lie carefully.

She must've sensed my doubt, because she tapped on her phone, then held it up for me to read. It was Kent's name and phone number. "Parking in the city is a bitch, so he drives a Prius. Try getting a large corner desk in a Prius."

I didn't write the number down. Not because I believed her but because, being good with numbers, I easily memorized it.

Izzy knew this about me, and she watched my face for proof I had faith in her. I wanted to believe her, too, so badly that whatever she saw there half convinced her. When she released a breath she'd been holding, all her anger went with it. "Kent had a couple neighbors help move the desk into his apartment. I don't remember their names, but Kent can give them to you. I'm not lying, Frankie."

Izzy and I had an unwritten rule: she tried hard not to screw up, and I tried equally hard to believe in her. I was straining to keep up my end of the bargain.

"Anne Wagner saw my truck."

"I can't explain that." She inched closer. "She couldn't have seen me. I wasn't there."

In Izzy's expression, I saw the little girl who had worked so hard to convince me spilling juice on her classmate was an accident, and that even if it wasn't, the boy deserved it for being a racist. I saw in her eyes the teen who stole the neighbor's puppy after she witnessed the man kick it, and then tried to lie about the yipping I heard coming from beneath her bed. That had always been my sister: Big heart. Poor impulse control.

Izzy dropped her head onto my shoulder, and immediately it began twitching. She lifted her head to look up at me. "You believe me, don't you?"

"Of course I believe you." My voice struggled to find a way around the lie.

I slid my hand closer to Izzy's, stopping just short. The tailgate warmed my palm. I wanted to cross that last inch, place my hand on hers, reassure her as I had so many times. But after everything that had happened the day before, I wasn't sure I was strong enough to believe her again. Worse, I resented her for asking it of me, and felt ashamed when I pulled my hand back into my lap.

"Would you have more faith in me if I hadn't killed that girl five years ago?"

I flinched, and my heart thumped. That was another unwritten rule of ours: We didn't talk about that night.

"Don't say that, Izzy."

"Don't say what? That I killed someone? Or do you not want me to talk about any of it?"

I whispered sharply, "Be quiet. Julian might hear you."

"See, Frankie, I'll admit to what I've done. So if I was guilty of this, wouldn't I admit that too?"

"You didn't kill that girl," I insisted.

"You only say that because you know if she's dead, you're responsible too." I must've blanched, because Izzy immediately apologized. "Sorry. It's not your fault."

"You imagined it." My voice held a confidence I didn't feel. Because Izzy was right: If Izzy hadn't imagined it, then I shared blame in what happened that night. I was as much a killer as my sister.

The shade had shifted since I'd climbed onto the tailgate, so that a sliver of sun now cut across my ankles. The spear of light baked the skin there. I pulled my feet back into the shadows.

"They'll figure out who really took Marina," Izzy said. "You'll see."

I was fairly sure I hadn't mentioned Marina by name. But I said nothing and finally grabbed her hand. There was no warmth in her fingers, which seemed little more than bone.

# 8

In my five years as a middle school teacher and lifetime as a math geek, I had learned one truth. Math will never lie to you. It can tease, frustrate, and steal your sleep, and sometimes it can be cruel. But it's honest. The answer is there, even if it's hidden. You want to know the greatest high you can get legally? It's that moment at two in the morning after a double shot of espresso when you can suddenly solve that equation that's been messing with you for weeks. That moment when you get it.

Like math, people can be frustrating, cruel even, but they are often dishonest and rarely offer the same clarity. I didn't get people. Even if Izzy had been telling me some of the truth, I sensed she'd kept parts from me. Why? I had kept her other secret for five years, so why did she think me incapable of keeping this one?

I dropped Izzy and Julian off at my parents', telling my sister I needed to pick up some brake pads for my Ford. Turned out I could keep my own secrets too.

I parked in front of the Italian restaurant near Mark's place. Mark lived in a one-bedroom cottage in downtown Petaluma, about fifty miles south of Cloverdale. Because it was Saturday morning and I was impatient, I made much better time than I should have.

I stepped out of my truck. Petaluma felt about ten degrees cooler than it had felt back home, but anxiety had me sweating. As I followed the sidewalk toward the entrance to Mark's, I plucked at the hem of my T-shirt, allowing air between it and the skin of my stomach.

The small complex had four units on each side, facing each other. The units resembled Monopoly houses, each of a similar shape and barely larger. A strip of lawn and a large apricot tree separated the rows. Mark lived in the third cottage from the street. I climbed the red steps of his home and knocked. No answer. Knocked again, more forcefully. I tried the doorbell but got no response to that either.

I frowned. I'd passed Mark's silver Honda Civic parked at the curb. If he wasn't home, he hadn't taken his car.

I pressed my ear against the door to hear signs Mark might be inside but avoiding me. That didn't make sense, of course. A day earlier, he had called me about us meeting. But at the moment nothing made sense, so maybe he had changed his mind. Or Izzy had changed it for him.

The curtains were drawn, but on the windows along the side I found a slight gap between two fabric panels. I stepped forward until my toes butted against the foundation. Leaned in until my nose nearly brushed the glass. Peered into the darkness. The thin shaft of light caught only the leaves of a potted plant and, next to it, a mug on its side. Anything else in the room was lost to shadow. No one seemed to be inside.

I started to turn away but something made me freeze.

*The mug.*

I again pressed my face to the glass and squinted. Had the mug been full or empty when it had been knocked onto its side? Had it been broken in a struggle? I looked for liquid pooling or shards of ceramic, but I couldn't see clearly. Too dark.

I considered my options. Mark had a programmable lock on the back door, and I'd been here when Izzy had used it. Without meaning to, I had committed the number to memory. Still, I hesitated. Izzy often accused me of not respecting her boundaries. To enter Mark's house now, even under the circumstances, felt like a violation.

Frustrated, I closed my eyes and inhaled deeply. Someone had abducted a seventeen-year-old girl. Mark wasn't returning my calls. And Izzy was lying to me.

*Guess now I'll have my own sins to account for,* I thought.

I opened my eyes and punched in the code.

Inside the cottage, the gloom deepened, all but one set of blackout curtains pulled tight. In the meager light and thick silence, I felt abruptly alone. I thought of Julian, who loved the dark. Often he would climb into my bed to tell me about a dream he'd had, or to ask for a story. He said the dark helped him imagine better. Under the current circumstances, I wasn't sure imagining better was a good thing.

I navigated the furniture mostly by touch, stumbling on a curled piece of carpet, until I found the lamp near the back of the living room. The knotty pine walls warmed in the sudden light. With the cottage measuring less than five hundred square feet, it was easy enough to see but not so bright that it might bleed through the edges of the curtains and alert the neighbors. I hoped.

I grazed the curtain's hem with my fingertips. Something about it bothered me. I looked closer, trying to find a stain or tear or other detail that might've pricked my subconscious. But I saw nothing.

I turned away from the curtains and took in my surroundings. A simple layout: in the living room there was a navy love seat, a rectangular oak table, and an accent table on which sat the lamp I had just switched on as well as a framed photo. I knew the one. It had been taken about a month after Izzy and Mark started dating. I picked it up. As many times as I'd seen it, why had I never before noticed the tightness in her smile?

Mark once told me it was her smile that got him. He and Izzy met in a grocery store's wine aisle. He had been buying a nice Alexander Valley cabernet, while she had been deciding between boxes marked red or white. Even my sister's happiest memories often revolved around alcohol.

I returned the photo to the accent table and checked out the upended mug. It turned out to be intact and empty, the table's surface dry. I touched the base of the plant next to it, then felt the soil. It felt like it hadn't been watered in a couple of days. Mark had a thing for plants. In the small space, in addition to the one on the table, I counted three others: a hanging ivy, a small spider plant on the TV stand, and a large ficus in the corner. Against the far wall there were two doors, both open. One led to the bathroom, the other to the bedroom. To the right was the kitchen, cramped and tidy.

I stood rooted in place, still worried I was crossing a line. How well did I know Mark? I knew he worked in an insurance office, but I wasn't certain what he did there. I couldn't say where he'd gone to school, or whether he preferred chicken or fish. But I knew Mark well enough to know he wouldn't want me going through his stuff.

Despite my misgivings, I stepped closer and peered into Mark's bedroom. In the corner, tucked against the wall just beyond the lamp's reach, I noticed a shape, the thickness and length of a small body. About the size of a seventeen-year-old girl.

Neighbors and consequences be damned, I flipped on the overhead light. In full light, it still looked like a body, hidden beneath a blanket. Not moving. Rolled up for easy disposal once the sun had set? Or covered out of guilt over whatever had happened here?

My heart's rhythm grew erratic, an almost painful pressure building in my chest. I forced myself forward, toward the shape. Hand unsteady, I reached for it. Reached for *her*? I touched the girl-sized form. Paused, confused. The shape yielded, soft. Too soft? I inhaled, steadied myself, and bunched the hem of the blanket in my fist. Before I could lose my nerve, I yanked. The blanket flew, like some perverted magic trick, revealing only a pillow and sloppily rolled sleeping bag. No dead girl.

Adrenaline still surging, I leaned in and smelled the pillow. I thought I detected the scent of lavender. The pillow didn't smell like my sister. Someone other than Izzy had spent the night here.

I stood and headed into the bathroom. On the counter I found another of Izzy's tortoiseshell barrettes. Next to it there was a tube of lip gloss. I skimmed the list of ingredients. Bis-diglyceryl polyacyladipate-2. Beeswax. Peppermint oil.

When Izzy was six, she had shoplifted a lip balm from a CVS. Her lips had swelled and reddened, and twelve-year-old me had convinced her it was because she had broken the law and was not an allergic reaction.

The gloss couldn't be Izzy's. And if the gloss wasn't Izzy's . . . I touched the tortoiseshell barrette I had assumed was hers. A match to the one I'd found in my truck the morning after Marina disappeared.

# 9

Still holding the barrette, I heard a voice behind me. "What're you doing in here?"

I jumped and turned to find a man studying me from the doorway. The stranger appeared to be in his late thirties, his brown hair in need of a cut and his T-shirt likely a medium when a large would've been a better fit. At least his shorts were baggy. He also held a leash, attached to a harnessed and rotund calico.

I decided to turn the question back on him. "What are *you* doing here?"

"I was walking Pancake when I noticed the lights on." I looked at the round cat. Pancake didn't seem like the exercise type. "Besides, I figured I should open the curtains and water Mark's plants."

The comment made me realize what had bothered me a few minutes earlier. With a houseful of plants that needed sunlight, why had the blackout curtains remained drawn? I could think of only one reason: Mark wanted to hide whatever had been happening inside his home.

"I'm Oliver, by the way." He gestured over his shoulder. "Just moved into the unit across the way."

I wanted to ask, *If you just moved in, why do you have a key?* Instead, I tried to smile, but my mouth was dry, my tongue tacky on the roof of my mouth.

"I'm Frankie," I said.

He took a couple of steps forward, five feet or so away now. It hit me that I didn't know this man. I'd allowed myself to be disarmed by Pancake, and now this stranger blocked my exit. I tried to sound casual when I asked, "Do you know where Mark is?"

He hesitated, his eyes narrowing. "Who are you again?"

"I'm his girlfriend's sister."

Oliver's face softened, and with that, my nerves settled. A little. "Oh. Izzy. Yeah, I met her. If you're her sister, I'm surprised you don't know—" He stopped, his expression clouding.

My pulse quickened. "Did something happen to Mark?"

Oliver seemed hesitant to share what, judging by his expression, could only be bad news.

Very bad news, it turned out. "Mark was in an accident."

If there had been an accident, why would Izzy keep it from me? We had just spoken, and she had seemed fine. Well, not fine exactly, but she hadn't acted so out of character that I'd suspected something like this. Then I realized I had yet to ask the obvious question. Maybe because I was afraid of the answer. "Is he okay?"

Oliver looked suddenly uncomfortable. "I think so?" He shrugged. Then he asked: "Shouldn't you know? He had to have an emergency contact."

Suddenly I wondered if Izzy knew at all. But she was at Mark's house, wasn't she? That's what she had said. She had to know. Unless she left before the accident? Or was her being here another lie?

I thought of Mark's car, still parked on the curb. "Unless he was walking somewhere and wasn't carrying his wallet or phone."

He lapsed into silence, studying me. "He was on foot," he said. "But even when I'm walking, I always carry my phone."

Pancake circled Oliver's leg, wrapping his ankle in the leash, before collapsing on his foot.

"Was Mark alone?" I asked.

He paused. "As far as I could tell, yeah. But, to be honest, I didn't see much."

The way he hesitated made me wonder about that. "You sure?"

He suddenly had a hard time maintaining eye contact. "I really should get going. It's supposed to hit upper nineties today. Don't want to get stuck running in that."

I nudged. "You must've seen something."

When he met my eyes, he looked conflicted. "I didn't see the accident, but—I heard it." He grimaced. "It was horrible, that a body could make that sound. The impact must've thrown Mark across the street, because he was lying in the road, almost in the gutter. Hit his head hard too. There was all this blood." He touched the side of his head near his hairline.

I found it harder to breathe. "What about the car?" *Please let me be wrong about this.*

"Didn't see the car," he said. "Bastard didn't even stop."

So it had been a hit-and-run. I tried to shake it off, force air back into my lungs. Coincidence, I told myself. I wouldn't become one of those people who assigned meaning to events that had none.

I ignored the tightening of my stomach. Pushed my shoulders back. Centered myself with a breath. Whether Mark's accident was related to that night five years before or a random occurrence, Izzy would need me. There were questions she would want answered.

A small voice inside me: *Unless she already has those answers.*

"Do you know where Mark was going?" My voice only slightly unsteady.

"Not sure. I just know wherever he was going, he was walking there. Otherwise he would've been headed in the direction of his car."

"Unless he was meeting someone on the street," I suggested. I pictured Mark in the road, the driver abandoning him there. Despite my resolve, my vision blurred at the edges. I blinked hard. Better.

Apparently less sure now, Oliver nodded slowly. "Yeah. I suppose he could've been meeting someone."

"But you didn't see anyone waiting for him? Like a car at the curb?"

"No. There was parking out front too." Confident again. "If someone had been picking him up, there would've been no reason for Mark to cross the street, not with spaces available much closer."

"What time did this happen?"

"I don't know. Five-ish?"

About the time I had talked to Izzy. "And you're sure he was alone?" I asked.

He shrugged. "Like I said, by the time I saw Mark, he was already down."

"What about before the accident?"

His eyes darted, settling on the front door. "Yeah." Definitely nervous now. "He was alone."

"What about Thursday night?"

This time he wasn't as quick to answer. "It's really not my place to say."

"It might help."

"How? Mark's hurt, or . . ." He didn't finish his sentence, but I guessed what word he omitted: *Or dead*. "It was a stupid argument. How's talking about it going to help him?"

"An argument?"

"He and Izzy fought, but I didn't hear what they were arguing about. Just raised voices, doors slamming, and all that."

Funny. Another thing Izzy hadn't mentioned. "And you're sure you didn't hear what the argument was about?"

His tongue darted across his lips. He was having a hard time looking at me.

"Even a single word might help." Or a name. Like Marina.

Oliver squatted to pet his cat, which I guessed was another tactic to avoid my eyes and my question. After a moment, he stood and finally made eye contact, though he spoke with obvious reluctance. "Mark might've said something about an accident."

Every muscle in me went rigid. "What kind of accident?"

He shrugged. "I'm not even sure that's what I heard." Backing off now. Likely not wanting to cause trouble for his neighbor. "And who knows? They could've been talking about a cooking accident, or maybe one of them spilled something."

Only I didn't think that was it at all. "Do you know what time this was?" I asked.

Uncertainty played across his face. "Eleven-thirty?"

"That sounds like a guess."

He squirmed and stepped out of the leash curled around his feet. Obviously done with my questions. "Look, I'll come back later to water the plants." He picked up Pancake and hurried away.

As he left, I did the math. Mill Valley was only half an hour south of Petaluma. If Izzy really had been at Mark's place at eleven-thirty on Thursday night, she still could have been in Marina's neighborhood about the time the girl was abducted. Or she could've been helping her friend move a desk in San Francisco, like she claimed.

Whatever was happening, I knew I had been wrong to dismiss the accident as coincidence. How could it be a coincidence when it had happened before?

# 10

Calling on the memory felt a little like picking at a scab to see the wound beneath. Not healthy, not productive. But I picked nonetheless.

Five years earlier, my sister was just about to graduate and I was months away from starting my first teaching assignment. We were at once settled and cocky about the possibilities that existed for us and our invincibility. Not normally an optimistic person, I had nevertheless given hope a foothold, and by the night of the accident I had allowed myself to grow stupid with it.

A lot of that was because Izzy had started to transition away from the party scene that had been such a large part of her high school experience. Or so I had believed at the time. In truth, she had only turned her attention to an older crowd, which brought with it the greater stakes of cars and freshly tasted freedom.

No one reveled in the taste of that more than my sister. Izzy had been a cranky baby, and from birth resented being held. But once she could move on her own, a switch flipped. The first time she scooted across the floor, she giggled for a solid five minutes. At eighteen, my sister glowed with her new freedom. The sobriety helped, too, as temporary as it turned out to be.

It was a Tuesday in early May. When she called, Izzy slurred. "Can you come get me?" As if I'd ever had a choice. I had gotten the same call several times before, and I had always gone.

After the initial moment of shock—I really had believed Izzy was doing better—I was annoyed: Who partied on a Tuesday? A few of her friends were in college now. Didn't they have homework? Jobs? One of my first thoughts had been about a bunch of kids shirking their responsibilities. Like I said, optimism had made me stupid.

Since Izzy had borrowed Mom's sedan, I had to take an Uber so I could retrieve both my sister and the car. On the ride, my irritation and concern grew, and it was a long, and expensive, ride, winding along Geysers Road in the dark.

Why hadn't Izzy called an Uber instead of me? And why hadn't I insisted she do that?

Those were the kind of stupid, pointless questions I had at first, when I thought that was just another night like so many others before.

About thirty minutes in, the driver slowed, glancing out the side window toward the mountains to the west.

"You sure we're in the right place?" he asked. Probably calculating how much he would've made picking up in-town fares instead.

"I'm sure." My feigned confidence reassured him, and he drove faster. From a distance, his headlights caught metal.

"This it?" he asked hopefully.

But it was a Jeep, not my mom's sedan. Frustrated, I felt myself flush. *Where are you, Izzy?*

"Keep driving," I said.

Finally, about a mile up, I spotted the car. The Uber driver dropped me off, eager to be rid of me, and I started walking. Gravel crunched beneath my feet as I navigated the shoulder between the asphalt and the cliff's edge. When I got closer to the car and saw Izzy leaning against it, the heat in my cheeks flared. I was done with this. Done.

Then I saw her face. Bloodless lips. A greasy sheen to her skin. Smudged mascara. In the night, her eyes were black, her arms tense bands wrapped around her chest. She was drunk, again, but I thought it might be something more this time.

She took a step toward me, but without the support of the car she faltered. She went down hard. Her head bowed, and she didn't get back up. Had she had more to drink since she had called? Or had I just not noticed how far gone she was on the phone?

My irritation disappeared. I dropped to my knees beside her and grabbed her wrist. Her pulse was weak, thready. That close, I could smell how the alcohol soured her breath.

I felt the blood drain from my face. "You okay?" Breathless. A stupid question since she obviously wasn't.

Izzy shook her head. She was trembling. She babbled, and it took her several tries before I understood her: "Got to find her."

Growing more alarmed, I checked her face and arms for signs of injury, my hands clenching into fists. She was having trouble keeping her eyes open.

I had never seen her that bad. "How much did you drink?"

She shrugged, but this set her off balance and she swayed. I threaded an arm around her back and used the other to grip her shoulder. "We need to get you to a hospital." I tried to pull her up, but she resisted with a flurry of slaps.

"No. No no no! Can't leave."

The moon cast scant light, but it was enough for me to clearly see her. She was terrified.

"Izzy." My voice was a warning. As her big sister, I'd used the tone often, and it always worked. But this time she was too far gone. "What's going on?"

I forced eye contact, but her gaze clouded, then wandered, her lids heavy. She started speaking rapidly then, her words running together so they became impossible to decipher.

"Slow down, Izzy."

She tried to stand but wobbled. She retched, and I moved just enough to avoid getting vomit on my sneaker. When I touched her forehead, it was clammy.

"Got to find her," she said again. She clawed at my arm, urging me toward the path below.

I shook my head. "We can't go down there." Izzy could barely stand on the hard-packed dirt. On the steep and uneven embankment, she would fall and break her neck. I noticed small abrasions on her arms and a small cut near her ear. While she had been waiting for me, had she already tried? I shivered at what could've happened.

"Got to," she said. More urgent now.

I wrapped my arms around her, a vise to keep her from the edge. She twisted against me, then swallowed suddenly. This time when she threw up, she got both of my sneakers and a pants leg.

"Damn it, Izzy." But my voice lacked heat. She stopped struggling, and I released her. I shook my feet and pants leg, then moved closer to the brush so I could rub my sneakers in it.

I returned to her, and held her face between my hands. Had she grown even paler? Were her cheeks cold because of the slight wind, or was her body struggling to regulate its temperature? With the sleeve of my sweatshirt, I wiped her brow, which had beaded with sweat.

"We need to get you out of here."

She became agitated again. "Stay." Even that single word she slurred. When she spoke again, she mumbled. A series of words that seemed to be all consonants and no vowels. Until the last word, which I only caught because she emphasized it. *Dead*.

"Dead?" My voice unsteady.

She pointed, though because her arm shook I couldn't tell at what. She spoke louder: "Find her."

When I didn't immediately move, Izzy stumbled forward. When I grabbed her, she thrashed against me and started sobbing. "I killed her."

I grew suddenly aware of the wind's bite and the night's darkness. She shifted in my arms to point at where she had parked. Pulling her with me, I walked to Mom's car. Started to examine it. I noticed a small dent above the car's bumper and brushed my fingers over it. I used my phone's flashlight to get a better look. A small ding, barely noticeable. I couldn't be sure it hadn't been there before Izzy had borrowed the car.

I continued to sweep the beam along the car, checking out the doors, the tires, the hood . . .

The hood.

There the beam froze, bobbling as my hand trembled. Another dent marred the steel, beneath a smear of what appeared to be blood.

Beside me, seeing the smear, Izzy's keening intensified. "Find her."

I nodded, unable to speak. Barely breathing, I opened the driver's door and grabbed the keys from the ignition. Then I forced Izzy into the backseat. It wasn't much of a battle. She teetered on the edge of consciousness. I buckled her so she remained upright, less likely to choke on her own vomit, then stripped off my sweatshirt and tucked it around her.

"You stay here." I again cradled her face in my hands, willing her to hear me. "I'll go look for her, but you stay here." I spoke slowly and stressed each word.

She nodded, or maybe her head had grown too heavy, causing her chin to dip against her chest. If there was an injured girl out there, I needed to do what Izzy had begged: I needed to find her.

I closed the door and locked Izzy inside the car. Then, still using my phone as a flashlight, I hurried as fast as was safe in the direction my sister had pointed.

Even as my heart pounded, I tried to calculate the most likely trajectory of a body thrown by a car. I started down the embankment, sideways, landing each step as carefully as haste allowed. My sneakers had decent traction, but I nevertheless found myself skidding on loose pine needles and damp leaves. I slowed. As I made my way down, I was forced to crawl, in spots. At other points, I grabbed nearby pines and boulders to steady myself.

I was thorough but quick in my search, anxious to be back with my sister. As drunk as she was, she could be at risk of permanent brain damage. Or death. If not for that smear of blood, I would've done a more cursory search, or just ignored my sister's pleading altogether. I could've convinced her I had already looked. Was Izzy even still conscious?

This thought renewed my fear. I needed to get back to her. The search was pointless anyway. There was too much ground to cover, and that ground was treacherous. My phone's flashlight would eventually die, and I would've wasted hours that could've been spent saving my sister.

Then the breeze shifted, and I caught the scent of recent death. It pricked the hairs on my arms and neck. An urge propelled me away from it, toward the safety of the car, but I pushed forward. The cuff of my jeans rose, exposing skin. Barbed weeds clawed at my ankles.

Thick shrubs hid whatever caused that stench—acrid, earthy, foul. As I approached, it grew more pungent. I switched to breathing through my mouth, but that only made it worse. Like I was pulling the decay deep into my core, where I might never be rid of it.

I switched to breathing through my nose again, treading carefully as I rounded the plants that blocked my view. There, the beam of my flashlight fell on the corpse, most of its damage hidden but its eyes flat. The only injury that showed was a jagged line at its throat.

A deer. It was only a deer.

My heart didn't stop hammering until I reached the car.

"It was a deer, Izzy," I said. When she didn't respond, I shook her awake.

She moaned, then murmured, "Found her?"

I sighed, brushing Izzy's hair off her shoulders and tucking in the sweatshirt that served as a makeshift blanket. "Yes. I found her."

The next morning, when I went to wash the blood from the hood of my mom's car, I noticed something I hadn't the night before. Stuck in one of the headlights, so fine as to be easily missed in the dark, were three long strands of human hair.

# 11

My parents, Fernando and Teresa Barrera, lived in a traditional one-story on the west side of Cloverdale. With my dad sick, I had stayed close, even during college, to help my mom with him and Izzy. Not that either of us would have admitted that to Dad.

I had hoped to have the conversation about Mark with Izzy at her apartment, but when I'd stopped there first, Piper told me Izzy was still at our parents' house.

I forced myself out of my truck. My mom was on the porch before I got off the sidewalk. The honeyed light made the world seem a better place than it actually was. Given my mood, a gray sky with nimbus clouds seemed more fitting. Instead, the sky was clear, and my eyes burned with tears I couldn't cry. What kind of message would it send if I allowed myself to fall apart?

"Beautiful day," I said, blinking. "How's Julian?"

She embraced me so tightly my spine ached, and my heart a little too. But I couldn't let her know Izzy was in trouble.

Her face split into a smile. "Amazing. He helped me make posole."

Julian *was* amazing, but I couldn't imagine him cutting up meat or roasting chilies. "And how exactly did he help?"

"He washed the cabbage and picked the limes from our tree."

"He'll be making it by himself in no time."

"You joke, but you could make it by yourself by the time you were ten. It's already obvious that Julian's going to be a genius like you."

Her happiness, while welcome, pained me. I hated keeping this from her. As she'd said countless times during our childhood, a lie by omission was still a lie. Most of those times she had been talking to Izzy.

"Where is the little genius?" I asked.

"He's in the backyard."

"How's Dad?"

Her smile widened. "He's having a good day."

My dad had been born just outside Morelia in Michoacán, my mom in the Northern California town of Eureka. His family migrated north, hers south, and they met as teenagers at a music festival near San Diego. Back then, my mom often told us, my dad was a musician with a full head of hair. Though he could've had the attention of any girl at the festival—my dad would always roll his eyes here—it was my mom he handed that red plastic cup of warm beer. My mom would whisper this—teens drinking at a music festival. How scandalous.

Despite decades of marriage spent raising two daughters—not to mention the hair he'd lost and the weight he'd gained—my mom still saw my dad that way: the wiry musician with the quick smile and long hair who had offered her that first taste of beer.

I was glad she saw him that way, because to see only the sickness in him would've broken her heart. Like it broke mine.

I steeled myself and asked, "Izzy still here?"

As expected, she nodded. "She's in the backyard with your dad and Julian."

My mom linked her arm through mine and led me to the backyard, where I would have to tell my sister about Mark and ask her why she had lied.

MY DAD AND IZZY were sitting at the patio table under the striped awning. My mom joined them, but I waited on the edge of the concrete, watching Julian, savoring that moment before he noticed me. On the grass beneath the shade of a redwood tree, he crouched with a tiny net. Probably hunting bugs.

Then he saw me, and he dropped the net and sprinted. He threw himself at my legs and looked up at me—"Mama!"—the fervor of his affection swelling my heart. I knelt, wiping away a smudge of either mud or chocolate and hugging him as fiercely as my own mom had embraced me.

I buried my face in his hair, mussed and sticky with sweat. Soon enough, my arrival would merit a slower approach from him. Acutely aware of how little time I had before that happened, I scooped him up, cradling his head the same way I had when he was an infant. My arms tightened on his back. These days he rode a little lower on my hip, and I wondered how much longer I would be able to lift him. I released him only when he started to wriggle.

"Abuela let me have pudding."

So the mystery of the smudge had been solved. I kissed his forehead, then licked my lips in exaggerated fashion. "Mmm . . . must be why you taste so sweet."

Julian giggled. "Noooo."

Julian's laughter fortified me. Or maybe I lingered out of procrastination. Izzy would not take my news or questions well. "I'm pretty sure I'm right. You tasted pretty sour this morning."

He licked my arm. Guess I should've expected that one. "Well, you taste like bug poop." Then he laughed.

I managed to keep a straight face, not easy despite my current mood. "No potty words." Still, I couldn't help myself. "What exactly does bug poop taste like?"

"Like you."

Maybe my mom was right: Julian *was* a genius.

After Julian returned to hunting bugs, I greeted Izzy and Dad, taking the open seat next to Mom.

"It's good to see you, mija."

"You, too, Dad."

I studied him, as I always did when seeing him for the first time on any given day. There was color in his cheeks, and he was grinning. Mom was right: he was having a good day.

"Julian keeping you busy?" I asked.

"Always. He's a spirited boy."

Spirited and stubborn, like his grandfather.

I turned my attention to my sister. "Hey, Izzy."

I wasn't sure if it was something in my expression or her own guilt, but she blanched. I couldn't tell her here, in front of our parents.

"Mom, Dad—I need to talk to Izzy alone for a minute."

A current passed between me and my sister. She pushed back her chair and stood, as if as eager as I was to be done with this particular conversation.

"We can talk in the kitchen," I said.

There, I waited for Izzy to settle on a stool at the counter before asking, "Would you like some water?"

"By the look on your face, I might need something stronger." She tried to laugh, but it lodged in her throat, and I winced. I didn't like when Izzy joked about that.

I started to reach for her, intent on reassuring her that I would protect her as I always had. But had I? Despite my continued efforts, the really bad things kept happening.

So instead I focused on a task I could manage. I turned from her and filled a glass at the sink, then moved to the freezer to pop a few ice cubes from the tray. When I babysat Izzy when she was about Julian's age, she would demand exactly three cubes in her water. Not two. Not four. If there weren't exactly three cubes floating in her cup, she would throw the cup and one hell of a tantrum. Izzy wasn't as picky now, but the habit stuck. I dropped three cubes into her water. As warm as the kitchen was, I expected they would melt to chips within a few minutes.

When I handed Izzy the glass, I squeezed her shoulder. "I'm sorry," I said.

She didn't ask why I needed to apologize. She took a long sip of her water, then set the cup on the counter. She traced a line in the condensation with her fingertip. A heart.

Finally, she took a deep breath and said, "Tell me."

I took a step closer, moving within reach in case she needed me. "It's about Mark."

I opened my mouth to tell her more, but I got out only the first few words before she collapsed against me, hands clasped against ears that didn't want to hear. Gently, I pried her hands free.

"You have to hear," I said softly. Then I told her the rest of it, and held her as she withdrew into her silence.

# 12

On the way to my parents' house, I had tracked down Mark to an ICU in Petaluma. Izzy and I headed there now. Needing time with her grief, Izzy hadn't wanted our parents to know, so I manufactured a less urgent excuse about a busted radiator and Mark needing a ride. In covering for Izzy over the years, I had lied to them so often that it came easily. Too easily. Why did they still trust me?

Though our dad was having one of his good days, and though they volunteered to watch Julian, I still felt horrible. For leaving Julian behind. For lying to my parents. And for watching Izzy's face for signs she might be involved in Mark's accident.

On the drive to Petaluma, Izzy remained lost in her silence. She stared out the window at the passing hills, fields, and auto dealerships, turning only occasionally to glance at my speedometer.

At the hospital's front desk, I asked for directions. In a reversal of our usual roles, Izzy led the way to the ICU. She nearly jogged, but her steps were erratic. Several times she stumbled.

Mark had survived the accident, though when we found him, I doubted I would've been able to tell, if not for the tubes and monitors signaling the fight to save him.

If my sister was a hurricane, all energy and exaggeration, her boyfriend was more like the sapling that might snap if the wind blew with enough force. Everything about Mark appeared faded, as if he had been left in the sun too long, and his brow was perpetually furrowed in either worry or thought.

Now, with Mark in an ICU bed, his face slack, the difference was even more pronounced. His right cheek was abraded, his right eye swollen, and he seemed to be held together by bandages and tape.

Izzy closed her eyes and took a long, jagged breath before opening them again. Sensing she wanted to be alone with Mark, I excused myself.

In the waiting area, I took a seat near a window and called the police. While I waited to be transferred, I noticed a small gray-brown bird landing in a nearby tree. A flicker? Sparrow? I wasn't good with birds. All I could say with certainty was it wasn't a duck.

After about a minute of watching the bird, I heard the call connect. "You were asking about the hit-and-run in Petaluma yesterday?" The officer's voice was deep, smooth, and immediately put me on edge. After years spent keeping secrets, I knew to choose my words carefully when talking to the police.

"Yes. Thank you." My voice cracked. To steady myself, I focused on the gray-brown bird. "The victim was Mark Kozlowski."

"Did you witness the incident?"

"No. Just checking on what might've happened."

"We're still investigating." In the tree, the tiny bird cocked its head, staring at me. Deciding if I meant it harm? "How'd you hear about the accident?"

Though he tried to sound casual, I sensed his interest. I realized he hadn't introduced himself, and it seemed awkward to ask for his name now. "From one of Mark's neighbors. Oliver." Had Oliver given me a last name? If so, I couldn't recall it now. "He lives in the unit directly across from Mark's."

"How do you know the victim?"

I chose a version of the truth that kept Izzy's name out of it. "He's a family friend."

The officer asked for my name and number, and I gave it to him. Since I had called from my cell phone, he already had both, and I hoped my honesty gained me points.

"We're trying to nail down a timeline leading up to the incident." The officer's voice grew friendlier, and if I hadn't been so practiced at keeping my secrets, I might've fallen for it. "Any chance you saw Mark before the accident, or were in the area around five o'clock yesterday?" A pause. "Any information, even if it seems insignificant, might really help us figure out what happened to your friend."

Wrapped in the smooth voice and careful wording were the real questions: *Are you involved? Do you have an alibi?*

If I had been the driver, would I really have risked a call to the police to gauge how much they knew? Maybe.

As I considered telling the officer about what I'd found at Mark's, the conversation played out in my head.

*Tell me again what you found, Ms. Barrera.*

*A barrette and a tube of lip gloss.*

In my head, the officer looked skeptical. *Hmm.*

*It's not just that. The curtains were closed.*

*And why is that unusual?*

*He had plants.*

*Plants.*

*Oh—and there was a sleeping bag in the corner of his bedroom.*

*I take it Mark wasn't a camper?*

*It wasn't his. The pillow smelled like lavender.*

Again: *Hmm.*

Even if the police did take me seriously, I couldn't be sure the evidence wouldn't lead to Izzy.

Near the window, the small bird tilted its head one way, then the other, the twin black beads of its eyes fixed on me. *What you gonna do, Frankie?*

"Wish I could help, but I was with my son most of the day." Except for the morning, when I'd been questioned by Detective Pratt, but it probably was a good idea to leave out that part.

I tried to steer the conversation back on course. "Can you tell me what happened?"

The officer answered quickly, as if I'd misunderstood his intentions and he had been willing to share all along. "I can tell you the driver was headed southeast on Keller Street toward Washington. Evidence suggests the car didn't slow down after hitting the victim." I wondered what that evidence was, but I didn't ask. I wasn't sure he would've told me. Besides, I already believed Mark had been hit on purpose. How would knowing there were no skid marks from sudden braking change that?

"Do you have a description of the car?" I asked.

This time the officer responded more slowly. "So far, the witnesses that've come forward didn't see the accident itself, only its aftermath. But like I said, we're still looking into it."

Before he could ask any additional questions, I thanked the officer and hung up. Outside, the bird quick-stepped on the branch and fluttered its wings, as if plotting a kamikaze run at the glass. I pictured its body falling broken to the earth.

*Don't do it.*

The tiny bird didn't understand, of course, but I felt a small sense of accomplishment, and relief, when it flew away.

"What are you staring at?"

I startled. I hadn't noticed Izzy approaching. "A bird."

"What kind?" she asked, her voice hollow.

*A lucky one.* "I'm not sure."

She sat beside me and pulled out her phone, which she cradled in her lap. She stroked the screen with her thumb.

"I should call Mark's parents." She glanced at me as if seeking approval. Grief had stained the whites of her eyes an angry shade of pink.

"You know the number?"

She leaned back in her chair. "No." Her voice cracked. "I should know that, shouldn't I?" She closed her eyes and began rubbing her temples in tight, furious circles. "Mark and I were talking about getting married. Having kids. Did you know that?"

I flinched. Kids? I was grateful Izzy's eyes were closed so she didn't see it.

"They're not close, Mark and his parents," she said. "I'm not sure he'd even want me to call them. Shouldn't I know that too?" She stopped rubbing, parting her lids slowly as if they were weighted. "But you know better than anyone, don't you? I can't take care of myself. How could I ever be a mom?"

"Don't say that."

Her laugh was half sob. " 'Don't say that.' Not, 'Oh, Izzy, that's not true at all.'"

"It's not true. But you're twenty-three. There's time."

Too late, I recognized what I'd said. Izzy's eyes glazed. "Is there? Bet Mark thought so." She paused, holding her breath. When she released it, her chest rattled. "Rachel probably did too."

We never said her name out loud. Never. The silence thickened so that it became a wedge between us.

"We don't know that she died." Though I kept my voice low, the corridor seemed to echo. "I only found the deer that night."

"That's all you wanted to find." I could tell Izzy needed the distraction of a fight. "Besides, I do know. Always have, even if you've never believed me."

*You were wasted, Izzy. Of course I didn't believe you.* "We shouldn't be talking about this here."

She stared at me with too-big eyes. "What would you do if I were involved in Marina's abduction?"

She made no attempt to keep her voice down. I glanced around, making sure no one had heard. "Are you?"

"What would you do?" she repeated. Harder now. More on edge.

"We'll figure this out. There's got to be a good reason . . ."

"What would be a good reason for abducting a child?" She shook her head. Purple-black smudges darkened the skin beneath her eyes, the telltale signs of exhaustion looking almost like bruises.

"I'm not involved. It was a hypothetical." I wasn't sure I believed her, but she continued, "I know what you would do . . . you would cover for me. Just like you did back then. And it would eat away at you until you hated me even more than you already do."

"I don't hate you." And I didn't. I hated myself. I fished out the tortoiseshell barrette I had taken from Mark's bathroom. I remembered how I'd worn the matching one while the officer had searched my truck. What would've happened had I left it in the cup holder instead? How close had I come to being arrested? "I found this at Mark's. His neighbor Oliver has a key?"

I phrased it that way intentionally. I hoped she would think Oliver was the one who let me in, which felt less like a betrayal. And I wanted an answer to whether we should be worried Oliver had a key.

"Oliver's cool," she said, distracted. She took the barrette from my hand, then clenched it in her fist. "Am I supposed to thank you for returning this?" She bit her lip as if confused, her head artificially cocked. Growing up, I had seen her use the same expression when questioned by our parents about missing homework, or by a neighbor about the soccer ball that took out a potted plant.

"So it's yours?"

She doubled down on the lip-biting. "Of course it is. You don't happen to have the other one? I might've left it in your truck."

Her eye contact grew shaky, but she squared her shoulders and held it.

"I do have it. At home." She released her breath in one sudden gust, her relief obvious. "Didn't realize they meant so much to you. You could probably pick up another pair at the grocery store for a few bucks."

I sensed Izzy constructing another excuse, but I was too tired to hear it. "I found lip gloss too."

"Oh?"

"It had peppermint oil in it."

She hesitated only a second. "Yeah, that's Piper's. I grabbed it by mistake, thinking it was mine. Must've left it there at the same time I left the barrette." She stood abruptly, her phone slipping from her lap and onto the floor. When she started pacing, she inadvertently kicked it underneath her chair. "The doctor's supposed to update me. Where's the damn doctor?"

I stooped to pick up her phone. "Probably taking care of Mark."

Near the window, Izzy stopped pacing, the fight draining from her. She shifted to face away from me and whispered, "Did you see the bruises?"

I nodded, then realized that with her back turned, she couldn't see the gesture. "I saw the bruises."

"He looked . . ."

I moved to her, and when I rested my hand on her shoulder, she recoiled.

"He's getting excellent care," I said.

When I stepped in front of her, I instantly recognized the expression she wore. Fevered. Restless. She wanted a drink. Badly.

The question lingered on my tongue. While my sister said she didn't want my protection, I needed to know. My hand clenched on Izzy's phone, but I kept my voice neutral as I asked, "If you had nothing to do with that girl, why did you lie about being at Mark's?"

I expected her to lash out. Instead, she slipped deeper into her anguish. "I only wanted to prove I wasn't the screwup everyone thinks I am." Her voice hushed. "But I ended up proving the opposite, didn't I?"

"What are you talking about?"

She pressed her lips together. Another expression I recognized. She wouldn't say more.

HALF AN HOUR LATER, the doctor finally arrived. A blur of bespectacled efficiency, Dr. Heckey gave an update in clipped prose. While Mark's brain CT scan didn't reveal major structural damage, he had been deprived of oxygen. There were positive signs: his eyes responded to stimulus, the doctor said, indicating some brain stem function. Efforts had been made to reduce intercranial swelling. They were keeping Mark sedated, but he was expected to recover.

Had the doctor's voice wavered on that last part?

When Izzy began to sway, I put my hand on her back to help keep her upright.

"Do you have any questions?" he asked, his tone softening.

When Izzy shook her head, he gave a curt nod, though his voice remained kind. "If you think of any, let me know. This is a lot to process."

"Thank you," I said.

Dr. Heckey paused for a moment to make sure Izzy understood. When she finally nodded, he strode down the corridor, back toward the ICU.

THOUGH IT WOULD LIKELY be hours before we would have more news, Izzy insisted on curling up in the waiting area chair to wait. I started to reach toward her with my left hand. Stopped suddenly, tucking my hand in my lap. Izzy's phone. I'd forgotten I still had it.

Palm tingling, I abruptly excused myself to use the restroom. There, I stared at the phone, considering. I knew Izzy's passcode. Julian's birthday. She had never tried to shield it from me.

I placed the phone, faceup, on the counter and leaned over the sink, then I turned on the tap to splash cold water on my face. My hands felt suddenly dirty, so I washed them too. Pear-scented dollops of foam slipped down the side of the bathroom sink, creating milky puddles in the basin.

When I picked up the phone again, shame burned my cheeks. I hadn't even given Izzy much of a chance to answer, had I? Given the circumstances, surely I owed her more time to explain before violating her privacy?

I retreated into the bathroom stall, bolted the door, and unlocked the phone.

I knew there were surveillance apps I could install, but I hadn't come prepared to betray my sister, and Izzy would soon notice her phone was missing. I started by checking her texts. She had recently cleared them. There were only a few left, all of them from today, and none of them significant. I shared her phone's location with mine, then deleted that text thread too.

Her call history remained intact, and one name there caused me to hold my breath. Ben. The man who had supplied the cocaine at that party five years earlier. Izzy had refused to talk much about what had happened that night—when I pushed, she would claim she didn't remember—but that detail she had shared. Why would she need to stay in touch with a man she had on past occasions dismissed as dangerous? A man who used drugs as a way to control attractive women. Unless, as I'd suspected earlier, she had started using drugs again.

The most recent call to Ben had been a couple of weeks earlier, so if he had provided her with drugs more recently, it had been arranged another way. The only calls since Thursday afternoon were from me, my mom, and Mark. I guessed if plans were made, they had been made by text.

I made note of Ben's number. From the area code, it was probably located in Marin County or San Francisco. But people relocated all the time, keeping cell phone numbers that no longer corresponded with their home addresses. Still, it gave me pause. What did it mean that Ben shared an area code with Marina?

I thought of the deleted texts. Izzy might've thought to erase those threads, but had she been as careful with the messaging apps in her social media?

I checked. At first I found nothing but random messages and shared photos. Then a message from bwesley420: A photo of snow, with the words, wanna play?

The bathroom door squeaked open, and my finger froze on the screen. I settled onto the toilet and peered under the stall's partition. The shoes were Izzy's.

"Frankie, have you seen my phone?"

My heart lurched. *Damn it.*

"No." I stared at that picture of snow, my hand clenched so that my knuckles turned white. "But I'll be out in a second. I'll help you look for it."

I expected her to leave, but she turned on the water at the sink. I heard splashing. She must've been washing her face.

I thought of Detective Pratt's search of my phone the day before. Heart thudding, mouth chalky, I navigated to settings. Scrolled to privacy. What if Izzy had turned off location services?

But when I clicked, the button was toggled to the on position. I selected *System services. Significant locations.*

It wouldn't let me access the information. I'd forgotten it required facial recognition. Under my breath, I swore again.

Outside the stall, the water stopped running. Izzy called through the door: "You okay?"

I bobbled the phone. It slipped off my palm, slick with sweat, but I caught it only a breath before it crashed to the floor.

With my elbow, I flushed. "Yeah."

I navigated back to settings and turned off facial recognition. Returned to *Significant locations.* As I studied the location data, my heart seized.

The night Marina disappeared, my sister had been in Mill Valley.

With my own phone, I took a few quick screenshots. Then I locked it and slipped both phones back into the pockets of my jeans, hoping Izzy wouldn't notice the extra lump.

# 13

Back in the waiting area, I slipped Izzy's phone under the chair and waited for her to find it. When she did, her brow wrinkled and she frowned.

"I thought I checked there," she said, to herself more than to me.

I averted my gaze so she wouldn't see my guilt.

By the time Izzy gave up waiting for more news about Mark, the sky outside bore the tint of a bruised plum. I dropped her at home to sleep and then drove to my parents' house to pick up Julian. Hours earlier, I'd filled them in about Mark's accident. Izzy had balked, but I pointed out that we couldn't disappear for half a day without explanation. At least I couldn't. Izzy had years of practice at that.

Julian had fallen asleep next to my dad. Julian's cheeks were slightly rounded and pink, my dad's creased and tanned, but they looked so much alike that I ached.

My mom insisted that Julian stay, so I returned home without him. It would've been selfish to wake him, settled as he was. Still, I missed him.

I changed into sweats and fell into my bed, exhausted. When I closed my eyes, they burned as if sandblasted. But my mind whirred, a machine at risk of overheating, parsing each fact. Each deceit.

After lying there for about an hour, I gave up trying to sleep. I sat up and texted Izzy's friend Kent—might as well check that alibi—then I got out of bed. As I awaited Kent's reply, I wandered the rooms, straightening shelves and cupboards disturbed the day before by the police.

When Kent's response came, it was anticlimactic. On Thursday night, Izzy had indeed been with him and his friend Jay. He helpfully provided Jay's number. I didn't reach out. No reason to make Jay lie for Izzy too.

Restless, I paced, considering how hard I would have to push Izzy before she shared her secrets. Pretty damn hard, I thought. If I knocked on her door at that hour, would she even let me in?

I solved that problem quickly: I wouldn't knock.

I grabbed my purse with its spare key to Izzy's apartment.

THE APARTMENT WAS EMPTY. No Izzy. No Piper. I worried at the implication of their absence. Cloverdale wasn't San Francisco. After midnight, where could they have gone?

My brain snagged on the flip side of that thought: The apartment was empty. Mine to search.

I headed into Izzy's room. There, I closed the door and flicked on the light. No reason to be stealthy. She was my sister, and I had a key.

I scanned her now brightly lit room and sucked in my breath.

It was tidy. Far cleaner than my own. Izzy had actually made her bed, sheets tucked in, throw pillows arranged. Since when did Izzy have throw pillows?

When she was in middle school, the year before I moved out, Izzy had crawled between heaps of clothing to reach her pillow. In our shared bathroom, she had encroached on my side of the counter with the determination of a wartime general. Most mornings I had to pick through her colored hair sprays, citrus-scented lotions, and tubes of gloss to find my toothbrush. So when had Izzy become . . . neat?

For a moment, a sense of disconnect made my head swim. Another secret Izzy had kept from me.

*No,* I corrected myself. Another detail I had missed. It was my responsibility to notice, not hers to say, *Hey, Frankie, I've started making my bed.*

I pulled open the closest dresser drawer. The jumbled mass of T-shirts reassured me slightly. Everything stored in messy balls, it looked as if she'd dumped her laundry basket into the drawer, then shoved it closed.

*So not a total transformation.*

After finishing a search of her dresser and small closet, I moved to her nightstand. No signs of Marina anywhere in the room. Then I heard the front door slam shut. I froze, listening. After years of sneaking out, Izzy had grown accustomed to shutting doors with more care. Unless she was upset. So was I dealing with an agitated Izzy—or Piper?

From the front of the house, a voice called out: "Izzy?"

I grimaced. *Piper.*

Izzy's roommate would've noticed the light seeping from

beneath the bedroom door. No use in pretending I wasn't there. I opened the door and walked the few steps into the dimly lit living room.

Piper had thick black hair, even thicker black liner, and lipstick so red it felt nearly hostile. Though it was a warm night, she wore a black hoodie and jeans. She had lived hard enough to have physical scars she worked to hide. Given her history, her armor wasn't surprising, but though I empathized, it didn't mean I liked her. Piper had never been good for my sister.

Half-shadowed by the table lamp, Piper crossed her arms. "What're you doing here?"

"Looking for Izzy."

"She's at Mark's." Her thinned lips suggested she was hiding something. Which she had to be, given that Mark was in the ICU.

I didn't call her on her lie. Either she knew and wasn't telling me, or Izzy hadn't told her yet. Which seemed odd. I felt my forehead crease.

There was no real hallway in the apartment, and the door was open. Taller than me, Piper had to do minimal neck-craning to see behind me into Izzy's room. "So—why were you in there with the door closed?" Her eyes narrowed.

"Just going through my sister's stuff."

She appeared surprised by my answer. Understandable. People were often taken aback by the truth, but I saw no reason to lie. There could be no other explanation for being alone in my sister's room, at least not one I could come up with quickly. It was a solid four hours past my usual bedtime, and I was exhausted. And cranky.

"Let me know if you hear from her?" I said.

She wouldn't, but it needed to be asked. "If I see her." Her expression guarded again.

"Great."

When I tried to move past her, she stepped backward and blocked the door.

"You don't like me."

I startled. Neither of us had said it out loud before. "Maybe. But I don't dislike you."

"Yeah, you do."

I had to give her points for being direct. No reason I couldn't do the same. "Okay, I do."

"Because of what happened five years ago?"

I couldn't hold Piper accountable for inviting Izzy to that party. There was no way she could've known what would happen. "Not for that."

"Then because I'm a bad influence?" When I didn't answer, she added, "You know she's an adult?"

I folded my arms across my chest. "What do you mean by that?"

"You act like she's your kid."

I opened my mouth to argue, but my denial would've been wasted. What did she know of it? Dad had gotten sick shortly after Izzy was born. By the time she was four, he'd lost the lower half of his left leg to diabetes and had started using a wheelchair. He had been fitted for a prosthetic leg, but never wore it—too uncomfortable, he said—and when Mom had suggested an equity loan on the house to buy a better model, he had refused. Prosthetic legs were only designed to last a few years, he had argued, and were they going to get a loan every time he needed a new one? Mom didn't tell him that she had needed to get a loan to keep up with the mortgage anyway. I did what I could to help, but the salary of a middle school math teacher only stretched so far. The one thing I had been able to do, though, was help with Izzy. I wasn't going to apologize to Piper for doing what I could to make sure Izzy always felt safe and loved. Even if I sometimes failed at that.

"I don't treat her like she's a child."

"Oh? Weren't you just ransacking her room?" she asked, smirking. "And aren't you always cleaning up her messes?"

I froze, suddenly immobile, fearful that even a flutter of an eyelash or twitch of my mouth would give me away. How much did she know? She had been at the party, but what did she know about its aftermath? They were best friends, after all. Other than the few months when Izzy left town, they'd spent little time apart since they were seventeen. Marina Wagner's age.

If Piper knew anything, she gave nothing away. "Don't get me wrong, Izzy isn't any better," she said. "She relies on you far too much. But she knows she screwed up, and she's trying. You have no idea how hard she's trying."

I thought of Izzy's unexpectedly tidy room.

Her eyes grew serious. "We both are. The drugs? That's not me anymore."

"Maybe. But even if I believe you, I remember what it was like back then."

The air between us seemed to grow colder. "Are you saying I'm responsible for all the shit Izzy did?"

"We both know no one can make Izzy do anything."

"Not for lack of trying on your part."

"I'm not going to apologize for looking out for my sister."

"Even if you're just doing damage?"

"Me?" I asked, incredulous. I remembered the night Izzy found Piper unconscious in a bathtub in a stranger's apartment, and she had to drag Piper out while some creepy guy tried to convince her to screw him. And there was the time Piper dropped off the planet for three weeks, and it turned out she'd driven to Baja to party. Meanwhile, Izzy was back home, so sick she couldn't eat because she thought her best friend had overdosed somewhere. "Aren't you the one who did the real damage to Izzy?"

My words came out hotter than I had intended, and I quickly regretted them. Though Izzy had always had issues with alcohol, her rock-bottom was a cliff far above where Piper had landed. While Izzy had experimented, Piper did Nobel-level research, addicted to heroin and living in a homeless encampment in southwest Santa Rosa. She ended up on Izzy's doorstep when one of the camp's residents she'd speedballed with got violent.

But Piper didn't flinch. "You're not the only one who knows things," she said. "I'm not the one who fucked up back then."

My stomach seized, and I felt suddenly shaky. "Oh?"

"I know about Rachel."

Even the dim light seemed suddenly too bright.

"I'm not sure what you mean."

Her trademark smirk reappeared, but now it chilled. "Do you forget I was there that night? I know things you don't. Things Izzy would never tell you because she's afraid of disappointing you."

"Izzy's not afraid of anything."

"True. Except for that." She stepped away from the door, but I made no effort to leave. I needed to hear the rest of it.

"Did she tell you about the game?" Piper asked.

"She said you played some stupid drinking game. I don't remember what it was called." I attempted to sound dismissive, as if those details had never mattered much to me. The truth was, Izzy hadn't shared them, mostly because she had blacked out early and regained consciousness just before hitting that deer.

*Or a girl.*

I had spent a long time searching for an explanation for those strands of hair I'd found in the headlight.

Piper's smirk deepened: "Paranoia."

"What?"

"That's what the game was called."

"That was five years ago," I said, as if it were no longer important, when really it was all I could think about.

Piper's full lips thinned, the red lipstick giving the illusion of a wound. "We played that stupid game, the situation got out of hand, and Rachel ended up dead," she said. "Have you seen how thin Izzy's gotten? What it's doing to her? Sometimes I come out to use the bathroom in the middle of the night, and she's up cleaning the apartment because she can't sleep. And it's already clean. Her hands are chapped, she's got insomnia, but it's fine, it's all fine, because she doesn't want her big sister to know what a fuckin' mess she is."

I felt as if I had been slapped. No, *punched*. Because Piper wasn't wrong. A week after the accident, Izzy had suggested she come forward, tell the police what she had done. But I had convinced myself she was imagining it—I'd never seen her that drunk—and before I conceded to myself that she might be right, Izzy had allowed herself to believe me. Together, we had wished it away. Or thought we had, but the unacknowledged truth had festered in both of us.

Suddenly I realized this was part of why I had never liked Piper: She reminded me of how I had failed my sister. Then, and now. "Just let me know if she comes back," I said.

This time, when I left, she didn't try to stop me.



BACK IN THE CAB of my truck, Piper's words echoed: *She doesn't want her big sister to know what a fuckin' mess she is.*

Truth was, it wasn't just Izzy who was a mess. I was just better at hiding it.

My shoulders sagged under the weight of the past couple of days. I wanted to shrug it off, make a to-do list of all the ways I could still save Izzy. Under pressure, that's what I usually did: I made a plan, then checked items off until the project was complete. But this list seemed impossibly long, and my abilities inadequate.

Whatever had happened out at Mercuryville in the hours before midnight, Izzy still suffered because of it. And I didn't have a clue as to how to help her.

# FIVE YEARS BEFORE

MERCURYVILLE, 8:34 P.M.

By the time the sky faded to cobalt, the moon a half disk of silver-white, everyone but Chuck and Rachel was on their second drink. Izzy had started her third.

"Why aren't you drinking, Rach?" Ben asked. "Warm vodka not your thing?"

"Alcohol's not my thing. It makes people stupid."

Izzy flushed in irritation. She knew Rachel hadn't meant the comment for her, but she felt her shoulders tense.

Tobin reached into his backpack and pulled out a sports drink. "Heads up." He tossed the bottle to Rachel. She reached for it too late and it landed at her feet, the blue liquid sloshing. He grinned. "Nice catch."

Her smile was wan. She seemed distracted. She had been that way since the moment they had arrived, when Izzy had noticed her blanch. She was tempted to ask Rachel if she was okay. Then she remembered Rachel's comment about alcohol making people stupid and went back to sipping her hard seltzer.

When Ben said they should all go for a hike, the interest was lukewarm. But everyone went because Ben was the one who suggested it.

On the hike, Piper and Izzy fell behind, Piper tracing their path with her flashlight. Once the others were out of earshot, Piper leaned in. "What do you think of Chuck?"

While Ben was clearly the most attractive, Tobin was more Izzy's type. But Chuck? "Why?"

Piper sighed, as if the answer should be obvious. "Well, Ben has a thing for Rachel, and I call dibs on Tobin. So that leaves Chuck." She elbowed Izzy in the side. "It's obvious he thinks you're cute."

"I thought you told me Ben used to live with Rachel's family."

"Yeah. So?"

"You don't think that's creepy? He's pretty much family, and she's so young."

She laughed. "She's at least six months older than you, and like you weren't checking Ben out too."

"I didn't live with him when I was in middle school."

She waved off my comment. "So what about Chuck?" When Izzy didn't answer, Piper shone the flashlight in her eyes. "Interested?"

Izzy blinked and pushed the flashlight away. "I don't remember you calling dibs on Tobin."

Even in the dim light, Izzy could see Piper's face cloud. "It's Chuck or nothing, Izzy."

Chuck seemed like a cool guy. He was smart, and not an

ass like Ben. But Izzy bristled at the attempt at matchmaking. She hadn't come out that night to hook up with some random guy. She had come to get drunk. Two totally different things. Most of the time, anyway. Piper talked like this was a clearance sale and Chuck was the last pair of jeans in Izzy's size.

"Thanks for your concern, but I'm good," she said.

Up ahead, Rachel screamed, the sound quick and sharp but stretched and blunted by the surrounding mountains. Piper froze on the trail.

Still irritated with her friend, Izzy turned to face her. "You afraid?"

She had every reason to be. It wasn't necessarily the smartest choice, heading toward a cry of alarm. And Izzy knew she could be reckless. *Just ask Frankie.*

When Izzy resumed walking, Piper hurried to catch up.

The others had stopped near a thick patch of brush. They stared at the ground.

"Is it . . . dead?" Rachel asked.

Tobin took a couple of tentative steps, gaze focused on a cluster of tall shrubs and wild grasses. When he leaned in, the weeds rustled, and he jumped back, swearing.

Ben laughed and slapped him on the back. "Not dead, then."

Now close enough to see what held their interest, Izzy winced. Mostly camouflaged by the thick vegetation, a deer struggled to stand, but it rose only inches before falling back to the ground. Had it been attacked in that spot, or had it pulled itself there to die? Even with the threat of six humans

so close, it stopped trying to flee. Its breathing was barely noticeable. Izzy could understand why Rachel had believed the
animal to be dead.

Izzy noted the lack of horns. "She's suffering." Izzy knelt and
cautiously reached for the animal. She didn't want to frighten
her. But the deer was beyond scaring. Izzy placed her palm
gently on the top of the deer's head, then looked up at Chuck.
"How can we help her?"

"I'm pre-pharmacy, not pre-veterinary science."

"Anyone up for some venison?" Ben asked.

No one laughed. Still crouched, Izzy scowled up at him.
"Shut the hell up."

This only made Ben's grin widen.

Chuck dropped beside Izzy and briefly examined the deer.
Hesitant at first, his touch grew more confident. He avoided
the deer's stomach, where blood had matted, instead leaning
in close to scan the injury with his eyes.

Rachel moved behind them but remained standing. "What
happened to her?"

"Pre-pharmacy, remember? Maybe animal attack?"

Izzy looked at Chuck. "What do we do?"

He shook his head. "Nothing."

"But she's in pain."

He touched Izzy's arm. When she glanced at his hand, he
removed it and wiped his palm on his jeans.

"We should kill it," Ben said. When Rachel gasped, he
shrugged, suddenly serious. "It's the most humane thing
to do."

Beside Izzy, Chuck exhaled. "Ben's right." He grimaced, as if he found agreeing with Ben on anything distasteful.

Everyone looked at Chuck. Ben reached into his pocket and pulled out a folding knife. He tossed it at Chuck, harder than necessary.

"Just give it back when you're done," Ben said.

# 14

Since the night of the hit-and-run five years before, I almost never woke gently. That Sunday morning was no different. I exploded to the surface, gasping. Through the slats of the blinds, a sliver of indigo indicated dawn remained at least an hour away. I checked my phone. I was surprised to see that Piper had texted me a couple of hours before.

Izzy's home. She's ok.

Relief flooded me, but, too on edge to fall back asleep, I headed to the bathroom. At the sink, I turned on the water and cupped my hands beneath the faucet. The first handful I splashed on my face, the second I drank.

Anxious to pick up Julian, I skipped the shower and instead used a washcloth on my face and arms. The coarse nubs of the terry cloth made me think again of Julian. Sometimes when I tried to wash his face, he would scrunch his nose and complain the fabric was too rough. In response, I would kiss his forehead, and he would say my mouth was too rough. Then I would tickle him, just a little because he didn't like more. He would blow a raspberry against my arm, and sometimes his giggling fits would overwhelm him so that his breath came in gulps. Then we would hug.

Next, I thought of Izzy, and how I still had no idea where she had been last night.

I finished my usual routine: teeth, moisturizer, lip balm. On my way out the door, I grabbed a granola bar and stuck it in my purse. Maybe later my stomach would settle enough for me to eat it.

WHEN I ARRIVED AT my parents' house, Julian raced out the front door, my mom a couple of steps behind him. In his fist he held a small orange globe, which he raised for my inspection.

"It's a . . . nec-ta-rine." He said the last word slowly, pausing on each syllable. Then he grinned, obviously proud of pronouncing the word correctly. "Abuela let me eat two."

My mom mussed Julian's hair. "A friend dropped off a bag. I'll send you home with a few."

"Thanks, Mom." I knelt down next to Julian, placed my palms on his cheeks, and kissed his forehead. "You've never had a nectarine before, have you?"

Julian's forehead wrinkled. "Remember? I had two."

I smiled. After the morning I'd had, it felt good. "You did say that, didn't you?"

When Julian found something new he loved, he would ask me if I loved him as much. *Do you love me as much as butterflies? Do you love me as much as cake? Do you love me as much as the color blue?*

So I saw the question coming. "Do you love me as much as nectarines?" he asked.

I pretended to consider the question before I kissed his forehead again, inhaling the scent of him. There was nothing special about that scent except for everything.

"I love you more than nectarines," I said.

"It's like a peach, but not fuzzy. One of them had a brown spot, but it tasted okay. Abuela says she's making jam with the other ones that have spots." He opened his hand and thrust it toward me, the prized fruit rolling on his palm. "You can have this one if you want."

After my late-night conversation, I still had no appetite. "That's very generous of you, but why don't you keep it?"

Julian looked relieved.

I heard my dad's wheelchair a second before the screen door squeaked open again. The creases beneath his eyes were deeper than they had been the day before, his skin paler.

"How's your sister?" he asked.

I kept the smile on my face, but now it felt forced. "Good."

"Come help me in the garage." It wasn't a request.

THE HOUSE WAS WHERE we gathered as a family. It was where we welcomed friends, cousins, aunts and uncles, and new neighbors we didn't know well, but whom we welcomed nonetheless because that's what the Barreras did. Inside the small house, we shared meals, slammed doors, and told family stories that always left one of us embarrassed, at least if we told them right. We cried and laughed and celebrated. But the garage had always belonged to me and my dad.

My parents owned only a single car, an older but meticulously maintained sedan that they kept parked in the center of the garage. Dad rolled over to crack the garage window overlooking the yard. By noon the interior walls would begin radiating heat. An hour later, the air would be stifling with it, until the early evening when the single redwood tree out back would shade the window, providing respite. I knew well the seasons of this space.

"What do you need help with?" I asked.

He tilted his chin toward the car. "It's been idling rough for a while. Thought you could help me replace the spark plugs."

"You sure it's the plugs?"

He nodded. "Should've replaced 'em a while back."

I pulled a box from the shelf and wiped off a layer of dust. My dad believed in always having a spare set of spark plugs and several quarts of oil on the shelf. It looked like this particular box had been there awhile.

I popped the hood and propped it open with the rod. "Julian keep you up last night?"

"Not at all. I'm not sure I want to give him back." He rolled next to me and leaned in. "Don't forget to disconnect the negative terminal on the battery."

Already done. I had changed my first set of spark plugs before I could drive. "Okay, Dad."

I used a towel and a generous spray of degreaser to wipe around the plugs, though the area was already clean. Still, we wouldn't want debris falling into the engine.

"You good, Frankie?"

"Always." With the socket, I turned the first plug counterclockwise until it loosened, then pulled it out and inspected it. Expecting to find soot or oily deposits. Some sign the plug was bad.

I held it up. "This looks good to me. Maybe there's a problem with the ignition system."

He shook his head. "No, the plugs definitely need to be replaced."

When I pulled a new plug from the box, my dad leaned in farther.

"Use the gap gauge."

I already had it in my hand. "Okay."

"They don't always come right from the factory. Best to check."

"I know, Dad. No shortcuts."

"That's right." He fidgeted, massaging his wrists, antsy.

"Everything okay with you?" I asked.

After a quick nod from my dad, I went back to work. I screwed the plug in, then tightened it. Reattached the plug wire. Moved on to the next one. If possible, this one looked even more pristine than the first.

I put the plug down and stared at my dad. "What's going on?"

He cleared his throat. "I wanted to talk about your sister."

My dad stopped fidgeting and pinned my eyes with his. Over the years, the intensity of that gaze had elicited countless promises and confessions. I crossed my arms, my standard defensive posture. Still, if I were the type to bet, I would've put the odds I would break in his favor.

"Tell me what's going on with her." His voice was abruptly as intimidating as his stare. The odds against me increased twofold.

"What makes you think anything's going on with her?" I held his gaze.

"Because I know my daughters." His expression softened. "I

know we relied on you a lot when Izzy was growing up. After I got sick. I think maybe we put too much on you."

I pulled a cooler from the shelf and set it next to Dad's chair, then sat on it. I shifted on the hard plastic, but there was no getting comfortable.

"Caring for Izzy has never been a burden," I said. It would've been truer to say it was a burden, but one I had willingly accepted. But my dad didn't need to hear that.

"It happened without us even realizing it," he said. "Your mom had taken that second job. We were still adjusting to the diabetes, and the complications. So when Izzy had the flu, or needed help with her homework, or wanted a snack, she went to you. And we let her."

"We're family. That's what we do, take care of each other." I took in his pallor, the slight waver in his voice. My throat tightened, and I swallowed. "You okay?"

"I'm fine, mija." He patted my hand. "Do you remember that time the dog came into our backyard?"

"What's that got to do with anything?"

"Do you?"

I nodded. It was a neighbor's mixed breed—wiry fur, severe underbite, and, that day, a single-minded purpose: to attack a stray tabby napping on our patio. Izzy had been a toddler, about the same size as the dog, and had taken to giving bits of her ham sandwich to the tabby. That cat loved ham, and Izzy loved that cat.

My dad continued, "The dog jumped the fence, went for that stray. Your mom was watching you two from the window, but it happened too fast for her to stop it. She was sure it was going to take off the cat's head, or hurt one of you girls."

The dog had charged and Izzy stepped in front of the cat, fists on hips, stomach jutting, lips pursed. She had stomped a foot. *Bad doggy.*

"When your mom got out there, the dog had run away, and you were standing in front of your sister, holding your side. Bleeding."

*Yeah, that one had hurt.* In reflex, my hand found the scar on my hip.

"Your mom found your sister, oblivious, yelling at the dog."

*Bad doggy. Bad bad bad.* Izzy had been a force, even then. Absolutely fearless.

"You were terrified, shaking, but still you stepped between Izzy and that dog."

"Mom was so angry with that neighbor."

He reached for my hand and squeezed it. "You've always put Izzy first. Even when it's hurt you. Like when you turned down that scholarship from UCLA to go to college closer to home. And like whatever happened when Izzy was eighteen."

I stilled and fought to keep my face neutral. "What do you mean?"

He waved off my question. "Like I said, I know my daughters. I don't know what happened back then—I don't need to know—but something changed, and I'm worried about you. You need to rely on us more."

"I do rely on you. You just watched Julian last night."

That penetrating stare of his returned. "Before that? How many times have you let us watch him overnight?" The answer came easily: twice. "Then when you come pick him up, you look so worried, like you think you've overwhelmed us."

I allowed myself a smile. "Julian overwhelms *me*."

My dad returned the smile, but it didn't light up his eyes as it usually did. "That's part of why I know something's wrong, that you've asked for our help this week. And . . ." He hesitated, then squeezed my hand again. "Izzy stopped by Thursday night."

A cold prickling raised bumps on my arms. "What time?"

"Late. Around ten. She wanted to borrow the car, said it was an emergency, but your mom was out with friends."

The tingling grew stronger, icy stabs on my skin. I tried to keep the worry from my face, but my lips pinched involuntarily. Izzy had come to borrow our parents' car, and when it had been unavailable, she had headed to my place for the truck. The significance of that struck me instantly. Her friend's desk wouldn't have fit in our parents' car. Izzy hadn't crafted her alibi carefully enough. What would have been her excuse if it had been our parents' license plate number on that AMBER Alert? The thought of that made me suddenly furious.

"Did she say why she wanted the car?" I asked, keeping the anger from my voice.

"You girls never tell me anything." There was amusement in his voice, but also a trace of sadness.

"You really want to know what Izzy's been up to?"

Though diabetes had taken its toll on my dad, as I studied his face now, what I noticed was his strength. Still, I wasn't sure he was strong enough for this. Parents were always most vulnerable when it came to their children.

He rolled closer so our knees touched, then leaned forward so we were closer still. "You need to take care of yourself, too, Frankie. Sometimes I think you don't do that enough. And maybe that's on us." When he sighed, I could hear the guilt in it. "But I also hope you can do what you did that day with the dog. What you've always done. Keep Izzy safe."

WITH JULIAN'S HELP, MOM convinced me we should stay for brunch. The hour I spent on the patio with my family made me nearly forget. During those sixty precious minutes, we ate nectarine-topped waffles and talked about the minor dramas of small-town life. Then, as we were clearing our plates, my phone buzzed in my pocket. I checked and saw Piper's name on the screen.

*This can't be good.*

When I answered, my sister's friend didn't bother with a greeting. "Where the hell is Izzy?"

I turned away so my parents couldn't read my expression and tried to keep my voice light. "Have you tried the apartment?" I asked.

"Of course I've tried the apartment. I ran by our place before I called you. Do you think I'm an idiot?" In her voice, anger mixed with worry.

I took a couple of long strides away from the house, hoping that put me out of earshot of my parents. "I thought she had that catering gig with you."

"No shit." Her tone grew more brittle. "Why do you think I'm calling? She should've been here a while ago. I thought maybe she got held up finding a ride, but when I went to the apartment, she'd cleared out."

"What do you mean, cleared out?"

When she sighed, it had a sharp edge. "Thought you were

the smart sister. Cleared out. She's gone. Packed a bag and everything."

"How do you know she packed a bag?"

"Uh . . . because her bag is gone. Why did I even call you?" Piper cursed under her breath and hung up.

I closed my eyes and counted, trying to relieve the pressure in my head. From the morning Izzy was born, I found myself shrinking, ceding room in our family so she could have more. She never asked this of me. In hindsight, I'm not sure she wanted it, since the attention she got wasn't always positive. But by the time I figured that out, our roles had been cast. I was the good daughter. The quiet daughter. The one who didn't require grounding or impromptu parent-teacher conferences. Years later, I could still slip easily behind that mask, even when I felt close to breaking.

Lately, though, that was getting harder.

Nerves abruptly raw, I dialed Izzy. She didn't answer. For a moment I stood there, fingers tight on my phone. Then I remembered setting up Izzy's phone to share its location with mine.

I tapped the info icon, hoping the tracking was still enabled. A map popped on the screen, Izzy's face marking her location.

She was at my house.

Normally I would've found her presence there reassuring, but with her a no-show for her job, my whole body twitched.

Behind me, I heard my dad's approach. I found myself unable to turn to face him. "Everything okay?" he asked.

That had become a popular question in our family. I shifted, offering him my profile. "Izzy didn't show up for work. I think she might be at my place."

He moved in front of me so he could study my face. Whatever

he saw there caused his lips to pinch. Then he waved toward the gate that led to the driveway, where my truck was parked. "We'll watch Julian as long as you need."

"I can't—"

He cut me off with another of his dad stares. "You haven't forgotten what we talked about already?"

I sighed. "I need to rely on you more."

"Besides, Julian will be happy he can help us make the jam. Now go. Before your mom starts asking questions."

I opened my mouth to object again, but he rolled away, deciding the matter.

AFTER A QUICK ROUND of goodbyes, I headed home to confront my sister. The drive took less than ten minutes, each second setting me more on edge. I parked in the driveway, then raced toward the porch. Before I reached the first step, I saw the small white square taped to my front door. It was a note, the handwriting unmistakably my sister's: Leave it alone.

When I checked my phone again, there was an alert that Izzy had stopped sharing her location with me.

Despite my best efforts at hiding it, it had been foolish to think Izzy wouldn't notice my attempt to track her. Still, though I didn't know where she was, I knew where she had been. I would start there.

I opened the screenshots I had taken of her location data and considered which spot I should check out first.

# 15

For the first few weeks after the Mercuryville party, I had reassured Izzy often: It was a deer, only a deer, and she hadn't killed anyone. It became a mantra, though one we quickly learned to stop repeating aloud. Silence turned out to be far more reassuring for us both. Months, then years went by, and no body was discovered in the Mayacamas. I began to think I had imagined those strands of hair, just as Izzy had imagined that what she hit that night ran on two legs.

But Izzy had needed her penance. She had been volunteering at a grief camp not far from Mount Tamalpais in Marin County for four summers, though I had found out about it only the year before. She let it slip at a family dinner. Her expression when she'd mentioned it told me she hadn't wanted me to know. Apparently she had a life I didn't know about. At the time, the accidental revelation had shocked me. It wouldn't have now. My sister had become more practiced at keeping her secrets.

A simple redwood sign marked the camp's entrance: CAMP SARAH. There were several vehicles in the small paved lot, including a white bus also bearing the camp's name. I parked next to it and started up an asphalt path cut into the mountainside. It was a short walk, perhaps a quarter mile, under a dense canopy that blocked even the harsh midday sun.

In the clearing, two young men with purple shirts and lanyards around their necks were making paper lanterns. When I asked to speak to the person in charge, the taller one pointed me toward a building.

"You'll want to talk to Jenny Hauser," he said, shielding his eyes to keep from squinting. "She's in the multipurpose room setting up."

I thanked him and headed inside. The space had a summer camp feel. One wall was stone, the other three painted a deep blue and decorated with murals of rainbows and stick-figure families. The floors were gray linoleum, the ceiling wood-beamed. Folding tables and chairs were stacked against the walls, next to pallets of bottled water and juice boxes. A tall woman with a broad face, even broader smile, and messy ponytail greeted me from behind a push broom.

"How can I help you?" She wiped her forehead with the back of her hand, then raked a couple of errant curls off her cheek.

"Jenny Hauser?" When she nodded, I returned her smile, though mine felt unsteady. "My name's Frankie Barrera."

I hadn't quite settled on how to start the conversation, but her face lit up at the mention of my name. "You're Izzy's sister."

I must've looked surprised, because she laughed. "She talks about you all the time."

"Good things, I hope." Half-kidding, half-fishing.

"The best." She gestured toward the water and stacked chairs. "Want to have a seat? Water?"

I shook my head. "I'm good standing, if you are."

"If you're good standing, are you also good walking?" she asked. "Camp opens in a couple of weeks, and there's still so much to do."

When I nodded, she clapped her hands with more enthusiasm than my acceptance warranted. I immediately liked this woman, with her messy curls and open smile.

"So what can I help you with, Izzy's sister?"

Since I wasn't sure what question to ask first, I started with one I hoped would get her comfortable talking to me.

"Tell me about this place. Is it yours?"

"Yep. All mine." She speed-walked toward another room, which turned out to be a kitchen. Forty-pound bags of rice, wheels of cheese, and flats of apples sat on an oversized steel island. "Help me with these, will you?"

We each grabbed a bag of rice, and I followed her toward a pantry just off the kitchen.

"Fair warning. Get me talking about this place, and I can talk for hours." Her laugh was loud, boisterous. Not what I would've expected from the founder of a bereavement camp.

We both set our bags down and returned to the kitchen for the apples.

"So—my story. When I was seven, we lived across the street from my school. My mom ran a day care out of our home, and every day at precisely two-thirty she would take the kids out into the front yard, and they would watch while I crossed the street." She started arranging the flats of apples in the pantry, taking more care than was necessary. "Then, one day, she wasn't waiting. I crossed the street. Went inside. The house was quiet. You'd think the kids would be screaming, or the dog would be barking. But it was . . . peaceful. Kids playing with blocks, the dog napping in the sun, and everything so damn quiet."

She paused here, her fingertips grazing the skins of the fruit. "I found my mom in the kitchen. She had been washing apples when she had a stroke. The water was still running in the sink, and the apples had scattered around her. On the counter, there was a knife and jar of peanut butter. The chunky kind, my favorite."

She led me back into the kitchen for more apples. "That's usually what she made me for an after-school snack: apples and peanut butter. So she hadn't been dead long." She wiped her hands on her shirt. "Now the cheese. Want to get that in the refrigerator before it gets sweaty."

Transfixed by her story, it took me a few seconds to get moving. As we put away the wheels of cheese, she launched again into her story. "Even though it's been thirty-five years, the details of that day are still so clear. But we never talked about it, me and my dad. Not even at the funeral. I was an only child, so no siblings to talk to either."

Through the worst of it, my sister and I had each other, and we had both of our parents. Now we had Julian too. My heart ached for seven-year-old Jenny.

"We never talked about her, and that's what I wanted more than anything: to talk about my mom. So ten years ago, I started this place, named after her, in case you haven't guessed yet. Figured I could honor my mom, and help other children who are going through what I did. Kids shouldn't have to navigate their grief alone. Even if they can talk to their parents or a therapist, sharing that loss with a peer, a friend, is different."

Groceries put away, Jenny grabbed a spreadsheet from the counter and a pen from the drawer. She began throwing open the cabinet doors, taking stock and marking her spreadsheet. I waited in silence for her to finish her task. When she was done, she put down the spreadsheet and pen and turned to face me. She crossed her arms.

"You didn't come to hear about the history of this place."

In a way, that was exactly why I'd come. If I hadn't been quite so worried about Izzy, I would've requested a tour. Camp Sarah was important to my sister, yet she had kept it from me. Worse, I hadn't asked her about it, because talking about this place meant talking about the guilt that had driven her here. Learning about it now from Jenny made me feel closer to my sister, and to the truth.

"So why'd you come?" she asked.

"This morning my sister took off. I'm sure she's fine, but that doesn't mean I'm not worried about her. We haven't been getting along lately."

Only the part about being sure Izzy was fine was a lie.

"You want to find her so you can talk it out. That's good. We don't always get the time we think we're owed. But I'm not sure how talking with me will help you find her. Camp's not for another two weeks, and I don't expect her until then."

Her answer gave me pause. According to Izzy's location data, she had visited the place several times as recently as a week before. Had I misjudged Jenny Hauser? If I asked for that tour, or poked around on my own, would I find my sister hiding in one of the rooms?

"That's odd," I said. "I was under the impression she had already been volunteering here this summer."

I studied the other woman's face for signs she might be preparing a lie, but, outwardly at least, she appeared relaxed. I noticed no tension around her mouth or eyes to betray her. "Izzy volunteered to clean the rooms, so she's made a few trips for that. But I haven't seen her for at least a week, and don't expect I will."

That tracked with the data I had from Izzy's phone. But that didn't mean it was the whole truth. A minute earlier, I had held information back too.

"I bet Izzy is good with the kids," I said.

Jenny nodded enthusiastically, allowing a couple of curls to escape from her ponytail. She tucked the stray coils behind her ears. "Izzy's great. Many of the volunteers have experienced a loss of their own, but even though your sister's never been through it, she understands."

Was she fishing too?

Jenny paused and cocked her head, and I wondered if she was about to reveal something significant. Instead, she said, "From what Izzy's told me, I think that's where she gets her empathy. From you."

I thought of the cat my sister had fed and protected, and the way she had brought me sopping washcloths that time I had a fever. They had soaked my pillow, but her face had been so earnest, I had accepted them.

"I think maybe *I* got it from *her*."

Jenny touched my arm, a quick gesture of comfort she must've used a thousand times in this place. "I'm sure whatever's going on with your sister, it will work itself out." Her expression shifted, as if a thought had just occurred to her. She motioned toward the door that led to the main room. "Here. Let me show you something."

I followed her into the main room. She stopped in the center of it and stared at the high spots on the walls, with their brightly colored drawings, paintings, and mosaics. One drew her interest more than the others. Artfully painted, it was something you might see framed in a small gallery, or at a county fair with a blue ribbon affixed to it. Like the artwork surrounding it, this painting featured a family, but instead of stick figures or round and happy faces, it featured a quintet of birds, rendered in pale blues, greens, and yellows. The brushstrokes were so delicate as to allow glimpses of the paper beneath.

"People think it's a sad place, this camp, and sure, there are plenty of tears," Jenny said as she craned her neck upward. "But it's also a place of healing. Even, sometimes, joy. The kids make friends, and many of them return the following year." Jenny pointed to the painting of the birds. "The girl who painted that was one of those. She was twelve when she came for the first time. Last year, when she turned sixteen, Marina became a volunteer."

My heart stopped, and I grew dizzy. Surely I hadn't heard that right. "Marina?"

"Marina Wagner." She said the name with a smile, which made me think she hadn't heard the news yet. "She's one of the girls Izzy helped most. That's why I wanted to show you this. It's a visual representation of all the good your sister does here."

So Izzy knew Marina. They were friendly. My anxiety ebbed, as I considered the implications. Anne Wagner might've been confused about what she witnessed. Izzy could've borrowed my truck because Marina needed a ride, or wanted to talk, and Anne hadn't known the plan. I could see that: it had been late, and Marina had slipped out of the house. Maybe the stairs had creaked, or the front door shut too loudly, and her mom, half-asleep, had glanced out the window.

Another possibility: Marina ran away because of problems at home. That could've made Anne angry enough to falsely report her daughter abducted. As Detective Pratt mentioned during our interview, AMBER Alerts weren't issued for runaways. Marina's mom might've seen the lie as the only way to get her daughter back. Look at all I had done for Izzy. Why would I expect less ferocity from Anne Wagner?

The weight I had been carrying in my chest shifted, just enough to allow me to breathe. Neither explanation offered a reason for Izzy to stick so steadfastly to her lies, not when the police were involved. At least not to me, already the keeper of her worst secret. And if Izzy had merely helped a friend, why did she seem so haunted by what had happened that night? Could it have started as an act of generosity, but then gone terribly wrong?

I tamped down the questions so they grew smaller, less important. If I looked too closely at either explanation, I felt an uncomfortable wriggling in my gut, that one that felt too much like doubt. So I clung to the explanations, imperfect as they were, because they allowed me to believe in my sister again.

"I'm glad Izzy found a friend here," I said.

For the first time since I'd entered the building, Jenny's face clouded. "Oh no, I haven't made myself clear," she said. "Izzy helped her, and Marina's a success story for sure."

I understood, or thought I did. It likely would've been inappropriate for a real friendship to form, given their different roles and six-year age gap. I figured that was what Jenny was struggling to say.

"I mean, they were friendly enough in the beginning." Jenny pointed again to the painting of the birds. "Izzy even helped with that. And she's definitely the reason Marina decided to volunteer as a junior counselor." She hesitated, her expression growing even more uncertain, but Jenny Hauser was a woman used to having difficult conversations. Unlike me. She found my eyes. "But after what happened last year, Izzy and Marina could never be friends."

JENNY HAUSER GAVE FEW details about the confrontation that would've made a friendship between Izzy and Marina impossible. She would only say that there had been an argument, that feelings were hurt, but that it wasn't her place to say more.

"When you find your sister, ask her," Jenny said. Her hand flitted across my arm again—a gesture of both comfort and goodbye—and then she returned to the spot where she had earlier abandoned her push broom.

Outside, one of the young men who had been assembling the lanterns waited. It was the tall one, all gangly limbs and Adam's apple. His hands were shoved in the pockets of his uniform khakis. When I passed him, he fell in step beside me.

"I overheard you asking Jenny about Marina."

I stopped and turned to him. "I was."

"I'm Blake," he said. "It's my third year here. I know Marina. Or knew her, anyway. I heard she's missing."

"I hadn't heard that," I lied, waiting for him to fill in the blanks.

Unlike Jenny, this young man seemed primed to talk about Marina. I just had to stay quiet and let him.

True to my impression, he started talking. "My first year,

Marina was fifteen and not a junior counselor yet. She hung out with Izzy a lot. I overheard you telling Jenny that Izzy's your sister?"

I nodded. "They were close, then?"

"Definitely. Some of the kids started calling her Izzy's puppy, on account of her following Izzy around all the time, but we put a stop to that real quick," Blake said, puffing his chest. Proud of himself. "You could tell Izzy liked her too. If she needed someone to set up an activity or help get lunch started, she'd always ask Marina first."

According to Blake, that was the year Marina painted the birds. It was also the year that Marina started opening up to the other kids about the sister she had lost. "Cancer, or so she said. That's what got my dad too." He went silent for a moment, then shook it off.

*"So she said?"*

He grinned sheepishly. "You caught that, huh? It's just, some-times Marina lies."

I could relate, but I felt suddenly uneasy. "About what?"

He shrugged. "Not big stuff, as far as I know anyway. Like she'll lie about going to see a concert, or where she lives. Stupid shit." He paused, letting the obscenity land. Testing me? Was I an adult like Jenny, or cool like my sister? "I think Marina doesn't like people knowing her business."

If that was true, I wondered how she'd feel about my con-versation with Blake. "Did it stay that way the next year? Their friendship?"

"At first. At the welcoming ceremony, Marina was right by

Izzy's side again, and at the second-day campfire. Then . . ." He hesitated.

"Then what?"

Blake looked over his shoulder before returning his attention to me. "Then the lantern ceremony."

"What's that?"

"The kids decorate these paper lanterns. Some write notes on them, or draw pictures. On mine, I always write my dad's name and a line from a song he liked." I waited for him to say more, but apparently those lyrics were between him and his dad. "After we decorate the lanterns, we gather near the lake and share stories about our loved ones, and we release the lanterns onto the water. It's really cool."

He moved closer and dropped his voice, though there was no one around to hear us. "So we were getting ready for that, and a couple of us noticed that Marina and Izzy were fighting." He pointed to a nearby manzanita. "Over there. Pretty far away, so we couldn't really hear much—something about Marina breaking the rules, I think. And at the end of it, Marina took a pack of matches from her pocket and tossed one on a pile of lanterns."

Blake made a whooshing sound and used his hands to mimic an explosion.

"Izzy and Marina both claimed it was an accident, like she meant to light a candle to see how it was going to look in one of the lanterns," he said. "But I saw the expression on her face when she lit that match. Man, she wanted to kill somebody."

# 16

Marina and Izzy sounded a lot alike, and that terrified me. With both of them stubborn and quick to anger, what would the aftermath of their fight look like? And if neither was the type to share her secrets, what chance did I have of finding either of them?

After exchanging numbers with Blake, I headed into town. Mill Valley was tucked into the slopes of Mount Tamalpais, just north of the Golden Gate, a small town known for its artistic heritage, redwood forests, and daunting real estate prices.

Since I didn't have friends or family in Mill Valley, I'd never had reason to visit. Still, as I drove past the restaurants, boutiques, and galleries, a sense of familiarity settled on me. Izzy had driven these same roads. According to her location data, she had made the trip at least three times in the past week. Including the night Marina disappeared.

The person Izzy had been visiting lived in a complex of cedar-shingled town homes on the shores of Strawberry Lagoon, an inlet of Richardson Bay. As I entered the complex, I slowed for a speed bump, suddenly on guard. Worried that my truck might get noticed. I still didn't know who Izzy had visited here, not for sure. One of the visits a couple of weeks earlier had corresponded with a call to Ben, whose area code could've put him in the neighborhood. I still hadn't been able to track down his address. But with the timing of the abduction, I thought this was the Wagners' neighborhood. I didn't know which I hoped for: that my sister had been visiting the home of a drug dealer, or that she had been in the area where a teen girl had been abducted.

Earlier, I'd searched online for the Wagners' address, but apparently Marina's mom liked her privacy. It made sense, considering Detective Pratt's comment during our interview: The family had it rough even before Marina went missing. People who'd experienced tragedy might be more inclined to hide.

In the nearby marshland, birds hopped and pecked, with their sharp beaks and bodies either snowy-feathered or mottled and plump, the feet at the end of their stick-like legs making tracks in the wet sand. In the overbright sky, they soared, glided, swooped. Had these marshland birds been what inspired Marina's painting? I could see her finding peace in their aerobatics and the squawks of the gulls. I could've used a little of that peace right then.

Though my truck wouldn't usually have been distinctive enough to get noticed, I drove a few blocks down and turned a corner. I hoped no one thought to check the plates against the active AMBER Alert. I had considered swapping my plates with those on my mom's sedan, but that seemed an admission of guilt. Plus it would've been really hard to explain to my parents—and the police—if I was pulled over again.

After I parked in a spot I hoped wouldn't get my truck towed, I googled Anne Wagner. I took a long look at the photo I found, then stowed my phone, grabbed a clipboard, and got out of the truck. Attached to the clipboard was a petition: *Save the Wetlands*. I hoped the fake petition and my best smile would keep me from attracting negative attention. The kind of attention that might get the police involved.

It was a beautiful weekend afternoon, and the homes here had views of the bay. Only a handful of homes had their blinds drawn. I started with those.

After knocking on four doors, I found her behind the fifth. She opened the door more quickly than any of her neighbors. Having a missing daughter obviously kept her on alert.

A thick smear of concealer did little to camouflage the shadows under Anne Wagner's eyes. Her strawberry blond hair, cropped just above her shoulders, appeared to have been combed with her fingers, or not at all. On the drive, I had convinced myself that Marina's mom had filed a false report, possibly out of anger. The woman in front of me didn't look angry. She looked like she was a short walk away from ending up in the bay.

Her face fell with the weight of her disappointment. I wasn't who she'd been hoping to see.

"Can I help you?" she asked halfheartedly. She didn't look capable of helping anyone.

My entire body tensed, my clipboard held tightly against my chest. This wasn't the face of a woman who knew what had happened to her daughter. Her distress was tangible, settling on my own shoulders. I shouldn't have come. I had allowed myself to believe Marina ran away, or that her disappearance was the result of a misunderstanding, because those explanations absolved Izzy. I had come to this woman's house more concerned with finding my sister than with finding her daughter. In my single-minded quest, I had intruded on a parent in mourning.

I should've apologized and fast-walked to the safety of my truck, but I remained frozen on the porch.

Why had I come here? What questions had I expected to ask? I couldn't mention that at the grief camp Blake said Marina sometimes lied or had burned lanterns decorated by grieving children. I couldn't ask about her other daughter, the one she lost to cancer. And I certainly couldn't mention Izzy.

The creases around Anne's mouth started to soften, and I realized my silence might be giving her the impression I had news to share. I had come here seeking information from her, and now I saw her dawning expectation that I might be the one with answers.

I finally managed to speak. "I think I have the wrong house."

But my hesitation made her suspicious. She gestured toward the clipboard. "What's that?" she asked.

"Just a petition. But I think I have enough signatures."

When I took a step back, she reached out and touched my arm. She barely grazed me, but her fingertips scalded. "Do you know something about my daughter?"

Whatever my original purpose, I now wanted only to help this woman. A few minutes of conversation could help me find answers that would lead me to Izzy, and then to Marina. Even if I had to lie to get those answers.

"I met your daughter at Camp Sarah. I volunteered there last year." It shocked me how easily I could lie to a grieving mom.

Her face grew suddenly sympathetic. "Have you lost someone too?"

I couldn't lie about that. I shook my head, using the clipboard I clutched as a shield. "I probably shouldn't have come. I didn't really know her well. I just—I heard what happened from one of the kids there. Blake."

She stared at me for a long moment. A hint of panic lodged in my chest. If Anne Wagner had glimpsed my truck Thursday night, had she also seen the driver? Though we'd never met, I suddenly worried she might think she recognized me. In the dark, Izzy and I resembled one another.

Then she stepped aside and gestured for me to come in.

A SEA OF BOXES flooded the Wagner living room, most partially full with their flaps unsealed.

"Moving in or out?" I asked.

"Out."

Was Marina happy about the move? If not, that might be a good reason for her to run away.

My cheeks grew hot. Here I was, invited into the Wagner home, still looking for excuses for Izzy.

"Mill Valley's expensive, and there's no need for a place so big, now that it's just me and Marina." Her face clouded as she realized: now it was just her.

She gestured for me to sit on the sofa, while she took the chair across from it. The living room was compact, the attached dining area large enough for only a small round table and four chairs. The walls were white, the carpet an inoffensive tan. All personal items and photos had been stowed in boxes. A blank slate for the next tenant. Guilty, I was glad I wasn't surrounded by family pictures. I set the clipboard with my fake *Save the Wetlands* petition on the cushion next to me.

"If you barely knew Marina, why are you here?" Her tone was flat, but it wasn't just small talk. She seemed genuinely curious.

I wasn't entirely certain why I'd come inside. "I guess—I want to help, and I want to know more about her, but it seems inappropriate to ask."

"I'm not sure I know her much better than you do." She closed her eyes, which had grown misty. When she opened them again, they seemed only slightly clearer. "She spends most of her time locked in her room, listening to music and painting."

"I saw one of her paintings at the camp."

"The birds. Her bedroom window looks over the bay. After her father left, and then her sister . . . I gave Marina the master. It gets the best light."

"She seemed to have friends at the camp." I didn't want to mention Izzy's name. If she didn't know it, I saw no reason to give it to her.

"Some." Her tone was curt.

"She had problems at the camp?" I held my breath as I waited for her to answer. Seconds ticked by with her blinking back tears and me not breathing.

Finally, she said, "After what happened last year, she wasn't going back."

"The thing with the lanterns?"

She nodded. So Blake had only half the story. Marina had been kicked out.

"The whole thing was her fault," Anne said. "Marina can be . . . headstrong. But she's got a kind heart."

"Do you mind me asking . . ." My voice trailed into silence.

"You want to know what happened? She and another camper snuck out after curfew."

I felt my brow furrow. That didn't seem like that big of a deal, especially given what Marina and the other kids at the camp were going through. Anne must've recognized my skepticism, because she added, "They might also have borrowed a volunteer's car."

*That would do it.*

Anne continued, "Then she set fire to the lanterns."

"So they sent her home?"

Now it was Anne whose brow wrinkled. "Oh. No. Leaving was Marina's decision. Jenny Hauser would never kick a kid out. She knows what hell these kids are going through."

"I don't understand."

"Marina was told she could stay, but not as a junior counselor. After all the work she put in, that devastated her. Marina doesn't have many friends."

"I'm sorry."

"Me too." She sighed, sending a tremor through her entire body. "It didn't help that she had that falling-out with the other counselor."

I sat still despite the sudden fluttering in my chest. "Oh?" To me, even that one syllable, carefully spoken, sounded suspicious.

She waved off my interest. "It was time for Marina to leave anyway. She'd outgrown that place."

"Any chance she ran away?"

I sat very still as I awaited the answer I very much hoped was yes.

She shook her head. "Marina was taken." There was no doubt in her.

Still, I pushed. "Are you sure? It was late. Probably happened quickly?"

She shook her head again, more violently. "I had a second glass of wine right before bed, so I was up an hour later to use the bathroom. That's always the way it is with me. You'd think I'd learn." She massaged her wrists in a nervous gesture, but she spoke carefully, as if making sure the details were remembered exactly right. "So I was in the hallway, and I noticed the light was on in Marina's room. I knocked. When she didn't answer, I tried the knob. She locks her door at night. Makes her feel safe, she says. But it wasn't locked. I poked my head in, but she wasn't there." This part of the story seemed difficult for her, and I waited while she steadied herself.

After a minute's thought, she went on. "I crossed her room to look out the window. I'm not sure why. It was more logical that she'd gone downstairs to get a snack, or that she hadn't gone to bed yet but had forgotten to turn out her light. Like I said, she doesn't have many friends. No one she would sneak out to meet in the middle of the night."

She paused again, and I nudged. "What did you see?" Expectant, I leaned forward, hoping whatever she said next would give me reason to doubt what she thought she saw.

"A white Ford truck. Someone in a hooded sweatshirt and jeans. And my Marina. Her abductor had his hands around her wrists, and she was struggling. Trying to beat her fists against his chest. I think she might've been crying. I ran down the stairs, out the door, but the truck was pulling out by then, and too far away to see more than a few numbers on the plate."

My only comfort was in her choice of that one word—*his*. It didn't prove anything, of course. Most violence against women is perpetrated by men, so it could've been an assumption on her part. I didn't ask, because I didn't want to put the idea in her head that the abductor might have been a woman. Like my sister.

"Anyone else see anything?"

"No. A couple of my neighbors have those doorbell cameras, and the police checked those too. None of them caught anything."

I stood, knees weak but still managing to keep me upright. "I should go."

"No, wait." She reached out, but her hand froze halfway to me. It trembled. "Those kids at the camp, maybe you can ask around? See if they know anything about Marina, stuff they might not share with the police?"

I balked at giving this woman false hope. Then I studied her face and thought maybe she needed it.

"I will," I promised.

Once the words were out of my mouth, they felt less like deception. I had already vowed to myself to find Marina, just not in the way her mom suggested.

Anne tried to smile, but her grief wouldn't hold it. "You'll need my number—" Her brow wrinkled. "I'm sorry, what's your name?"

I bit my tongue, the tang of blood instant, and I swallowed the grimace that threatened to give me away. My name. Should I give Marina's mom a fake name, knowing she would distrust me if I contacted her later? Or give her my real one, hoping she hadn't already heard it from Detective Pratt?

"Frankie."

I waited for the flash of recognition, but, thankfully, my name seemed to mean nothing to her.

"What's your number, and I'll text you mine?" she asked. A moment after I gave it to her, my phone pinged. I felt like such a fraud. "You'll tell me as soon as you hear anything?"

Before I could answer, she shot up from her chair, her hands forming fists. I tensed.

Was this it—the moment she recognized my name?

But then she relaxed her hands, and I realized she had only been holding her tension there, as if she were squeezing an invisible stress ball.

"Do you have a few minutes?" Her expression turned expectant. "My neighbor, he's helping look for Marina too." Hope energized her, and she didn't wait for my response before unlocking her phone to text. Her neighbor, presumably. "We can talk. Make a plan."

The situation felt close to spiraling. I moved closer to the door. "I can't stay. I need to—" Just in time, I stopped myself before I could finish that sentence: *I need to pick up my son.* I could think of nothing crueler to say to a mother who'd lost two children. "I need to get to work."

She stilled, the spasm of hope-fueled energy sapped. "Oh."

Her desperation was so thick in the room that I nearly relented and offered to call in sick to my nonexistent shift. But the best thing I could do to find Marina was find my sister.

"You can take his phone number, at least?" she asked. "In case you can't reach me? He's wonderful. He even lived with us for a while after his dad died. He's the one who told us about the camp."

The way she clenched the phone, I doubted I would need to make use of his number. Still, I told her to text it to me. My phone pinged again. When I saw the number, my pulse quickened.

*That can't be right.*

I must've remembered the number incorrectly. The number of the Wagners' helpful neighbor only *seemed* familiar. But I had always been good with numbers, and had memorized this one instantly. It wasn't one I would forget.

Tears finally breached her eyelids, and she swatted at them, as if aggravated by her own grief. "If you can't reach me, you can always try Ben."

# 17

The boxes stacked in the room seemed to sway, threatening to topple and bury me beneath them. But it wasn't the boxes. It was me, suddenly unsteady on my feet. Anne Wagner knew Ben, the man who had thrown the party the night of Izzy's hit-and-run, and he was helping search for Marina. Desperate people didn't always make smart decisions. After all, here she was talking to me.

The room grew tighter, the walls moving toward me like a horror-movie trap. If I didn't get out of this home and away from the responsibility of this mother's grief, I might be crushed. I nodded a goodbye, abandoning my clipboard. I didn't want her to notice my suddenly shaking hands. She deserved more than that, but it was all I could offer. My head felt as if it had been piped full of helium.

When I tried the door, it seemed stuck, but it was only my sweaty palms unable to gain traction. On my second try, I got it open, aware of Anne staring. Even through her grief, her attention was a laser. I didn't want that attention. I raced toward the steps, tripping on the first one.

Then a man stepped in front of me. He offered his hand to keep me from falling. I stepped back to be farther from it.

"Ben Wesley," he said.

His brown hair was slightly long, his brows and lashes thick. His manicured stubble shadowed a too-sharp jaw. I might've described him as beautiful except for that jaw and his eyes, at once both warm and predatory, like a dog that might bite. Though his clothes and hair were dry, he wore the brackish scent of the bay.

So this was Ben, the man Izzy spoke of with both awe and dread, before she stopped talking about him altogether. Apparently, though, she hadn't stopped talking *to* him. What did it mean that she had called him in the weeks before Marina disappeared?

I wasn't about to introduce myself to this man, but I didn't need to. My sister and I shared the same nose and jawline, and even if we hadn't, Anne Wagner had just texted him my name. Only my first name, but I was pretty sure Izzy would've mentioned me at some point in the past five years, and taken with the resemblance, it would be enough for him to make the connection. How was he going to play this?

I got my answer a second later. "So you're Izzy's sister."

He smiled broadly, exposing lower teeth that overlapped slightly. Intentional, I thought. This seemed a man who owned his flaws. At least the physical ones. I was certain that most people found that smile charming. Despite my aversion to him, even I felt an unwelcome tingle at his attention.

Anne had joined us on the steps. She moved behind Ben, holding his arm to steady herself.

"And you're Ben." Manipulator. Drug dealer. A co-conspirator in Marina's abduction?

"Izzy told you about me, then."

I fought to keep my expression neutral. "I know who you are." *What you are.*

"So, Frankie Barrera, what brings you here? It's quite a drive from Cloverdale."

I ignored the question, eager to be out of there. "It was nice to meet you, Ben," I lied, "but I was on my way out."

Before I could take a step, he shifted in front of me. Little more than a repositioning of his body, it was subtle but as calculated as that smile.

"No, really, what are you doing here?" Since he had his back to Anne, she couldn't see the shift in his expression. The smile remained in place, but it was pulled taut now, his eyes half-hooded.

"I'm going to help Anne find her daughter."

He raised an eyebrow in either amusement or recognition of the hidden threat in what I'd said. Hard to tell which. "I wasn't aware you knew Marina."

From behind him, Anne spoke. "She knows Marina from that camp."

"Oh? I know Izzy volunteers there, but I didn't know you did too."

Rather than double down on my lie to Marina's mom, I went on the offense. "Anne says you're also looking for Marina." My voice artificially friendly. "Do you have any ideas where she might be?"

"Not yet. But we're hopeful we'll find her."

I wanted to ask him if he sold drugs to my sister, and to warn him away from her, but more than that, I wanted to leave. "Do you mind?" I gestured for him to move.

"Of course," he said, but he didn't move. "While you're here, we have some beautiful trails. You should check them out. One warning, though: There are mountain lions out there. Coyotes, too, and rattlesnakes."

"You're quite the tour guide."

"Just want you to be careful."

"Thanks, but you don't need to worry about me." My composure started to splinter, and I couldn't stop myself from adding, "And, Ben? A warning for you too: stay away from Izzy."

He laughed. "Isn't that her decision?"

"I'm surprised you'd want to stay in touch. After what happened the night you met."

Ben's lips thinned. A blink later, the faked half smile snapped back into place. But I had seen the shift. My own half smile was genuine. But the satisfaction I got from unnerving him lasted only a few breaths. Too late, I realized Ben had a weapon—Anne—standing behind him, and he immediately pointed her in my direction.

"I passed your truck on the way in. White Ford, right?"

Anne stepped forward, her pallor gone, her cheeks flushed a deep pink. She spun to face him.

"White Ford? What are you talking about?" Her voice cracked. I tried to push past them, but she turned on me and planted her legs wide, using her body as a barrier. "What is he talking about?"

I could've answered that thousands of Californians drove a similar truck, but she would've seen through that. The other drivers hadn't come to her house fishing for information about her missing daughter.

When I made another move to get by, she grabbed my arm.

"Who are you?" When I didn't respond, she dug her nails into my skin. "Who the hell are you?" My skin was pinched between her fingers, and I twisted free, as gently as I could. I didn't want to hurt her more than I already had.

"I haven't lied about who I am or my purpose, only about having met your daughter."

She wasn't letting me off the hook. Here was someone she could blame for this unthinkable thing that had happened. "Where is she?" Her pitch was fevered. "Where did you take her?"

The only way out was to point Anne at another target. "You should ask Ben."

She swiveled, more confused than suspicious, and I took advantage of her distraction. I ran down the steps, missing one, nearly stumbling. Anne followed, the sound of her footsteps swallowed by the slight wind. But I heard her breathing, ragged and quick.

"Wait." The agony in her plea stopped me. Winded, I turned to find her less than ten feet away. I didn't think she had yet dialed the police, but she clenched her phone in her right hand. "Are you a mom?"

Not wanting to lie again, I said nothing.

"She's a good girl, Marina." Her voice taut, near the point of snapping. "She treats her floor like it's a hamper, she's a terrible driver, and she's moody as hell sometimes. But she's also artistic. Kind. Funny. And she's everything to us."

A shock went through me when I realized what she was doing: she was humanizing Marina, as if I were a person who could hurt her.

"I would never—" My voice broke.

"I can't lose another child. If you're a mom—"

I thought of the daughter she'd lost to cancer and wondered how Anne Wagner remained upright. Judging by the way her body trembled, that could change at any moment.

"I just want her back. I won't call the police. If you bring her back to us safely, I won't ask questions. Please."

I saw in Anne Wagner's face my own memories—Izzy hospitalized with meningitis as a child, Julian jumping off the couch and breaking his wrist the year before. Witnessing their suffering had always been far worse than experiencing my own. I knew Marina's mom had lied about not calling the police, but my desire to reassure her was abruptly stronger than my fear of arrest.

"I don't have your daughter," I said. "But if there's anything I can do to bring her to you, I'll do it."

Anne Wagner's expression faltered, and I thought I might've convinced her. Then she started lifting her phone.

Out of time.

Pulse quickening, I sprinted back to my truck, determined to find Izzy before either of us could be arrested.

# 18

Back in the quiet of my truck, the memory of Anne Wagner's words echoed.

*I can't lose another child . . . I just want her back.*

But there wasn't time to replay that conversation. I drove quickly away from the complex. Too quickly. At the entrance, I hit the speed bump at least ten miles an hour faster than I should have. The tires lifted, the front of the truck finding air before landing hard. Metal scraped. I gritted my teeth and slowed.

Still, I hit Highway 101 in minutes. While I headed north, checking my mirrors often for police cruisers, I risked a quick call to my parents. Assured by them that Julian was fine, I turned my attention back to Izzy.

I had been going about this all wrong. I had been retracing Izzy's steps as if a cold trail might lead to her. It was time to stop reviewing GPS data and start looking at what I knew about my sister.

Who was Izzy? Where might she go?

My first mistake had been believing Izzy might go anywhere. She wouldn't. She didn't own a car. She could've rented one, but if she became a suspect, the police could easily track her through the rental company. Plus, she wasn't yet twenty-five. That might make it harder to rent a car. As far as borrowing a vehicle, she often used my truck and our parents' sedan, but I could think of no one else she might approach. So her mobility would likely be limited to ride shares, public transportation, and places she could go on foot.

Another factor to consider: Izzy didn't trust easily. As far as I knew, she trusted only six people: Our parents, Julian, Piper, Mark, and me. And the last couple of days had proved that she kept secrets even from us. Piper seemed the most logical choice for a confidante, but she had seemed genuinely anxious when she called me. If her concern wasn't feigned, that left no one on my list.

Unless she trusted Ben. He didn't seem like someone who could offer Izzy the kind of support she needed, but that didn't mean he wouldn't be there with the wrong kind of help. Especially if they were both involved in this.

Then there was her friend in San Francisco who had lied about the desk. Kent. I didn't think she would've trusted him with a secret like this, but maybe he would give her a place to stay for a few days while she figured things out? But with rents what they were in San Francisco, Kent probably had roommates, and I doubted he would cover for her if he knew the police were involved.

Next, I considered work friends, or someone from Camp Sarah. That didn't feel right either. Casual friends, even the well-meaning kind, weren't likely to risk their own livelihoods, their lives, for a potential criminal.

She might have a trusted friend I didn't know about, or her relationship with Ben might run deeper than I suspected, but without leads into those theories, considering them was wasted energy.

I shook my head to clear it. My instincts were telling me Izzy was most likely alone, or with the girl she had taken. So . . . with no car, no friends, where might Izzy go?

A hotel was out. Easily tracked, unless she paid cash, and Izzy was broke. Would she stay at someplace questionable, that maybe didn't care so much about ID?

Then it hit me: There might've been only six people Izzy trusted, but those of us she did, she loved with a fierce loyalty. What would she sacrifice for our parents, and Julian? How many times had she forgiven Piper? And, if I was being honest, me?

Mark was on that list of six. While he was in the ICU, she wouldn't go far from him. She would stay close, in case he needed her. I'd read more than one story about a fugitive caught upon returning to a familiar place. Under stress, Izzy would do the same.

She would go to Mark's place. It was empty, and she had a key. Eventually the police might search it, but unless they'd developed new leads, it wasn't on their radar yet. For now she would be safe there. That's where she would go.

I switched off my phone in case the police were tracking me. I didn't want to talk to them until I talked to Izzy.

IN DOWNTOWN PETALUMA, I parked in a public lot up the street from Mark's complex, choosing a spot away from the other cars. I hoped it would help me avoid anyone who had seen the AMBER Alert, as well as the attention of Oliver and his cat.

The late afternoon heat kept many people inside, and the ones I passed showed no interest in me. At Mark's place, the curtains were drawn, just as I'd left them on my last visit. At the back door, I tried the code I'd used to enter the last time. But someone had changed it. My sister was here.

I moved to the front door and began pounding. Waited. Pounded again. I tried the knob, but it wouldn't budge.

I called for Izzy, not too loudly and just once. If she was inside, as I suspected she was, she would've heard my knocking and would be listening for me to announce myself. Calling out a second time would only alert the neighbors—and give them reason to remember her name.

Getting no response at the front door, I circled the unit slowly, trying the windows and looking for gaps in the curtains. The one I had peered in before was now closed.

*Definitely here.*

I walked briskly back to my truck and dropped the tailgate. There, secured to the sides of the truck with bungee cords, was the heavy-duty bag containing my father's tools. I unzipped the bag and selected a torque wrench, then stuffed it in my waistband.

A woman walking down the street would draw minimal attention. But put a torque wrench in her hand, and passersby might take a second look. Pulling the hem of my T-shirt to cover the wrench, I headed back to Mark's.

I rapped on the front door, three times in quick succession. When there was no answer I slipped the torque wrench from my waistband and considered the homes on either side.

The windows were open on the house to the left, alternative

rock playing inside. The volume of the music was too low to serve as cover. The house to the right was quiet. Empty? I couldn't be certain, but it seemed the better choice.

I walked the corridor between the two homes until I reached the rear.

*Sorry, Mark's landlord.*

I swung the torque wrench against the window. It splintered. A second swing shattered the glass, shards tumbling inward. I knocked free the jagged pieces that still jutted from the wood, then hoisted myself through the now-empty frame and curtains. On my way in, a glass fragment I had overlooked nicked my arm. I winced, then dropped to the floor in the kitchen.

Though I tried to reposition myself so I wouldn't fall head-first, my landing was clumsy. To keep from falling, I grabbed the counter. Steady now, I glanced at the wound on my arm. Blood beaded, but it was only a scratch.

I dabbed at it with the hem of my T-shirt and stepped into the living room. On the sofa, Izzy sat cross-legged with a large glass bottle wedged in her lap.

"Mark's going to be pissed about that." Izzy made a *tsk*-ing sound, then took a drink. She wasn't slurring yet. I wondered how long she had been at it.

I sat next to her. I wanted to take the bottle from her, but I resisted. If I did, she would only pick it up again.

"I wouldn't have broken in if you'd answered the door."

"I would've answered if you hadn't gone through my phone. Maybe next time remember to turn back on my facial recognition."

This was a game we could've played all evening, so I ended

it. "I'll have the window replaced before he gets home. Any word on that?"

She shook her head and took another drink.

"I was worried about you," I said.

"You're always worried about me."

I raised an eyebrow and tilted my head toward the bottle.

She raised it in a toast. "Fair point."

"I met Marina's mom."

"And how is Anne?" She tried for casual, but I could tell my revelation unnerved her.

"We're done with this, Izzy. You need to tell me everything."

She lifted the bottle to her lips, paused, then set it on her lap without drinking.

"I've been thinking the same thing."

It was my turn to look surprised. "I went to Camp Sarah too. Jenny Hauser said you and Marina were friendly, but that you'd had a fight last year."

Her face darkened, but she didn't respond.

"I thought maybe Marina had run away and you'd helped her," I continued. "But then I talked to Anne, and she said whoever took Marina was rough with her."

Izzy's anger flared. "That's not true."

"Then tell me what is."

She put the bottle on the coffee table, but continued to stare at it. "The truth. That covers a lot of territory. I don't know where to start."

"Let's start with where's Marina?"

"I don't know."

"I thought you were going to be honest."

"I am being honest. I've been looking for her too. I didn't know her mom saw your plate that night, and then Mark's accident . . . I've been trying to fix it, but I don't know where she is."

"Did you let someone borrow my truck? Someone like Ben? Is that it?"

She unfolded her legs and shifted to face me. "It was me," she said. "I took Marina."

Though I had suspected those words were coming, I felt like I'd been sucker-punched. "Why?"

"Because she asked me to." Her gaze wavered but she steadied it. "When she called me Thursday night, I couldn't refuse. Not after what I'd done to her sister."

I could think of only one person who would inspire the kind of guilt to make my sister steal my truck and then lie about it. "The girl you hit with your car?" Too late, I realized I had stated the hit-and-run as fact. I'd never done that before. "But her name was Rachel Stroud, wasn't it?" As if I would ever forget the name.

She nodded. "Different fathers."

"I thought she died of cancer. That's what Marina told people at the camp."

"You've been busy." She smirked. "Marina lied. Sisters do that sometimes."

I tried to minimize the damage of my earlier words. "We can't even be sure Rachel's dead. We don't know—"

She cut me off. "She's dead. But it's more than that."

"What are you talking about?"

"That wasn't all we did to Rachel that night."

Even before Izzy started her story, I knew what it would be about. Piper had warned me. The day before, on my visit to the apartment, she had gotten upset, and she'd said things I had dismissed as unreliable. But I hadn't forgotten what she'd said.

*We played that stupid game, the situation got out of hand, and Rachel ended up dead.*

# FIVE YEARS BEFORE

It was Ben who suggested the game. Paranoia. After what had happened with the deer, no one felt much like playing, but everyone agreed anyway. Most of them had grown accustomed to doing whatever Ben suggested.

The rules were easy to remember, but Ben went over them twice. A question was whispered to the person on the right. The answer to that question had to be the name of someone in the group. The person answering would say the name, and then a coin would be flipped. If it landed on heads, the question would be revealed. But if it came up tails, the person named would have to drink, and the question would forever remain a mystery.

Ben was especially adamant on that last part: If someone revealed the question despite the coin landing on tails, Ben warned, he would hold them down and force them to drink a whole bottle of vodka.

"I don't care if that shit kills you, those're the rules," he said.

They gathered to sit on flat rocks and trampled weeds to form a lopsided circle, two lanterns and the plastic bags that held the alcohol at its center. Tobin, though shivering, took off his sweatshirt so Rachel had a dry place to sit. Piper joined the circle last because she'd needed to empty her bladder and she got momentarily lost on the way back. Everyone else waited, drinking more slowly than they had been before, still thinking about that deer.

Ben started the game by whispering in Rachel's ear.

*Of course*, Izzy thought. There was no way he would let someone else go first.

Ben whispered his question to Rachel, who answered with a name of someone in the group. Then Rachel to Tobin, who did the same. Then Tobin to Chuck, and Chuck to Piper, and Piper to Izzy. Which brought it back to Ben.

The first round went quickly, once everyone figured out the rules. Though everyone had been hesitant to play, the game became a welcome distraction. In the beginning anyway. Talk of the dead deer faded. More drinks were shared. Even Rachel, so tense earlier, seemed to relax. But when the second round started and Ben whispered his question, Rachel laughed nervously. "Can I pass?"

"Spoken like someone who's never played a drinking game before."

Her cheeks flamed, and Piper's jaw gaped. "You've never played a drinking game before?"

Ben nudged her. "Come on, Rach. Answer or down the whole damn bottle."

She bit her lip as she glanced around the circle. "Um . . . I guess . . . Chuck?"

"Sounds more like a question than an answer," Ben said.

Even in the dim lantern light, Izzy noticed her flush deepen. "It's an answer. Chuck."

Ben reached across Rachel and punched Tobin on the knee. "Go ahead, Tobin. Flip."

Tobin grimaced at the punch, but flipped the quarter, caught it, and slapped it on the back of his hand. Then he extended his arm so the coin glinted in the light of the lantern.

"Tails." Ben sounded disappointed. "That was a really good question. Too bad we'll never know what it was. Guess you're drinking, Chuckles."

Chuck's expression telegraphed his annoyance at the nickname—Ben was more Tobin's friend than his—but he poured a shot of vodka into his paper cup. Ben made a *tsk*-ing sound and grabbed the bottle from him. "You can do better than that." He added another shot to the cup, and Chuck sipped, but Ben was having none of that. He hit the bottom of the cup, forcing the vodka down the other guy's throat. Chuck gagged, then sputtered.

"What the—?"

Ben feigned surprise. "Dude. It's only a game." He nudged Rachel. "You're up."

Still looking uncomfortable, Rachel placed her hand to Tobin's ear. Unlike his sister, Tobin didn't hesitate before answering: "Izzy." He flipped the coin. This time, it was heads. He said, "The question was 'Who's most likely to pass out tonight?' "

Izzy tossed an empty seltzer can at him. "Hey." But it was a playful gesture.

He smiled and shrugged. "You're one drink ahead of us, and you weigh like a hundred pounds."

"You'd be surprised."

He held her gaze a few seconds, then leaned toward Chuck. He whispered his question. Chuck also named Izzy. But that time it was tails, and the question remained a secret. Izzy poured herself a shot and downed it. The way Chuck avoided her eyes made her think the question had something to do with sex.

Ben threw a rock across the circle, hitting Chuck in the knee. "You're up, Chuckles."

"Hey!" But it wasn't Chuck who objected. It was Rachel.

"Looks like Rach has never been to a party either. Can't recognize it's all in good fun." Ben threw another rock at Chuck.

Chuck bristled, but he leaned to whisper in Piper's ear. It was loud enough that Izzy, who sat on the other side of her, overheard: "Who's the most likely to spend their life in a dead-end job?"

Piper laughed. "I can't say myself, right?" she asked. When Ben shook his head, she glanced from Izzy to Ben as if deciding. "Okay. Then Ben."

It bothered Izzy that Piper almost named her, mainly because it would've been a valid choice. Izzy finished the seltzer she had been drinking before the game started. The buzz in her head became a dull throb.

Tobin flipped, and the quarter landed on tails. Ben drank, apparently unperturbed that he would never know Chuck's question. Chuck, on the other hand, looked disappointed.

When Ben had drained his cup, Piper whispered her question to Izzy: "Who would make the worst porn?" Izzy picked Chuck but then Ben smirked, and she regretted it. The coin landed on tails. Again, Ben poured an extra shot into Chuck's cup.

Rachel continued to look as if she wanted to bail on the game, shifting in her seat as Izzy asked Ben who among them he found the most attractive.

Smirk still firmly in place, he said, "Chuck." And Izzy's suspicion was confirmed: Ben had a target. He wanted Chuck to drink. No, she corrected herself: he wanted Chuck pass-out drunk.

The coin was flipped. Tails. Chuck poured himself a light shot, and drank quickly before Ben could add another. Before the game started, Chuck hadn't kept pace with the group, nursing his lone can of seltzer. Still, he had consumed five shots in the game and seemed an inexperienced drinker. When he put down his cup, he swayed.

Ben's smirk finally slid from his face, but his eyes glittered. He was enjoying this. There was something about Ben since the incident with the deer. To Izzy, he seemed nearly envious that Chuck had been the one to kill it. Izzy didn't think it was the incident itself he envied but that Chuck had possessed the stomach to do something Ben couldn't.

When Ben leaned in to Rachel, he was so close that he brushed against her breast. Tobin noticed. Izzy could tell he didn't like Ben touching his sister. It was less clear how Rachel felt about it. Her face was turned, hidden in shadow.

When Ben whispered in Rachel's ear, she shook her head. "That's not cool."

"You know the rules." Ben gestured toward the bottles

of vodka. "You answer honestly, or you drink a whole one of those."

Izzy opened her mouth—about to say that Ben himself lied in his own response only a moment before—but Rachel spoke before Izzy could get the words out. "That wasn't one of the rules." There was unexpected steel in her voice.

Ben's face darkened. He didn't appreciate the challenge. "Of course it was. And good girl that you are, I know you'd never break a rule."

Reluctantly, she answered, "Chuck."

Tobin glanced from his sister to Ben, and back again, before he tossed the quarter in the air. He called it: "Heads."

"So, Rach," Ben goaded. "What was the question?"

Softly, Rachel answered, " 'Who's the most likely to become a pharmacist?' "

Tobin grimaced. "That's screwed up."

Everyone waited for Chuck to react. Ben pushed: "You want out, Chuckles?" For a minute it looked like Chuck was indeed going to leave. But he remained quiet, and the round continued.

The questions grew darker—Who would you smother with a pillow? Who was most likely to die alone?—and they all got drunker. But no one else named Chuck, even to the questions where he was the obvious answer.

Then it was Izzy's turn to ask her next question to Ben. She chose one that didn't fit Chuck at all: "Who's most likely to flunk out of college?" But she knew what would happen.

"Chuck," Ben answered.

Tobin flipped the coin. When it landed on heads, Izzy exhaled in relief. Then Ben said, "The question was 'Who's the most likely to have sex with a dog?'"

Izzy bolted to her feet. "That's not what I asked."

Ben shrugged. "Sorry if I misheard." It was clear he wasn't at all sorry. "But it makes sense, right? Who else would have sex with him?"

Chuck stood. He was steadier on his feet than Izzy expected. He left without acknowledging Ben's comment, turning before he could witness the anger this lack of reaction brought. With no target for his acrimony, Ben changed the rules of the game. "Let's ask our questions out loud. For fun. So, Rachel, have you ever had sex?"

Tobin glared. "That's not the game."

"New game. What's the answer, Rach? And blow jobs count."

Rachel picked herself up off the rock. "I'm not answering that."

"Please tell me I haven't been wasting my time," Ben drawled. "Never played a drinking game. Never partied. Never broke a rule. Never had sex. What have you done, Never Girl?"

Rachel left the circle, Tobin right behind her. Ben followed at a lazier pace, calling out: "Come on, Rach. It's only a game."

# 19

In the living room of Mark's cottage, Izzy told me what she remembered from that night. It had started with a game. A drinking game, because at that age what other kind was there?

She told me how Rachel had stormed off, and if she had only headed toward the car instead of down the trail, the night would've ended differently. But another thing Rachel never did: She never drove while drunk. Plus Ben was her ride.

If Izzy had gone after Rachel, that might've changed things too.

Instead, she stayed with Piper, drinking. Not long after Rachel stormed off, Izzy's head swam, her mouth sour with the taste of sickness, as she clutched a bottle she didn't remember finishing. The last thing she clearly remembered was talking to Chuck. Then, what seemed like only seconds later but was really a couple of hours, Izzy regained consciousness behind the wheel of her car, Rachel standing only a few feet in front of her, haloed in her headlights. The next moment, Rachel's body slammed into the hood of her car before it bounced off and landed somewhere in the thicket below.

IZZY SAID BEN HAD called Rachel the Never Girl, and in a way, Izzy and I had made that come true. Because of us, she became the girl who was never found. Never came home. Was she also the girl they never talked about? Whose name they never mentioned? Had Marina invented a sister who died of cancer because the truth was somehow harder for her to contemplate?

I got Izzy a glass of water, three ice cubes, and sat across from her on the sofa again. A pale light seeped from the edge of one curtain panel, but the room otherwise existed in shadow. In the tight space, I felt suddenly claustrophobic, like there were bad things on the other side of the door pushing to get inside.

"If Ben is such a jerk, why were you in touch with him? Is he involved in this?"

She didn't look at me but past me. "He's not involved, but he saw me that night. When I was leaving Marina's, I noticed him on his balcony. Watching."

"Why hasn't he gone to the police?"

"Ben would never turn me in."

I thought about his casual mention of my truck to Anne, and the story Izzy had just told me. "You sure about that?"

She nodded, then took a large drink of the water, still eyeing the bottle on the table. It was tequila, I now saw. The same cheap brand she'd favored before she stopped drinking the last time. "He might know my secrets, but I know his too. Besides, like I said, Marina wasn't abducted. She texted me, asking for a ride."

I wasn't ready to let it go. "You still haven't said why you were calling Ben the day Marina disappeared. Or why her mom saw Marina struggling with her abductor."

Izzy hesitated, then set down her water and reached into her pocket. She pulled something out and then tossed it onto the coffee table. A small bag containing white powder.

"That's not good, Izzy."

"I know."

"It seriously messes with your brain's chemistry. You can have seizures. A stroke."

"I know."

"You could die."

Despite the alcohol, her eyes were surprisingly clear. "I haven't used it yet," she said. "But that doesn't mean I don't want to. Badly."

"We need to flush it."

Absurdly, I wondered if that was even okay. Would it clog the pipes? Pollute the water system? I didn't know. I just wanted it away from my sister.

She nodded, and before she could change her mind, I took the small bag of powder and headed to the bathroom. I dropped it in the bowl and flushed, waiting until it spiraled out of sight before returning to the living room. Though away only seconds, I half expected Izzy to be gone. She buzzed with an unfamiliar energy, as if she were planning something. Something I wouldn't like.

I perched on the arm of the sofa and studied her face. There, I saw all the versions of her she'd been before: the fussy baby, the independent toddler, the reckless teen. I wanted to talk to her more about the cocaine, to make sure she fully understood the risks, but there wasn't time. Not now.

"Tell me about Marina."

She stared at the bottle like she wanted to climb inside. "After Rachel died, I needed to know her family was okay." She laughed harshly. "As if they could be okay, after losing her like that. I didn't know what I could do for them, I only knew I wanted to do something. I set up second social media accounts—I couldn't

use my own name or photo, because Tobin knew me—and I followed them. Ben, too, and Chuck. I didn't interact with them. I
could never do that. But I watched. Waited for Rachel's body to be
found, or for a chance to help them."

"That made it better for you?"

"Not at all."

When she reached toward the table, I hoped it was for the
water. Instead, she grabbed the tequila, nesting it in her lap. Her
hands in a choke hold around the neck of the bottle, she continued, "Then I saw that Anne had posted about signing Marina up
for Camp Sarah. I just—I wanted to help, like I said. I thought if I
could volunteer there, maybe I could help Rachel's sister. Or if not
her, the other kids. I could . . . atone, maybe?"

Izzy twisted the cap, first loosening it, then tightening it, then
loosening it again. The motion seemed to calm her.

"The first time I saw Marina, she looked so lost. I told myself
I was only going to reach out in a general way, not get too close,
but when I saw her sitting at the art table by herself, I couldn't stop
myself. I wanted to make her feel better."

"But last year, you guys fought."

She nodded. "I felt guilty, not letting her know what happened
to her sister, especially since she was older by then. More able to
handle news like that," she said in a strained voice. "But I also
worried what would happen if I told her the truth. If she were
pissed at me, who would be there for her? She doesn't have many
friends."

I remembered her mom saying the same thing.

"I thought maybe if I could point her in the right direction, at
least, she might be able to tell her mom, and then her mom could

call the police. They could finally find her body." She released a deep jagged breath. "So I told Marina that I'd met Rachel, and that we had partied a couple of times up by Mercuryville. Just that, nothing else. But of course she asked a lot of questions: When was that? Who else was there? Stuff like that. I kept everyone else out of it. Told her it was just us and some random people I didn't know well."

"How did she react when you told her?"

"She said Rachel never partied. I thought maybe she didn't believe me, and I wasn't going to push. But I'd forgotten how rebellious Marina could be. She snuck out, and convinced another camper to go with her. They stole a volunteer's car and drove out to Mercuryville." She sighed, her whole body rattling. "Stupid. They were never going to find her body in the dark, especially after all these years. But maybe she just wanted to feel closer to her sister?"

"So that's why you fought last year. But what about Thursday night?"

Izzy unscrewed the cap and lifted it to her lips. She closed her eyes and took a long swallow. "We weren't fighting. Marina was upset. She texted me, but she wouldn't say why."

When I had checked Izzy's phone, there had been no texts from Marina. But it made sense that she had cleared them. Of course, it didn't matter that she had deleted the texts on her phone. They would also be stored on the phones of whomever she'd texted. And even if that person cleared their texts, too, the cell phone company would have the records, wouldn't they?

She continued, "I assumed it was about Rachel, of course, but honestly, I didn't ask questions. I was just grateful she'd reached out. I was glad she didn't hate me for not telling her sooner."

I could see the rest of that thought reflected in her face: *like I've hated myself for the last five years.*

"When I got there, Marina was waiting on the curb with a bag. Sobbing. When I tried to comfort her, she pounded my chest with her fists. She didn't want to be comforted. At first I couldn't even tell what she was saying, she was crying so hard." Her eyes glazed. "She kept repeating herself until, finally, I made sense of what she was saying: 'They've found Rachel's body.'"

SINCE FINDING THOSE STRANDS of hair tangled in the headlight, I had been expecting those words, but hearing them now left me shaken.

"When?" I asked.

She shrugged, capping the tequila and dropping it to the floor. The amber liquid sloshed as the bottle rolled under the coffee table. "They told the family Thursday."

"What did she say happened?"

"At first she would only say they found her sister, then she begged for a ride. Crying the whole time. I asked her where she wanted to go. She said wherever. For the first half of the drive, she wouldn't say more, even when I pushed." Izzy's gaze slid to her lap, her shoulders hunching as she retreated into herself. It was a posture of defeat I wasn't used to seeing in my sister. It worried me.

I rested my fingertips on her knee. She had more to say on that, but I could tell she wasn't ready. I steered the conversation to what I hoped was a safer subject.

"Where'd you go?"

When she found my eyes again, hers were glassy. "Here."

The barrette. The lip balm. The signs that someone had been camped out on the floor. "When's the last time you saw her?"

"I was supposed to pick her up here Friday," she said, her voice husky with alcohol and suppressed emotion. "But when I got here, Mark was gone. And so was Marina."

"She hasn't tried to contact you?"

She shook her head. "I've been texting her. Called her a couple of times earlier today. Her phone might be dead, or she's turned it off. It goes straight to voice mail."

I had believed that if I found Izzy and convinced her to talk to me, I would finally get my answers. But Izzy didn't know everything. Marina's whereabouts were a mystery to her, too, and old memories that might've helped guide us had been erased by alcohol.

"Why're you telling me the truth now?" I asked.

"I figured I owed it to you to tell you first."

*First.* If I was first, who would be next?

Izzy squared her shoulders, bracing for whatever choice she had already made. Then she said, "I'm going to the police."

"Let *me* go," I said quickly, but she was already shaking her head.

When she spoke, her voice held a hint of irritation. "Stop trying to cover for me."

She wrapped her arms around herself but didn't look away. "That's not all Marina said. She brought up what I told her last year. About partying with Rachel. She asked again about who else was there, and again I lied. Told her I didn't remember their names. She asked if Rachel seemed to know them. I said they seemed to be strangers to her too." She paused and inhaled deeply. "Then she said, 'If they didn't know Rachel, why would they want to kill her?'"

# 20

A few days after the hit-and-run that killed Rachel, Izzy and I had
returned to that remote stretch of Geysers Road. We had gone
looking for evidence that what Izzy remembered had happened.
We had hoped to find new memories too. Or I had anyway. Maybe
Izzy had always preferred that most of that night remained lost
to her.

To help her remember, I had even borrowed our parents' car
and parked on the same shoulder that Izzy had chosen days before. That afternoon, a thin fog had hugged the base of the Mayacamas. Staring at those mountains from the front seat of the car,
our breath fogging the windows, we had talked about the party.
Back then, Izzy had mentioned the game only in passing, giving
me a vague list of names and claiming she couldn't remember
more. I had believed her.

When we had finished talking, we had trekked down the
mountain to the spot where I'd discovered the deer. Then we had
visited the clearing where Izzy and her friends had gathered. A few
crumpled seltzer cans had still littered the hard-packed dirt. The
afternoon had been damp, water beading on our outer layers but

not penetrating to the skin. Still, Izzy shivered. The haunted look she gave me that day remained the clearest thing in my memory.

That afternoon was the most we had ever talked about the party, until this one.

When I was certain Izzy was done talking, I leaned in and rested my hand on top of hers.

"It was an accident," I said.

"Was it?" Her eyes burned with a new fervor. "I didn't accidentally get drunk. The keys didn't accidentally find their way into the ignition."

I couldn't argue. We had both screwed up that night. "What are you going to tell the police?"

She pulled her hand away. "I'll leave you out of it."

That she would think that was my concern made me stiffen. "I don't care about that."

"You want to compare stories, then? That's what you're asking?"

The tension in my shoulders became a throb. "I'm not saying we should align our stories," I snapped. "I only want to know what you're going to say."

"Isn't that the same thing?"

I sighed, exasperated. "Not really." But maybe she was right.

"I'm going to tell them about Marina, and what I remember about the hit-and-run." When I opened my mouth to give her a hundred reasons why that last part was a bad idea, she quickly added, "I have to. What if Mark's accident is related? If they're going to investigate that properly, they need to know what happened back then."

"I don't like it. I understand telling them about Marina. That will help her get home safely. The party, though . . ."

"I need to know what happened too."

The thin ribbon of sunlight at the edge of the curtain had started to fade as evening approached. Despite the deepening gloom, my eyes had adjusted enough that I could clearly read Izzy's face. There was no talking her out of this. And I wasn't sure I should.

"Where do you want to go?" I asked

"I don't know." Her voice unsteady. Was her resolve wavering too?

I ran through the options. Rachel had died in rural Sonoma County. Probably the sheriff's office on that one. Mark was here in Petaluma. And Marina had been reported missing from Mill Valley. That reminded me I had Detective Pratt's contact information.

"How about we call the detective who questioned me?"

Izzy nodded enthusiastically, as if it might go easier with someone I'd already met. I wasn't at all sure that was the case, but I turned on my phone and found Pratt's number.

BEFORE IZZY CALLED DETECTIVE Pratt, she opened the curtains and put the tequila in a kitchen cupboard. Then she asked me to leave.

"You can't be part of this," she said. "If you're gone too much longer, Julian will start to worry. Our parents too."

"I can't leave you here by yourself."

"Because I can't handle it? Or because you think I'll leave again?"

My face flushed. "Because you're my sister, and you're in trouble."

There was another reason for my hesitation, one I was grateful Izzy wasn't able to guess. Though she claimed to have shared all she remembered, she had said the same five years earlier. I had always believed that was my superpower: understanding Izzy. When she was thinking, she bit the inside of her lip, which caused an almost imperceptible thinning on one side. When she lied, I often noticed it in her hands first, the way she might scratch the underside of her wrist or bite her nails or rub her fingertips together. In contrast, her happiness always rested in her eyes. She could fake a smile, but true joy made her eyes blaze.

These were tics I had learned to recognize, or so I had believed until she had lied to me recently with such ease. Did I believe her—really believe her—or was my judgment clouded by my desire to restore my faith in her? I watched her hands but they gave nothing away.

"That night, I didn't call you to get me out of it," Izzy said, her voice hushed. "I wanted you to find Rachel."

"I looked. You know I did."

"You looked until you found that deer, and that gave you the excuse you needed to leave."

"If I had stayed longer, you could've died."

"Rachel did die."

"And it would've been better if you had too?" Frustration sharpened my voice. "By the time I got you to the ER, you were barely breathing. A couple of times you stopped entirely. They were talking about intubating you."

At the hospital, I'd parked the car in the darkest corner. We couldn't have people noticing the blood on the hood and getting curious. Though, in hindsight, maybe a blood-streaked car wasn't an oddity outside an emergency room.

I remembered carrying Izzy in because I couldn't find a wheelchair. Inside, they'd almost immediately started talking about sticking a tube down Izzy's throat, into her windpipe, and hooking her up to a ventilator.

"If we'd stayed longer, we might've been able to save her."

I wanted to shake her. "Did you not hear me? You. Stopped. Breathing."

"You don't know that I wouldn't have survived it. I'd been drunk before."

"But that was the first time you'd been so drunk you ran someone over."

In trying to get through to her, I had gone too far. Her lips pinched, but she gave no other indication that I had wounded her.

"What about whatever you noticed on the headlight?" she asked.

I froze, heart racing. "What?"

"The next day. You were washing the car. I went out to offer to help, but I stopped when I saw you. Squatting next to the car, the sponge dripping in your hand, staring at one of the headlights."

When I didn't respond, she crossed her arms. "It seems you have your secrets too," she said. "You're such a hypocrite."

*My secrets have been about protecting you. I've never killed anyone.*

I bit the inside of my cheek to keep from saying the words aloud, because by prioritizing Izzy's life that night, I left a young woman out there, dying. I was at least as responsible as my sister, because I had been sober. Even had Rachel already been dead, by leaving that night I had denied her family closure for five years. Still, I stood by my decision.

*Keep Izzy safe,* my dad had told me. I would continue to do that, no matter how fiercely Izzy fought against it.

# 21

I grabbed the torque wrench I'd used to break the window and, against my better judgment, left Izzy to make her call to Detective Pratt. Back in the parking lot, as I approached my truck, I sensed movement behind me. I spun and scanned the lot. I saw no one. Apparently Izzy's story had made me jumpy.

I moved to the rear bumper, intending to return the wrench to the bag of tools. The bag was gone. Someone had stolen it.

I swore under my breath. After throwing the torque wrench in the backseat, I settled in the front. Should I report the tools stolen? The more expensive tools that I'd borrowed from my dad I'd stowed in my garage. What was the value of the ones that had been in my truck? Several hundred dollars? The bag itself was worth nearly as much. That might be a lot for me and my parents, but it wasn't enough to attract much interest from the police.

*Not worth it*, I decided. I engaged the brake pedal. Hit the start button. The engine rumbled.

A second later, the fuel light flashed, and I checked the gauge: empty.

I pushed the button again, killing the engine, then I dropped my head onto the steering wheel, teeth clenched so tightly my jaw ached.

*Damn it.*

Taking a breath, I pushed away the tension and self-pity. No time for that. Reaching across the console, I fumbled in the glove box for a flashlight. It had been a while since I had replaced the batteries, but when I toggled it on, a soft beam of white light fell on the floorboards. A moment later, it flickered, but the light held. I pulled an old sweatshirt off the passenger seat and hopped out of the truck.

Immediately I caught the scent, faint but acrid. Gasoline.

I dropped to my knees, using the flashlight to peer underneath the truck. In the few seconds I had run the engine, a wet spot had stained the asphalt. Definitely a leak. Fuel tank, most likely.

When my dad had his old Econoline, he kept a bar of Fels-Naptha soap in his glove box for just such occasions. Once when we'd been driving back from the coast, a rock bounced off the road and punctured the van's tank. My dad had climbed under the van and rubbed a thick coating of soap over the hole. That fix got us home.

I didn't have a bar of Fels-Naptha, but I did have access to an auto parts store. First, though, I would have to see what I was dealing with. I laid the sweatshirt on the ground and slid under the truck, flashlight clenched tightly in my left hand. The beam glinted off the steel and caught a bead of gas on the tank. The bead stretched, dripped. When I strained to see better, the spot where my neck and back met began tingling. I would be able to fix it easily enough, but I was pretty sure a rock hadn't done the damage.

Someone had deliberately punctured the tank with a sharp object. Like a knife.

The flashlight pulsed, its batteries fading.

Inside my head, unease snapped like a rubber band. I got to my feet and debated: Call a tow truck, or fix it myself? On my phone, I did a quick search. There were three auto parts stores within half a mile. I chose the one closest to a gas station and set off in that direction.

IT WAS A SHORT walk, but it gave me time to think. There was no question the fuel tank had been sabotaged. Though I felt the truth of that in my gut, I doubted I would be able to convince the police of it. The question they would have was the same one I did: Why?

Why had someone stolen my tools?

Why had someone pierced my fuel tank?

The tools weren't worth much, and there were more permanent ways to disable a vehicle. If the saboteur had slashed the wiring harness instead, that would've been a much harder repair. The damaged tank was an inconvenience, and it pissed me off, but it could've been worse. Much worse.

Which was probably the point, I decided. Someone wanted the memories I'd been dredging up to remain buried. This was my warning.

Had Mark's hit-and-run been a warning too? I couldn't help but connect the two events: a few days earlier, Mark had been nearly killed half a block from where I now stood. It wouldn't have been hard for that same person to find me here too.

I couldn't guess who that person was, not until I knew more. Without all the variables, an equation wasn't solvable. Those were the rules. And I couldn't get this answer wrong.

As I walked, the evening heat pressed against me, though that alone wasn't the reason for the sweat that dampened my neck, or my erratic heartbeat. I was scared—by all that had happened, certainly, but also by my decision, which had only solidified when I'd found that gas stain on the asphalt.

Despite the threat, I couldn't let it go. I wasn't just protecting Izzy. I was protecting us all—Julian, my parents, even Marina, a girl I had never met. Because someone who would hit Mark with a car and sabotage my truck wasn't the kind of person who cared if more people got hurt.

AT THE AUTO PARTS store, I bought a fuel tank repair kit, some medium-grain sandpaper, batteries for the flashlight, and a gas can. I filled the can at the nearby station.

Back at the lot, I replaced the flashlight's batteries. Before starting the repair, I hesitated. Scanned the lot. Waited another minute. Finally convinced I was alone, I again slid under the truck. Using the sandpaper, I scuffed the metal surrounding the hole, then cleaned it with alcohol and my now-ruined sweatshirt. Focused as I was on my task, I felt vulnerable. My back burned. My whole body itched. I couldn't shake the feeling I'd had when first entering the lot: that someone was watching. My hand shook so that when I opened the tubes to mix the epoxy compound, I bobbled one of them. I caught it and forced my hand to steady.

*Focus, Frankie.*

I smeared a layer on the hole in quick, thick swipes. Eager to be done.

"Need a hand?"

I jumped, nearly hitting my head on the undercarriage. I scrambled out. Ten feet away, a man was watching me. Silver hair. Glasses. Wiry build. I squinted to see his face more clearly.

When I glared, he took several steps back. "Didn't mean to startle you."

"Thanks, but I've got it." It came out more brusque than I had intended, and the man held up his hands.

"Sorry." He didn't sound sorry. He sounded irritated. "You should be more grateful when someone offers to help."

"I said thanks, didn't I?" This time I intended the edge to my voice. I almost added, *And don't tell me what I need to do.* But since I was a woman alone with a stranger, I bit my tongue.

After the man drove away, I waited for the compound to harden and cure. The incident with the stranger left me unsettled, and when I transferred the fuel from the can to the tank, gas splashed on my hands.

*Careful,* I reminded myself, blotting my hands on my sweatshirt.

I fired up the engine and checked for leaks. There were none.

From that first sniff of gasoline to the moment I shifted my truck into gear, only about an hour had passed. Not much time, I told myself. But with Julian so far away and my sister currently confessing to the police, to lose even a minute seemed a risk.

I pulled out of the lot, passing a large trash bin. On the ground next to it, a black bag had been dumped. I recognized it immediately. It was the one that held my dad's tools.

I got out of the truck and approached the bag. I half expected to find a note taped to it, or the knife used to puncture the tank staged among the tools inside. When I unzipped the bag, carefully, I saw only a jumble of screwdrivers, wrenches, and pliers. Nothing ominous at all. Still, my heart banged, and afraid of what other surprises might still be hidden inside, I left the bag on the ground where I'd found it.

# 22

I took Julian to Hamburger Ranch, where he inhaled a chili cheese dog and I forced down half a patty melt. It was an extravagant dinner for an ordinary Sunday, but there had been nothing ordinary about that day. I ate a couple of sweet potato fries, usually my favorite, before I finally surrendered, throwing my napkin on the table. With the appetite I didn't have, I probably should've gone with the salad.

After finishing his own dinner, Julian started on my fries, dunking them in thick swirls of ketchup, half of which transferred to his cheek. We would eat only green things the next night, I promised myself.

Back home, Julian and I burned some calories with a game of hide-and-seek. When he asked to hunt bugs in the dark and I refused, he started to fuss. After he brushed his teeth and settled into bed, I placated him with his stack of Eric Carle books. We made it through all of them before his eyes finally closed. I planted a few extra kisses on his forehead.

I stayed there awhile, waiting for Izzy to call. Watching Julian sleep usually calmed me, but that night, it didn't help.

I got up, grabbed my laptop from my bedroom, and set up at the kitchen table. Though I'd searched these particular names countless times in the past—always anxious that new information might implicate Izzy—I typed them in again now, one by one.

*Ben Wesley.*

*Rachel Stroud.*

*Tobin Stroud.*

*Piper Lange.*

*Chuck Romero.*

And then, reluctantly, *Isobel Barrera.*

There was nothing new since the last time I had searched months before. The articles about Rachel still listed her as missing, not yet connecting her to Mercuryville or the bones found a few days before. It looked like that detail had been shared only with the family.

In my search, I easily found a phone number for Chuck, who worked as a pharmacist in Allentown, Pennsylvania. I saved the number in my phone.

That left Tobin's number. I navigated to one of those sites advertising access to cell phone information and paid a few extra dollars for the premium report. I saved his number too.

I wasn't sure if I would call either of them, but it gave me purpose while I worried about Izzy. After texting her several times and getting no response, I turned the ringer up as high as it would go and went to bed.

I WOKE UP AT five to my phone ringing. I grabbed it, knowing by the ringtone who it was before I answered. Izzy.

"How you doing?" I asked, clearing my throat.

"Good." She paused. When she continued, her voice hitched. "Actually, I'm not good."

I sat up in bed, pulling my blankets around me, and rubbed my eyes. "Tell me."

"I told Detective Pratt everything about Marina." Her voice broke again. She was having a hard time getting the words out.

"She didn't believe you?"

"I don't know." Her breath came in quick bursts.

Knowing she was on the verge of hyperventilating, I kept my voice calm despite the chaos swirling inside my own head. "Take your time. Breathe."

I heard her inhale deeply.

"Where are you?" I asked. "Do you need me to get you?"

"I'm back at Mark's. They had me come in for an interview and they dropped me off after."

"Who's *they*?"

"First it was Pratt. She asked a bunch of questions about Marina. Then after I mentioned hitting Rachel with my car, they called in someone from the sheriff's office. Another detective, Jim Kaplan. A deputy was the one who gave me a ride home." When she exhaled, it came in a drawn-out hiss. "I think it's bad. Really bad."

I wanted to reassure her. I knew the police had no reason to arrest her—yet. It was almost impossible to convict on a state-ment alone, and the authorities wouldn't want to jeopardize the investigation by arresting her too early. They would wait until they had corroborating evidence. But after Izzy's confession, she'd become a suspect. They would be working hard to connect her to Rachel's death.

"I don't know what I'm supposed to do, Frankie."

I heard the fatigue in her voice. "You been to sleep yet?"

"No."

"You need rest," I said softly. "Tell me why you think it's bad. What did you say to Pratt?"

"I told her Ben saw what happened. And now that she knows the phone number Marina used to call me, she can check those records, and mine."

"Marina didn't use her own phone?"

"She has one of those phones you can pick up at a convenience store. The kind you don't need a plan for? She didn't want her mom being able to find her."

"You really think Ben will back you up?" I asked.

"He will." She sounded irritated at the question. I welcomed the shift. I would rather have her irked at me than teetering on the edge of despondency. "I know you don't like Ben, but he's not a totally bad guy."

"He sells drugs."

"I've taken drugs. Does that make me a bad person?"

It wasn't the same. "Of course not." I hoped she heard the sincerity in my response. "But he also started that stupid game, and threw me under the bus with Marina's mom."

"I'm not saying he can't be an ass, but you don't know what he's been through."

"We've all been through stuff." Izzy should know that as well as anyone.

"I know. I'm just trying to get you to understand." Impatient. *Good*, I thought. "I was at his place once, and I saw this weird painting on the wall. Dalí's *The Great Masturbator*, he said. He told me how Dalí's dad showed his son photos of people with venereal disease and gross stuff like that. As a lesson. When I asked Ben why he would have something like that on his wall, he said as a reminder that like Dalí's dad, his dad was a dick too."

*Shocking.*

We were getting off track, but I found myself curious about Ben's childhood. "Did he say how?"

"He just said his dad liked to give him lessons, too, but they usually involved a belt. So Ben's loyal to those who are loyal to him."

What about those who weren't? "So Ben will back you up, and Pratt probably believes you."

"Yeah. Since it's looking to the police like Marina ran away, they've called off the AMBER Alert. And Pratt said helping Marina would be considered contributing to the delinquency of a minor, which is a misdemeanor."

"That's all good news."

"It is." Izzy did not sound like someone sharing good news. "Marina's still out there."

"I know."

Izzy got quiet. Even the background noises—the rustling, clicking, breathing—stopped, as if the world no longer existed on the other end of the line. "You still there?" I asked.

"I think the detective from the sheriff's office, Kaplan, thinks I killed Rachel." Her voice was little more than a whisper.

"Isn't that what you went there to confess?"

"On purpose."

I pulled the blanket more tightly around me, clenching a section of it in a fist beneath my chin. "He said that?"

"Not exactly. He just asked if Rachel and I argued that night."

"Did you?"

A couple of seconds passed. Then: "No." But I didn't like that hesitation. "I'd only just met her. I'm not saying I liked her, but I didn't dislike her either. I was just kinda . . . neutral about her."

When I inhaled, I caught the scent of fabric softener I'd used when I had washed the blanket Thursday morning. Back when tasks like doing the laundry seemed important.

"You need to tell me exactly what you told Kaplan."

"I told him the same thing I told you: that I got wasted, regained consciousness in the car, and hit Rachel." She paused. "I'm sorry. He asked how I got home, and I mentioned you."

"I don't care about that."

She continued as if I hadn't spoken. "I told him I didn't mention Rachel to you right away. I didn't want to involve you like that. But then he asked why. If I was so concerned about Rachel, why didn't I tell you about her? I said I was too drunk, my thoughts were all jumbled. That I didn't think to tell you." Her words tumbled from her in a rush. "But I could see right away he didn't believe me. He said something like, 'So you were sober enough to find your keys, start your car, realize you hit someone, and identify that someone as Rachel. Then you were able to call your sister and ask her for a ride. But—what? Forty minutes later, when you should've been more sober, you didn't think to tell your sister you killed someone?'" Izzy had burned through her earlier calm. She was panicked now. "I told him I drank more after I called you. That part isn't a lie. I had to steady my nerves, after what I'd done."

I wanted to ask her how much she'd needed in order to *steady* herself, but there was no point.

"That's when he started asking about my relationship with

Rachel." Another pause. "What if he's right and we were fighting?" Frustration raised her pitch. "I'm not sure we weren't, not with how little I remember that night. We were out there for almost four hours. Why can I remember only about half of that?"

The smell of the fabric softener had grown cloying. I released the blanket. "You were drunk."

"I'd been drunk before. Many times." Her laugh was harsh, desperate. "I need to know if I killed her. Intentionally, like that detective thinks. I need to know what happened that night."

# 23

I wanted Marina found. I did. But the police were investigating that, and my priority was now helping Izzy figure out what happened the night Rachel died. Was I selfish for prioritizing my own loved one above someone else's? Probably. Still, Marina had family, neighbors, and police looking out for her. Izzy had me.

So while Izzy slept, I considered my next step. Even with the three-hour time difference, it was too early to call Chuck Romero. If I could believe Izzy's story, he would have the least information, having left the party early, but it was easier than starting with Marina's brother, Izzy's hostile roommate, or a guy who could be a bastard. Plus, right now Chuck was the only one I was sure hadn't killed Rachel.

I DECIDED MY NEXT step would be to make Julian chilaquiles, just like I had the last morning our lives had been normal. Normal sounded good right then.

With my music played low so as not to wake him, I gathered the ingredients on the counter, then set to work husking and rinsing the tomatillos. I roasted the pile of small green fruit in a pan with jalapeños, onion, and garlic, then tossed them in a blender with cilantro, salt, and a squeeze of lime. I left them unblended for the moment, still mindful of Julian sleeping in the next room.

I cut some store-bought tortillas into strips and threw them into a skillet with preheated oil. Distracted, I'd set the flame too high, and the oil splattered onto my wrist. My skin throbbed, and I swore, too loudly. I took a step toward the sink, intending to run cool water on my burn, but my elbow caught the handle of the skillet. It toppled off the stove, splashing my shirt. I could feel the oil's heat through the cotton. The tortilla strips fell into a soggy heap at my feet.

I ignored the mess and hurried to the sink. Turned on the tap. Stuck my arm under the faucet. Pulled the hem of my shirt into the water too. I waited for relief to come, but my skin felt as if it were in the pan, sizzling. I gritted my teeth and closed my eyes.

When I opened them, I found that Julian had padded into the kitchen. Holding Mr. Carrots by his ears, he rubbed his eyes with his fists.

"I'm hungry," he said.

And it all became too much. Izzy. Marina. Rachel. My throbbing wrist and a blooming headache.

"There's cereal," I snapped, using a towel to pick up the pan and throw it in the sink.

It landed harder than I'd intended, and Julian's eyes widened. I suddenly felt like crap. I was always so careful with him, but now he looked scared. Because of me.

Tears pricked my eyes. "I'm sorry," I said. But even that had an edge to it. I was failing him, just as I was my sister.

He stood there, unmoving, eyes still wide. When I shifted to more directly face him, my arm scraped the faucet. I winced and bit my lip to keep from swearing again.

"Why don't you go get dressed and I'll pour you some Cheerios?" My voice still didn't sound quite right. I couldn't lose it. Not here, with Julian watching me.

He hesitated. "With sliced bananas?" he asked tentatively.

I forced a smile. "With sliced bananas."

After Julian left, I found a couple of ibuprofen tablets and went to my own room to change my now-sodden shirt. Passing the mirror above my dresser, I caught a glimpse of my face: jaw clenched, eyes shadowed. That wasn't me. That wasn't the face I wanted Julian to see staring back at him.

*Get it together, Frankie.*

I inhaled until air filled my lungs. Then I plucked a dry T-shirt from my laundry basket and headed back to the kitchen to slice bananas for Julian's cereal.

AFTER BREAKFAST, TEETH-BRUSHING, AND a quick combing of Julian's sleep-mussed hair, I walked Julian to preschool, trying to ignore the throbbing in my wrist.

Back home, I took a couple more ibuprofen and applied antibiotic ointment to the burn. Then I retreated into the backyard to sit on the covered swing there, my legs crossed under me. Later the heat would likely make my skin sticky, but unbearable afternoons often made for beautiful mornings. I tried to forget how I'd snapped at Julian. But there was no forgetting that look on his face.

Inhaling deeply, I caught the sudden scent of damp earth. Sprinklers, I guessed. Someone watering their lawn.

My throat closed, and my head throbbed at a memory.

A month after Rachel had gone missing, a summer storm hit Cloverdale. The air had thickened with the heat and unexpected rain. At that point a missing persons report had been filed, but the police hadn't found evidence to suggest Rachel might be at risk. In the days before she went missing, she'd talked about moving out. Getting her own place. And she was an adult. Add to that Piper's account of how, a week after the disappearance, she'd seen Rachel drive by in a blue sedan—even if Piper hadn't gotten a license plate, and she didn't know Rachel enough to be sure it was her.

Now that I knew Izzy had shared her secret with Piper, I suspected the story was misdirection. But then? I thought only Izzy and I knew the truth of that night. I wanted to believe Piper, despite the hairs I'd found in the headlight.

The day of the summer storm, though, the rain had triggered an image of Rachel, alone out there in the shadow of the Mayacamas, unable to shield herself from the rain. That was the day I acknowledged, to myself at least, that Rachel would never come home. While Rachel's family continued their futile hoping, I'd crawled into bed with a migraine. A well-deserved punishment, I'd thought at the time. Now, as I smelled wet earth again, my head ached with phantom pain.

After rubbing my temples for a moment, I punched in the number for the Allentown pharmacy where Chuck Romero worked. The man who answered the phone put me on hold. A minute of canned music later, another man's voice greeted me with a robust, "Hello. This is Chuck Romero. How can I help you?"

Though I had planned what I would say, I felt unexpectedly anxious. I introduced myself, adding that I was Izzy's sister.

"Hold on," he said abruptly, before returning me to an instrumental version of a ballad I couldn't quite name. Midway through the bridge, the line clicked open again. "Sorry about that. Thought I should take this in the back. Izzy okay?"

There was a time when my answered phone calls always started the same way—*Is Izzy okay?*—but hearing the words from a stranger jarred me. I responded on autopilot. "She's fine." But of course she wasn't. If my sister really had been okay, I wouldn't be calling this stranger in the middle of his workday.

"It hasn't made the news here yet, so I'm not sure if you've heard, but Rachel Stroud's body was recently found off Geysers Road."

He gasped. "No, I hadn't. Tobin and I are still in touch, but just birthday texts and the like." He paused to consider what I'd just told him. "That's horrible."

I agreed that it was. "The reason I'm calling is because Izzy doesn't remember a lot about the night Rachel died, and I'm helping her fill in those blanks. And since you were there . . ."

"Not sure how much help I can be. I left early." Chuck sounded more guarded than he had a moment earlier. Had I been wrong to believe this would be an easy call?

"Izzy told me. But anything you can remember would be helpful."

"How do they know Rachel died the night of the party?"

Not the response I'd been expecting. "What do you mean?"

"If Rachel's been dead for five years, and I'm guessing she has been since she's been missing for that long, how can the police pinpoint it to an exact time frame? Any evidence has to have deteriorated long ago."

My practiced script went out the window. Certainly it was okay to tell Chuck, since Izzy had already told the sheriff's office? "Because Izzy remembers hitting Rachel with her car."

"Holy crap."

*Holy crap indeed.* "So if there's anything you can remember, even if it seems insignificant, it would really help Izzy."

I wasn't sure my appeal would work. As Tobin's friend, his allegiance was probably to the Strouds. As Izzy told it, she'd met Chuck for the first time that night. Why would he want to help a young woman he'd met once five years before?

"Izzy was kind to me that night. I would've liked to know her better."

Chuck's characterization of Izzy made me emotional. Not enough people recognized that about her. They often saw the drinking, the recklessness, the temper, and then they could see nothing else. Hadn't I been guilty of that on occasion too?

"How about Rachel?" I asked. "As Tobin's roommate, you must've known her."

He was slow to answer. "I knew her, but mainly through Tobin." I heard a rustling of what sounded like paper. "Look, I wish I could help, but I was only there for the first hour or so, and I really should get back to work."

I thought of Izzy, depending on me. "Please, Chuck."

"I'm sorry."

I sensed he was close to hanging up, and the next time, he would be less likely to take my call. "If you don't talk to me now,

I'll get on a plane to Pennsylvania this afternoon. And when I get there, I'll be cranky, because last-minute airfare is terribly expensive. You'll have to get a restraining order to keep me away from your work and off your doorstep."

I hoped he didn't question me on that, because having Julian meant I couldn't really jump on a plane on a whim.

After a moment he said, "Why would you come, when I've told you I don't know anything?"

"For Izzy."

"That's ridiculous."

"You have people you love there in Pennsylvania?"

Chuck hesitated. "I got married last year, actually. She's pregnant." Despite the conversation we were having, I could hear the smile in his voice.

"Congratulations. If your pregnant wife was in trouble, would you fly to California if someone had information that might help her?"

"I told you—"

I interrupted. "Would you?"

No hesitation this time. "Yes. But I don't know anything useful. I swear."

"Have you ever heard of that guy, John something, arrested in Florida somewhere for killing his neighbor?"

I was being deliberately vague because *John something* didn't exist. The story was a fabrication.

He hesitated. "I think I might've heard something about it. He had a machete or something, right?"

*Sure, let's go with that.* "I think so. The police weren't even looking at anyone else, because they had the weapon, and the two men had often argued about a bush that might've been planted on the wrong side of the property line."

"Yes," he said emphatically. "I remember this story now. It was in Pensacola."

I was glad he couldn't see the look on my face. *Really?* "So this neighbor was arrested—"

He interrupted. "But it was really the wife who killed him."

Had I somehow made up a story that had really happened? While Chuck continued talking—adding details about the wife— I pulled my phone away from my ear and put Chuck on speaker as I did a quick Google search. No machete-wielding murderers in Pensacola, though I did get quite a few hits in Miami.

"Then you must remember how the police figured that out."

He was silent, then, "Another witness came forward?"

The lie was pretty much telling itself at that point. "Exactly. But this witness didn't even realize she had useful information. She just happened to overhear the wife's phone conversation in a grocery store where she asked someone if it had been taken care of, then a few days later this shopper saw the wife on the news crying about her husband."

"It wasn't a grocery store," Chuck corrected. "It was a coffee shop."

"Of course," I said. "The woman wasn't even sure that what she'd overheard was significant, but she came forward, and the police traced that call to the person the wife had hired to kill her husband."

"Still, I don't know anything that can help you."

I groaned. "Come on, Chuck. You've spent more time avoiding my question than it would've taken to answer it."

I could almost feel Chuck thinking. "Okay. But I've got to get back to work. I take lunch in half an hour. Can I call you back then?"

I stifled another groan and told him I would be anxiously awaiting his call.

I HAD LAUNDRY TO do, the bathroom needed cleaning, and the breakfast dishes still needed washing. I ignored all that, holding my burned arm in the swing and remembering the last time I had shared the swing with Julian. After he'd fallen on the patio, it was here I had dabbed antibiotic ointment on his abraded skin. The same tube I'd just used on my wrist. I thought of all the scraped limbs I had bandaged in the past few years. As soon as he could crawl, Julian had been drawn to sharp corners and rough surfaces. He was clumsy and curious, born to poke things that didn't want to be poked, and each time his curiosity got him hurt, his mouth would wobble in surprise and the tears would come. And then the next day he would do it again.

As a small child, Izzy had been the same. I wished our current problems could be solved as easily, with a smear of ointment and a bandage.

My phone buzzed. It was Chuck. I had half expected him to blow me off, but here he was, calling exactly thirty minutes after he'd disconnected.

"Thanks for calling me back," I said, swinging gently. The movement soothed me. Almost made me forget the burn and the look on Julian's face when I'd snapped at him.

"Like I told Izzy back then, I can't really remember much."

I planted my feet on the ground to stop the gentle motion. "Izzy?"

"She called me about seven months after that night. I'd just started dating Angela—that's my wife—and I was about to start pharmacy school in Pittsburgh. Then Izzy called, and I was back in that clearing, drinking warm vodka and being bullied by Ben. It was not a place I wanted to be."

"Izzy never mentioned that."

"It was a short conversation. She asked what I remembered from that night, trying to fill in the holes in her memory like you're doing now, but there wasn't much to say."

"Tell me what you told her."

"It was a long time ago."

I could feel him slipping away, eager to leave the memories behind. "Start with Rachel," I prodded. "What was she like?"

"Quiet, I guess. Nice."

When he didn't offer anything more, I prompted. "Tell it like a story. So you and Tobin arrive at the party . . ."

He sighed. "We didn't arrive together. Tobin and I took separate cars, but we got there at the same time. Ben brought Rachel, and Izzy brought Piper. I'm pretty sure Ben took Piper home, though. That's what I heard the next day anyway. Not sure what happened to Rachel." He paused. "Well, I guess I do know what happened to Rachel now, don't I? But as I said, I left early."

"Izzy mentioned you were the first to leave."

He scoffed. "I should've left as soon as Ben suggested that ridiculous game. I had a test the next day, but honestly? I stayed as long as I did because I thought Izzy was cute, and like I said, she was kind to me. Talked to me. I know that doesn't sound like much, but I wasn't usually the guy women talked to at parties. Which is why, for the most part, I didn't go to them." The statement was devoid of self-pity. Delivered matter-of-factly, the way he might describe rain being wet or the sun being hot. "I never expected I'd have a shot with Izzy, but she intrigued me, and so I stayed. Until Ben started playing his own game, trying to get me drunk. No point in sticking around for that."

"What about Rachel and Izzy? Did they get along?"

"Well enough, I guess."

"You don't sound convinced."

"Ben's a bastard, but he's a good-looking bastard."

"Okay."

"I mean, I don't understand the charm myself. Being a bastard would be a deal-breaker for me if I were a woman. But a lot of women seemed to like him. When we were roommates, Tobin would tell me stories, and I would cringe. Anyway, that night it seemed like Rachel and Ben were a thing, but he was also flirting with Izzy. So Rachel and Izzy were never going to be friends."

"What about Tobin? He left early too?"

"Yeah, he got back to the apartment shortly after me."

"You stay in touch with anyone else from that night besides Tobin?"

"Just that one call from Izzy. And like I said, Tobin and I aren't close like we used to be."

"You must've talked about that night."

"Not really. He left early, too, so at first, what was there to talk about? That stupid game?" he asked. "And by the time we knew Rachel wouldn't be coming home—that she wasn't just staying with a friend somewhere—I'd already moved out." He paused, and for a moment I thought the call had dropped. "Besides, Tobin didn't like to talk about it. Not that I blame him. Can you imagine what it was like for him, losing his sister like that?" I thought of Izzy and shivered.

On the other end of the line, I heard a knock. "Look, I have to go," he said brusquely.

He hung up before I could ask anything else.

# 24

Tobin Stroud held an entry-level job on the digital delivery team of a San Rafael software company. Even after speaking to a representative in the department, I didn't fully understand what that meant, but I did know he would be working a half day. Off at noon. I was told the rest of his afternoon would be spent planning Rachel's memorial service. Though the family had been grieving for years, they only now had a body to bury.

"It will be nice for the family to finally have closure," the assistant overshared.

Nothing about the family's situation could be called *nice*, but I thanked the assistant for the information.

Before I headed to San Rafael, I called Julian's preschool and asked if there was room in the after-school program. There was, so I signed him up. If I hurried, I would probably be only a few minutes late, but traffic on U.S. 101 could back up midday. Better to be safe.

The international company's local headquarters looked about as I had expected. A long three-story building with nearly as much window as wall. Newer trees in front with thick foliage. Carefully tended flowers, mostly red but with an occasional burst of pink or white. The asphalt and sidewalks looked as if they had been scrubbed clean. Maybe they had been.

Outside the main entrance, on a small patch of lawn the shade of a putting green, I sat on a bench and waited. To blend with the office workers, I wore a pair of cropped slacks, a cap-sleeved blouse, and sandals. The bench was positioned in direct sun, so that even in the lightweight cotton I quickly grew uncomfortable. Perhaps the company preferred that visitors didn't linger. At least the ibuprofen had dulled the pain in my wrist.

By the time I spotted Tobin leaving the building, the base of my ponytail was damp and sweat streaked my temples. In contrast, Tobin's ruddy face was clean-shaven, and his dress shirt still held its crease. He wore his hair expertly styled but short, which called attention to ears that seemed almost elfin. I rose from the bench and approached.

When Tobin saw me, he stopped, but his gaze was wary. Izzy had described his eyes as smart, but there was something lost about them now. The whites were cast with pink, and the ruddiness I'd seen from a distance seemed to be due to barely repressed emotion. Anger or grief, I couldn't yet tell.

"Tobin Stroud?" I asked, though I knew from the photos I'd found online that it was him. When he nodded, his brow furrowed. "I'm Frankie Barrera. Izzy's sister."

The lines on his forehead deepened. "Has she heard from Marina?" There was a hint of anger in his voice. His question made clear he knew about Izzy's involvement in Marina's disappearance. Did he also know about her role in Rachel's death? I didn't think so, since it was still so early in the investigation.

I was grateful for that at least. Tobin already seemed irritated by me.

"She hasn't," I said.

His lips thinned. "Then why are you here?"

His eyes fell to the bandage on my wrist, but he didn't ask about it. Probably didn't want to encourage conversation.

"I actually hoped to talk to you about Rachel." I stilled, watching for his reaction.

"I'd rather not." He started walking, but I kept pace. He shot me a glance, his lips so compressed that they disappeared into his face.

I quickened my step so I could get in front of him again. I queued up the tone I used to placate difficult parents at my middle school. "I'm sorry that my sister helped yours run away. I'm sorry about—" I stopped myself before I could mention Rachel. "Everything."

"My mom said you were at her house."

"That's part of the everything I'm sorry about. If something happened to Izzy—" I choked. "I can only imagine how you and your family are feeling. I only want to help."

He must've recognized the sincerity in my apology, because his lips reappeared. "How can you help?" Suspicious. Which I guess was better than irritated. At least he appeared open to listening now.

"I'm not sure I can," I said. "But if we can talk for five minutes . . ."

When he exhaled, I recognized the surrender in it. Still, he said, "I have to pick up my mom in twenty minutes, and that's about how long it takes to get to her house from here."

"We can sit in your car. Just five minutes. Please."

He shook his head. "It'll be an oven in there." He pointed to the anemic shade of a nearby tree. "There."

SINCE THERE WASN'T ENOUGH shade for us both, I stood in the sun. I didn't want to give Tobin any excuse to deny me the full five minutes. He checked his watch. Apparently I was already on the clock.

"I was hoping you could tell me what happened the night Rachel disappeared."

"You mean the night she was *killed*. What does that matter?"

"Not sure it does, but Izzy doesn't really remember much about what happened, and she'd like to. I'm sure you would, too, given that's the night your sister died."

"Understandable that Izzy doesn't remember much. She was pretty wasted."

Though there was no accusation in his words, I bristled. "She didn't drink that alcohol by herself."

He acknowledged the comment with a curt nod. "The truth is, I don't remember much about that night either." His smile was rueful. "I was pretty wasted, too, and it was a long time ago."

"What do you remember?"

His smile slipped. "Ben suggested we get together out on Geysers Road. Not sure why. There were better places to party, especially since Izzy and Rachel were the only ones not yet old enough to drink. I was the next-youngest, and I'd just celebrated my twenty-first a couple of months before. We could've just gone to Ben's town house, like we had before."

"Then why didn't you?"

"He said he wanted to do something different, since it was the first time for Izzy. An initiation, he called it. But, really? He just wanted to prove that all of us would go where he told us to."

"The whole he-says-jump, you-ask-how-high kind of thing."

He nodded. "You've met him, at my mom's. You know what he's like."

"He's a bit of a jerk."

His defense was swift. "That's not what I meant. He just likes to be in control, and for the most part we let him. Back then, anyway. He was older and he brought the drugs."

I couldn't tell which came across more clearly: Tobin's admiration for the man Ben had been, or his pity for the man he'd become. "You've known him for a while?"

"For years before that night. My mom knew his father, so when he died, Ben came and lived with us for a while. Ben had just moved into his own place in the complex a couple of months before Rachel died."

I prodded. "So Ben suggests Geysers Road, and you all follow him there."

His eyes went glassy. He rubbed them roughly, as if angry with them. I'd seen his mom make a similar gesture. Pratt was right that first day: The family'd had it rough. "I'm still not sure why this matters."

"It was Rachel's last night," I reminded him.

For a few seconds, his eyes lost focus. "You don't need to remind me of that. The last five years have been hell. And now, with Marina gone—" His voice caught. He cleared his throat. "We caravanned to that place. We drank for a while." He paused. "Then

Ben suggested that game. Casually, but I could tell he'd been planning it all along."

I wondered at that hesitation between mention of drinking and the game. "Why do you think he was planning it?"

"He likes to make people uncomfortable."

My opinion of Ben stood, but I was careful to keep the judgment from my face.

"I heard he was pretty rough on Chuck and Rachel."

"Chuck, definitely. Rachel, not really."

"What kind of questions were asked?" Even as I spoke, I realized I was asking to double-check Izzy's story. The thought brought the blush of shame to my cheeks.

"We were a bunch of drunk college kids. Sex and insults, mostly. One I remember: Someone asked who would be most likely to have sex with a dog. That one was Chuck. Ben tried to make sure every answer was Chuck. He wanted him to drink."

"Sounds like"—*Ben's a creep*—"he didn't much like Chuck."

"It's not like that," Tobin insisted. "But Ben was an alpha. You know how that is."

"He targeted Chuck because he was weak?"

He shook his head quickly. "Not at all. Chuck's brilliant, and Ben flunked out of art school. Ben's always been a little threatened by anyone who's smarter than him. That's probably why he was bothered by you too."

"I wasn't aware he was bothered by me."

He shrugged. "Maybe I'm wrong. But when my mom told me about your visit, and how Ben reacted, that's how it sounded to me."

I considered my next words carefully. "Whatever Ben said

to Rachel that night seemed to upset her, at least from what I've heard."

His eyes grew soft, like a man remembering. "Rachel was special. She didn't have the grades I did, and people often wrote her off because she was pretty. But she had such a gentle way about her. Unless you made her mad." He tried to laugh but choked on it. "Marina's like that too. Fiery when pushed. But Marina's slower to forgive, whereas Rachel would forget all about it before you could get the apology half out. So, yes, she stormed off that night, but she calmed down as soon as Ben said he was sorry."

"So they kissed and made up?"

He frowned. "Why would you say that?"

"They were dating, right?"

He shook his head vigorously. "There might have been some casual flirting, but Ben was like an older brother to us both."

In the heat, my blouse stuck to my back, all my exposed skin feeling as if it were being slowly baked. "The comments he made about Rachel still being a virgin don't sound brotherly."

His expression darkened. "It's obvious you've made up your mind about Ben. I wonder how you'd feel if I was nearly as judgmental about Izzy."

Instantly I was transported to other times Izzy had been threatened, whether it was that stray dog or the repercussions of her own bad choices. My desire to protect my sister had never originated in my conscious mind. It came from somewhere deeper. An involuntary firing of my brain's synapses. A coiling of my body. An almost painful pressure. Now I fought the urge to tell this grieving man to shut the hell up.

I inhaled, the air hot and thick. *High road*, I reminded myself.

"We're not talking about Izzy," I said.

"Aren't we?" His tone a challenge. "She took my underage sister. It doesn't matter if the police now say Marina called for a ride, she's a damn kid. And now she's out there, vulnerable, just like Rachel . . ."

His breath hitched and he blinked rapidly. The lost look returned. "So to answer your question, I followed Rachel and Ben that night, but when things seemed cool between them, I left."

Abruptly, it made sense. He wanted to believe in Ben, because if he wasn't the good guy Tobin thought him to be, then it had been a mistake for Tobin to leave Rachel alone with him. My hand twitched, the urge to comfort him strong. His pain was as palpable as the heat. But I sensed any kindness from me would be refused.

"After that, I hung out with Piper and Izzy for a while. I think." His forehead wrinkled as he tried on the memory to see if it fit. "I don't think I was that wasted, not like your sister, but honestly? I don't remember driving home. If not for Chuck, I wouldn't even be able to tell you what time I got back."

"What time did you get back?"

His shoulders jerked in an impatient shrug. "Eleven. Eleven-fifteen," he said. "The time didn't seem important. Not then. But I think that's right. You can check with Chuck. He's got a better memory than me."

I didn't point out I'd already talked to Chuck, or let him know that I planned on double-checking the timeline as soon as I got back to my truck.

"If I'd stayed, it wouldn't have happened," he said. "I would've been able to protect her."

The sun continued to scald the back of my neck. Tobin couldn't have protected his sister from being hit by a car, but how could I tell him that without implicating Izzy? Since she had already confessed to the sheriff's office, if evidence was found connecting her to Rachel's death, Tobin would find out soon enough. Better that I wasn't the one to tell him.

"You don't know that," I said.

A shadow crossed his face. "If I find out her death wasn't an accident, I'll kill whoever was responsible." Delivered less as a threat than as a statement of fact.

A lump rose in my throat, but I spoke around it. "Is there any reason to suspect it wasn't an accident?"

He checked his watch and scowled. "It's been well over five minutes. I'm going to be late."

"Thanks for talking to me."

Though Tobin claimed to be in a hurry, he waited for me to leave. When I glanced in my rearview mirror, I saw that he remained beneath the tree, hands stuffed in his pockets, still watching me.

# 25

I tried to make the rest of the day as normal as I could for Julian. After I picked him up from preschool, we went to the library and then the park. We had dinner with my parents. Leftovers, which meant Julian got to use the microwave.

It was nearly ten when we left, and Julian fell asleep on the way home, his head lolling against the side of his booster seat. After slinging his backpack over one shoulder and readying my house key, I scooped him from the truck. Julian heavy on my hip, I unlocked the door and nudged it with my elbow. It wasn't until it had started to swing open that I noted the glow from the living room, and realized what it meant. Though I'd left well before dark, the tabletop lamp had been switched on, its soft white light cast on the old recliner I often used for reading.

Seated in that recliner was Piper, sipping liquid from my happy face mug. Her other hand rested in her lap, partially covering a lump of white. When she shifted, I saw that the lump was Mr. Carrots.

Julian's weight doubled in my arms.

"Hope you don't mind that I helped myself to some water."

"I very much mind." I didn't like her holding Mr. Carrots. "How'd you get in?"

She put the mug down on the coffee table and folded both hands around the rabbit. "Izzy's key."

I was beginning to rethink the wisdom of handing out spare keys. "And why're you here?" My gaze darted between Julian's rabbit and her face. I had questions for Piper, but I preferred to ask them on my own terms. I didn't like unexpectedly finding her in my home, holding Julian's rabbit.

She stared past me to the open door. "I don't suppose you'd be willing to close the door?"

"Why would I, when you're about to leave?"

I freed my keys from the lock but stopped in the doorway. Shifting Julian's weight to my left side, I awkwardly patted my sweatshirt pocket. No phone. Jeans pocket. There it was. I pulled it out. Swiped it to unlock.

Piper looked amused. "You really going to call 911 on me?"

I tapped the phone icon. It was a bluff, but I was angry. "Unless you tell me why you're in my house."

She stood quickly, the rabbit dangling from her left hand as she crossed the room. I stepped back, the wood of the doorframe cutting into the soft spot between my shoulder blades. She smirked.

"Shit, Frankie, chill. I wasn't this uptight when I found you at *my* place." When I stepped away from the door, she pushed it closed.

I gestured toward Mr. Carrots. "Give me the rabbit."

She handed it to me. Irritation made my neck tingle.

"You might want to put Julian to bed. This could take a while."

"I'm good." With the door closed, the room had grown too

dark. I used my shoulder to toggle the switch for the overhead light. In the sudden illumination, I noticed the redness in her eyes, and the creases beneath them.

"I heard you talked to Rachel's brother," she said.

"Chuck too."

"Why?"

"Just trying to fill in the gaps in Izzy's memories."

"Does she want that?"

"Yes."

"You sure?"

In my head, I heard Izzy: *I need to know if I killed her. I need to know what happened that night.*

"I'm sure."

Piper leaned forward. That close, I could nearly taste her breath, equal parts sour and sweet. "I think someone gave Izzy Rohypnol that night. Maybe me too. I don't know."

Skeptical, I arched a brow. Back when she was drinking regularly, Izzy sometimes lost time. I wasn't convinced binge-drinking alone wasn't the reason for the blanks in her memory.

"What're you talking about?"

"I drank a couple of shots of vodka and about half of one of those horrible hard seltzers." She grimaced. "Nothing worse than that crap at room temperature. Point is, you know better than most my tolerance. That was nothing for me. Like, nothing. So why don't I remember anything after the first hour?"

When Julian stirred, I pressed him more firmly against me and began rocking from side to side.

"What do you remember?" I asked.

"Izzy finally told you about the game, right?"

I didn't respond, and she laughed. "Still keeping her secrets, I see. It's okay. I was there, remember? The thing is, how she tells the story isn't exactly how it went down." She stopped suddenly, her lips pursing. "For fuck's sake, put the boy down. You're going to throw out your back."

Julian stayed where he was, pressed against my shoulder. "You were saying?"

She sighed. "Yeah, you're not stubborn at all. Anyway, you know she and Chuck hooked up that night, right?"

My surprise must have shown, because she smirked again. "When Rachel, Ben, and Tobin went to get high in the woods, or whatever it was they were doing, Izzy went after Chuck. She didn't come back for at least twenty minutes, and when she did, her face was flushed. Like I'm an idiot and couldn't figure that out."

Holding Julian had started to make my back ache, but I drew resolve from his weight. "She never told me."

"See? There are things you don't know. So why don't you and I play our own game? You ask me anything and I'll tell you the truth. But you've got to do the same."

I was starting to really feel Julian's weight in my back, but I wasn't going to admit that to Piper. "What could I know that you don't? Izzy tells you far more than she tells me."

Her face darkened. "You'd be surprised."

"Fine. I'll play. Do you know what happened when Rachel, Ben, and Tobin went into the woods?"

"You wasted a question. I don't. But to prove I'm a good sport, I'll tell you what happened before."

"I know that part. Ben was taunting Rachel about being a virgin."

"That's half-true. He said those things, but it really was just part of the game. Izzy exaggerates that part. Rachel wasn't even that angry."

"I'm not sure I believe that." Even though Tobin told me the same thing.

She threw up her hands in mock surrender. "Hey. This was my idea. Why would I lie?"

"Because you're Piper."

She laughed at that. "Fair. But I'm not lying now. Rachel left the circle because she didn't like the game, not because her feelings were hurt. At least, not badly enough to stay angry at Ben. That was their cycle. Rachel's signature exit was to storm off. And Ben—no matter how much he played at being an asshole, he always followed."

I shimmied so Julian rested higher on my torso and pressed his head into my neck. "Be back in a second. Don't steal anything."

"Back hurting, huh?"

It hurt like hell, my burned wrist, too, but I shook my head. "I don't know where this conversation is going, but I'm pretty sure it won't be appropriate for a four-year-old."

I tucked Julian in and returned to find Piper back in the recliner, happy face mug in hand. "My turn," she said. "What do you remember about that night?"

I ran through the details quickly. How the Uber driver had nearly given up as the traffic thinned, a dozen cars becoming several becoming a single parked Jeep. Then nothing but empty road, until finally we had arrived at my mom's sedan. How Izzy had insisted she hit Rachel with her car, but when I'd searched, I found only a dead deer, partially hidden by a boulder. How drunk Izzy had been. I didn't mention the hair I'd found the next day. No matter what game we were playing, I didn't trust Piper that much.

Piper blanched, her body coiled with tension, hands tight on the mug. I wasn't used to seeing her like that.

"You okay?" I asked.

She nodded. "I've just never heard that story before."

"A couple of days ago, you told me you knew about Rachel."

"Let me rephrase: I've never heard the story from someone who was sober when it happened. When Izzy tells it, she uses a little less . . . detail."

"Back to the Rohypnol. Why would someone do that? And who?"

My face must have betrayed my skepticism, because she jerked forward, her eyes feverish. "That's two questions, but I'll allow it. Because I don't know."

"Come on. You're always willing to give an unqualified opinion."

"Okay, not facts here, but opinion? You're right. I always have one of those." She kept her voice light, but she seemed distracted now. More worried than she had been before. "Chuck was pre-pharmacy. He might've had connections. Not the type, though. Tobin? Maybe." She waited a couple of beats before continuing. "Then there's Ben. The pharmaceuticals guy. He scored the cocaine, no problem. All I can say is, it wasn't Izzy, and it wasn't me."

As much as I disliked Piper, I thought she was telling the truth. I didn't think she was involved in any of it. But I was less certain about Izzy. Was I entertaining the crazy theory that the drinks had been spiked because that gave Izzy an excuse for whatever else she'd done that night?

When Piper continued, she spoke with growing urgency, as if willing me to believe her. "As for why . . . who the hell knows? It's known as the date rape drug, right? But I don't think that's it. Maybe it was a prank. Or maybe someone wanted us to forget something else."

She stood abruptly. "I think that's enough sharing. Now that you know what happened, you need to stop this."

"As always, we disagree."

Piper gestured toward Julian's bedroom. "He important to you?"

I frowned. "That's a ridiculous question."

"What if something happened to Izzy? Or to your relationship with her?" she asked. "What would happen to him then?"

My blood went cold. "He has nothing to do with this."

Her cocked eyebrow made me wonder how much she really knew. "We're allies, Frankie, not enemies. We both want the same thing: to make sure Izzy stays sober and out of prison."

"Izzy's not going to prison." I tried to sound confident. "All they have is her statement. She shouldn't have gotten behind the wheel that night, but it was an accident. Besides, any physical evidence was lost years ago." I couldn't stop myself from thinking: What if it wasn't? What if a scrap of clothing, a mark on our parents' car, or the way Rachel's bones had fractured somehow connected Izzy to the hit-and-run? And what if one of the four witnesses then told the police how drunk Izzy had been?

Piper drew a deep breath, released it. "You don't get it. I'm not sure it *was* an accident."

"Of course it was."

"Remember how I told you Izzy can get creative with how she

tells that story?" When I nodded, Piper said, "That night—she got mean. Said things to Rachel that she wouldn't have sober. Hell, that she wouldn't have said if she'd had even a couple fewer shots."

I didn't want to believe her. Didn't want to know more. Still, I asked, "Like what?"

"Rachel and Tobin's dad left their mom when they were young. Just didn't come home one day. The only time they heard from him again was when the divorce papers came, which I'd mentioned to Izzy. One of Izzy's questions—well, it had to do with that."

"No."

She shrugged, as if she didn't care if I believed her. "Ask Izzy. She might not tell you the truth, but you'll be able to tell if she's lying, right?"

I shook my head. "She would never be that cruel, even drunk." I was angry now. Izzy saved stray cats and helped friends detox. She volunteered at a bereavement camp. She wouldn't deliberately hurt someone who'd lost her father.

"You sure?" Piper asked. "You've never seen Izzy angry? And angry *and* drunk? That's a potent combination."

Of course I had seen Izzy angry. We were sisters, and we fought. More often than was probably healthy. Once, she tore all the pages out of my math book because I wouldn't let her have ice cream for dinner. But she had been five, and she'd outgrown that.

"There's no way Izzy deliberately hit Rachel with her car."

The smile she shared with me was a sad one, wilted at the edges. "Pretty confident, for someone who wasn't there that night."

"I don't have to have been there to know what Izzy might do. It was an accident."

"Normally, yeah, I'd agree with you. But the cocaine, the alcohol, the Rohypnol . . ." Her voice trailed off. Her face showed no obvious signs she was lying. Something in the back of her eyes chilled me.

"She wouldn't run someone over."

"Keep telling yourself she's not capable of that. But if the police figure out what Izzy did, they'll arrest her." Piper leaned forward. Shadows distorted, the lamp's halo shrinking, growing, shrinking again like the throbs of a heart. "Do you want your curiosity to be the reason for that?"

# 26

After Piper left, I moved to the patio, keeping the door open so I could hear if Julian awoke. The moon was waxing crescent, the stars stark in a near-black sky. I easily found the two stars at the Big Dipper's bowl. With my eyes, I traced a line upward and landed on the North Star. Though Julian couldn't yet identify the constellations, he was fascinated by them. The last time we had studied the sky from the patio, Julian had wriggled free of the blanket we shared, turning in circles on our small patch of grass, his face upturned, until he'd made himself dizzy.

He had giggled. *There are more stars when I spin.*

I had put off calling Ben because, frankly, I didn't want to talk to him, but after my conversation with Piper, I knew it was time. I turned on the outside light, settled in the swing next to the lemon tree, and punched in Ben's number.

He answered immediately. "It's late," he said. There was no irritation in his voice.

"Should I call back tomorrow? Say, at five a.m.?" I kept my voice low in case Julian surprised me. Ninjas had nothing on four-year-old boys.

"Now's good. Though I'm surprised to be hearing from you at all, considering how our last conversation went."

"You mean when you threw me under the bus by mentioning my truck?"

He laughed. "Self-preservation. You seemed bent on outing me to Anne."

"If you have nothing to hide, what could I possibly tell her to make you so defensive?"

When he answered, he sounded amused. "Have to say, I'm intrigued by this conversation. Like, why are we having it? Something up with Izzy?"

I shivered at his casual mention of her name. "Izzy's fine." I had no desire to share that information with this man. "Any word on Marina?"

"That's why you're calling?"

"No. Just worried."

"We haven't found her yet, but we're getting close, I think. A friend of mine thought he saw her in town."

"I'm guessing you know Izzy helped her run away."

"She filled me in."

It shouldn't have surprised me that my sister had reached out to Ben—his number had featured prominently in her call history—but somehow it did. "She called you?"

"Of course she did. She's always believed in confession, your sister." Something bothered me about his tone, but I couldn't quite figure out what it was. "That's why keeping the secret about the hit-and-run has been so hard on her." He must've sensed the shock behind my silence, because he laughed. "I've known about that almost since the night it happened. You wouldn't let her go to the police, so she had to tell someone. And you'd be surprised how open people are when they're high."

Though night brought relief from the triple-digit temperatures of the afternoon, the air remained thick, almost fetid. "Izzy could've gone to the police. I wouldn't have stopped her."

"Really? And when she went to the police yesterday, you didn't try to stop her?" Despite his words, his tone was light, playful. "She's always done what you've asked." *Not even close,* I thought, but I didn't interrupt. "That night five years ago, she told you what she'd done, and you covered it up. You tried to convince her it never happened, and eventually she let you believe you had."

Suddenly the doubt that had been a seed buried deep for the past few years grew into a plant with poison-tipped thorns. Was Ben right? How much of what was happening was my fault? Fifty percent? Seventy-five? Or was it all my fault, and Izzy just the scapegoat I used to make myself feel better? Back then, she'd listened to me more than she hadn't. So when I told her to abandon Rachel, what else could she have done?

Ben continued, voice gruff. "When you kill someone, you don't forget that."

"Personal experience?"

He laughed again, but he didn't answer the question. "Izzy didn't need to tell me she'd helped Marina run away. It was pretty obvious to me that Marina wasn't being forced into the truck."

"If you saw what happened, why did you let Anne believe her daughter had been abducted?"

He sighed. "You're a bright girl. You can figure that one out."

I almost corrected him: *Woman, not girl.* But then it hit me. "You did tell her."

"Indeed. I told her Marina left voluntarily. Even described what I'd seen from my balcony, which was an emotional teenager being helped into the passenger seat by a friend. Izzy even helped with Marina's seat belt."

"But Anne didn't believe you."

"Not even a little bit."

"Why not?"

"It didn't fit her narrative. She saw something different, and one of us had to be wrong. It was easier for Anne if that was me."

So that was why he had been so cavalier about the abduction when I'd met him at the Wagner place. Not because he was involved. Because he knew Marina hadn't been taken by force.

As if reading my mind, Ben said, "If I thought she had been abducted, do you really think I would've let you leave that day?"

"If she didn't believe you, you could've told the police."

He snorted. "Why would I do that? From Izzy, you must know about my . . . hobby. And with Marina's disappearance reported as an abduction, more resources were brought to the search."

The longer I sat there, the more sour the air seemed. I knew the sense of smell could evoke memories, and I expected the reverse was also true. Dredging up these memories, I could almost smell the deer carcass I'd discovered. At that moment, had Rachel's body been close to me too? If I'd looked harder, would I have found her hidden under a nearby tree? And would she still have been alive?

I switched to breathing through my mouth, but the stench of

the memory lingered. "What happened between you, Tobin, and Rachel the night she died?"

"Izzy asked that too. On several occasions." There was that tone again. I realized now why it bothered me. He sounded almost proprietary, as if Izzy were a pet whose tricks amused him.

I struggled to keep my annoyance from my voice. "What did you tell her?"

"Nothing. It really wasn't her business, and it certainly isn't yours." There was a sharpness in his voice now. "Look, I didn't hurt Rachel. To be honest, I don't remember much of what happened." I was getting tired of hearing that. "Tobin left, then I did, but Rachel stayed."

"But you were her ride."

"Don't know what to tell you." He paused, as if trying to decipher the motives of a girl long since dead. "You picked up Izzy. So you know my car was gone by then. I'd parked just up the road from her, but it was gone when you got there, right?"

*Yes*, I thought. The only car I'd seen had been the one Izzy had borrowed from our parents. But I didn't want to give him the satisfaction of an answer. "I don't remember," I said, mimicking his tone exactly.

He laughed. "I see where Izzy gets it." Then he grew abruptly serious. "When I left, everyone was gone but Rachel and your sister. If I were you, I don't think I'd want to know what happened."

First Piper. Now Ben. Still, I pushed. "Everyone has a different interpretation of the game you played."

He sniffed. "That again."

"Is that why you and Rachel fought?"

"Rachel and I didn't fight. We never fought. Not like you're suggesting."

I shrugged in reflex, though there was no one to see it. "Like I said, different interpretations."

"I'm not saying Rachel didn't get irritated with me. I can be irritating." He didn't need to convince me of that. "But I can also be charming, and she always forgave me."

"From what I've heard, you were more irritating than charming that night. You seemed to be especially hard on Rachel and Chuck."

"Not at all." He sounded almost bored. "I've explained about Rachel. We had history. We quarreled, but never seriously. But Chuck? Yeah, I might've been a little harsh that night. That dead deer you found. How do you think it died?"

Though I found the question odd, I answered it. "A car, maybe. A mountain lion could've done it too."

He laughed, and I sensed he knew something I didn't. "Close enough," he said. "The deer was prey. Any number of predators could've taken it out. Chuck was like that deer. Nice enough, but soft. I did him a favor."

"How's that?"

"Did you know deer aren't exclusively herbivores? These scientists—I'm not sure where it was; someplace cold as shit, I think—anyway, they put up these cameras and found Bambi apparently likes to snack on baby birds. They pluck them right out of the nests like they're a pile of berries or acorns. Scientists caught them raiding more nests even than foxes or other predators." His voice grew so low that I strained to hear. "See, deer can adapt. They have a little predator in them, too, given the right circumstances."

"So you were helping Chuck adapt."

"Or maybe I was just having some fun with him." He exhaled. "This chat was entertaining, Frankie. Really. But I'm busy, and it's late."

It gave me a small measure of satisfaction that I disconnected first.

All the talk of dead things made me again aware of the smell. I untucked my legs to stand, anxious to be away from it. Then, glancing down, I noticed it: a large rat at the base of the lemon tree, its body bloated and stiff-legged beneath the yellow glow of the patio light. A gift from the neighbor's cat and the source of the odor. I hoped it wasn't also an omen.

# FIVE YEARS BEFORE

MERCURYVILLE, 9:22 P.M.

Ben's voice boomed, carrying as wordless echoes to where Izzy and Piper shared the blunted edge of a large rock. In contrast, Rachel's anger was quieter, harsh whispers filling Ben's pauses. Izzy couldn't hear Tobin at all. She got the impression he had followed his sister more as a gesture than as a challenge. Ben didn't seem the kind of guy who would've appreciated a challenge.

Izzy checked her phone. No texts, but the battery had drained to twelve percent. She excused herself, as much to escape the distant fight as to get her portable charger from the car. Or, rather, Frankie's portable charger. The month before, her older sister had insisted their mom stash it in her glove box. *You never know when you'll need it*, she'd said.

Frankie's compulsions usually annoyed Izzy, but at the moment she was grateful for them. Not that she would ever tell Frankie that.

For the walk to the car, Izzy took a bottle of vodka with her. No reason to stop the party just because that stupid game had pissed off Rachel.

At the top of the slope, Izzy found Chuck in his car with the door open, his phone lighting his face. She pulled up short.

"You're still here?" she asked. She flushed, at the obvious nature of the question and the way she slurred. She quickly shook it off. Why should she care what this stranger thought of her?

"I didn't want to get on the road until I sobered up."

She leaned against the car and held out the bottle. "So I guess I don't need to share?"

He shook his head and tapped his phone, pausing a video he'd been watching. "It's all yours."

She uncapped the bottle and swallowed a shot's worth. Wrinkled her nose. Wished it was tequila instead, or at least that the bottle was colder. Then she motioned to his phone, which showed a bunch of random shapes and letters.

"I think I've seen that episode."

Chuck smiled. "Studying for o-chem," he said. He had a nice smile, Izzy decided. Not as flashy as Ben's, or as confident as Tobin's. But nice. "I'm happy to teach you about *Avogadro's constant* if you'd like."

"I think I'll pass."

When Izzy took another long drink, his forehead wrinkled. "The party seems to be winding down," he said. "You need a ride?"

Now he sounded like Frankie. She scowled. "I'm not leaving for a while, but thanks."

"Oh," he said, as if suddenly remembering something. He stood, and from the pocket of his jeans he pulled out the knife he had used to kill the deer. "Since you're going back down there, if you see Ben, can you give this to him? I certainly don't want to ever talk to him again."

Izzy took the knife, which had a faux-wood-grained handle, its silver blade tucked inside, a flick of the switch away from being released. Folded, it was nearly the length of her hand. Did it still have blood on its hidden blade?

As if reading her thoughts, Chuck said, "Don't worry. I cleaned it."

She nodded. Paused. Then: "I'm sorry you had to do that."

"I am too."

She shook the bottle so the vodka sloshed. "Sure you don't need this?"

"I'm sure." But the dark look spread so it consumed the whole of his face. "Listen, I really don't mind giving you a lift. I could drop you off at home, then bring you back here tomorrow to get your car."

"It's my mom's car."

She groaned inwardly. *Why did I say that? It makes me sound like I'm still in high school.*

"Well, then, I could bring you back to get your mom's car."

She shook her head, which made her dizzy. She was really feeling the vodka, that familiar floating sensation taking hold. "I've got to give Piper a ride."

"I could drive her too."

Izzy gestured toward his phone. "Thought you had a big test tomorrow?"

"It's not until the afternoon. If I picked you up at, say, nine, I could still be back in plenty of time."

"I'm not really a morning person." She sipped at the vodka and studied his face. "Why do you care how I get home?"

"I don't care how you get home. Just that you do."

On impulse, she leaned in and kissed him, hard. Surprised, he pulled back, his face turning red. Izzy grinned. "Never been kissed before?"

Immediately he tensed. For a moment Izzy thought maybe he hadn't been kissed before, and that her words had hit too close to home. But that couldn't be right. Then his expression clouded, and she realized her question and its flippant delivery had reminded him of the game.

"These people aren't always nice," he said. As if she needed to be reminded of that after Ben's behavior. "Be careful."

She wiggled the knife. "If things go bad, I've always got this."

But even as she said it, a shiver traced her spine. She couldn't stop herself from remembering the knife's earlier purpose, or from feeling that that act had somehow tainted the blade, and with it, the night.

# 27

The next morning, I dropped off Julian at preschool, then picked up Izzy and drove her to the hospital. After having been intubated for four days, Mark had finally been taken off the ventilator. Though he hadn't regained consciousness, the doctor expressed optimism at the reduced swelling in Mark's brain and his ability to breathe independently of the machine. There was even talk that when he came out of sedation he might be moved out of the ICU and into a bed in another part of the hospital. It was a welcome bit of good news during a week that had left me feeling like I'd been kicked in the teeth.

After a couple of hours of alternating between Mark's bedside and a chair in the waiting area, I convinced Izzy to come with me to the cafeteria. I tried to recall the last thing I'd seen her eat, but all I came up with was that bottle of tequila. Her jeans seemed even looser on the hips than they had been the morning I'd found her sleeping in my truck. Were they the same jeans? Was she also wearing the same shirt?

When I asked if she was okay, she nodded. But her head wobbled, as if not connected properly to her body. She tried to order only coffee, but I forced a granola bar on her. So as not to appear a hypocrite, I grabbed one, too, though my stomach roiled at the thought of eating it.

We chose a table away from the window. Izzy said the sun's glare gave her a headache.

I had already given her some details of my conversations from the day before, but I had saved the more difficult questions. When we'd settled, I asked the first of these as gently as I could.

"Piper said during the game, one of the questions you directed at Rachel was about her father abandoning her."

Her cheeks flamed. "That never happened. Not that I recall, anyway."

The thought came, unwanted but difficult to ignore. That memory lapse seemed too convenient.

"You didn't ask a question that Piper might've interpreted that way?"

Izzy picked at her granola bar, sending flakes to the tabletop. She flicked one in my direction. "Like I said, I don't remember. But so what if I did? There were a lot of awful things said that night."

"I'm just trying to make sense of what everyone's told me."

I felt Izzy pulling back. It was a pattern we often repeated: I advanced, she retreated, right up to the line where pushing harder might damage our relationship. And then, sometimes, I still nudged.

"Piper also thought you might've been drugged, with something like Rohypnol," I said.

Izzy continued picking, building her small pile of crumbs.

"No one drugged me. I almost wish someone had, because at least that would make it less my fault."

"Tobin and Ben both downplayed how upset Rachel was."

"That doesn't surprise me. Tobin wouldn't say anything that might cast Ben as a bad guy, and Ben would never admit to being an ass to his girlfriend."

"I'm getting mixed messages about that."

"About what?"

"The girlfriend thing."

There was awkward silence, and then she said, "Are you saying I lied?"

"Not at all. Chuck and Piper mentioned the relationship too. I'm just wondering what caused the difference of opinion."

"It isn't a *difference of opinion*. Whoever told you that they weren't together is lying."

"But why would they do that?" At Izzy's glare, I waved off the question. "When Piper came to my house, she mentioned you and Rachel didn't really get along."

"She didn't make much of an impression. I've told you that. We certainly had no reason to argue."

"Piper thought you might have had a thing for Ben."

Her eyes flashed. "My roommate needs to keep her mouth shut."

I wanted to stop badgering her. I wanted to reach out and hug her, even if she fought it, but then I reminded myself this was what she wanted. She had asked me to find answers. If she didn't like the questions that got me there, that was too damn bad.

"What about Chuck? Piper said you guys hooked up."

She laughed, a bitter sound not at all like her usual laughter. "I'm definitely going to need to talk to her. But, yeah, we hooked up."

"Let's talk about the timeline—"

She interrupted. "Why are we talking about this again? I've already told you everything."

"You were the one who wanted help filling in the blanks, Izzy. That's all I'm trying to do." When she didn't respond, I pressed, "Tobin said he was home by eleven. That sound right to you?" I had confirmed the timeline with Chuck, but I waited for Izzy's response.

Her eyes were suddenly too bright. "I guess so."

"Any idea when Piper and Ben left?"

"No." She screwed her eyes closed in obvious frustration.

"Ben mentioned that earlier that night his car was parked nearby," I said gently. "But it wasn't there when I arrived."

"Damn it, Frankie." She grabbed the granola bar off the table and tossed it toward a nearby garbage can. It ricocheted off the rim and landed on the floor. "I don't need another interrogation. I've already had a couple of those this week." She sounded tired, and when she stood to properly dispose of the granola bar, she moved slowly.

"I'm sorry. I'm just trying to sort this all out." I pushed my still-wrapped granola bar toward her. "You need to eat."

On the table, her phone vibrated. When she glanced down, her brow furrowed, confused, as if she didn't recognize the number. But though I got only a quick look before she snatched the phone off the table, it seemed familiar. While Izzy answered the phone, I started to scroll through my contacts.

"Hello?"

At Izzy's sharp intake of breath, I paused in my search to study her expression. She covered her shock by clearing her throat, offering a half smile, and waving away my interest. She mouthed Piper's name, but I had seen the number. It wasn't Piper's.

"I'm glad you called," she said, standing. "How've you been?"

She mouthed, *Sorry*, and moved away from the table. Since I could no longer hear her conversation, I analyzed her body language. She bowed her head, left hand cupped around her mouth for privacy.

Pulling my gaze away from Izzy, I returned to scrolling through my contacts.

I stopped abruptly, my finger frozen above the screen. Though the number had been immediately familiar, confirmation of the caller's identity hit hard, a gut-punch.

I was staring at the screen—wondering what it meant even as suspicions burrowed—when Izzy sat back down at the table. She took a sip of her coffee.

"So that was Piper?" I asked, still hoping she might tell me the truth.

She nodded and looked away. "She was checking to see if I'm up for some catering shifts."

Her voice was steady, giving no indication of her lie, and the ease with which she told it made me doubt all the answers she had given me before.

I considered calling her on it, but it was better if she thought I believed her.

"Can I borrow your truck later?" she asked.

"Sure. For what?"

I watched while she constructed her fiction. "I'm going to pick up a shift." Grimacing, she pushed away the coffee, as though she found it suddenly distasteful.

"With everything that's going on, you sure that's a good idea?" Still watching.

"It'll be a good distraction. Thanks."

"You know I'd do anything for you." Sincerely delivered, it was admittedly an attempt to stoke guilt.

Izzy's expression remained mostly neutral. I might've thought she was telling the truth if not for the slight spasm at the corner of her mouth. That and the number that I could now place as belonging to the volunteer at the grief camp.

## 28

Izzy had finished most of the granola bar but was sticking to her lie when Julian's teacher called.

"Nothing to be too concerned about," Candace said, which immediately put me on edge. Apparently Julian had a stomachache and needed to be picked up early. My mom was working and the neighbor I sometimes called for emergency babysitting was out of town. I was just under an hour away, so I told her I could be there in forty-five.

"That'll be okay, I guess," she said. I could picture her wringing her hands, slathering them with sanitizer. Sick kids made Candace nervous.

I made it in forty-three minutes. Breaking the speed limit seemed a minor offense compared to my past ones.

At home, Julian squirmed when I took his temperature—normal—then asked for a juice bar—grape, not strawberry. He also requested that a blanket fort be erected in the living room. I brought in the dining room chairs, a couple of pillows, and the comforter from my bed. He supervised from the couch, with enough enthusiasm that I began to doubt he'd ever been sick.

The fort wasn't my best effort, but the supervisor seemed

satisfied. As soon as I tucked in the last corner, he scrambled in with Mr. Carrots and a couple of plastic dinosaurs. I brought the tomato soup and grilled cheese.

While Julian nibbled around the crust on his sandwich, I kissed the top of his head.

"Mama, do you love me as much as grilled cheese?" he asked.

I pretended to consider it before answering, "Much, much more." As I watched him eat, I smiled. "Feeling better, I see."

He shook his head, eyes wide. "My tummy hurts." He inhaled the rest of his sandwich.

"Do you know why it hurts?"

"I think I have the flu." He started in on his soup. When he dribbled on Mr. Carrots, I handed him a napkin.

"And how long has your tummy hurt?"

"Since workbook time."

*Ah.* Julian hated workbook time. "Very specific." I suspected his "stomachache" had as much to do with the current upheaval as it did the dreaded workbook. I felt a throb of guilt in my burned wrist.

He put down his spoon and lifted his bowl like a cup. A minute later, done slurping, he wiped his tomato soup mustache with the back of his hand.

"I think I might be better soon."

I pointed to his napkin, which he used to clean his hand. "I'm glad." I took his empty bowl and plate. Reaching beyond the fort to the coffee table, I placed them there.

"Why was Aunt Piper here?"

I cringed. I hated that he called her that, but she was Izzy's friend, and he had known her as long as he'd been alive.

"Last night?"

He nodded. I worried what he might've heard, and was angry at myself for not putting him to bed sooner.

"She just came to visit," I said.

"She never visits."

*True enough.* "She came to talk." I steeled myself. "Did you hear what we talked about?"

He shook his head, but pulled Mr. Carrots against his chest. A gesture of self-soothing. He'd heard something. I struggled to keep the irritation off my face. It wasn't for him.

"It's okay if you did and you want to talk about it," I said, resting my hand on his knee. "Maybe you heard something you didn't understand?"

"You were fighting." His face was earnest. Trusting.

"We were arguing."

"About Aunt Izzy?"

That he phrased it as a question gave me hope that he hadn't heard the worst of it.

"Yes. Sometimes adults don't agree."

"What did you not agree about?"

I inched closer, searching for words he would understand. "Remember the other night when you wanted to hunt bugs, but I said it was already dark? And then you got upset and said we could turn on the porch light?"

"You said the bugs were sleeping. But they weren't, because I heard them." His tiny forehead wrinkled, the same way it had when I'd told him no. "Aunt Piper wanted to hunt bugs, and you wouldn't let her?"

I smiled. "It's actually the opposite. I wanted to do something, but Piper didn't want me to."

I couldn't bring myself to refer to her as Aunt Piper.

"What did she want you not to do?"

"I called a couple of Aunt Izzy's friends so I could ask them some questions."

I got the response I expected. "Why?"

With a four-year-old, that one word often led down a rabbit hole. I chose my words carefully to avoid repeated use of it.

"Aunt Izzy wants to remember something from a long time ago that she's forgotten."

"Why?"

I sighed and tapped Julian's stuffed bunny. "If you lost Mr. Carrots, wouldn't you want to remember where you'd put him?"

His grip on the bunny tightened. It seemed I had driven the point home.

I added, "Aunt Izzy wants to find her memories."

"I hope she remembers where she put them."

I hoped so too.

Seeing Julian's lids start to droop, I grew aware of my own exhaustion.

"Nap time?" I suggested.

"You too?" he asked hopefully.

Though I still had calls to make, I could think of nothing more appealing. Clutching Mr. Carrots, Julian tucked himself next to me on the pillow in our fort, and we both quickly gave in to sleep.

I WOKE BEFORE JULIAN. Normally I would've woken him, too, but I let him sleep.

I called Izzy first. Mark had been transferred to a hospital bed but hadn't regained consciousness. She asked if it was still okay to borrow my truck, and could she stop by after visiting hours ended. We agreed on ten, because Julian would be asleep by then. Izzy wouldn't be up to entertaining a four-year-old.

Piper was next. I wanted to follow up on some of the comments she'd made that I now doubted. The question Izzy supposedly posed during the game about the divorce of Rachel's parents, for instance. And, honestly, I wanted to remind her to stay away from my home. I didn't want to expose Julian to more conversations like the one we'd had. When she didn't answer, I left a voice mail.

I poked my head in the blanket fort to confirm Julian was still sleeping. Then I moved into my bedroom, closed the door, and dialed the number I had earlier seen pop up on Izzy's screen.

Blake didn't answer. Rather than leave a message, I called back. On the third try, he picked up.

"Hello?"

I decided to get straight to it. "Why'd you call my sister?"

"What? Who is this?"

Buying time, I suspected. When we'd met, I'd seen him enter my name in his phone. He knew damn well who it was. "Frankie Barrera." I kept my voice friendly. "We met a couple of days ago at Camp Sarah."

He pretended to consider the name a moment, before saying, "Oh yeah. You were asking about Marina."

"You called earlier. Spoke with my sister, Izzy."

"Hmm," he said, as if trying to remember. "Today?"

"Come on, Blake." I switched from friendly to authoritative. Maybe he would respond better to that. "We both know you called Izzy this morning. Was it about Marina?"

"Hmm."

I closed my eyes to keep from losing my patience. "Let me rephrase. You called about Marina. What did you say?"

He laughed nervously. "Shouldn't you ask her?"

I pushed. "You know where Marina is, don't you?"

"I didn't say that," he said, too quickly.

I lied just as quickly. "Izzy mentioned that's what you guys talked about."

"She did?" Dubious.

"How else would I have known you called?"

That one seemed to stump him. Then he said, "I don't know. Maybe you saw my number on her phone?"

*Point Blake.* But I couldn't concede now. I scoffed with what I hoped was conviction. "I just happened to be with her when you called? Then why didn't I call you earlier?"

There were several reasons, of course. I had still been hoping Izzy would tell me the truth. Julian had been sent home from school with a faked stomachache. And I'd had no idea what I would say.

"I didn't call her," he said. "How would I even have her number?"

Now I was the one stumped. A second later, the answer came. "Marina's the one who called."

As soon as the thought occurred to me, I knew I was right. Marina had left her phone at home so her family couldn't trace her, and she probably hadn't wanted to use her secret burner phone in case it was being tracked. Maybe she'd even lost it, or the battery had died. That made sense. According to Izzy, her calls to Marina were going straight to voice mail. "She borrowed your phone," I said.

His silence told me I was right.

When I spoke next, I softened my voice. "I only want to help her. If you know where she is—"

He cut me off. "It's not like that."

"Like what?"

"I don't know where she is. I ran into her, at the camp. She'd come to talk to Jenny. The camp founder, you know?"

"I remember Jenny."

"Yeah, well, she came to talk to Jenny, but Jenny's not here. Family reunion or something down in Pasadena."

"How'd she get to the camp?"

"I don't know. An Uber?" he said, as if I were dense for not figuring that out on my own. But if she didn't have a phone on her, how would she have requested a ride?

"She didn't mention where she was staying?" I asked.

"A friend's house, but she didn't say which friend."

"And you didn't ask?"

"She's, like, nearly an adult. Why would I ask her that?"

With Marina's mom claiming her daughter didn't have many friends, where would she go? "For someone who doesn't want to be found, that's a pretty high-profile move. Showing up at the camp like that."

"Not really. The staff doesn't show up until Thursday, except for Jenny sometimes, if someone's dropping off supplies or whatever. So Marina would expect to find Jenny there alone. But Jenny's got that family thing, like I said, so she asked me to stop by and sign for a delivery." It felt like the truth, but I didn't know him well enough to be sure of that. The past few days had shown me how easily I could be fooled. "Besides, Marina knows Jenny wouldn't rat her out."

"Why not?"

"Because Jenny's cool."

It still seemed an odd move to me. Blake obviously believed differently, but I couldn't imagine Jenny risking the camp's future by helping a runaway, no matter how "cool" she was. Even if she escaped legal consequences, parents would think twice about trusting their children to her care. Not to mention Marina's safety should've been Jenny's primary concern.

"I hadn't realized Jenny and Marina were close," I said.

"They're not especially close, but Jenny's tight with all the kids. Like I said, she's cool."

I still wasn't buying it. "Did she tell you what she wanted to talk to Jenny about?"

"She wanted to borrow money. I didn't have any cash, or I totally would've given it to her." He paused. "But I opened the kitchen and gave her some food. A couple of bottles of water."

For a day, at least, Marina wouldn't be hungry. "Did you call the police? Her family?"

"No."

"What about her call with Izzy? Did you hear any of that?"

"No." But this time his voice wavered. It sounded like a lie.

I didn't push, because I could guess what my sister and Marina had talked about. Immediately after their conversation, Izzy had asked to borrow my truck. The last time she had borrowed it, she had used it to meet Marina.

# 29

The sun setting on Mount Tamalpais washed the sky in an amber light, darkening to crimson where masked by the clouds. I couldn't appreciate its beauty, though, reminded as I was of the falling night. I reached across to the passenger seat, seeking reassurance from my fully charged phone and the flashlight with its fresh batteries. Just because I planned on being out of there before full dark didn't mean I hadn't prepared.

After talking to Blake, I had called Detective Pratt.

"We're not getting any hits off the burner phone, but we'll check out the camp," she'd said. "The family will be relieved there's been a sighting. That she's okay."

I assumed she would talk to Blake too. Maybe even call Jenny Hauser in Pasadena. Didn't matter. I'd done my part.

A few hours later, when I checked back, I was told the police had found no indication that Marina had returned to the camp. I would've been mollified except for one detail that continued to trouble me. Why had Marina gone there to talk to Jenny?

The truth was, I didn't believe she had. As a former volunteer, Marina would've known the camp was closed, and likely empty.

As Blake had told me, Jenny returned only sometimes. And if she intended to ask for money, why would a cash-strapped Marina take an Uber? An Uber that would've been easily tracked in an app. An Uber that Blake hadn't seen, and that she'd had no phone to summon.

With Marina now classified as a runaway and nearly eighteen, she wouldn't be law enforcement's priority, and they certainly didn't care about clearing Izzy in a years-old hit-and-run. So I found myself dropping Julian off at my parents' and heading to Camp Sarah.

The only vehicle parked in the lot was the small white bus. I pulled in behind it, so my truck could no longer be seen from the road.

I got out of the truck, pocketed my phone and flashlight in my sweatshirt, and started walking. The trail leading up the hill to the camp seemed longer than it had on my previous visit. Sunlight dappled the earth in spots, but my steps were mostly lost in shadows. My mouth tasted sour, dusty. I wished I had a bottle of water, but when planning the trip, it had seemed wise to keep my hands free.

The gloom deepened. The silence pressed, broken only by the chirp of hidden insects. The similarities to the night Izzy had killed Rachel caused my heart to thunder. I didn't want to remember, but the images intruded, flashes that seemed at once surreal and more tangible than the trail at Camp Sarah. The memories tangled, coming out of order. The deer, discovered in the thicket of weeds and trees and thorny bushes. The nearly deserted road. The blood on the hood of our mom's car. My legs unsteady as I scrabbled down the mountainside, uncertain what I would find. My sister's screams. Her skin, tinged with blue. Cool, then cold.

Disoriented, I closed my eyes and counted to ten, as if a child's trick would work now. Surprisingly, the pause slowed my heart. When I opened my eyes again, I saw the oaks, pines, and manzanitas of Camp Sarah, not the rugged terrain at the base of the Mayacamas. Still, something about the memories bothered me in a new way. As if I'd missed something back then. Something important.

Almost reluctantly, I tried to bring back the memories, but they were distant now. No longer as vivid.

At the clearing where Blake and his friend had sat making paper lanterns, I stopped. I surveyed the buildings for signs of light or movement. They remained as still as the air.

I approached the main building. I had no intention of breaking in. Entering Mark's or Izzy's homes, even breaking Mark's window when I knew Izzy was inside, was different. That had been family. There was no gray area here. I was trespassing. Still, if someone was inside, the door would likely be unlocked.

I tried the knob. It wouldn't turn.

As I rounded the building toward where the campers bunked, I patted my pocket, worried I might've dropped either my phone or my flashlight. Both remained in my sweatshirt, two reassuring lumps. I was considering taking my phone out to make sure I had service when something caught my attention. Inside one of the buildings. A flicker? But as soon as I turned my head, it was gone. If it had ever existed.

I moved toward where I thought I saw the phantom light. I stood, unmoving, staring at the windows.

There. Definitely a flicker, like a lighter or a match. Then out again. If it had been earlier in the day, or if I'd been using my flashlight, I would've missed it. I was suddenly grateful for the darkening sky.

I considered what to do next. Should I knock to avoid startling whoever was inside? I was trespassing, after all, and that seemed the reasonable action. I didn't want to barge in only to find someone waiting with a gun.

Problem was, I wasn't feeling especially reasonable. I could go in quickly and catch the person unawares. And hope they were unarmed.

I moved quietly to the cabin closest to me and peered in the window. It had a connecting door. To a hallway or a bathroom? I circled the building carefully, wincing when I stepped on a pile of old leaves. They crackled softly.

I stopped. Listened. When I heard nothing, I continued my exploration. There appeared to be a back door in the rear of the cabin. If someone was inside the other cabin and wanted to escape, that was the route they would choose. Inside, there wasn't much in the way of furniture. The beds didn't have mattresses, and there was a single dresser pushed against the wall.

Decision made, I approached the cabin where I had seen the glow. I knocked. The person inside had three options: answer, hide, or flee. In that situation, I knew which choice I'd make. There wasn't enough furniture to provide camouflage, and alone in the woods, if it were me, I would never respond to an unexpected knock.

I quickly moved to the back of the cabin, hoping my instincts were right and that my knock would send her fleeing in that direction. When the back door creaked open, I was waiting. But I wasn't expecting the burst of pepper spray.

It wasn't a direct hit, but my eyes suddenly felt as if they'd been set on fire. Better than being met with a gun, I supposed, but that didn't stop the burning, an intense and searing pain. More than once in the past, I had touched my eyes after dicing chilies. This was worse. Far worse. Worse even than the wrist I'd recently burned.

I blinked, trying to see through the tears. Breathing harder, I inhaled too deeply, and my lungs blazed too.

I felt more than saw her, a blur I thought had to be Marina. She pushed past me, and I grabbed for her arm. But, disoriented as I was, my fingertips grazed the tail of her shirt instead.

"Marina," I choked. "Wait." Even those two words started a coughing fit.

I stumbled after her. There was no way I could catch her, but I hoped she would at least stay within shouting distance. Once I was again capable of shouting.

Finally, I managed, "I'm Frankie. Izzy's sister." That started a new round of coughing. When it stopped, my lungs and throat were raw.

I pricked my ears. A quiet had returned, the only sound my own labored breathing. I thought maybe Marina had stopped running.

Though it was hard to talk, I swallowed. Cleared my throat. Tried again. "I just want to talk."

The words, strangled as they were, echoed. Suddenly I worried: What if we weren't alone out here?

With my vision compromised, I risked only short, slow steps. I felt the panic building in my chest. If I could barely walk, how would I be able to drive? If I couldn't see, if someone was out here with us, how could I protect myself, let alone Marina too?

"I'm sorry about your sister," I called, my voice lower now, in case someone was listening. I hoped I spoke loud enough for Marina to hear. I strained to remember the best things I'd heard about Rachel. "I never met her, but I've heard Rachel was kind, and gentle. Your brother, Tobin, mentioned she could be fiery, but that she was quick to forgive. He said you inherited some of that spirit."

From somewhere in front of me, her voice came, nearly a whisper. "You've talked to Tobin?"

"Briefly."

"He okay?"

I stopped walking. "He's worried about you. I talked to your mother, too, and Jenny Hauser. I'm not sure why you've left home, but there are a lot of people who care about you."

I could sense her taking a few hesitant steps in my direction. "You're really Izzy's sister?" She sounded suspicious, but a second later she said, "I guess you do kinda look like her. You know, except for her piercings, and you being a lot older."

*A lot older?* But I supposed it was a fair point. For a seventeen-year-old girl, six years represented a third of her life.

"You were supposed to meet Izzy here, right?"

"No." Confused. "I mean, I called to ask if I could borrow some money, but I didn't tell her where I was."

"Why not?"

"She started asking a lot of questions, and I realized if we met, she would just tell my mom. So I hung up."

"Why don't you want to go home?"

I blinked hard several times. Through the tears, I could make out a shape, a blur of green and gray, so still I wasn't sure if it was Marina or a bush. Then the bush moved, drifting toward me. Marina, then. She stopped before she got too close.

She didn't answer my question, instead asking, "How'd you know I was here?"

I didn't want to tell her Blake had helped me figure it out, even if he hadn't meant to. The truth was, just like when I'd found Izzy at Mark's place, Marina hadn't had a lot of options. "There weren't many places I could think of that you might go."

"Why do you care what happens to me?"

I debated how much to tell her before deciding if she was going to trust me, she needed the truth. At least, the truth as I knew it. If I lied, she might see through me. Izzy had always been the better liar.

"Izzy's in trouble."

"So you're here for your sister. Not me. Not really, anyway." Her voice cracked. "That's how it was when Rachel was around too."

"I'm here because of you both." My nose was running. Damn pepper spray was making my whole face seep and burn. I wiped my nose with my sleeve, then grimaced. Gross. "Can we go inside?" I gestured to my face. "I need to rinse off a little."

"Sure." She didn't apologize for spraying me. When she stepped around me, back toward the cabin, she kept her distance. Still wary of me, I guessed.

I shuffled behind her, arms outstretched, trying not to trip or be knocked out by a low-hanging branch.

WHILE I CLEANED UP in the bathroom, Marina watched me from the doorway. I half expected her to bolt, but curiosity rooted her in place. Or maybe it was like I'd thought earlier: she really had no other place to go.

When I was done, I followed Marina back to the bedroom where she'd been hiding out. Without their mattresses, the two twin beds consisted of metal frames crisscrossed with straps. I sat on the edge of one, while Marina paced.

After a few minutes, she said, "They found Rachel's body a couple of days before they told us, but they had to make sure the teeth matched." Her voice was hushed, full of so much pain that each word was as clear as if she had shouted.

"I'm sorry," I said again.

"You asked why I left home? That's why."

"That must've been devastating news for your entire family."

"You don't understand."

I leaned into the silence, waiting for her to say more. She stopped pacing and sat on the bed across from me.

She forced herself to finish. "But Izzy understood. She knows what it's like, being a child in a house full of adults." When she shifted on the bed frame, it creaked. "Rachel was almost seven years older than me, and Tobin a few years older than that. When I was young, it felt like there was the three of them—Mom, Tobin, Rachel—and then there was me. They read the same books. Laughed at jokes I didn't understand. They had this whole life before I existed. And after too. I was in bed by nine, but they were downstairs, always together. Watching TV. Talking. When it would get loud, my mom would shush them. 'Don't want to wake Marina.'"

I started to reach out, to offer the comfort she obviously needed, but before I could, she laughed, a sharp sound utterly lacking in joy. "I sound like a bitch, don't I? Talking about my dead sister as if I resented her? But I did." She breathed deeply, her body shaking. "I'm a terrible person."

"You're not," I insisted.

She went on as if she didn't hear me. "You know why I was crying when Izzy picked me up?" Her voice shaky too. "Because before last Thursday, I'd started to get my mom back, and Tobin. He'd always been Rachel's brother, but finally he was becoming mine too. The three of us would do family dinners, and we'd started to share our own jokes. Tobin was even tutoring me in history."

Marina's voice was thick with emotion. Eyesight still blurred by the pepper spray, I couldn't quite see her face. I didn't need to, though, to tell she was crying. "Then the police came to tell my mom and Tobin about Rachel, and when they knocked on our door, do you know what my mom did? She sent me to my room. Like I was a kid again. I found out that my sister was dead by listening through a crack in my door."

She stopped abruptly, unable to continue.

"They need you, you know."

She shook her head.

"They do." Cautiously, I moved from my bed frame to hers. "Izzy's probably talked to you about me, right?"

When she nodded, I continued, "I'm always doing stupid stuff like that with her too. I'm sure she's complained about it. How I think I'm right all the time. How I think it's my job to protect her, when she's quite capable of protecting herself." I still wasn't sure that last part was true. But I wanted nothing more. "The point is, even if I act like that, if something happened to Izzy . . ." It was my turn to choke on my words. "That's why I'm here, for her but for you too. Because if Izzy needed help and I wasn't there, I'd want someone to do whatever they could to help her, like I'm trying to help you."

My words came out tangled, and I wasn't sure they made sense, but she seemed to understand. "She told me how sappy you can get." This close, I could see the suggestion of a smile forming. She swatted at her tears with the back of her hand.

I asked gently, "Did you see what happened to Mark?"

She nodded slowly. Wary again. "It was an accident."

Sensing her sudden nerves, I was considering my next question when the bed creaked again. Neither of us had moved. So not the bed.

Beside me, Marina tensed. She'd heard it too.

My voice as low as I could make it, I whispered, "Anyone else here?"

She shook her head.

"You're sure no one knows you're here?"

She nodded.

The creak again. This time I recognized that it came from the other side of the back door. Someone was trying to open it.

I froze, heart jumping into my throat. Had we locked it?

I strained to remember if Marina had. But, no, she had entered first. It would've been up to me to lock it behind me, and I hadn't. My eyes had burned, and at the time I'd been focused on remaining upright.

Against the door, a sudden thud. A rustling outside of it. No attempt at stealth now.

From my sweatshirt pocket, I pulled out the flashlight. Held it like a weapon. I wished I'd brought my dad's, which was the length of my forearm. The one I held was only the size of a water bottle. It felt lighter in my hand than it had before.

I leaned in toward Marina. "Pepper spray?" I whispered.

She tried to hand it to me, but I shook my head and pointed to her chest, mouthing the word, *You.* My still-hot eyes reminded me of both my vulnerability and her aim.

Slowly, I stood. Watched the door. It remained closed. No more thumping. No more sound of any kind.

I pulled out my phone. If I called, how long would it take for the police to arrive?

I gestured with my head toward the front door. Marina stood, too, and we both took a step.

I stopped, Marina so close that she walked into my back, nearly toppling me.

"What—?" she said, a little too loudly. I put a finger to my lips.

What if that was the reason for the silence? That the person had decided it was better to approach from the front?

I punched in the numbers. Before I could hit send, something banged against the back door, louder this time. A rattle followed.

My brow furrowed. Alarmed still, but also curious. I put the phone back in my pocket, but my finger hovered over the switch on the flashlight. Should I risk turning it on? We'd grown accustomed to the dark, and with my clouded vision the light probably wouldn't help.

When I moved to the back door, Marina grabbed my arm. I gently removed it, then pressed my ear against the wood. Though faint now, I could again hear the rustling.

I pointed at the pepper spray she held, then toward the door. She nodded. Then, in one quick motion, I switched on the flashlight with one hand and opened the door with the other. A few feet away, a raccoon reared and chittered, nearly a growl, before deciding against a fight. It abandoned the trash can and skulked off, its round body disappearing quickly in the brush.

With Marina pressed against my back, I blinked rapidly and scoured the darkness as best I could, but there were no larger predators waiting. Not within the range of the flashlight's beam, at least.

# 30

The encounter with the raccoon was enough to convince Marina that camping alone out there wasn't her thing. Or at least that's the excuse she gave for agreeing to come with me.

Though my vision had improved, I asked Marina if she would drive. She knew her way home better than I did anyway.

Once we were back on the highway and both breathing normally, I risked again broaching the subject of what had happened to Mark.

"Back at the cabin, you mentioned the hit-and-run was an accident," I prodded.

"Yeah." The headlights of a passing car lit her face. The nerves were back.

"Can you tell me what happened?"

The car passed, her face returned to shadow. For a moment I wasn't sure she would answer, and when she spoke, her hands tightened on the steering wheel.

"It's my fault." Her voice was small. "Is he okay?"

I didn't want to lie to her, so all I said was "He's doing better."

That seemed to settle her. She glanced quickly at me—trying

to decide if she should say more?—then returned her eyes to the road.

"Why do you think it was your fault?" I asked.

"Because it was." She sighed, as if deciding something. She risked another quick glance in my direction, then she said, "Izzy left to go get us some food. Mark's nice, but I don't know him like I know her, and after she'd been gone awhile, I started to get nervous. I'd lost my burner, so I used his landline to call home."

With all the people I had talked to, why had no one mentioned this? I opened my mouth to ask, but then closed it again. I could see Marina thinking. Deciding. I tried to be patient with her. Not my strong suit.

Finally, she answered my unasked question. "Before it could connect, I hung up. After all, nothing had changed." Her voice hitched. "Izzy knew Rachel was dead, didn't she?"

She wasn't asking about now. She was asking about then.

When I hesitated, she said, "You don't have to say. I know you want to protect Izzy." Her eyes remained on the road, as bright as the high beams. "I figured it out when I was at Mark's place. Last year, she told me about drinking with Rachel the night she disappeared. I didn't believe her. Rachel never partied."

"But you borrowed the volunteer's car and went looking for her anyway."

"So stupid. Even if Izzy had been telling the truth, what would I have found after four years? That's what we fought about, when I set fire to the lanterns. I thought she was bullshitting me."

I studied her face, so intent on the road. Izzy had told the police about the hit-and-run. There was no reason to keep it a secret from Marina. "What made you figure out Izzy knew Rachel was dead, even before the police found her body?"

"I overheard her and Mark fighting about it, and she knew more details than I'd given her. So when she was out getting burgers, I did it again. I ran away."

Suddenly I understood. "Mark followed you."

"He ran after me. And a car—" She couldn't finish the sentence.

"Did you see what happened?"

She shook her head. "I heard him behind me. His footsteps. Then someone screamed. He landed in the street right next to me. Bleeding. Head just . . . crushed. By the time I looked up, the car was gone. But it was an accident. I know that much. I ran into the road without looking, and he—he would be okay if I hadn't done that."

I looked at Marina, but I didn't see her as I had a moment before. Instead, I saw the girl on the "missing" flyer, with clothes she didn't seem quite comfortable in and an awkward smile that made her seem impossibly young. I saw Izzy, too, when she was seventeen, and imagined Julian at the same age. I wanted to believe it was over. That with Marina safe, all of our lives would return to normal. But they hadn't been that way for five years, so why should I expect that to change now?

Marina shifted in the driver's seat as she pulled the truck onto the exit ramp. I recognized the route I'd taken only a couple of days before. We were a few minutes away now.

She continued, "What I said earlier . . . it doesn't mean I didn't love my sister. Even when we were fighting, even when I hated her, Rachel was the only one who understood me, you know?"

I thought of Izzy. "I know."

"I was only twelve when she disappeared. If I'd been older, maybe I would've understood her too. Maybe I could've helped her not be so sad."

A shiver pricked my spine. "Why do you think Rachel was sad?"

"I don't know. She didn't talk about it."

"No—I mean, what makes you think she was sad? Was she crying a lot? Something else?"

She went silent. She frowned, and I thought she might be remembering. "It's going to sound stupid."

"I'm sure it won't."

She hesitated. Then she said, "She stopped bringing me Takis."

I felt my brow wrinkle. "What?"

"Takis. They're like chips?"

I smiled. "Yeah, I know. Izzy loves those." Julian too. Once, when Izzy had left behind half a bag, I'd found Julian with red dust on his face, a crumpled bag beneath his pillow. He'd claimed Mr. Carrots was responsible. "But why did that make you think Rachel might be sad?"

"It was a thing she did, you know? If I failed a test, or one of my friends said something mean, or I spilled a soda on one of my drawings, Rachel would get the Takis and come into my room and we'd talk about it. But right before she disappeared, she stopped doing that."

I reached across the console and squeezed her shoulder. It was a reflex, one I'd so often repeated with Izzy, and the second I did, I worried how Marina might react. She didn't seem to mind, though, and when I let go, she looked at me from the corner of her eye.

"You don't know why?" I asked.

She hesitated. "I was twelve."

"Any guesses?"

She shook her head, but there was hesitation there too.

I nudged. "You sure?"

Even in the meager light, I could see her cheek flush. "You probably already think I'm a bad person. For what I said about Rachel, and for worrying Tobin and my mom by running away."

"You're not a bad person, Marina."

"You don't know me."

"I know enough."

"I went through Rachel's stuff." She shot me another look to see my reaction. "A few weeks before she disappeared, I went in her room when she wasn't home. She had this box with stuff in it. I found some birth control pills. I think she had a boyfriend."

The truck slowed, and I checked the speedometer. We were going ten miles under the posted limit. I didn't point it out. If Marina needed more time before she faced her family, I would give it to her.

"I heard she and Ben were a thing," I said.

She went quiet and I could nearly hear her thinking. When she spoke, her voice was soft. "I wondered about that."

I watched her, surprised. "You did?"

She nodded. "After Rachel disappeared, our family kinda fell apart. Not right away. Mom called the police the next day, but everyone thought Rachel was with friends. We believed eventually she wouldn't be sad anymore and she'd come home. And when she didn't, and none of her friends knew where she was, we started thinking maybe something had happened to her."

Her voice had grown so soft that I leaned closer to hear. "We made posters. The police thought they had a couple of leads. But we never found her, until—"

Her voice hitched. She didn't need to finish the sentence. She'd been about to say *until her body was found*.

I nudged gently. "So what made you think Rachel and Ben might be dating?"

Seconds passed, and then she said, "We had hope, but Ben— from the beginning, he was messed up. Like, way more messed up than I would've expected him to be. If they were just friends, he wouldn't have cared as much, right? But that might've been because of the phone call."

"Phone call?"

"The day before she disappeared, I heard her on the phone with him. She didn't want to go to Mercuryville. That's what I heard: '*No, Ben. I don't feel up to it.*'" She glanced at me with haunted eyes. "I'm the one who convinced her to go. And do you know why? So I could have our mom to myself for the night."

"It's not your fault. None of it."

She rubbed her nose with her sleeve before shooting me a sheepish look. "Sorry about the pepper spray."

"Don't be. If a stranger approaches again, I hope you'll do the same. As long as you no longer consider me a stranger."

She tried to smile, but it faded before it could wholly form. I thought she might say more on the subject of Ben and Rachel, but instead she asked, "How pissed do you think they're going to be?"

I squeezed her shoulder again. "They're not going to be angry," I reassured her. "They're going to be so, so happy to see you again."

We pulled onto the street where the Wagners lived. The rising moon reflected on the bay, the birds from my earlier visit gone now. When the birds returned in the morning, Marina would be there to see them from her bedroom window. Her mother would make pancakes, or whatever was her version of the chilaquiles I made for Julian. They would argue, and they would continue to mourn Rachel, but I was pretty sure they would be okay. For them, maybe some version of normal was possible.

Marina parked and handed me the keys. Her eyes drifted to the town home she shared with her mom.

"I'm still pretty sure they're going to be pissed," she said.

When she got out of the truck, I took her spot in the driver's seat. I waited until the door opened, and then a minute longer as Anne and Tobin wrapped themselves around Marina. Anne melted around her daughter, but Tobin's posture was rigid, his arms wide as if shielding her from the bad things that might do her harm. He looked up and our eyes locked. His expression suggested he thought I might be one of those bad things.

# 31

When Izzy showed up at my door at ten, I told her about Marina. I expected her to say she no longer needed to borrow my truck, but she held out her hand and asked for the keys.

I gave them to her. After she left, I tried Piper again. She had even more questions to answer now that I'd talked to Marina. She didn't pick up.

I checked all the window and door locks a second time. Then I stripped the comforter and pillow from my bed and arranged them on the floor in Julian's room and, eventually, fell asleep.

The next day, I awoke with a plan. Piper would be working a wedding at a private estate north of Guerneville. I knew from Izzy that she planned to set up, and that she was always the first to arrive. If I hurried, there was a chance I could catch Piper alone.

Since Izzy had yet to return my truck, I walked Julian to pre-school, then took an Uber to my parents' house to borrow their car. When I declined my mom's offer of a hot breakfast, she forced a nectarine and a piece of pan dulce on me.

It was an hour's drive, though I shaved a few minutes off that.

I paused at the gate and tried Piper again. When she didn't answer, I checked the gate. It wasn't locked, so I let myself in.

The private road was potholed dirt with patches of gravel. Hard on the car, but when I got to the end of it, I saw why the residents didn't mind. The sprawling house with its wall of windows sat among redwoods. To the right, a muted sun reached through gaps in the trees, dappling the house with golden light. To the left, a path lined with Mason jars disappeared into the grove. Beside it, a second road—narrow and even more gouged—led deeper into the woods.

There were no cars in the driveway. Since it was a weekday, it made sense that the residents might be at work, or picking up last-minute items for the wedding. But I didn't see the catering van either. Was I at the wrong place? The gate hadn't been locked, but it had been closed. Was I trespassing? Again?

I swore under my breath and quickly checked the address I'd plugged into my phone. It matched. But that didn't mean someone wouldn't come home and wonder what the hell I was doing at their house. After all, I hadn't been invited. It suddenly seemed a very bad idea to be there.

I restarted the car and began a U-turn in the driveway. Mid-turn, as I drew closer to the rutted side road, I caught a flash of yellow. I stopped. Focused my eyes. There, at the end of the road, the catering van was parked.

Relief flooded me. I backed up and pulled in beside the house, out of sight, or so I hoped. If the residents came home, I would prefer they didn't see the car right away.

I approached the spot where the path and side road began, running parallel to each other. Path or road?

Path, I decided. With my history, I knew how dangerous un-expected cars could be to pedestrians.

On the path, I noticed an electronic candle had been dropped into each of the Mason jars, and light strings had been wrapped around the trunks of several of the trees. At the end of the path, an arch of dried wildflowers draped with white ribbon connected two redwoods.

Here, there were fewer trees, though a few of the giants still loomed hundreds of feet overhead. At their bases, flat green leaves and cones lay scattered on the ground. In the clearing, rows of chairs faced a freestanding arch, decorated with the same white ribbon and wildflowers. Beyond that, a small red barn, and several hundred feet to the left, the yellow van. Its rear doors were ajar. I headed in that direction, assuming I would find Piper inside.

She wasn't, at least in the back of the van. There were a few chairs and a long table, but anything else that had been brought had already been unloaded.

I checked the front of the van next. She wasn't there either. The keys were in the ignition, and a phone rested on the passenger's seat. Piper's? I called her number. A second later, the screen displayed my name. Or a version of my name anyway: Izzy's fake mom.

*Funny, Piper.*

Unless she had scaled one of the redwoods, there was only one place left where she could be. The red barn.

As I walked in that direction, the wind stirred, warm and thick with the scent of the redwoods. When I found Piper, what would I say? I had allowed myself to be convinced she might be an ally, if not someone I trusted then at least someone focused on Izzy's best interests. But now I wondered. I worried.

Inside the barn, wood tables and chairs with plaid cushions had been arranged on either side, the center left clear for the movement of the guests. The next evening, the tables would likely be covered with burlap runners or cotton tablecloths, then adorned with table garlands or floral centerpieces and whatever stemware and place settings the couple had chosen. The chandeliers and light strings would be illuminated. Music would be played to encourage dancing. But now the tables were bare and the barn dusty. There was no magic in here yet.

It was a large open space with few places to hide. When I called out, an echo was the only response. Had Piper knelt behind one of the tables to pick up a stray nail or fix a wobbly table leg? As unlikely as that was, I squatted to check. I cleared most of the floor quickly, but there was one spot where a chair bumped up against a support beam that required a closer look. No Piper.

I looked up toward the rafters. This wasn't a working barn, and any space once used to store hay had been torn down years before.

Around back, then? I crossed the barn to a second door, which was cut into the left wall. Shadow pooled beneath it. My hand fell to the knob.

Something caused me to freeze. The feeling that something was out of place.

I sucked in my breath as I realized what it was. The shadow. Its border was irregular, and denser than it should've been.

It seeped.

I jerked my hand back and balled it against my chest. Beneath my fist, my heart thudded. The shadow that wasn't a shadow advanced a quarter inch. Then half. I stepped back, still holding my breath.

I pulled my phone from my pocket and checked the signal. Two bars. I released the air from my lungs, then took a step. Hand back on the knob, I turned it. Then I yanked the door open, which smeared the blood and brought Piper's body tumbling across the threshold of the barn.

MY EYES GLAZED, MY brain obscured by fog. Piper had been stabbed. That would've been obvious enough by examining the body, but it was made even clearer by the knife still wedged in her chest. I felt for her pulse while struggling against my surging nausea. I pressed my hand against the wound that didn't have a knife protruding from it. A sob lodged in my throat. She was dead. I hadn't saved Rachel, and I wouldn't be able to save Piper.

My hands slick with Piper's blood, I fumbled my cell, but I managed to keep it in my hand long enough to dial 911.

The dispatcher answered, but before I could respond, I grew aware of a soft shuffling outside the barn. Footsteps. How close? The sound seemed to come from a distance, but even with the door open, I couldn't be sure.

How much noise had I made when I opened the door? Since? Then I remembered how I'd called out for Piper when I'd entered the barn, and a chill shot through me.

I nudged the body back outside and gently closed the door. Even though she was past saving, guilt welled at leaving her alone again with her killer.

*I'm so sorry.*

But maybe the person shuffling closer wasn't her killer at all. It could be the homeowner returned from an errand, or a member of the catering staff.

I turned off my ringer and turned down the volume, but I kept the line to 911 open. In silence, I waited. Hoping to be reassured by a scream. But the person outside remained as quiet as I did. With the door closed, even the shuffling was muted.

I quickly scanned the barn. As before, there were no places to hide.

*Think think think.*

The car was too far away. I couldn't make it even across the clearing to the shelter of a redwood trunk.

My eyes landed on the chair in the corner, next to the support beam. I wiped my phone and hands on the inside of my T-shirt. Then I checked my feet. I hadn't stepped in her blood, so no footprints would give me away.

I speed-walked, not trusting myself to run, my eyes darting between the unfamiliar floor and the open door at the front of the barn, sure the ten seconds it took to cross that space would be enough for the killer to round the corner and see me.

Near the beam, I slowed my pace even as my heart thumped. I tucked myself between the beam and the chair, forcing my breaths to remain shallow even as they fought to explode from my chest. Making myself small, I felt foolish. I would be seen clearly if someone expended a few seconds of effort.

If the killer had heard me, he would expend those seconds. I would be discovered quickly.

*Please, don't let him have heard me.*

I heard footsteps again, though I couldn't be sure it wasn't my heartbeat.

I sensed him at the entrance to the barn. For an unbearable moment I felt him, like the disturbance in the air before a lightning storm, and I grew suddenly certain he felt me too. Was it my imagination, this feeling? Hidden as I was, I could see no part of him. I couldn't even be sure it *was* a *him*. On that one, I was just playing the odds.

I listened and inhaled, as if I could identify the killer by the way he breathed or smelled, improbable at that great a distance. But when I inhaled, all I caught was the acrid tang of Piper's blood drying on my shirt.

I didn't move from my spot until I heard screaming. The homeowners had returned, only a minute ahead of the police.

# 32

Piper's blood stained my shirt, so I called Izzy for a replacement. I asked her to drop it off at the front desk of the sheriff's substation. I didn't tell her the reason I needed it, even when she asked.

"Just clearing up something," I said. "We'll talk later."

I sensed she wanted to push, but she agreed to drop off the shirt and pick up Julian at preschool.

Asking for the second part of that favor set me on edge. Izzy had relapsed recently, and if I hadn't taken our mom's car, I would've relied on her instead.

"Maybe you can watch Julian at our parents' house," I suggested.

I knew she saw through me, but she agreed anyway.

"That's probably better than taking him to the apartment," she said. "Piper doesn't really like kids."

I closed my eyes, and wished we both still lived in Izzy's reality, where Piper remained alive and I wouldn't have to tell her the truth. I cleared my throat, but when I spoke, my voice still rasped. "Thanks, Izzy."

"You sure you're okay?"

*No, I'm not okay. Someone killed your best friend. Stabbed her at least twice, not bothering to remove the knife from her chest.*

Later, what could I possibly say to my sister that wouldn't seem inadequate, especially with her hold on sobriety already so slippery?

"I'm fine," I said. I'd been telling that lie a lot lately.

She hesitated. Recognizing the lie? I knew she would call me on it later, but by then, I wouldn't have her friend's blood on my shirt.

THE RIVER SUBSTATION LOOKED like any other building in downtown Guerneville except for the small sheriff's sign, its arrow pointing toward a faded green door. A blond deputy with a severe topknot led me up a ramp and through that door, before directing me to have a seat in one of the hard-backed chairs against the wall.

There I stayed for fifteen minutes, give or take a year, until the blond deputy reappeared. She brought me into an interview room and left me there. It wasn't much different from the one at Cloverdale PD, where Detective Pratt had first asked me about Marina. How long ago had that been? Only five days? Each of those days settled on my shoulders like a stone. Carrying that extra weight, it was a challenge to remain upright.

Though the air conditioner chugged, sweat slicked my stomach, and the crust on the inside of my shirt grew damp. A rusty stain transferred to my skin. I plucked the hem away from my body to allow chilled air between me and the fabric.

I wanted out of that damn shirt.

Half an hour later, I got my wish, trading the blond deputy

my soiled shirt for the clean one Izzy had dropped off at the front desk. It was pink and read SAVE THE UNICORNS. Izzy's, not mine. An attempt at humor, I guessed. I grew suddenly light-headed.

The detective who finally arrived appeared to be on the tail end of his forties, dark hair showing its first gray streaks, wire-framed glasses crooked on his sharp nose. He introduced himself as Detective Jim Kaplan. The same detective Izzy had talked to.

"How're you doing?" he asked, almost too friendly. It made me think I might be a suspect. "Sorry to keep you waiting, but I had to drive up from Santa Rosa. Need some water?"

"No, thanks."

"Let me know if you change your mind." His smile was professional, cool. "I know it's been a rough morning for you, so let's see if we can get you out of here as quickly as possible."

The way he said it made me wonder if the "quick" way was to be booked and transferred to the jail.

Kaplan started by verifying a few personal details, like name, address, and date of birth. Then he leaned in and laced his fingers in front of him on the table.

I steeled myself. *Now we begin.*

"How did you come to be at that house today?"

"Piper is—*was* my sister's roommate. She wasn't returning my phone calls, so I figured I'd catch up with her at work this morning."

"You two close?"

"Not really."

When Kaplan leaned farther, his glasses slipped down the bridge of his nose. He peered at me over the top of the frames. "But you drove quite a ways just because she hadn't called you back, and you knew her work schedule."

"We were planning a surprise party for Izzy." Only a few questions in, and I had just told my first lie. "As for the schedule, Izzy and Piper sometimes work together." *Worked*, I corrected silently.

"Was your sister scheduled to work with Ms. Lange today?"

"Not with setup, but she's supposed to help with the wedding tomorrow." Would there even be a wedding? No couple wanted to get married at a murder scene. At least not the kind of couples who were into rustic barn weddings.

Kaplan adjusted his glasses. "Does Ms. Lange usually do setup alone?"

"I'm not sure, but I think so."

"The tables look heavy."

"She has a cart, I believe." I almost added that he could ask Izzy about that, but I didn't want to bring my sister into it again. "It's not a huge company, so there's not a lot of staff."

He nodded as if this meant something, which caused his glasses to slip again. "I know you told the deputy what happened, but if you could please run through it again."

I told him about arriving at the front gate, which was closed but not locked. I mentioned spotting the yellow catering van, which was nearly empty and had its rear doors ajar. I described walking through the clearing before coming upon the empty barn. Then I told him about finding Piper's body on the other side of that door.

"What made you open the door?" he asked.

I paused, remembering. "There was a shadow. But it was really blood." Seeping through the crack. A dark blot on the ground.

I hadn't realized I'd said the last part aloud until Kaplan asked, "So she was still bleeding when you found her?"

My palm fell to my stomach, pressing against an imagined stain. I couldn't speak for a moment, but the detective waited.

"Yes."

"So you opened the door and found the body." When I nodded, he asked, "What happened next?"

"I heard footsteps. I closed the door. Softly, so he wouldn't hear."

"He?"

"It's just a guess." But even as I answered, I wondered: Had the footsteps sounded heavier? Was there a reason my subconscious had assigned that identity?

His glasses had reached the tip of his nose. With his index finger, he pushed them back up the bridge. "Tell me more about your relationship with Ms. Lange."

"I've known her for about six years, through my sister."

"She has you listed in her contacts as *Izzy's fake mom*."

"She thought I treated Izzy like a child." *Thought*. Piper had been dead only a few hours and already the past tense came more easily.

"Tell me about that."

I shrugged, even as my internal alarm sounded. Where was Kaplan going with this? "Not much to say. There's a large age gap between me and my sister. I helped raise her." I wasn't going to apologize for that.

"So you and Ms. Lange often argued about that?"

"Not often." Lie number two.

"Tell me about Rachel Stroud."

The air conditioner's rattle was good cover for my suddenly thunderous heart. If I lied, this detective with his ill-fitted glasses would see through me immediately. I felt the truth in that as certainly as I felt the recirculated air on the back of my neck.

"I didn't know Rachel."

"But Ms. Lange did, right? And your sister?"

"They met, but I'm not sure how well they knew each other."

When Kaplan's glasses slipped this time, he took them off and placed them on the table. "How'd they all get along?"

"Good, I guess. Again, they weren't my friends."

He tapped his glasses on the table before perching them again on his nose. "We found a voice mail you left yesterday." He looked down at his notes, squinting, and quoted that message. *"I have some questions about our conversation. Some things I'm having a hard time believing. Call me.* Then you paused before adding, *And don't stop by my house again. Ever."* He spoke in a reasonable voice that I knew didn't reflect the tone I'd used. I'd spoken quietly, but I'd been irritated at the time. "That sounds like you'd have a hard time being in the same room as Ms. Lange."

"I've already said we weren't close."

When I didn't expand on that, Kaplan said, "Tell me about this conversation you two had."

"She stopped by late and rather unexpectedly." I hesitated, unsure what to say. I couldn't use generalities, like I had with Julian. I doubted Kaplan would be appeased by my bug-hunt analogy. There was also no denying the information might prove useful to clearing Izzy.

But what if it hurt her instead?

"Piper was"—*don't say angry*—"not happy that I had called an old friend of hers. Tobin Stroud."

"Marina Wagner's half brother?"

I nodded. "As you probably know, my sister gave Marina a ride, and she felt guilty about that. I was helping Izzy retrace the girl's steps. Piper thought I should leave it alone."

Though it was a lie, it fell close enough to the truth that it sounded believable.

"Anything else?"

"That was it. She didn't stay long."

What if they had proof that wasn't true? GPS data that put her at my house for over an hour? A neighbor who saw what time she arrived and left?

"Tell me what happened the night Ms. Stroud died."

How much had Izzy told the sheriff's office about that night? She had said she would keep me out of it, but I had never cared about that. I only cared about not offering a story that would contradict my sister's.

"My sister called me. Late. I don't remember what time. She needed a ride. She and some friends had been hanging out at this spot on Geysers Road." I paused, to see if he wanted me to provide a more exact location. When he didn't ask for one, I continued. "Izzy had been drinking. The others, too, or so I've been told, but my sister was the only one there when I arrived. By Uber. My driver was not happy about the distance."

I adjusted in my seat, trying to dodge a draft of air that now seemed too frigid. "I found Izzy standing next to our mom's car, which she'd borrowed for the night. She was nearly incoherent. She said she'd hit someone with her car, and there was some blood on the hood." And the strands of hair I found the next day, but I didn't share that detail with Kaplan. "I searched, but all I found was a deer carcass. I assumed at the time that's what she hit. The deer. It was dark, and Izzy was pretty out of it, so after about fifteen minutes I left. Took my sister to the hospital."

Story finished, I leaned back in my chair. But Kaplan remained silent. Even looked a little bored.

Finally, I asked, "Do you know about the Rohypnol?"

He stared, adjusting his glasses, but still said nothing.

"Piper told me recently that she believed that Izzy might've been drugged, and that's why she got so sick. Why she can't remember everything that happened."

With nothing more to say, I folded my arms across my chest and waited for Kaplan to fill the silence. It took him a while, but he did.

"I appreciate the tip about the Rohypnol, and your candor about the incident with the car. You sure there's nothing you want to add?"

"There's nothing I can add. That's it. That's all I know."

"Last week, Ms. Stroud's body was found. A few hours ago, Ms. Lange was stabbed to death. What do you make of that?"

"I'm not sure what you mean."

"You a big believer in coincidence?"

I thought of Mark's hit-and-run. I had been convinced it was connected to Rachel's death five years earlier, but it really had been an accident. Someone driving too fast. Mark running into the road. Tragic, yes, but still a coincidence. "My opinion on that is evolving," I said.

"Here's what I think." He adjusted his glasses. "Two young women who knew each other, killed in a similar way. It's more likely than not that they're connected."

I shook my head. "They knew each other, but their deaths weren't similar."

"You're right. Similar might be the wrong word." Kaplan's eyes narrowed almost imperceptibly. "A better choice would be identical."

# 33

The deaths of Piper and Rachel weren't similar. They were identical. That's what Kaplan had said. But it didn't make sense, no matter how many times I repeated it to myself.

Not similar. *Identical*.

Piper and Rachel had both died young, and they'd been casual friends. They had both been killed in remote locations, though Mercuryville was far more distant than the Guerneville estate. But Piper had been stabbed, and Rachel had been hit by a car. Similar? Yes. Identical? Not so much.

So Kaplan had misspoken. Of course that was it. That was the only explanation.

But then the detective continued, and I understood. After piecing together the lies and half-truths of the others who were there that night, it was time for Rachel's story to be heard, even if she was no longer around to tell it. He showed me the photos, watching for my reaction even as I squinted to make sense of what I was seeing.

But like the stories of the others near Mercuryville that night, Rachel's remained an incomplete version. Forensic specialists still needed to complete their tests, Kaplan said. But the examination had already uncovered certain irrefutable truths.

He tapped one photo. A broken wrist, he told me. A fresh injury, since the bones had shown no signs of healing.

He flipped to a second photo, where thin striations marked the bone. I cocked my head, trying to decipher what part of the body had been photographed, and what those narrow lines meant. Then Kaplan explained: Rachel had been stabbed in the chest, hard enough that the knife marked bone.

That word made my ears ring. Stabbed. Like Piper.

The third photo showed a skull. Fractured, like the wrist. There were more tests to be done, Kaplan reminded me. But a theory had started to form. Beyond those three photos, he wouldn't elaborate. He just studied me, sharp eyes camouflaged by ill-fitting glasses, as if I already knew what that theory was.

But, of course, I did know. Kaplan believed Izzy had killed both Rachel and Piper. Maybe he didn't have enough evidence yet, since he hadn't brought Izzy in too. But maybe when those next tests came back that would change, and he would arrest my sister.

Unless . . .

*No.*

I tried to shake off the thought, but it was stubborn. Could Kaplan think I was involved too?

I DROVE BY MY parents' neighborhood without picking up Julian. I slowed to turn, but when I put on my blinker, my hand started shaking. So I went home instead.

It was only a temporary reprieve. I couldn't leave Julian there for another night, and I still had my parents' car. I couldn't leave them for too much longer without transportation, especially while they had Julian. But I barely made it to the couch before my knees gave way. I was nearly spent. What energy remained I needed for my conversation with Izzy.

When I called my parents, Julian got on the phone first. As always, he talked about bugs, describing a green one he'd found burrowing in the dirt. According to Julian, Abuela had taken a photo and they were going to try to find out what it was. There was also mention of a scratch that hadn't really needed a bandage but got one anyway, and ice cream, because most summer days at my parents' house included ice cream. Then he said he missed me, and I immediately felt like crap. Would Julian complain of another "stomachache" at school the next day because I'd been spending less time with him?

After I said my goodbye to Julian, I asked my dad if Julian could stay for dinner. Soon he would want an explanation, but for the moment he hesitated only slightly before he said, "Of course, mija. Whatever you need."

I spent my first kid-free hour torturing myself. While half listening for Izzy to return with my truck, I used my laptop to search phrases like *parental rights for felons* and *will a mom lose custody if arrested*.

I knew I was spiraling, but I was incapable of stopping it. When I finally heard my truck pull into the driveway, I closed my laptop, took a breath, and waited for her to come inside.

A minute passed. Then two.

*I should go outside,* I thought. I might've been delaying a difficult conversation, but there was no avoiding it entirely. I called myself a coward and went to greet my sister. My truck was parked next to my parents' car in the driveway. The driver's door was open, the keys in the ignition, but Izzy was gone.

I was getting really sick of my sister disappearing on me.

I walked to the edge of my property and scanned the sidewalk and road in both directions. Had a ride-share been waiting? Had Izzy left on foot? Had she gotten a ride?

I patted my pockets, but my phone was on the kitchen counter. Keys first, then Izzy.

I returned to my truck and reached for the keys. On the passenger's side, a McDonald's bag had been crumpled and tossed on the floor, next to an empty water bottle. I stretched but couldn't quite grab them.

I sighed—*My truck isn't a garbage can, Izzy*—before moving to the other side of the truck. I opened the door to retrieve the trash. Noticed wadded napkins in the compartment on the door. Grabbed those next. Figured I might as well check the backseat too.

I folded the seat forward and quickly inspected the backseat but saw nothing. Then I glanced at the floor. There, I saw only organic debris—a thin layer of dirt, a few small branches, flat green leaves. Nothing I couldn't pick up with a few swipes of the vacuum later.

There was a sudden prickling along my neck. *Flat green leaves. Redwood needles.*

I struggled to keep my thoughts in order, but they scattered, like those tiny leaves on the floorboard of my truck. As a quiet unease rose in my chest, I bent down and picked up a tiny segment of branch. There was nothing special about it. I had once seen an albino redwood, with white needles instead of green. Those were rare. But this? Trees like the one that had shed these needles could be found all over Sonoma County.

It could be coincidence that similar redwoods grew on the property where Piper had been fatally stabbed.

It *was* a coincidence.

The tingling on my neck became a burning. The unease in my chest surged. Because though I could easily make a case for coincidence, I knew these needles hadn't been in my truck before Izzy had borrowed it. Julian rode in the backseat, and though he buckled himself in, I always double-checked his straps. And his backpack always rested at his feet in that very spot.

I told myself that maybe I tossed his backpack on the floor-boards without noticing the debris. But my inner skeptic pointed out that today I had noticed immediately.

Maybe the needles had come from another source. It seemed reasonable, especially given how calm Izzy had been when we'd talked earlier. She couldn't have lied to me so easily, right?

My inner skeptic didn't even bother responding to that last part.

Quickly, I went to the garage and retrieved the car vac. Switched it on. Ran the nozzle along the floorboards. Suctioned up every last fleck of dirt and redwood needle. As I emptied the vacuum into the garbage, I told myself it was no different from the hundreds of times I'd cleaned my truck in the past. I was just getting rid of a little debris. Not evidence.

Next, I pulled out a large plastic bucket and a bottle of car-washing soap. Squirting the soap in the bucket brought back memories of the morning I had washed my parents' car. When I had pulled those strands of hair from the headlight. It turned out Rachel hadn't even died from the hit-and-run, or at most it had been only a contributing factor. Five years earlier, what damage had I done—to the investigation, to Rachel's family, and to Izzy? What damage was I doing now?

As I filled the bucket with water, I wondered how many times I was willing to do this. How far would I go to save my sister? Considering the pattern had repeated, I was pretty sure I'd already gone too far.

# 34

Once I finished washing the truck, I returned the bucket to the garage, then went into the house to retrieve the keys to my parents' car and my phone. Izzy hadn't called, and I didn't plan on calling her. My sister's abrupt exit had made it clear she didn't want to talk to me, even if I had no idea why. That was fine with me. I wasn't in a rush to talk to her either.

When I pulled in front of my parents' house, that turned out to be a problem. Izzy was sitting on the front steps. Her knees were drawn close, arms folded on top, forehead resting on her wrists.

I could've asked her why she had dropped off the truck without checking in, or grilled her about the debris I'd found on the floorboards. If I'd been a more forgiving person, I could've told her about Piper—if she didn't already know about that—and then taken a seat beside her to offer comfort. And I would. Soon. But not yet.

Because the moment I saw her, I realized how angry I was with her. It wasn't the disappearing act, or even the redwood needles, that suggested she might be hiding yet another secret. What I was most angry about was that because of those secrets, I had been driven to search online for what happened to a child if a parent was arrested.

Of course, I blamed myself more than Izzy. I was self-aware enough to realize this, and to know that for every mistake Izzy had made, I'd made one nearly as significant. In some cases, my mistakes were worse. When Izzy had called me for a ride five years earlier, I was the one who left Rachel behind. Several days ago I had tried to talk my sister out of going to the police. I had just vacuumed up what might be evidence of a crime.

But *I* hadn't killed anyone.

I meant to push past Izzy, but when I got close, she lifted her head to look up at me. Her nose was red, her eyes swollen.

"The reason you were being interviewed. It was because of Piper, wasn't it?" Her eyes blazed, and I realized it wasn't just grief that made her voice tremble. She was as angry at me as I was at her. Of all the scenarios I had considered for why Izzy had left my house so quickly, that was one that hadn't occurred to me.

"Yes," I said.

Her jaw went rigid. "Let me guess. You didn't tell me because you were *protecting* me."

My own anger flashed. "I didn't tell you because I was at a police station, and it wasn't something I wanted to tell you over the phone."

"It was better that I hear about it from a casual friend in a text?"

She went still. Quiet. My sister gave away her moods by the depth of her silences. When she was content, they felt airy and light, bubbles easily popped. When she was bored, they were lazy and bloated and stalled quickly. But when she was upset, the quiet spread black and thick like hot tar, ready to trap or burn or suffocate. During those moods, the greatest danger she posed was to herself. Izzy was in one of those hot-tar moods now.

We were dangerously close to saying things we couldn't take back. I was the one who crossed that line first. "You sure you didn't already know about Piper being killed?"

"What are you talking about?"

There was a moment when I could've covered by saying I only meant that someone else might've told her. Instead, I doubled down. "I found redwood needles in my truck."

She fell silent, then said, "Really? You actually think I killed my best friend because—" She stopped to catch her breath. "Because you found some needles in your truck?"

The way she said it made it sound ridiculous, and maybe it was. But I was too frustrated to take it back.

"Why did you need to borrow it?"

She glared at me. "Why does it even matter?" She shook her head angrily. "Okay, you want to know? I needed to run some errands. Fix that window you busted, for one. Move some of my stuff into Mark's, since he'll need help when he comes home." She thrust out her phone. "Here. Check it, like you did before. See where I've been."

My hand twitched, and I almost took it. Who the hell had I become?

"I'm sorry about what happened to Piper." My voice hitched. The pain on Izzy's face left me nearly undone. If the circumstances had been different, I would've been next to her, arm around her shoulders. Though I had helped raise Izzy, I didn't know how to navigate the current situation. I didn't know what to do with my emotions, which filled me near to bursting.

"What *happened* to Piper is that someone killed her." Her voice grew louder, and I looked around to make sure my parents and Julian weren't near enough to hear. Thankfully, the front door remained closed. "Someone stabbed her to death, and you think it was me. Because of some damn redwood needles." She gestured over her shoulder. "Mom and Dad have a redwood tree. Maybe I got them here, or from one of the other thousand places they grow in the county. If I'm even the one who tracked them into your truck."

"I considered that."

She laughed harshly. "Glad you considered that before judging me guilty. Makes sense, I guess, since the police probably think I am too."

She must've seen the truth of that on my face, because she asked, "What did they say?"

"They asked about your relationship with Rachel. Mine too." But I wasn't done talking about how Izzy had lied. So many times. "What else haven't you told me?"

She stood and moved closer, her face only a foot from mine. The air between us seemed to grow colder. "You're not my mom. You're my sister. For once, can you just be that?"

"I've always been that."

She shook her head, her eyes still bright. "You want to smell my breath? Make sure I haven't been drinking?" She opened her mouth and exhaled sharply. I couldn't help myself. I didn't lean in but I inhaled, almost reflexively. No alcohol. Not even the telltale scent of a breath mint.

"You ask what I haven't told you. Well, what haven't you told me?"

I frowned. "I tell you everything."

"Oh? You told me about the hair you found the day after Rachel died? What about how you used your key to search my apartment, broke into my phone?"

"I'm sorry about that. I overstepped." I tried to sound contrite, but I didn't pull it off.

"What about Piper being killed?"

"I already told you I planned to tell you about that, but you left before I could."

"Why didn't you tell me you were planning to confront Piper? And how about your excursion to Camp Sarah looking for Marina? You didn't tell me about that, either, did you?"

"I was trying to—" I stopped.

But Izzy knew what I had been about to say.

"You were trying to protect me." She said this as if it were an obscenity. "That's what a parent does for a child, not what a sister does."

I felt the heat rise in my face. "Okay, Izzy, you want me to treat you like an adult? Maybe you should start acting like one."

From the backyard, I heard Julian's laughter, loud and full, as it always was. In contrast, it made what I had just said seem even uglier.

Izzy's voice dropped to a hiss. "That's what I've been trying to do. I started volunteering. Got a job. My own place. I went to the police, which I'd like to point out you tried to stop me from doing. What the hell do you want from me?" She took a breath, but it did little to calm her. "That you still treat me like a child is on you. Not me."

I couldn't deny she had a point. But I was armed for battle and wasn't yet ready to lay down my weapons. In my head, I prepared a list of all the times Izzy had indeed needed saving, but before I could deliver it, Izzy's tears started again.

"I always thought you knew me best, Frankie. But if you think I could kill Piper, you don't know me at all."

I squared my shoulders and tried to form the words. *I'm sorry.* But they lodged in my throat. As often as I'd been wrong, I should've been better at apologizing. I swallowed and tried again, but the words remained stuck, a bitter lump that prevented me from saying anything. So I stayed silent, failing yet again. Apparently, *that* I was good at.

The front door opened, and Julian ran through it, Mom a second behind him. Julian wrapped himself around us, binding Izzy and me together within his small arms. His sudden arrival prevented my response to Izzy's comment. Probably a good thing, because I had no idea what I could say to that.

# 35

After Izzy and I both turned down our mom's chicken and rice—in itself nearly a sign of the apocalypse—she offered us a ride home. Izzy climbed into the front seat, while Julian and I took the back. The ten minutes to Izzy's neighborhood were even more unsettling than the hours I'd spent earlier at the sheriff's substation. Neither of us was up to pretending everything was okay, so we rode in awkward silence. I was grateful for Julian's presence. With him next to me, our mom was less likely to ask the hard questions.

When we turned in to Izzy's complex, Mom slowed abruptly. My heart banged, because at the same instant, I saw what she had. Parked along the curb were two white cars with light bars and green lettering: SONOMA COUNTY SHERIFF.

"I wonder what's going on," she said, curious, nervous even, but not worried. Did she think a burglar alarm had been triggered? Or that someone had reported a domestic disturbance?

Whatever she believed, she wasn't thinking that the deputies had come to arrest her daughter.

The only question was which daughter. The location suggested they'd come for Izzy, but I had been the one who had recently spent hours in the interview room. I tried to catch Izzy's gaze but she wouldn't look at me.

Beside me, Julian squirmed, straining to see what had gotten our attention.

My voice low, I said, "Let's turn around. You can just drop Izzy off at my place."

Izzy's face settled into stone. "No. Let me out here."

Julian stretched tall enough to see out the front window. Without their lights strobing, sheriff's cars didn't hold quite the allure of a dump truck or fire engine, but his eyes widened nonetheless.

"Police!" He looked at me for confirmation, then started sounding out the word on the side of the car. "Shhh . . ." His forehead wrinkled.

Usually I would've worked with him on it. Helped him sound it out. "Sheriff," I said.

When Izzy unbuckled, I leaned forward in my seat.

"Would you like me—" I began.

She cut me off, her voice harsh. "I'm good."

She opened the car door, and our mom touched her arm. "You sure it's safe? I think Frankie's right."

Izzy's jaw twitched. If anyone else had said that, she would've erupted. Beneath her anger, I sensed fear too. "Frankie's always right."

Even our mom couldn't miss the bitterness there.

Maybe I wasn't right. This time, I wanted to be wrong.

Izzy turned to our mom. "It's fine. Piper was"—she glanced at Julian—"in an accident earlier, and they're probably here to talk to me about that."

Mom's eyes grew large. "Is she okay?" Then, remembering Julian, she said, "Call me later."

When she got out of the car, our mom backed out of the driveway. I wrapped myself around Julian so he wouldn't see Izzy being handcuffed.

WHEN THE PHONE RANG less than an hour after I came home, I thought it might be news about Izzy. After I had told our mom a parent-friendly version of what had happened to Piper, she had gone home to find Izzy a lawyer. I offered to help, but she had shaken her head. "Not this time."

Expecting to hear our mom's voice, I was instead greeted by a relative stranger. "Is this Frankie Barrera?" the man asked. Though I'd heard the voice only once before, I recognized it immediately, even if there was less hostility in it this time. When I confirmed who I was, he introduced himself. "This is Tobin. Rachel and Marina's brother. Is this an okay time to talk?"

*Not really.* "How'd you get this number?" I realized how rude the question sounded. As a woman, how many times had I been advised to be polite? It was right up there with being told to smile more. I'd never really cared for either piece of advice.

He seemed taken aback. "I got the number from Marina. I hope you don't mind me calling? I know our last talk wasn't exactly . . . friendly."

"Now's fine." Even as I worried about Izzy, it seemed being polite was too deeply ingrained for me to abandon it entirely. Besides, Tobin might want to share news about Marina. That, at least, was worth me taking the call.

"I wanted to thank you for convincing Marina to come home."

"Oh." Here he was, thanking me for bringing his own sister home, when mine had just been taken away. His timing kind of sucked. "I'm glad she's safe. Everything going okay?" When my eyes blurred, I rubbed them hard. The past several days I had spent so much time focused on this man's sister, but now it was hard to remember why that quest had been so important. All I could think of was Izzy.

"She and Mom are working through some stuff, but what mother and daughter aren't?"

I thought of my own mom, who had needed a saint's patience to raise Izzy and me. I made a note to take her out to dinner when this was all over. When Izzy was back home.

Tobin continued, "I don't want to keep you. I just wanted you to know that we're both really glad she's back."

I paused. I wouldn't be talking to Tobin again. Now was the only chance I would have to ask questions, even if they might no longer matter. "Before you go, I was wondering . . . Marina mentioned Rachel had a boyfriend before she died."

"What does that have to do with anything?" Abruptly, he became more guarded.

"I'm not sure it does, but I thought, with Piper being stabbed—"

He interrupted. "What?"

"You didn't know about Piper?"

His voice was thick when he said, "No. What happened?"

As I told him, I could hear his breath growing heavier on the other end of the line. I couldn't bring myself to tell him about Izzy.

When I was done, he said, "That's horrible. But that just makes it clearer that Rachel's boyfriend had nothing to do with it."

"So Rachel was dating someone?"

"I'm not sure." Hesitant now. "She never confirmed it with me."

"But you obviously have an idea who it was."

He was silent for a moment, then he said, "I always thought she and Chuck had a thing."

"What made you think that?"

"I don't know. He just seemed weird around her. Awkward. But I might've been imagining it." Or maybe he wasn't. "Besides, it doesn't matter, because Chuck lives in another state. He's married, with a baby on the way. Even if he had done something to Rachel, which I know he didn't, he's not around now."

I wasn't nearly as confident as Tobin. If my call had triggered Chuck in some way, he could've booked a plane ticket and made it to Guerneville in plenty of time to kill Piper. I thought back to our conversation, but nothing from it stood out. He seemed like a nice guy. Or maybe, because he had also slept with Izzy, I just wanted him to be innocent.

Then I remembered what Ben had said about the deer stealing birds from their nests. Ben claimed he had tormented Chuck because the other man was weak. He needed to adapt. How effective had Ben been in making Chuck less like the plant-grazing deer and more like a bird-eating one?

Still, I thought it was more likely Tobin was protecting Ben.

"You're sure Rachel wasn't involved with Ben?"

"Because you helped Marina, I'll say this one more time." He talked slowly, as if talking to a petulant child. "Ben was like a brother to Rachel. He has his faults. The drugs, for instance. His sense of humor sometimes, sure. And he's definitely an alpha type. Overall, though, he's a good guy. He's been there for my family for years. He wouldn't hurt Rachel."

Funny. He had claimed the same thing about Chuck.

Sensing I'd pushed as much as I could, I thanked him for the call, adding, "Tell Marina I said hello."

He paused. "I don't think I'll do that," he said. "Look, as I said, my mom and I are both grateful that you helped Marina, and I've answered your questions. Even if, frankly, you have no place asking them. But from now on, I think it would be best if you and your sister stayed away from my family."

It was only after I hung up that I realized if Chuck really had hooked up with both Rachel and Izzy, that might give my sister one more reason to dislike Rachel.

LATER, AS I WAS getting Julian ready for bed, my mom called. From her greeting, I knew to take it in the other room. The call lasted only a couple of minutes. My mom was too frantic to talk longer. As it was, it took a few attempts for me to understand what she was saying.

The knife the police had recovered from Piper's body had belonged to the catering company. And Izzy's prints were on the handle.

# 36

When Izzy was Julian's age, she nearly drowned. We were visiting Howarth Park in Santa Rosa, which had a carousel, pony rides, and a small train that looped around a section of the grounds. It also had a playground surrounded by an expansive lawn, and acres of trails and hills dense with trees.

But Izzy's favorite spot had always been Lake Ralphine. Even then, it hadn't surprised me that my sister would be drawn to a place that was so large and dangerous.

That morning, intending to feed the geese that lived at the lake, Izzy had twice attempted to smuggle a bagel, which our mom took from her. But Mom hadn't noticed when Izzy stuffed the bagel in her pocket the third time.

The geese could be aggressive, and our mom always got nervous when they came waddling toward her. She called them devil birds, not at all affectionately. Though only four years old, Izzy was quick. She could get in trouble in the time it took someone else to draw a single breath.

The park was crowded that day, so our mom parked in the only spot available, one close to the lake. Before Mom could stash her keys and unbuckle, Izzy had clambered over the seat, thus evading the child locks. She opened the passenger door and took off running.

I ran after her, but the moment before I caught her, she leaped off the dock, toward a gaggle of geese. I'm still not sure why she did that. She had always been impulsive, and four-year-olds don't always need reasons.

I jumped, too, but I landed several feet away. It took only a few seconds to swim to her, but in those seconds, Izzy sank. I dove beneath the water. Hooked my hands on her arm. Tugged her upward. When she surfaced, she gasped. Coughed up lake water. Then her forehead had wrinkled and she had frowned. Apparently I had scared the geese away. That was the first time I realized Izzy didn't always appreciate being rescued.

I waited until Julian was asleep, then sneaked into his room with my blanket. Wide awake, I hoped the sounds of his breathing would calm me. But as I lay there, eyes closed, sleep eluded me. Because Izzy had been right. I had been treating her like the toddler version of herself who had needed shielding from that dog, or the preschooler who had jumped in the lake, or that seven-year-old who had run away. She was still impulsive and she still occasionally made bad decisions, but she was also an adult.

As I had so many times in the past five years, I thought of that night near Mercuryville. Izzy imploring me to find Rachel, clawing at my arm, urging me over the embankment. She had called me for help, but instead of listening to her, I had convinced her she couldn't trust her own memory.

Eventually, the magic of Julian's breathing worked and started to lull me into sleep. As I drifted, I felt as if I were being pulled into the depths of Lake Ralphine, just as my sister nearly had been twenty years before.

I AWOKE WITH A headache. I attacked it with two ibuprofens and a cup of coffee. By the time Julian got out of bed, it had subsided enough that I was fairly confident my head wouldn't actually explode.

Julian lingered over his bowl of cereal until the flakes grew soggy. It was a chore getting him to brush his teeth and change out of his pajamas. After he had rejected his fifth outfit—because it made him look like a three-year-old, he said—I figured out what was going on: he didn't want to go to school.

Since I'd already claimed the title of World's Worst Sister, I figured there was no harm in adding a Bad Mom honorable mention. I called the preschool and told them he wouldn't be in that morning.

After a particularly productive bug hunt—Julian identified a caterpillar, a roly-poly, and a couple of bees—we headed to Cloverdale Regional Library. Julian took his time choosing a small stack of books, and nearly as much time picking the perfect spot on the carpet. That's where we were, cross-legged in a corner of the library, when I got news from my mom. It wasn't the news I was expecting. Mark had regained consciousness and could finally have visitors.

The thing Izzy had most wanted, and she wouldn't be there for it.

I offered my parents a ride to Petaluma, but Mom insisted on driving her own car. My dad hadn't slept well, she said, and she wasn't sure how long he would last at the hospital.

The air outside was swampy, but Julian and I found a bit of shade outside the hospital entrance to wait for my parents. When they arrived, the four of us headed inside together.

Dad rolled in first, Mom behind him. She greeted Mark with a careful hug. Julian and I hesitated in the doorway. The corridor held the barest scent of disinfectant. Would Izzy want me there? I didn't know. But Mark was family, and what kind of big sister would I be if I left a room every time my little sister willed it?

Julian tucked himself behind me, eyes fixed on Mark in the hospital bed. The large scrape on Mark's cheek, raw and pink when I'd last seen him, had formed a scab. His formerly swollen brow now showed the hint of bruising. But the most significant change was in his eyes, half-open and slightly softened by pain medication.

When he noticed how Julian's own eyes widened at the sight of him, he attempted a smile. "Hey, Julian," he said, voice hoarse. "Everybody."

Julian stepped out from behind me, but his hand clutched the hem of my T-shirt. His upper lip always became more pronounced when he was anxious, almost beak-like. It was part genetics, part the tension in his jaw. Staring at Mark, Julian's beak protruded more than usual. I had prepared him, of course, but he had never before been to a hospital. And how could I adequately prepare a four-year-old for what had happened to Mark?

My dad rolled closer to Julian. "You want to go get something to drink from the cafeteria?"

Julian didn't answer, still transfixed by Mark's injuries. He took a few more tentative steps. "You got in a car accident."

When Mark nodded, he winced. "Yeah."

"Does your face hurt?" Julian asked.

His laugh rasped. "My everything hurts."

Julian nodded, then turned his attention to my dad. "Do they have lemonade in the cafeteria?"

My dad smiled. "We can check."

Julian nodded again. Once he and my dad were in the hallway, my mom looked from me to Mark, and back again. "Lemonade actually sounds good," she said. "You two probably have some talking to do." Then she left the room. I was starting to suspect my parents knew more about their daughters than they let on.

The sun-faded look Mark always wore was more pronounced now, his abrasion and bruising standing out in stark contrast. I remained standing next to the machines that still monitored his heart rate and respiration.

We made awkward conversation, Mark talking about his aches and how glad he was to be rid of the feeding tube, me updating him on Julian's progress in school and a dining room remodel I was considering. Then I finally asked, "You heard about Piper?"

He started to nod, then remembered it hurt. "I talked to your mom on the phone earlier."

"Then you know about Izzy."

"Yeah." Each word seemed to tax him. His chest rose and fell in an irregular rhythm. When I glanced at the monitor, he smiled. "I'm fine. Just tired."

He didn't seem fine. His pulse rose and fell without an identifiable pattern. "I should let you rest."

He reached out and touched my arm. The simple gesture quick-ened his heartbeat and made him grimace. "Wait. The day of the hit-and-run, we were supposed to talk."

"I assumed it was about Marina?"

He started to shake his head, then winced again. "I would never betray Izzy like that," he said, which made me feel like crap. "Actually, I wanted to ask . . ." His voice trailed off, and he closed his eyes for a second. I checked the monitor again. No alarms or erratic patterns. When he opened his eyes again, he said, "You know Izzy better than anyone, so I wanted to ask if, you know, you thought she would say yes if I proposed."

My breath caught. All this time worrying, thinking Mark meant to tell me Izzy was drinking again. A grin started, until I realized I had done what I always did. When Mark had called, I'd immediately thought the worst of Izzy.

"If I say no, you're still going to ask her, aren't you?" I teased.

His smile grew sheepish. "Hey, I gotta take my shot. Before she realizes she's out of my league." I congratulated him, and he in-stantly became serious again. "I was recently reminded we shouldn't wait to say the things that are important."

Did he know about the rift between Izzy and me? How could he, with Izzy in custody?

The ping from the pocket of my jeans gave me an excuse to avoid thinking too long on that. I pulled out my phone and checked it. *Marina?* While I'd given her my number, I hadn't thought she would use it, especially not so soon, and definitely not after the conversation I'd had with her brother.

Meet at 2:15 town center corte madera?

I checked the time before typing: Ok. What's up?

I didn't want to be asked for a ride when I got there. That hadn't gone so well for Izzy the last time.

Want to show u something.

Apparently Marina hadn't gotten her brother's message about his family avoiding ours. When I looked up, Mark was studying me with those fuzzy eyes of his.

"Was that about Izzy?"

"No."

"You gotta go?"

I shook my head. "I've got a few minutes."

"You haven't asked me about the accident."

"I didn't think you were up for it yet."

"I'm fine." But even as he said it, pain flashed on his face.

"What matters is you're recovering," I said. "Besides, Marina already told me what happened. That it really was just an accident."

He paused. "Maybe."

Surprised, I asked, "You don't think it was?"

"I don't know. Not for sure." He shifted in his bed, which brought new tension to his face. After a couple of steadying breaths, he continued. "I didn't see the car. All I remember is Marina running across the street. I tried to stop her. I didn't look before I ran after her. Stupid, I know. I wasn't thinking. I was actually worried about her getting hit. Then—nothing. I don't even remember the impact."

"Then why do you think it wasn't an accident?"

His pause stretched. Worried our conversation might be harming him, I checked the monitor again. His heart rate had risen, but not enough to trigger an alarm.

"It's not so much what happened that night as the week before."

"What happened?"

"Ben came over looking for Izzy. He did the whole buddy routine, but I knew he was selling to Izzy."

I thought of the cocaine Izzy had shown me the day I'd tracked her down to Mark's place. The photo of snow bwesley420 had direct-messaged her on Instagram. "If it helps, she gave the coke to me." Realizing how that sounded, I quickly added, "I flushed it."

"It wasn't the first time she almost used. But it was the closest she came, I think."

Mark's skin had taken on a waxy sheen, its undertones gray as if he'd just been plucked from the Petaluma River. I worried he wasn't as fine as he claimed to be.

I took a step toward him. Should I fluff his pillow? Get him some ice chips? When I offered these things, he managed a laugh, though it came out sounding more like a cough. "I'm not pregnant, Frankie. And I'm fine." Dubious, I shot him a look, and he exhaled sharply. "Truth is I feel like shit."

I moved so I could better see the monitor and the door. "So when Ben came over, I'm guessing you guys didn't make plans for a bro weekend."

"I might've called him loser scum, and he might've threatened to kill me."

Before I could ask how serious Ben had seemed about his threat, my parents and Julian walked into the room, Julian holding a small paper cup.

"No lemonade, but they had apple juice," my mom announced. She turned her attention to Mark. Her brow knitted. "You sure you're still up to having visitors?"

He smiled, a hint of pain at its edges. "What is it with you Barrera women?"

Remembering Marina's text, I hugged my parents. "We've got to go," I said. Then I grabbed Julian's hand and left before my parents could ask me any questions about where I needed to be.

# 37

Marina was seated beneath a yellow umbrella outside the vegetarian restaurant. She sipped a bottle of ginger ale and picked at a stack of what looked like battered green beans. When she saw me and Julian, she smiled, but not enough to show teeth. I returned the smile. When I sat across from her, Julian in the chair between us, she pushed the plate of green beans toward me. I shook my head. A couple of minutes outside, and already I felt like I was melting. I brushed away the sweat with the back of my hand.

"Not hungry." My stomach grumbled in protest, but I doubted I could keep down even the simple green beans. Since Izzy had been arrested, anything stronger than water turned my stomach.

Julian grabbed a handful, then made a face. Not a fan, apparently.

I introduced Marina to Julian as "Izzy's friend from camp."

"Nice to meet you," he said solemnly, as he had been taught to do.

Her smile became a real one. "Nice to meet you too."

"Izzy's my aunt," he said, and my heart seized. He decided to give one of the green beans another try, but ended up making the same face.

"You doing okay?" I asked Marina.

She nodded, then tucked a strand of blond hair behind her ear. She had the same slightly elfin ears as her brother. The same pale skin. I wondered if Rachel had shared the same traits. It must be strange for Marina to be approaching the age of her once much older sister. After Marina's next birthday, she would celebrate ages Rachel had never reached.

"Thanks for coming," she said. "I know it's really far for you to drive, but I don't have a car and I'm, like, grounded for forever. She even has Ben watching the house while she's at work, to make sure I don't leave." When I cocked an eyebrow, she shrugged. "This doesn't count. Ben just dropped me off, and she's meeting me on the way home to pick a dress for Rachel's"—she glanced at Julian—"thing. My mom should be here in, like, fifteen minutes. That's why I had to be so specific with the time, you know?"

Julian squirmed in his seat. "Who's Rachel?"

"My sister." Her voice caught in her throat.

Julian stabbed a green bean into the table, the batter curling, then shredding on the hard surface. He grinned at the smooshed green bean as if he had just created art. "Izzy's my mom's sister."

Her smile grew sad. "I know."

"I'm glad you reached out," I said. "Izzy and I are both here if you ever need to talk."

But Izzy wasn't here. She was probably in a cell at the Sonoma County Jail, or stuck in an interview room while she awaited charges. Or had they already charged her? The heat felt suddenly unbearable.

Marina reached under the table. She pulled out a notebook and set it on the table. It was spiral-bound and had a brown cover, faux-leather, the edges of which were frayed, the corners bent. The writing on the cover indicated it was a sketchbook, not a notebook.

Marina didn't offer it to me. Instead, she fidgeted, her hands clasping and unclasping on top of the sketchbook.

"I don't think Izzy—" She looked at Julian again. "You know." So she'd heard that Izzy was a suspect in Rachel's death. I must've looked surprised, because she continued, "Izzy was cool to me, even when I wasn't so cool to her. Tobin, Ben, my mom . . . they all think she . . . you know . . . or at least knows more than she's saying."

There was such sincerity in the girl's voice that my own doubt earlier seemed even more of a betrayal. I risked a look at Julian, but he had moved on from green bean art to engineering and seemed less interested in the conversation than the structure he was building with his green beans.

"When we were packing, I found this in one of the boxes with Rachel's stuff." Marina slid the sketchbook toward me. "It's mainly self-portraits, but some of it . . ." Her face scrunched in the universal expression of distaste. "It shows what I told you, about how sad she was before she . . . disappeared." Her voice trailed off, and her shoulders slumped and she folded in on herself.

"You sure your mom would be okay with me having this?"

She snorted. "She wouldn't be okay with you having anything

that belonged to Rachel," she said. Julian perked up at that and Marina quickly added, "Sometimes my mom's not very good at sharing."

Julian nodded as if he understood the feeling exactly. "I have to share most things, but I don't have to share Mr. Carrots, because he's special to me."

Marina said, "I don't think my mom would mind sharing this, though. I don't think she would like to look at it." Marina finished her ginger ale and began peeling the label. Bits of it stuck to her fingertips. "There're some pictures in there. Some dates too. And some of the pictures are . . . Well, maybe something in there will help the police figure everything out."

Julian's eyes grew wide. "The police?"

Whatever was in the sketchbook, I would have to stash it someplace now that it had drawn his interest. Marina shot me a look of apology.

"Why not give it directly to them?" I asked.

She sat up straight again. "If someone had something that would help my sister, I'd want to see it first, you know?"

I couldn't imagine how a couple of drawings would help Izzy, but the gesture warmed me.

Marina glanced around somewhat nervously. I checked the time on my phone and saw that we'd been talking for nearly fifteen minutes. When Anne arrived, I knew the last thing she would want to see was me sitting with her daughter.

I reached across the table and squeezed Marina's hand. "Thanks for trusting me with this."

Then I left, sketchbook tucked under my arm, Julian's sweaty hand in mine. Halfway to the truck, he tried to pull away.

"Ow, Mommy."

"Sorry, pumpkin." I loosened my grip only slightly.

EVEN THOUGH I'D CRACKED the window, the cab of the truck felt as if its thermostat had been set to broil. I turned on the air-conditioning, then tossed the sketchbook on the passenger seat. After I double-checked Julian's straps on his booster in the back-seat, I buckled my own seat belt. I ignored the sketchbook. Loitering could lead to another confrontation with Anne or, worse, get Marina in trouble. Better to spend time studying the sketches at home, where I could pour myself some ice water and sit in front of a fan, away from Julian's growing interest in Rachel's drawings.

Julian complained less than I thought he would on the ride home, primarily because he slept through the second half of it. Once home, I turned on the fan in the living room, poured us both glasses of water, and helped Julian haul out his sets of building blocks. Apparently stacking green beans had reminded him he hadn't played with the blocks in a while.

When I was confident Julian was fully immersed in his building, I started flipping through the pages in Rachel's sketchbook.

At the center of the first page, Rachel had used a pencil to sketch a smiling face, its chin resting on two hands. Though Rachel had lacked Marina's talent, the drawing was clearly a self-portrait, the long hair colored with alternating strokes of red and yellow crayon. Rachel's hair had been long, too, and copper-colored. Lighter than Tobin's, darker than Marina's. Pencil smudges suggested she had erased the lines many times in her quest to get it right. Even then, the proportions were odd. The fingers too thin and tapered to sharper points than was natural. The eyes too large and set wide. The paper around the head was filled in almost entirely with pictures of flowers. She had printed thumbnail photos of daisies, sunflowers, and tulips on regular copy paper, then had cut them into circles, each about the size of a quarter. The flower dots had been affixed to the thicker stock of the sketch paper. She had probably used liquid glue, because several of the flowers bubbled as if too much had been applied. In the corner, written carefully in the same shade as the tulips, were two words: Easter Brunch. I did the math on the date. Rachel would've been about eleven.

As the drawings progressed, they improved. Liquid glue was replaced by glue sticks. No more bubbling. The collages grew more complex. The fourth page had a Victorian theme, with beads, lace, and an old wedding photo featuring a bride artificially colored with ice-blue eyes and too-pink cheeks. But the center of the page was taken up by another self-portrait, this one in profile, head haloed by a veil similar to the one worn by the bride. This time, the features were more realistic. In the corner, she had written: Janice's Wedding.

At the middle of the book, a page had been torn from the sketchbook, the edge of it still clinging to the spiral coil that held the book together. By then Rachel had grown confident enough to sketch full-body portraits. The first of these featured Rachel dressed like a cat, surrounded by photos of horror movie villains, spliced together to look like filmstrips. Halloween Party. Other pages followed. Camp Days. Driver's License. Christmas Eve. By tracking the dates, I watched Rachel age, her talent grow. On these later pages, an occasional photo of someone else would appear. I recognized one girl as a young Piper. But Rachel remained at the center of every page.

Then came Day at the Beach. This page featured Rachel in a bikini. The drawing took up nearly the whole page. Crowded in the corner as if it were an afterthought, there was a smaller sketch, a giant head with the tip of its nose pressed against the ground. A grasshopper straddled its profile. A bare-shouldered woman emerged from it, her face hovering near a man's waist. Cuts on the man's knees. Sexual undertones unmistakable. Drawn even more carefully than the portrait of Rachel. At once, it seemed both out of place but also exactly right.

Confused, I felt my forehead pucker. The way she had been drawn made me suddenly doubt Rachel was the artist. Had she sketched any of them?

I quickly flipped to the next page, the last that had been filled. I blinked rapidly to better focus, sure I hadn't seen it correctly on first glance. But when I looked again, I realized I had. This one was worse than *Day at the Beach*. Far worse.

Marina wouldn't have understood that, of course.

On this page, instead of photos printed on copy paper, glossy snapshots had been used. Pasted along the bottom border was a panoramic shot of mountains. The collage also included smaller photos of wildflowers, a rusted structure, a tree, and a sign: MERCURYVILLE. 1/2 MILE CITY.

The longer I stared at the page, the faster my heart raced. As Marina had mentioned, in this drawing Rachel wasn't smiling. But I don't think the artist was aiming for sad. I think he aimed for seductive.

Because the snapshots and her expression weren't the first

things I noticed. That would be what she wore: a bra and panties. Marina might've believed it to be another bathing suit, but I suspected that wasn't what the artist had intended. The undergarments were white. Virginal. Instantly it reminded me of Ben's question during the game.

*So, Rachel, have you ever had sex?*

In the corner of the page, in the same careful script, the artist had written a single word: Paranoia. The game they had been playing that night.

Below it was the date: two days *before* Rachel had been killed.

I picked up my phone to call Izzy. Then I remembered she wasn't home.

# FIVE YEARS BEFORE

After his fight with Rachel, Ben left, taking Piper with him. By then Chuck and Tobin had been gone for more than an hour. That left Izzy with Rachel, with only one car between them.

*Shit,* Izzy thought. *That means I'm going to have to give her a ride home.*

Izzy had stopped drinking as soon as Piper left, but her head still buzzed. She figured she'd be okay to drive in another twenty minutes or so. She gestured toward the unopened sports drink next to Rachel.

"Do you mind?" Important to hydrate if she was going to avoid the next day's hangover.

Rachel picked up the bottle and handed it to her. Since the night had blown up, neither of them had really talked much. With Ben and Piper gone now, too, the silence grew even more awkward. The knife Izzy had forgotten to return to Ben rested on the ground between them.

*Maybe I'm sober enough to drive now,* Izzy thought.

She twisted off the cap of the sports drink and drank half.

She offered the rest to Rachel, but the other girl shook her head, grabbing a can of hard seltzer instead.

*Sure*, now *she drinks*.

But Rachel took only a few tentative sips before putting the can on the ground at her feet. Then she turned to face Izzy, as pale as she had been when they had first arrived, the pink in her cheeks muted.

"I'm glad everyone else is gone," she said.

Izzy studied Rachel's expression to see if she was joking. Only a few sentences had passed between them the entire night. But her face was serious, her mouth set in a grim line.

What was Izzy supposed to say to that? Uncomfortable, she sipped the sports drink so she wouldn't have to answer, then started picking debris off her jeans to occupy her hands.

Dark, quiet minutes stretched. Then Rachel leaned forward, a curtain of red hair cascading to shield her face. Her voice low, she said, "You haven't asked me what that fight with Ben was about."

"I'm not nosy like that."

That wasn't entirely true. She'd been curious.

"Everyone's nosy like that," Rachel said. "They just don't admit it."

In the light of the twin lanterns, Izzy's eyes blurred. The dark pressed against her back. In that moment, the night had been reduced to the two of them and their pair of lanterns. Nothing more. The only reminder that a world existed beyond them was the earthy scent of wildflowers and hidden things decaying, carried by the breeze.

"I figured it was your business," Izzy said.

"The fight was about some pictures I found."

Izzy drained the last of the sports drink and tossed the bottle with the other recyclables. "What kind of pictures?"

"The kind that cause fights." Rachel hesitated, resting her hand near her pocket. "I'm not sure what to do."

Izzy shrugged. "I'd say do whatever feels right."

Rachel straightened, the curtain of her hair parting, exposing a face that had grown paler, even her cheeks the color of chalk now. "We were supposed to come out here a couple of days ago. Did you know that?"

Izzy nodded, growing abruptly light-headed. Maybe she wasn't as close to being sober as she'd thought. She blinked, long and slow, to shut out the stars.

"Piper said you bailed because of food poisoning."

"It wasn't because of bad chicken," Rachel said. "It was because of the picture."

She shifted to face Izzy, as if deciding something. After several seconds, she said, "I didn't want to come here because I thought maybe he had something planned."

"Like what?"

Rachel reached into her pocket and pulled out a folded sheet of paper. Slowly, she unfolded it. The edge was ragged, the paper clearly ripped from a spiral notebook.

"There were these sketches. One of them was of this place." She fidgeted, tearing off flakes from the edge of the paper. "This one, though . . . it's worse."

When she held it up for Izzy to see, her hand trembled. The lantern cast shadows, so Izzy leaned in to better see. Immediately she recoiled. It was a drawing of Rachel. Naked. Her body had been shaded with red pencil, her hands and face a pale pink, hands darker. But in the most private spots, the shading had been done with such a heavy hand that it cut grooves into the paper. In the sketch, Rachel's chest was the color of blood.

She quickly refolded the picture and stowed it in her pocket. "When I saw it, I threw up." Eyes suddenly wide and too bright. "I'm not being dramatic. I actually threw up."

She appeared on the verge of being sick again. Izzy felt her own stomach curdle—one part vodka, two parts disgust.

"Anyway, I'm not sure what he'd planned for tonight," Rachel said. She closed her eyes, as if even this small part of the world were suddenly too much for her. "Like I said, I'm really glad it's just us now."

# 38

As I walked Julian into Candace's classroom, I realized that a week earlier when I'd followed the same path, I'd been worried about getting to the grocery store. Whether Julian would enjoy his field trip. What Mark wanted to tell me about Izzy. Then the police cruiser had pulled up alongside my truck at the gas station. Had it really been only seven days?

The afternoon before when I'd closed the sketchbook, I had debated whether to drop it off with the police. What did it prove? It wasn't like one of the drawings had been titled *My Plans to Kill Rachel*—though maybe that last page came close. I decided I wanted to talk to Izzy before I did anything.

Thankfully, that was now possible. She'd been released the night before. Our mom had been the one to get the call, and the one to pick her up from the jail. Apparently there were insufficient grounds to make a criminal complaint. A witness they'd had was no longer sure. The knife had multiple prints on it, not just Izzy's. Mom had tried to sound optimistic when relaying the news, but I heard the unspoken words: Izzy was free, but it was likely temporary.

The night before, Izzy hadn't wanted to go back to the apartment, so my mom had dropped her at Mark's place. When I knocked, she didn't answer. I checked the time. Hospital visiting hours had started forty-five minutes earlier, so I was pretty sure that's where she would be. I considered heading to the hospital.

*No,* I thought. *Give them space.*

Though patience wasn't something that came easily to me, I sat on the steps and waited. An hour later, she appeared, her frown signaling she wasn't happy to see me. Still, she unlocked the door and ushered me into the living room. She perched on the sofa, arms crossed, waiting for me to speak. Her face was stony, but I could tell by the way her gaze drifted to the sketchbook that she was curious.

"They released you."

Her arms tightened around her torso. "Surprised?"

There was no way I was getting out of this without apologizing.

"I shouldn't have thought you capable of hurting Piper," I said. Judging by her clenched jaw and the parentheses that framed her mouth, it wasn't enough, so I added, "I'm sorry."

I let that hang in the icy space between us for a moment. Then I asked, "Have you seen Mark?"

"This morning. He knows about Rachel, obviously, from before his accident. And Mom told him about Piper while I was . . . you know." She looked away. "I'm glad she did. I wouldn't have wanted him to hear about it from someone else." I suspected that last part was a dig at me. She faced me again. "He proposed. But you probably knew that." She sounded both irritated and happy.

"Congratulations."

She gave a curt nod. "I said yes without thinking. But I can't marry him, even if I want to. Even when I was with him in the hospital, so happy he was doing better and that he'd proposed, I kept an eye on the door." As if this reminded her she needed to do the same now, her gaze drifted toward the entryway. "I keep expecting to be arrested again. I hear a sound outside and I immediately hold my breath, sure it's the deputies come to take me back there."

"They can't really think you killed her."

"Why not? My own sister did."

I flinched. *Fair.* "What did they say?"

"They said they had a witness, but turns out the statement had inconsistencies. Then there's the knife." She paused, chewing on her lip. Thinking. "They may have released me, but they made it clear I was still their primary suspect in Piper's murder."

When her eyes fell again on the sketchbook, I offered it to her. "Then it's time we focused their attention elsewhere."

IZZY TOOK HER TIME with the book, spending several minutes on each page and sometimes doubling back for a second look. In her focus, I sensed how desperately she wanted the answers to be in those pages. I wasn't sure if her lingering meant she had found those answers, or that she hadn't. Two pages in particular held her interest: *Day at the Beach*, and the one with the photos of Mercuryville.

Finally, she rested the book on her lap, open to the last page.

I leaned in and tapped the date with my finger. "Why two days before?" I asked.

"The six of us were supposed to meet up two days earlier, but then Rachel ate some bad chicken or got the flu. Something like that. So we rescheduled." Izzy slowly traced the snapshots with her fingertip. "Ben said he knew this cool place, where the cops would leave us alone. But until the day we went, he wouldn't tell us where. He was all about surprise. Theater. And when he did tell us where to meet, none of the rest of us had heard of Mercuryville. Except Piper. She knew."

"Unless someone was lying."

She continued making lazy circles on the photo of the Mayacamas Mountains that had been stripped across the bottom of the page. "It seems a stupid thing to lie about. Why would any of us care?" She paused. "At least until after Rachel died, but there was no way that was planned."

The circumstances of Rachel's murder didn't seem premeditated to me either. Still, I wasn't sure. Someone had created this collage. Someone had made plans that had ended with Rachel dying.

"It's not like it was private property," I said. "If Ben was dating Rachel, he might've told her. Then she might've told her brother, who might've told his roommate."

Reluctantly, she nodded. "Yeah. Maybe. But that means anyone could've done it, and that doesn't help, does it?" She closed the book and tossed it on the table. Probably sick of looking at it. I knew I was.

"You're closer to this than I am, Izzy. Who do you think drew those?"

She didn't hesitate. "It's either Tobin or Ben. It has to be. They were the only ones who lived in that house."

"Ben makes sense," I said. "It was his location. His game."

She nodded. "And he was likely dating Rachel. Though not everyone agrees on that. If this is his work, it certainly suggests there was at least . . . *interest* . . . on his part." She wrinkled her nose in distaste.

"What about Tobin?"

"Maybe." She didn't sound convinced.

"He didn't like Ben and Rachel together," I pointed out. "Five years later, he still won't admit they were."

"Then why would he kill Rachel, but idolize Ben? And another thing . . . whatever happened, it might not have been consensual."

"It definitely wasn't," I snapped. "Rachel's dead." I took a breath. "Sorry. Not about you."

She waved off the apology. "But we agree it's definitely not Rachel's sketchbook?" She was grasping here. Considering all angles. How had I not seen earlier how much my sister had matured?

She picked up the book again and opened it, this time to the other page that had earlier caught her interest. *Day at the Beach*. As she studied it, her brow furrowed.

"Rachel was missing for five years," I said. "She was an adult, so the police might not have searched her room. But her mom definitely would have."

"Yeah." When she exhaled, I heard the frustration in it. "When Piper did her disappearing act a couple of years ago, I went through all of her stuff. Even her toiletries. As if I'd find a clue in a bottle of Suave shampoo. And she was just my friend, not my kid. If this book was in Rachel's stuff back then, Anne would've found it." She looked uncertain. "Plus the drawings are damn creepy. No way Rachel did those herself."

"So either Tobin or Ben left the sketchbook behind, and somehow in the move it got mixed in with Rachel's stuff? That's our theory?"

"That's what I think."

I hesitated, then asked, "What about Chuck?"

She shook her head, still staring at the page. "No," she said firmly.

"We can't rule him out, Izzy. He was Tobin's friend. He must've been over there all the time. Maybe he got off on being in Rachel's room, alone with the book. He might've forgotten it, or stashed it after someone nearly caught him, and then never had the opportunity to return for it. Plus Tobin said he suspected Chuck was hooking up with his sister."

"No," she repeated, though she remained distracted. I recognized the expression. She was thinking.

I held up my palms in a gesture of surrender. "Okay, so back to Ben. Mark said Ben threatened him about a week before the hit-and-run. Is there something there that might help us figure this out?"

My fuel tank had been sabotaged with a knife, the weapon of choice for the killer. It seemed reasonable to assume it was all connected.

"That was just male posturing. If I thought it was more than that, I would've gone to the police as soon as I heard about the accident." Abruptly, she grabbed her phone. When she spoke, she was nearly breathless. She'd made a connection. "Ben did go to art school. And he's obsessed with Salvador Dalí."

She tapped a few words in the browser. Hit search.

I thought about it. After a minute, I said, "This isn't art. This is . . ." My voice trailed off as I searched for the right word. "Perverse." But a new thought came. "If the person who made this is the killer—"

"Of course it's the killer's." Eyes fixed to her screen, she clicked on one of the links.

"—then wouldn't he be the kind of sick bastard who might have other trophies too? Ones that are more damning?"

A new intensity blazed in her eyes. I thought maybe, for the first time, she glimpsed freedom—and justice for Rachel and Piper. She held up her phone, excited.

"*The Great Masturbator.*"

"Um . . . what?"

She tapped the sketchbook open in her lap. I looked at the image on Izzy's phone, then at the drawing, and back again. The sketch in the book had been crudely done, but now that Izzy had found its inspiration, the resemblance was unmistakable. The head with its nose pressed to the ground that had been drawn in the corner of *Day at the Beach*. It had mimicked the painting that Izzy had seen in Ben's home.

Then, just as quickly, the light in my sister's eyes dimmed. "It's got to be Ben. But it's still not enough."

*Unless.* "Do you know enough to get Ben arrested on drug charges?"

"Probably. But he'll do almost no time, if any." But a second later, she understood. I recognized the moment it happened. Her eyes widened. She gasped. And she nearly smiled. "If they search his house, they might find other evidence."

"Damn," I said.

Izzy looked confused. "Damn?"

"Looks like I'll have to shell out money for a bridesmaid's dress after all."

# 39

The tall oaks shadowed the playground, while on the distant hills, similar trees were reduced to blots on a canvas of fawn and green. The sun caught the leaves of a vineyard bordering the park, turning them a golden green. For the moment, Julian had the play structure all to himself.

I had dropped off the sketchbook at the sheriff's office on our way to the park, and now there was nothing to do but wait for Ben to be arrested. Drug charges would come first, but I had faith murder charges would follow. When they searched Ben's house, the police were bound to find evidence tying him to Piper's stabbing at the least, and maybe Rachel's too.

As I watched Julian scramble up the ladder that led to the slide, I felt an unfamiliar surge. I thought it might be hope.

I should've known not to trust it.

"Lovely afternoon, isn't it?"

I recoiled at the voice even before I turned to find Ben walking toward me. He stopped before he got too close, but I moved between him and the structure where Julian was playing.

I took out my phone and unlocked it.

If Ben was disturbed by the action, he gave no indication. His face remained stony, his eyes flat. Almost sociopathically so. "Next, you're going to ask how I knew you were here. You're a creature of habit, Frankie. You were almost too easy to find."

I tapped the phone icon. Navigated to the keypad. Stabbed out the numbers 911. As my finger hovered over the icon to connect the call, my eyes darted to his hands. Both at his sides. I scanned the pockets of his jeans. No bulge that might suggest a gun. Or a knife. But it could be tucked in his waistband.

I hit the connect button.

"Guess we don't have much time now, do we?" He seemed irritated but not at all concerned.

A voice came to me, tinny and as if from a distance, and I realized I hadn't brought the phone to my ear. When I did, Ben advanced a couple of steps. I widened my stance but stayed rooted in my spot. If I had to face down Ben, better to do it as far away as possible from the play structure.

I gave my name and location to the dispatcher, but even before I hung up, I realized how ridiculous I had probably sounded. Ben hadn't threatened me, not directly. In hindsight, I realized it had been foolish to think he might've brought a gun with him. If he intended to shoot me, he wouldn't have introduced himself so brazenly.

Unless he wanted to see my face when he killed me?

But no. Ben had been right. I had well established routines, ones he had learned about through his friendship with my sister. Ben could've ended me at a location much less public than City Park.

I felt Julian's presence like a burning between my shoulder blades. I risked a glance over my shoulder just as he crested the play structure. He waved, then seated himself on the slide. Usually I would position myself closer, ready to scoop him up if he descended too quickly, or catch him if his hold on the ladder faltered. Now the best thing I could do to protect him was to stay where I was. Act as a wall between him and the man who had killed two women.

"So tell me, Frankie. Why did you tell that detective I killed Rachel?" When I didn't answer, he scowled. "We both know who really killed her."

I hadn't intended to engage, but I couldn't help myself. "Yes, we do." I matched his glare with one of my own.

He seemed amused by my attempt to stare him down. "Think logically. Not with your emotions." He paused, perhaps allowing me time to do just that, before continuing. "I wasn't there. I was with Piper."

"Convenient that your alibi is now dead."

"Not convenient at all, actually. I didn't like her much, but that's one thing she would've been good for: telling the cops I didn't do it. So why would I kill her?"

"You tell me. Or better yet, tell the sheriff's office. Detective Kaplan is a really good listener."

I looked toward Julian again. He had moved to the taller slide on the other part of the structure. I couldn't see him as well now.

"Would you like to move closer? So you can see him better?"

Suddenly I worried that he had a friend with him, someone who might've approached from the other side. Maybe a customer he had offered drugs to in exchange for a quick kidnapping.

I took several steps back and adjusted my angle so I could see Julian again. From the bottom of the slide, he looked up, and a new worry sprouted: Julian would soon grow curious or bored.

When that happened, he would run to my side. Just because I now believed Ben didn't have a gun didn't mean I would bet Julian's life on it.

"Think about it," Ben said. "Really think about it. Izzy's got a temper. As her sister, I know you've seen it."

I had seen it. Many times.

He continued, "Izzy and Rachel were the only ones there. And Rachel didn't stab herself."

"You're right," I said. "About Rachel, I mean. She didn't stab herself. You did."

"How exactly would I have done that?" he asked. He put on a good show of frustration, but I saw through it. "And why?"

"The police will figure that part out." I scanned the street for a police cruiser. None yet. Out of the corner of my eye I saw that Julian was standing now. Looking in my direction. "I have some ideas, though. You and Rachel were dating."

Unlike the last time we talked, he didn't deny it. "So? She was eighteen. That's legal, and certainly nothing I'd kill to cover up."

"Judging by the sketches I saw, your fascination with her started years before."

"Those sketches mean nothing," he said.

And that was the moment I knew he'd done it. I had dropped the sketchbook off at the sheriff's office on the way to the park. He wouldn't have been questioned yet. So how could he dismiss the drawings so quickly if he hadn't seen them?

"I have to say, I can see why you had to drop out of art school."

Ben seemed calm, serene even, his eyes as cool as rocks in a winter stream. It was the expression of a man no longer concerned about convincing me he wasn't a monster, but not so careless as to admit it.

"I dropped out of art school because I found my calling elsewhere," he said. "Besides, I studied digital media, not portraiture." Abruptly, he offered a smile, as lifeless as his eyes. "Ah, look, we have a visitor."

Julian was suddenly at my side, tugging on my arm. "You said you would slide with me."

Then he noticed Ben smiling down at him, and he froze, fingers wrapped around my arm.

At only four years old, could Julian recognize it too? That the expression worn by this man was somehow wrong?

"Think about it, Frankie. Who was the last one there that night? Who really killed Rachel?"

With that, Ben shoved his hands in his pockets and walked toward the curb, unconcerned about the police cruiser that had just parked there.


THE POLICE DIDN'T ARREST Ben then. The arrest happened later.

As I had expected, the drug charges came first. Detective Kaplan said Ben likely returned to Mercuryville after dropping Piper at her apartment. Or maybe she had returned with him. There was no way to question a dead woman, but I thought Piper had to know more than she'd let on. Ben probably wouldn't have been as quick to kill his alibi otherwise.

Ben stabbed Rachel, and she fled, right into Izzy's car. The body was likely dragged away from where it had landed, because her bones were discovered half-buried far down the mountain, by a dog that had slipped its leash. If not for that, she might've remained hidden another five years.

Ben said he was innocent, of course, offering an excuse to counter each of the claims against him. When they asked about the sketchbook, he said it wasn't his. They never found any Rohypnol. I was beginning to wonder if Izzy was right, and that Piper had lied about that.

Ben tried to explain away the photos of Rachel that seemed to be taken without her awareness. They weren't his, he insisted.

He had a harder time explaining the knife the authorities found.

# 40

After Ben was arrested, Izzy asked if I would drive her to the spot where it all happened. Izzy invited Marina, too, but she declined.

"I don't want to think of her like that," she said. In a box with some letters Ben had written Rachel, Marina had also found some of her sister's CDs: alternative rock, eighties pop, rap. "That's how I want to remember her. Earbuds in, tuning me out ninety percent of the time. But being there when it counted, you know?"

When Izzy recounted this part of the conversation, I sensed she meant me to take a lesson from it.

Marina had transferred Rachel's music to her laptop and made a playlist. She texted us a link to it, and that was the music we queued up for the long drive to Mercuryville.

As we pulled away from the house, I asked, "You're sure you're up for this?"

Izzy shot me a look, and I took one hand off the wheel in a gesture of surrender. "Okay, okay. No mom talk. If you say you're ready I believe you."

I returned my hand to the wheel and merged onto U.S. 101.

On both sides, spears of brush and rows of wine grapes marched along tree-darkened hills.

"Why do you think he did it?" Izzy asked.

I didn't need to ask who she was talking about. "He was obviously obsessed, so maybe he just snapped." I shrugged. "You know him better than I do."

"I thought I did." With its thick covering of clouds, the sky looked more white than blue, an oak tree's gnarled branches silhouetted against it. "He's always been an ass. I'm not going to deny that. It's just . . . he seemed to really care about Rachel, in his own way."

"That's not a way I'd ever want anyone to care about me."

I reached into the backseat and grabbed a bottle of water. I uncapped it and took a drink. Among the swaying weeds jutted an old barn touting DR. PIERCE'S MEDICAL DISCOVERY, its siding weathered, its roof rusted. Though I had passed it thousands of times, I had never thought to research what it was the good doctor had discovered. I glanced at Izzy, who was staring out her own window. As familiar as that old barn, but still so much I didn't know about her.

"Do you know the history of that barn?" I asked, trying to lighten the mood.

It had already slipped behind us on the highway, but she knew which barn I meant. She had passed it thousands of times too.

"Something about a cure for tuberculosis?" she said, her mood remaining dark. "Sometimes I think I remember something about that night, but I don't know if it's a real memory or just the way I wished it had happened."

"Like what?"

"Like Rachel, during the game. I think someone asked her who she thought was most likely to change the world, and maybe she said me." It was her turn to shrug. "Piper said Rachel and I fought that night, but I don't remember that. I've never felt that way about Ben."

"Good thing."

"Before she died, Piper told me how I was jealous that night, but honestly? I remember going with Rachel when she needed to go to the bathroom, because she was afraid of rattlesnakes. I remember bringing a bottle with me in case I needed to bash a snake in the head." She laughed, then I felt her grow serious again. "I'm pretty sure that happened. Why would I do that if I didn't like her?"

That question triggered something in my brain. A memory of my own, but one just out of reach.

"Is that why you want to go back? To see if you remember something?"

I knew it wouldn't happen. Time and the drugs had robbed her of those memories forever.

"I know that's not possible," she said. I glanced at her sideways before returning my attention to the road. "It just pisses me off, not remembering. Like Ben took something from me that wasn't his to take."

A hawk floated above us, riding the current. It reminded me of the birds Marina had painted.

"I'm sorry."

"You're not responsible for what he did."

"I took something from you too. We should've gone to the police that night. You wanted to, but I was more concerned with getting you to the hospital. Maybe if we had, you would've—"

She cut me off. "I would've died. You saved my life." Her voice was suddenly urgent. "Never apologize for that."

The hawk dipped, turned. Then it disappeared behind us. It had been our companion for miles, and I felt a sentimental pang at its absence.

I took the exit toward Geyserville, then turned left onto California 128 E. Here, the clouds grew more sparse, revealing sun-brightened sky. In the sudden glare, I squinted.

"At least we don't have to worry about losing Julian, now that they've arrested Ben," Izzy said. Though she intended to reassure me, I tensed. Losing Julian had always been my greatest fear, and it was too soon to let go of that.

"And Marina seemed good?"

"Her mom will never like me, but yeah, they're both doing good."

We rode in silence for several minutes. I could feel her thinking as hard as I was. Oaks on both sides reached across the road, casting shadow on the asphalt. I turned left onto Geysers Road. We drove in silence for a while. The Mayacamas Mountains towered, a patchwork of dried brush, fire-blackened trees, and new growth. Oaks, pines, and conifers consumed the mountainside.

"A little farther," she said. But I didn't need her directions. Even though it had been dark that night, I remembered.

MERCURYVILLE. 1/2 MILE CITY.

I drove a few more minutes, then parked the truck in a turnout next to a gated driveway, just up the road from where I had stopped that night. WESTERN GEOPOWER. The sign looked old, faded, as did the warning against trespassing, but the sign advertising the use of cancer-causing chemicals was newer.

I finished my bottle of water, then uncapped a second one. I offered it to Izzy, but she shook her head. Her eyes were wide, her look haunted. I capped the bottle and tossed it in the backseat.

We got out of the truck, the gravel crackling beneath our feet. When we approached the gate, I noticed a jumble of locks on its post—I counted at least nine—and a perimeter protected by rusted barbed wire. But the gate was low and easy to jump.

"Is this where the others parked?"

"Ben and Tobin parked here." She pointed to the spot where I'd found our parents' car. "Chuck was over there, where I parked."

"Did you climb down the embankment over there or jump the gate and take the path?"

"We jumped the gate."

I did the same now, hoping I wouldn't get shot. Izzy followed in silence, the only sound the crackle of gravel, as I imagined Rachel's last night.

AT DUSK, ACCORDING TO the stories I'd been told, Rachel and Ben had arrived first, with the others only moments behind. They would've jumped the gate and followed the road to where it snaked down the slope. Later that night, I would use the light from my phone to search for Rachel's body. But earlier, the six friends would've expected the darkness. They would've carried flashlights or lanterns, in addition to the plastic bags that contained the alcohol. Ben likely stashed the drugs in his pocket. Cocaine for sure, and possibly Rohypnol.

The road narrowed and sloped downward, cutting into the mountainside. Had Rachel and Ben been arguing already?

No, I decided. According to Izzy, when the game started they had been friendly, sitting next to each other. As they made their way down the trail, Rachel would've stayed close to Ben, her flashlight aimed at the ground. Snakes are active at night, hunting in weeds like those that grew next to the path. Rachel wouldn't have wanted to be surprised by the sudden strike of a rattlesnake.

Now birds trilled sharply, the air heavy with the scent of heat-baked vegetation. But then the trees would've blurred into the purple hues of the thickening night.

As the mountainside started to flatten, a rusted structure listed to one side. It looked like an inverted top, boxed in by metal posts and crossbeams. Mining equipment? Something else? Whatever purpose it once served, that night it had been the landmark used to orient six friends to their chosen drinking spot.

We stopped where they had played their game, until Ben had asked Rachel the question that abruptly ended it.

I glanced at Izzy, and she understood what I wanted. She pointed in the direction Rachel had headed after fleeing the circle.

Off the path, the ground was uneven. Though she was angry, Rachel would've had to be more careful here. The weeds grew to knee-level in spots, hiding rocks and other obstacles that might cause someone to stumble.

I stopped near an oak tree. At night and under the influence, I doubted Rachel would've gone farther. She, Ben, and Tobin likely stopped here.

What had Ben said? *I'm sorry? I care about you?* Whatever it was, according to both Ben and Tobin, Rachel's anger cooled quickly.

Then Tobin left, and Ben stayed.

This was the point where events grew murkier. Everyone agreed that Chuck and Tobin were already gone, and that Ben, Rachel, Izzy, and Piper remained. Some time later, though, Ben left, and Piper hitched a ride with him.

Why had Rachel not gone with them? The obvious answer was that the fight between her and Ben had been paused, not finished. As soon as Tobin left, it had started again. Had Rachel confronted Ben about the sketchbook? Had he then stabbed her, leaving her unconscious in the brush for hours, before she stumbled up the mountainside and into Izzy's car?

That didn't sound right. Rachel was stabbed with such force that it marked her bones. Blood had been smeared on the hood of my mom's car. And Rachel had been running. She had been actively terrified. As if her attacker wasn't far away.

I turned to Izzy, my skin prickling, though not from the heat. Earlier, Izzy had asked why she would accompany Rachel to relieve herself if there was animosity between them. Now I realized why the comment had disturbed me.

"Ben drove Rachel here that night, right?"

"Yeah."

"Why would she willingly go with him if she was afraid of him?"

She furrowed her brow as she considered my question.

I continued, "Whatever happened that night started and ended here."

In the turnout on the road above us, a vehicle pulled in and parked. I looked up and understood suddenly that it had never been Izzy's memories that held the key to what had happened to Rachel. It had been mine.

At the top of the mountainside, it was the Jeep I had spotted alongside the road five years earlier.

Of course. That had always been the only explanation that made sense. Someone had returned that night.

Tobin got out of the Jeep and waved at us. Only Izzy waved back.

# FIVE YEARS BEFORE

Izzy opened her eyes. She didn't remember closing them. When had that happened?

She looked around but saw no one. Where was Rachel?

Izzy's eyes blurred. When she tried to stand, her bones felt as if they were made of rubber. So she sat again. It was darker than she remembered. Wasn't it? Then she saw why. There had been two lanterns at the center of the circle, but now there was only one. Where was the other lantern? Had Rachel taken it?

Izzy squinted as she tried to take in her surroundings. Between the branches of an oak tree, light danced. The second lantern?

She blinked and pulled open her eyes. They felt tacky, as if coated with a thin layer of glue. They tried to close again, so she let them. With her fist, she rubbed her eyelids, wiping away a crust that had formed at their corners. Had she been sleeping again?

The light she had glimpsed next to the tree had disappeared. Her eyes darted, and she found it again. It had moved farther to the left, toward the path that led up to the road. The glowing orb floated, but it no longer danced. Pinned to the night, it beckoned. Finding it seemed abruptly urgent.

This time when Izzy tried to stand, her rubber bones supported her weight. She took a couple of tentative steps that felt more like swimming than walking. She bent to reach for the lantern, then winced. Up close, the light seared her eyes. Too bright. She turned away and blinked to clear the halo.

She abandoned the lantern. The dark receded under the strobe of the moon. She risked a few more steps. Liquid seemed to slosh inside her head, but her footfalls were solid. She felt suddenly invincible, the far-off path glowing. In the distance, the lantern bounced again. She couldn't let it get away. She followed, tracking it.

Halfway to the light, she heard the voices. Two of them. One belonged to Rachel. The other lower so she couldn't quite identify it. Definitely male.

Izzy's steps became more careful, her thoughts clouded. Why had she left the lantern behind? She couldn't remember. At night, it could be dangerous out here. Tobin had said as much when they had arrived.

Izzy's forehead creased. Strange that he would say that. As if he had been here before.

With that thought came recognition. The second voice was Tobin's.

"What're you doing with Ben?" she heard him ask. He sounded confused.

Izzy was confused too. *Ben?* Ben wasn't there. She'd seen him leave. Hadn't she? She shook her head to clear it, but a surge of vertigo made her sway.

She inched closer on wobbly legs, head spinning. Through the branches of a tree, she could make out shapes. Tobin with hands in his pockets. Rachel with arms crossed. When Izzy took another step, leaves crackled beneath her sneakers.

She froze, instinctively understanding that to be caught would be bad. Very, very bad.

But Rachel's raised voice masked the sound of the crunching leaves. "That's none of your business."

Rachel started to walk away, but Tobin grabbed her arm.

"He's too old for you," he said.

She shrugged off his hand. Despite the distance between Izzy and the siblings, she clearly saw the rage on Rachel's face. It was hard to miss. "Don't touch me," she said.

"It's wrong," Tobin insisted. Izzy took another couple of steps to hear better. "Ben's like a brother to you."

"Well, you *are* my brother." She spit the words as if she found them distasteful.

Tobin went quiet. Time stretched. Finally, he said coolly, "What do you mean by that?"

"I found the sketches."

He waved his hand in a gesture of dismissal, the lantern bobbling and catching the suddenly hard planes of Rachel's face. But when he spoke, his voice wavered. "It's art. Like *The Birth of Venus* or *Sunbathing in the Dunes*."

"You're not an artist." Her voice caught in her throat. "You're a pervert." She paused, letting her breathing settle. "During that game tonight, do you know what I almost asked? *Who here is most likely to draw naked pictures of his sister?*"

Even in the dim light, Izzy could see the subtle shift in

Tobin's expression. His jaw tensed, and when he spoke, his voice hardened. "You're disgusting."

"*I'm* not the one who drew those pictures."

Tobin stepped back as if she'd slapped him. "I don't understand you." His voice softened. "It's like Patti Smith and Robert Mapplethorpe. Camille Claudel. Lizzie Siddal. You should be flattered to be my muse. To know I love you that much."

She recoiled. "Those *muses* you mentioned? They were the artists' lovers, Tobin. Not their sisters."

His face darkened. The hand that didn't hold the lantern clenched into a fist. "That's not—"

She cut him off. "Besides, *they* had talent."

Tobin stilled again, and for several seconds all Izzy heard was the faint clicking of nearby insects. When he spoke again, he sounded hurt. Nearly keening. "Remember that day at the beach, when you got so sunburned that it blistered, and I had to put aloe vera on your back for a week? Or Halloween, when that creep wouldn't leave you alone, and I faked a family emergency to get you out of there? I've always taken care of you— that's what those sketches represent—and now you . . ." He paused, breathing heavily. "*You're* the pervert, Rachel. Thinking I would ever want to . . ." He paused again. Shook his head. "It doesn't matter. You're not going to remember this conversation tomorrow anyway."

Rachel retreated a few steps. "What do you mean?"

"The sports drink I gave you. I put something in there to help you forget this horrible night."

He delivered the words calmly, as if he were speaking of a favor he'd done her, but Rachel's eyes widened.

"You tried to drug me?" At the word "tried," he cocked his head, and she added, "I didn't drink it."

*No*, Izzy thought in horror. *I did.*

"We can still fix this," Tobin said. "I'm sorry if you misunderstood—"

"*Misunderstood*?" Her pitch sharpened. "You said you wanted to help me forget this night. What exactly did you want me to forget?"

"The game. What a jerk Ben was tonight. The dead deer."

She shook her head. "No," she said firmly. "You couldn't have known about that beforehand, and you came prepared. And that sketch . . ." She inhaled sharply. "Did you plan on raping me tonight?"

"You're sick."

But even drugged, Izzy sensed the truth in Rachel's accusation.

"*I'm* sick?" she sneered. "I'm not the one who drew those pictures or tried to drug my sister. You said Ben was like family, but you and I are *blood*."

She put every bit of her revulsion in that last word.

Trembling, Tobin seemed unable to speak. He set down the lantern.

"From the beginning, you bought into all of Ben's moody artist crap." His tone, slightly regretful, made Izzy uneasy. She felt herself sway again, and her stomach heaved.

*Do. Not. Throw up.*

Izzy brought her fist to her mouth and bit down on her knuckle. Her mouth tasted sour.

Tobin put his right hand in his pocket. "Even after he

dropped out of art school, started selling drugs, you defended him. But me? I've done nothing but take care of you, and you say these horrible things."

"You've always been jealous of Ben."

When Tobin pulled out the knife, his hand trembled. Izzy's legs threatened to buckle. She dropped the hand she'd been biting, bile rising, and grabbed for the nearby tree. But she'd misjudged. The tree was just out of reach. She had nothing to steady her. She struggled to remain standing. If she fell, or if Tobin heard her, she was sure he would kill her.

"I'm sorry," he said.

Less than ten feet in front of her, Rachel backed away, but Tobin matched her step for step. "What the hell, Tobin?" Her voice trembled as violently as his hand did.

"This is what I'm talking about, Rachel." His voice hitched. Grief mingling with anger. "Before you started dating Ben, you never swore. And these . . . things you're saying about my *art*. It's because you're with him. You shouldn't be with him."

"You just don't want anyone else to have me."

Tobin grabbed Rachel by the wrist, and Izzy thought she heard bone breaking. Rachel screamed. In the light of the lantern, her eyes widened. When she stumbled, he embraced her so she wouldn't fall. Then he slid the knife into Rachel's chest, and the screaming became a rasp. He leaned in and kissed her forehead gently. Then he stabbed her twice more.

Rachel fell to the ground, her head hitting rock, and Izzy did too. She spread herself across a patch of dirt and grass, rocks jabbing her stomach.

Near her, something scuttled in the brush, and Tobin's attention snapped to the spot where she'd been standing a moment before. She held her breath for so long that her lungs began to sting.

Then Tobin wrapped his arms around Rachel and started dragging her farther down the slope. Leaves crackling. Branches snapping. Body thumping.

Izzy waited until the crunching-sliding sound grew distant, and then she started crawling up the slope, praying Tobin's back remained turned. Hoping he wouldn't abandon his sister's body to look for evidence. Or witnesses. The rough terrain abraded her palms and bit through the knees of her jeans. Heart pressing against her ribs, the sour taste growing stronger, she risked a glance over her shoulder. The ball of light from Tobin's lantern had waned, now no bigger than a lighter's flame.

Izzy started to turn away from that distant light when she sensed movement. Her head snapped back in that direction, and she grew suddenly dizzy. For a moment, she wondered if Rachel might still be alive.

*No*, she decided quickly. No way could Rachel survive an attack that brutal.

Izzy closed her eyes against the vertigo and began climbing again. When she neared the top of the slope, she shot to her feet and stumbled upward and broke into an awkward jog toward her mom's car. She knew she was in no condition to drive, but maybe she could make it half a mile up the road. Then she would call Frankie. Her sister would know what to do. She always knew what to do.

# 41

Thoughts fought for space in my brain, tangling. While I worked to unravel them, Izzy was already halfway up the steep and uneven mountainside, moving as blindly toward Tobin as she had toward that lake when she nearly drowned. Once again, oblivious to the danger. She hadn't put it together like I had.

When the Uber driver had dropped me off that night, there had been only two other vehicles parked alongside the road: our parents' sedan, and the Jeep parked a mile away. I hadn't considered that, even had Tobin returned to the apartment he shared with Chuck, he would've had just enough time to sneak out and make the trek back to Geysers Road.

In a rush, it all made sense. When I had approached Tobin at his work, he had been reluctant for me to see his car. He had waited for me to leave so I wouldn't know which vehicle was his. The references to Chuck having a thing with Rachel, too, had come from Tobin. No one else had mentioned the possibility of a relationship between the two of them, nor had they mentioned Chuck acting "odd" around her.

When they had played the game, according to Izzy, Tobin had

laid his jacket on the ground for his sister, even though it left him shivering. When Ben and Rachel went off for their private talk, it was Tobin who followed.

And the night I found Piper in my home, she had paled when I told her about seeing the Jeep that night. She hadn't thought much of Ben. If it had been him, she would've had no problem sharing that fact with me, and the police. But she liked Tobin. She would've wanted to check it out before she accused him of murdering his own sister.

Then there was what Marina thought she'd heard the day before her sister disappeared.

*No, Ben. I don't feel up to it.*

Had Marina misheard? Had Rachel really said, *Tobin, I don't feel up to it?*

I remembered thinking that Tobin blamed himself for his sister's death. And he did, but not because he didn't prevent it—because he caused it.

And now, with Piper dead, I was the only one who knew about the Jeep being here that night.

I raced after Izzy, but by the time I reached the top of the slope, she was already by Tobin's side.

"I'm glad you're here, actually," she said. "I wanted to apologize."

"Oh?"

"I could've done more to help Rachel that night."

The heat blasted my face. Izzy was inches from him. At his hip, his T-shirt bulged. I tried to keep my voice neutral. "You here to say goodbye to Rachel too?"

He studied me. "I heard you two invited Marina up here. That was kind of you, to include her."

Keeping a few feet between us, I tried to catch Izzy's eye, but she was focused on Tobin. "Marina's great," she said.

I wished I had a weapon. But with a man Tobin's size, and with my own inexperience with weapons, anything I might have had likely would've been used against me instead. "We should probably go," I said. "We wouldn't want to intrude on your grief."

Izzy finally looked at me. She'd heard something in my voice. But I feared Tobin had heard it too. His gaze grew more intense. Darkness rippled at the back of his eyes.

"You aren't intruding at all. It's comforting to be able to share the experience with someone who knows what really happened that night."

Was there a threat buried in that? I looked past him, toward the road.

"Honestly, we've been here awhile, and I'm getting hungry." I grabbed Izzy's arm. Tension caused my fingers to dig into her flesh, and she winced. I could tell she didn't know why I was acting the way I was, but she trusted me enough to take her place by my side.

After staring at me a moment, Izzy said, "I'm actually starving too. I skipped breakfast."

She'd told me earlier that because of nerves, she'd finished half a box of cereal that morning. She might not know what was happening, but she was going along with it.

I took a step, but Tobin blocked the way. He cocked his head, studying me. The intensity of it felt like knives on my skin. "I heard Ben is still insisting he's innocent."

I understood then. The sketchbook had been planted for Marina to find. The drawing of the Dalí painting crowded in the corner. The one that had seemed out of place, but which Izzy easily identified. Then the knife that had been left for the police. When Rachel's body was found—when I started asking too many questions—Tobin must've known someone had to take the blame. He had played us all. But now I feigned ignorance. "Is he? It doesn't matter. We all know he did it."

Tobin's posture held no tension, his face relaxed too.

"Right?" he said. "Who else would do such a horrible thing?"

After he'd defended Ben so fiercely before, I got the feeling he was toying with me now. That his facade was cracking. When his hand settled near his waist, a chill traced my spine.

Time stretched, his darkening expression warning me there would be no coming back from whatever came next. He looked at his Jeep, then back at me. Finally, he said, "You've figured it out."

There was no response I could give that would help me. "I don't know what you mean."

His smirk told me he didn't believe me. He crossed the few feet that separated us, then sighed deeply and draped his arm on my shoulder. He pulled me to him, squeezing hard enough that I flinched.

"I didn't mean to hit Mark, you know. I thought Marina knew more than she did." So when Marina had called home from Mark's place, caller ID had likely displayed Mark's number. It would've been easy enough for Tobin to trace that to Mark's address. But with both his sister and Mark moving so quickly, he had misjudged his target. He seemed relieved to finally be sharing his secret. "But looks like I won't have to kill my sister after all. Which is good. That would ruin my mom."

After the night five years before, I had done a lot of research on what happens when a pedestrian and car collide. I knew the bumper would crash into the legs, throwing the body against the hood before it was then thrown into the road. The head would hit hard—the hood, the windshield, the asphalt. Or the pedestrian could be knocked beneath the car, in the path of its tires. Skulls were often fractured. Pelvises broken. Organs ruptured.

That this man had, on an impulse, tried to inflict that kind of damage on Marina, and that he had nearly killed Mark, enraged me. And that he had stabbed Rachel and Piper—I fought for breath, even as terror surged at the certainty that he intended the same for me and Izzy.

Heart knocking, I shifted in his grasp, becoming a shield between him and Izzy. He still held me so tightly I could barely breathe, but I straightened my spine. It took effort, building the illusion that I was okay, when all I wanted to do was give up my fight against gravity and collapse. I hardened my jaw and tilted it in defiance. My body language lied. It said that whatever happened next, I was ready. But I knew my eyes gave me away. They widened and burned with unshed tears, more angry than sad.

*Better me than her.*

Tobin reached into his waistband and pulled out a knife, still holding me tightly despite how I fought against him. When Izzy saw the blade, she stepped forward.

The rest happened in seconds. Tobin released me abruptly and shoved. I stumbled, landing on the ground several feet away. I scrambled to my feet, but he was already reaching for her—one hand still fisted around the hilt of the knife, the other empty and open. He meant to stab her.

But the angle of the blade was wrong. Up instead of out. Understanding what he intended, I lurched toward them and grabbed for his arm, but too slowly. Too late.

When Tobin's fist and palm landed on Izzy's chest, he twisted his head slightly so that our eyes locked. Then he turned back toward her and pushed.

# 42

Less than five feet from the cliff's edge, Izzy staggered backward, arms flailing to find my outstretched hand, but even as I lunged forward, I remained just beyond her reach. She skidded, and then there was nothing under her but air.

She fell, fingers grabbing, wind pushing her toward the mountainside below.

My body vibrated as I stumbled to the edge. Afraid to look. Needing to look. My face felt hot, my neck clammy. In my veins, adrenaline pulsed.

I saw her, about thirty feet below. She was still. How long had she been in the air before landing? I prayed she had fallen on a spot of wild grass and rolled down the slope. The mountainside seemed to be nothing but jagged rocks and steep drop-offs.

I felt a tap on my shoulder. When I turned, Tobin was still holding the knife in his right hand, his other extended palm up. He demanded my phone and keys. I didn't care about either. At the moment, all I cared about was my sister, likely unconscious thirty feet down the slope.

My eyes darted, settling on each part of the world around me:

the golden slope with its patches of brush. The weeds. The road glimpsed just over his shoulder.

He noticed my interest and shook his head. "No one can see us from the road, and even if they do, you really going to leave your sister to die down there? Like you did Rachel?"

At my feet, a small weed spiraled, all green leaves and tiny purple flowers. Yellow flowers sprouted from barbed shrubs, and wild grasses grew as high as our knees. I fought the urge to pulverize all of it with the toe of my sneaker.

I tried to get him talking until I could figure something out. "You came here to kill me. Why?"

He shook his head. "I didn't come to kill you. At least, I hoped I wouldn't have to. Just had to be sure. But then I saw that look of recognition on your face."

Apparently that was all he felt like saying, because he stepped forward, all coiled energy, and I saw his intention in the slight twitch in his right shoulder. The way he planted his feet. All in an instant, but my reaction was just as fast. He blocked the road, so there was only one direction to go. Down. Even if I ended up falling, at least I wouldn't be alone down there. I would have Izzy.

I jumped back, turned quickly, and stepped onto the slope, letting momentum pull me toward where my sister waited. I had nothing to lose, and that made me reckless. The grasses slapped at my knees, small rocks jutting from the earth in odd spots, but I stumble-ran down the slope.

My breath exploded from my lungs in ragged bursts. So loud that it took me a moment to realize Tobin wasn't behind me.

Reaching Izzy, I stared up toward the spot where he had been standing. He wasn't there. Then suddenly he came into view again. He paused, for no longer than it took me to draw a breath, and then he started down after me.

His steps were more careful than mine had been. He had the advantage. I scanned for weapons, but then I heard it. The crunching of weeds. My attention flashed to the spot where I'd seen my sister. Less than ten feet away now. She was struggling to sit. Her hand flew to her head, and she winced.

Before I could ask, she rasped: "I'm okay. Just shaken up."

"You sure?"

She nodded, but when she tried to stand, she flinched. I rushed to close the gap, but she extended her arm, palm out, in the universal gesture for stop. "I rolled most of the way. Ankle might be sprained, but that's better than being dead, right?"

She tried to play it off, but I saw how much even a slight movement cost her. She limped a few steps.

"So what's the plan?" she asked.

*Hell if I know.* "Move."

We needed to get to the truck. "Phone?" I asked, reaching for Izzy to offer her support. She shook her head and took the lead, advancing slowly sideways through the knee-high grass, wincing whenever her foot caught a fissure in the earth.

As she walked, she patted her pockets. Finally, she said, "No phone. What happened to yours?"

With a tilt of my head, I gestured in Tobin's direction. "He took it."

Tobin was closer now. Maybe twenty feet away. He had adjusted his course so that he came for us on a diagonal, and with his longer stride and two good ankles, he was closing the gap quickly.

We had to get back to the road. We needed to move as quickly as we could up the mountainside. But I hesitated.

It was Izzy who started moving first. On the rough terrain, her gait was awkward as she favored her injured ankle, and sweat beaded her brow, but she clambered up the slope quickly.

Muscles burning, I ran, too, Izzy beside me. She stumbled, and I grabbed her elbow again. This time, she didn't fight it.

Tobin was less than ten feet away now. In his effort to move faster, the hand holding the knife had relaxed at his side.

My toe jammed against the root of an oak tree. I lurched forward, hand still clamped to Izzy's elbow, nearly taking her down with me.

A plan started to form. A really bad plan. But it was the only one I had.

I released Izzy and took a step back. I placed my palm in the small of her back, urging her forward.

Then I slowed. Tobin grew so near that I could hear his footfalls, heavy and quick. I stopped abruptly and turned. Instead of heading away from him, I raced forward. My hands shot out in front of me, and I planted them on his chest, just as he raised the knife. He nicked my arm, but I pushed as hard as I could. He faltered, then he fell, and gravity pulled him down the slope.

My gaze dropped to the wound. The scratch welled with the promise of blood. But it was a minor injury. A couple of Julian's bug Band-Aids, and I'd be as good as new.

The larger threat was Tobin, who still held the knife and was already halfway to his feet.

I sprinted, catching up with Izzy. Together, we scrabbled up the mountainside.

With my legs on fire and Izzy's sprained ankle, I didn't know how we managed to ascend the slope, or why Tobin didn't follow more quickly. Maybe he thought a thirty-second delay didn't matter, since he had my keys. But the Barreras had a thing about spares, one of which was hidden on the inside of my bumper.

When we reached the truck, though, I quickly realized the spare key would do us no good. The tires were pancaked on the ground. All four of them flat.

They had been slashed. We were stuck.

"Can we drive on them?" Izzy asked, breathless. She swayed. How much longer could she remain standing?

"Not far."

The flattened rubber would cushion the rims for a while. If we drove at a slow speed, we could make it a short distance before the wheels were damaged. But we were miles away from . . . anything. In his fully functioning Jeep, Tobin would catch up with us in no time.

Which meant we needed to disable Tobin's Jeep too.

I reached in the backseat for the bottle of water I had discarded earlier. When I started jogging down the road, Izzy followed.

THOUGH IT WAS ONLY a short distance, my lungs and legs cramped. When we reached Tobin's Jeep, luck was, finally, with us. Probably cocky because of the remote location, Tobin hadn't thought to lock his Jeep. I pushed the release to open his fuel tank.

Damn it. Tobin had a locking gas cap. So much for luck.

When Izzy noticed, too, she said, winded, "Can't we let the air out of his tires?"

I squatted, then swore again as I shook my head. The Jeep had run-flat tires. Even if we let the air out, Tobin would be able to drive much farther, and faster, than we would.

I inhaled sharply and closed my eyes: *Think, Frankie, think*. Tobin had to be close. How close?

When I opened my eyes again, Izzy had already grabbed a rock. She pounded the gas cap. After several blows, the plastic shattered.

At my expression of surprise, she arched a brow. "You do finesse, I break things."

If there had been time, I would've hugged her. Instead, I opened my bottle of water and removed the gas cap. I emptied the bottle into the tank. Since water was heavier than gas, it would sink to the bottom. The Jeep wouldn't start, at least not until the tank was emptied and filled with new gas.

I allowed myself a breath, but it was small cause for celebration. We had no real advantage. We had just leveled the playing field.

Tobin wasn't far away. Taking cautious steps because he knew he had us. I thought of Rachel, and the terror she must've felt running up this slope, stabbed and bleeding. Into the front of Izzy's car.

I realized, suddenly, we did have a weapon. One that weighed several thousand pounds.

I reached inside the Jeep and released its emergency brake. Shifted it into neutral.

"Push," I shouted.

But Izzy had already moved to the other side of the vehicle. It was pointed in the right direction: facing the embankment. Toward where Tobin picked his way through the brush. I threw all of my weight against the Jeep's frame. On her side, Izzy did the same. The Jeep rocked, moving only inches. I worried suddenly that our strength wouldn't be enough. But then it started to roll. One foot. Two. Aided by our adrenaline and the vehicle's momentum, it picked up speed.

Understanding the danger, Tobin quickly looked left, then right, but boulders and a steep and uneven terrain prevented quick movement. He jumped to the left. Faster than I thought he could move. But not fast enough.

The Jeep clipped the lower half of his body. Pinned him beneath its front tires. His scream echoed. When the rear tires ran over him, he was past screaming.

The Jeep crashed against the rusted framework that had been pictured on that last page of Tobin's sketchbook. A relic from the past. Below us, Tobin remained unconscious on the ground not far from where he'd stabbed his sister.

# 43

After all I had risked to find the truth, it was impossible to let it go. I spent several weeks poring through transcripts, talking to Kaplan, even calling Chuck again. A math geek to the core, I couldn't leave a problem half solved. I could be every bit as stubborn as my sister.

In his interview with Detective Kaplan, a now-paralyzed Tobin insisted there had been nothing inappropriate about his relationship with his sister. When shown the sketchbook I had turned over to Kaplan, Tobin said it was Rachel who first encouraged his interest in art. She gifted him the sketchbook after a classmate bullied him. The bullying didn't bother Tobin—his classmates were often intimidated by his intelligence—but he reveled in his sister's attention. He and Rachel had always shared a special bond.

According to Tobin, she posed for the first drawing in her bedroom. In detail, he described how she rested on the bed, chin on the back of her hands as he sat cross-legged on the floor, pencil in hand. Studying her. Later, when he showed her the drawing, he was patient as she pointed out what parts he hadn't gotten quite right.

After that, he got in the habit of walking into her bedroom without knocking. She didn't mind, even if she was dressed only in a bathing suit or that thin T-shirt she wore to bed, the snug one that clearly showed her breasts. Not that he noticed. He was her brother. Sometimes she would get an odd expression on her face or ask him to leave, but mostly she would just cover up so they could talk. He loved their conversations. When it was just the two of them, together.

Then came the afternoon he caught her undressing. He averted his eyes immediately, of course. But she made it clear she didn't want him in her bedroom again.

Of course he understood. She was upset, as any girl would've been in that situation. Still, he decided it was best to hide the sketchbook. He didn't want to make her uncomfortable.

That time frame fit with when he had started the full-body sketches. Kaplan asked about the missing sketch, the one that left a jagged edge of paper jutting from the spiral rings. Tobin said he couldn't remember the subject. But I could guess what he had drawn.

Tobin claimed Rachel's death was an accident. At first he tried to blame Izzy for hitting Rachel with the car. But then Kaplan pointed out that Rachel had been stabbed with enough force to leave striations on her bone in several places. Tobin still insisted he was innocent. He had always been stronger than people thought, he said. He never intended to kill her.

Kaplan asked him why, then, did he have a knife.

Tobin pointed out that the knife wasn't even his. Ben had brought it, then given it to Chuck to kill the deer. He only borrowed it. That part of the county could be dangerous in the dark.

Kaplan asked why he didn't try to get help for his sister after he "accidentally" stabbed her, or after Izzy hit Rachel with her car. Why, instead, he dragged Rachel farther down the slope. That last part had been a guess on Kaplan's part, but Tobin confirmed it.

He claimed he wanted to hide her. After all, he said, he had seen what some wild animal had done to that deer.

Tobin mentioned how he heard me that night, as I trampled the brush in my quest to find his sister. He would've called out, he told Kaplan, but I never got close enough. Besides, even though it was clearly an accident, he was concerned about how it might look.

Rachel's head resting in his lap, Tobin stayed with her until he heard me leave.

His story finished, Kaplan asked a final question. How did he explain what happened to Piper Lange?

At that point, Tobin stopped talking.

# FIVE YEARS BEFORE

AFTER MERCURYVILLE

It had been seven weeks since the night Rachel hadn't come home. When talking about her, Piper and the others used the word "disappeared." But Izzy never used that word. She knew.

In the days that followed, Tobin told the others his sister hadn't been quite herself in the months before they'd gathered out by Mercuryville. At the time, it hadn't concerned him, he said, but in hindsight maybe it should have. She was even talking about moving out of state, he said. He added that she also hadn't been doing well in her classes, and no one could dispute how badly that last night had gone. For one thing, Rachel had hated that stupid game.

These conversations always left Izzy with a sense of unease. Eventually, being in the presence of the others made her physically ill, and she abandoned the group, except for Piper.

No matter how Frankie and the others tried to convince her, Izzy knew Rachel would never return. She wasn't out there, somewhere, starting a new life. She had died, left behind on that remote slope near Geysers Road.

Izzy didn't have all of her memories, but she remembered

the impact. And she had seen her sister washing their mom's car the next day. She had seen her pluck those strands of human hair from the headlight.

Sometimes, like now, Izzy would lie in bed, curtains and eyes closed, and strain to remember how those hairs had gotten there. What had happened in the hours before?

No matter how hard she reached for them, those memories evaded her. Even moments she could recall easily at first started to fade.

Except for the sight of Rachel when Izzy's car hit her. There would be no forgetting that.

Lying on her bed, Izzy felt the familiar queasiness. There was still one thing she hadn't told Frankie. Soon there would be no getting around it. She would have to tell her the truth about what else had happened that night.

Still, she knew Frankie would fix it. She always did.

# 44

The cardboard box still had a bit of room, so I tucked Mr. Carrots among the Lego tubes and picture books. When I touched one of the stuffed rabbit's ears, rubbed to the stitching and stained with jelly, I felt a twinge in my chest. How long before Julian would ask for him? A day? A week? While Mr. Carrots had been Julian's favorite companion for much of the past year, he had been recently replaced in Julian's affections by a handful of plastic dinosaurs he kept in his pocket.

Mr. Carrots stared back at me with his one good eye as I folded the flaps to close the box.

"Sorry, Mr. Carrots, but you had a good run."

"Are you talking to Julian's rabbit?"

I turned to find Izzy standing in the entryway to Julian's room.

"I was."

"Thanks for letting me move in for a while until Mark's home. Without Piper, the apartment . . ." Izzy's voice cracked.

Before everything that had happened, I had been planning to rip out the flooring in the dining room, and maybe invest in a better table. Now Izzy was sewing curtains to cover the glass in the French doors, and I had bought a gallon of blue paint. Izzy's favorite color. "You can stay as long as you need."

Her gaze locked on mine, and her eyes turned suddenly somber. "Thank you. For, you know, all of it."

Together, we packed another box to store in the garage, then when we were done we dropped the tailgate of my truck. After a while, Julian ran over and pulled a plastic brontosaurus from his pocket. He held it up for my inspection. "His name's Steve."

"That's a nice name."

Julian squinted in the sun, and with his scrunched nose and flushed cheeks, he looked just like Izzy had at his age. I hadn't thought my heart capable of swelling and breaking at the same moment, but as I stared into Julian's eyes, it did both.

I cleared my throat. "You want to go play with your dinosaurs while I talk with Aunt Izzy?"

Julian nodded, but paused after taking only a few steps. "Do you love me as much as dinosaurs?"

I answered without hesitation, my voice cracking. Just a little. "I love you as much as all the things."

He grinned before his face grew thoughtful. "Do you think Mr. Carrots could play too? I think he'd like Steve."

So maybe the changes would be smaller ones, and I could bear them after all.

After unpacking Mr. Carrots for Julian, and with the roar of dinosaurs coming from the living room, I again joined Izzy on the tailgate—the tailgate where so many memories had revolved around plastic cups of beer and, later, Izzy's eyes glazed by something stronger.

She looked through the open front door to the living room,

where Julian and his dinosaurs were either waging a great battle or throwing a raucous party. Hard to tell.

Izzy smiled at the chaos on the other side of the threshold. "Thanks for letting me spend time with him."

"Of course." I aimed for nonchalance, but Izzy saw it. Sober, finally, she saw through me a lot easier now.

When I had believed Izzy might go to prison, I had tortured myself about what might happen if she did. All those Google searches about parental rights. I meant it when I said now, "I would never keep Julian from you. Not now that you're clean." I meant it fully, but my heart seized nonetheless. After raising him for four years, I wasn't sure I would be able to let Julian go.

Izzy grabbed my hand. It was clammy, and that made me worry. But just for a second. "I'd never keep him from you," she said. "You're the only parent he's known. Besides, you raised me. I can't think of anyone I'd rather have raising him."

In the past, I might not have believed her. Recently, I'd realized that part of my drive to protect her came from the feeling that I had failed—if I had helped raise Izzy, wasn't I to blame for her choices? I smiled. "I did do a pretty good job with that, didn't I?"

"Eh. A work in progress."

She released my hand and looked away, her voice soft when she spoke again. "I'm not ready yet. To help raise him. It might be a while."

It might be a while. She had said nearly those same words the night she had shown up at my door four years before, a son she hadn't bothered to name wrapped in a yellow blanket. Another mess for her big sister to clean up. A mess that was both my greatest blessing and the cause of my deepest fear.

"Chuck's the dad, isn't he?" She nodded, but she didn't ask how I knew. We were trying to do better about not keeping secrets. "After I talked to him, and he mentioned you had tried to call him about the same time you were pregnant, I figured it out." I paused before asking, "You going to tell him?"

"I tried once. I'll try again, but not yet."

I didn't push. Instead, I grabbed her hand again, wrapping it between mine. Her fingers felt delicate, breakable, like Julian's that first night. Like then, I tried not to press too tightly. It felt close to forgiveness. "But you're good?"

She nodded. Too enthusiastically? "I think I might have to go back. To rehab. I haven't felt so strong lately."

I squeezed her hand. "You're strong for knowing that."

I hopped down from the tailgate. "Shall we see if Mr. Carrots is getting along with his new friends?"

Izzy jumped down and grabbed my hand, and together we walked toward the boy we both loved, who presided over an army of dinosaurs and one threadbare bunny on the living room floor. He looked up, and the sun caught his face through the open door, and I realized I had been wrong earlier. In this light, he didn't look like Izzy alone. There were parts of both of us reflected there. The best parts.

# ACKNOWLEDGMENTS

BOOKS ARE A collaborative process, and I'm blessed to work with the best collaborators. Chief among them is my brilliant agent, Peter Steinberg, whose faith in my writing has steadied my nerves on too many occasions to count. I would also like to thank Yona Levin and everyone at Fletcher & Company. I'm so lucky to have landed where I did.

I'm grateful, too, to David Highfill, for his insightful editing and support, along with Tessa James, Aryana Hendrawan, Rachel Weinick, Dave Cole, Jessica Lyons, Nancy Singer, and the rest of the William Morrow team. I'm thrilled to be working with all of you.

There are only a handful of people I trust with my messiest pages and craziest ideas. Thank you, Crissi Langwell, Ana Manwaring, Jan M. Flynn, Dana Rodney, Mary Keliikoa, and Anika Scott. Thanks, too, Lisa Ostroski, Patty Hayes, and Gina Blaxill, with a special shout-out to Dawn Ius for insisting I write even when I'd much rather have been napping with the cat. You all deserve medals, but accept my gratitude instead.

With this sophomore novel, I finally found my community, and I'm deeply appreciative for you all. As I've often said, people who love books are among the most generous people in the world. Thank you to members of the International Thriller Writers, Sisters in Crime, and, especially, the 2020 Debuts. We've been in this together since the beginning, and I'm inspired by the resilience and talent in each of you. There's no one else I would rather share this journey with. And, of course, thank you to the readers, booksellers, and libraries who've supported my work. I quite literally could not have done this without you.

I'm also grateful to Retired Lieutenant Tom Swearingen of the Santa Rosa Police Department for continuing to be patient with my questions and thorough in his responses. As always, any mistakes are mine.

Undying gratitude also goes to the generous friends and colleagues who endure book talk without complaint and make every day brighter: Alena Wall, Dory Haessler, Wren Herman, Dean DeRosa, Denise Barredo, Holly Clarke, Karen Jacobsen, Kari Kincaid, and Jason Turner, who is the reason Frankie and Izzy live in Cloverdale.

As always, I'm grateful to my parents, Ron and Norma, and stepdad, Rob, who helped Frankie fix her truck. Also thanks to my extended family and amazing in-laws. While there are too many to list individually here, your support means everything to me.

Of course, I couldn't do any of this without my incredible husband, Alex. Being married to a writer isn't always easy, but you put up with it all—even when I ask to read "just one more paragraph." (Even though you know it's never just one.) Thanks and much love also to my amazing children, Maya and Jacob, who think nothing of brainstorming with me about the best places to dump a body, while also making this world a happier, funnier, better place.

Finally, this is a book about sisters, which makes me think of my own, Michelle. You may no longer be around to read this book, Miki, but you were in my thoughts every day of its creation.

Discover another gripping thriller
by Heather Chavez . . .